'One story nests within another, like the set of Russian dolls that Martin owns … Kate Atkinson has that priceless Ancient Mariner ability that keeps the reader turning the pages'
Spectator

'While Kate Atkinson could give a masterclass on creating believable and intriguing characters, she also knows more than a thing or two about plotting … another class act'
Mirror

'Deft and funny prose sums up each character sharply and endearingly … blends humour with page-turning action … masterfully controlled'
Time Out

'Whatever she does is done to the highest of literary standards. She has produced an engrossing, enjoyable, complex novel packed with intriguing characters, vividly imagined scenes and a compelling plot'
Times Literary Supplement

'Such a joy that Kate Atkinson has produced another flawless, upbeat mystery after her success with *Case Histories*'
Good Housekeeping

ONE GOOD TURN

A Jolly Murder Mystery

Kate Atkinson

BLACK SWAN

TRANSWORLD PUBLISHERS
61-63 Uxbridge Road, London W5 5SA
a division of The Random House Group Ltd
www.booksattransworld.co.uk

ONE GOOD TURN
A BLACK SWAN BOOK: 9780552772440

First published in Great Britain
in 2006 by Doubleday
a division of Transworld Publishers
Black Swan edition published 2007

The author and publishers are grateful to the Society of Authors as the
Literary Representative of the Estate of Laurence Binyon, for permission
to reproduce short extracts from Binyon's poem 'For the Fallen'
(September 1914).

Kate Atkinson has asserted her right under the Copyright, Designs and
Patents Act 1988 to be identified as the author of this work.

Addresses for Random House Group Ltd companies outside the UK
can be found at: www.randomhouse.co.uk
The Random House Group Ltd Reg. No. 954009

The Random House Group Ltd makes every effort to ensure that the
papers used in its books are made from trees that have been legally
sourced from well-managed and credibly certified forests. Our paper pro-
curement policy can be found at: www.randomhouse.co.uk/paper.htm

Typeset in 11/14pt Melior by
Falcon Oast Graphic Art Ltd.

Printed in the UK by
CPI Cox & Wyman, Reading, RG1 8EX

8 10 9 7

*For Debbie, Glynis, Judith, Lynn, Penny,
Sheila and Tessa.
For the way we were and for the way we are.*

I owe a debt of gratitude to Martin Auld, Malcolm R. Dixon (Assistant Inspector of Constabulary for Scotland), Russell Equi, Major Michael Keech, Sheriff Andrew Lothian, Dr Doug Lyle and Dr Anthony Toft for telling me things they knew and I didn't. Apologies if I have misunderstood that information or, occasionally, wilfully misused or distorted it.

Thank you to David Robinson and Donald Ross at the *Scotsman*, to Reagan Arthur, to Kim Witherspoon and to Peter Strauss and to Little Brown, US, and Transworld, UK.

Thank you also to David Lindgren for trying, and usually failing, to explain corporate law to me and, more importantly, for being a lawyer who lunches.

Thanks also to Alan Stalker and Stephen Cotton for coming to the rescue in hard times.

Last but not least, thank you to the writer Ray Allan for graciously allowing me to steal a story from his life.

Male parta, male dilabuntur.
(What is dishonourably got is dishonourably squandered.)

(Cicero, *Philippics*, II, 27)

Tuesday

1

HE WAS LOST. HE WASN'T USED TO BEING LOST. HE WAS THE kind of man who drew up plans and then executed them efficiently, but now everything was conspiring against him in ways he decided he couldn't have foreseen. He had been stuck in a jam on the A1 for two mind-numbing hours so that it was already past the middle of the morning when he arrived in Edinburgh. Then he'd gone adrift on a one-way system and been thwarted by a road closed because of a burst water main. It had been raining, steadily and unforgivingly, on the drive north and had only begun to ease off as he hit the outskirts of town. The rain had in no way deterred the crowds – it had never occurred to him that Edinburgh was in the middle of 'the Festival' and that there would be carnival hordes of people milling around as if the end of a war had just been declared. The closest he had previously got to the Edinburgh Festival was accidentally turning on *Late Night Review* and seeing a bunch of middle-class wankers discussing some pretentious piece of fringe theatre.

He ended up in the dirty heart of the city, in a street that somehow seemed to be on a lower level than the rest of the town, a blackened urban ravine. The rain had left the cobbles slick and greasy and he had to drive cautiously because the street was teeming with people, haphazardly crossing over or standing in little knots in the middle of the road, as if no one had told them that roads were for cars and pavements were for pedestrians. A queue snaked the length of the street – people waiting to get into what looked like a bomb hole in the wall but which announced itself, on a large placard outside the door, as 'Fringe Venue 164'.

The name on the driving licence in his wallet was Paul Bradley. 'Paul Bradley' was a nicely forgettable name. He was several degrees of separation away from his real name now, a name that no longer felt as if it had ever belonged to him. When he wasn't working he often (but not always) went by the name 'Ray'. Nice and simple. Ray of light, Ray of darkness. Ray of sunshine, Ray of night. He liked slipping between identities, sliding through the cracks. The rental Peugeot he was driving felt just right, not a flashy macho machine but the kind of car an ordinary guy would drive. An ordinary guy like Paul Bradley. If anyone asked him what he did, what Paul Bradley did, he would say, 'Boring stuff. I'm just a desk jockey, pushing papers around in an accounts department.'

He was trying to drive and at the same time decipher his *A–Z* of Edinburgh to work out how to escape from this hellish street when someone stepped in front of the car. It was a type he loathed – a young dark-haired guy with thick, black-framed spectacles, two days of stubble and a fag hanging out of his mouth, there were hundreds of them in London, all trying to look like French existentialists from the Sixties. He'd bet that not one of them had ever opened a book on philosophy. He'd read the lot, Plato, Kant, Hegel, even thought about one day doing a degree.

He braked hard and didn't hit the spectacles guy, just made him give a little jump, like a bullfighter avoiding the bull. The guy was furious, waving his fag around, shouting, raising a finger to him. Charmless, devoid of manners – were his parents proud of the job they'd done? He hated smoking, it was a disgusting habit, hated guys who gave you the finger and screamed, 'Spin on it!', saliva flying out of their filthy, nicotine-stained mouths.

He felt the bump, about the same force as hitting a badger or a fox on a dark night, except it came from behind, pushing him forward. It was just as well the spectacles guy had performed his little paso doble and got out of the way or he would have been pancaked. He looked in the rear-view mirror. A blue Honda Civic, the driver climbing out – big guy, slabs of weightlifter muscle, gym-fit rather than survival-fit, he wouldn't have been able to last three months in the jungle or the desert the way that Ray could have done. He wouldn't have lasted a day. He was wearing driving gloves, ugly black leather ones with knuckle holes. He had a dog in the back of the car, a beefy Rottweiler, exactly the dog you would have guessed a guy like that would have. The guy was a walking cliché. The dog was having a seizure in the back, spraying saliva all over the window, its claws scrabbling on the glass. The dog didn't worry him too much. He knew how to kill dogs.

Ray got out of the car and walked round to the back bumper to inspect the damage. The Honda driver started yelling at him, 'You stupid, fucking *twat*, what did you think you were *doing*?' English. Ray tried to think of something to say that would be non-confrontational, that would calm the guy down – you could see he was a pressure cooker waiting to blow, *wanting* to blow, bouncing on his feet like an out-of-condition heavyweight. Ray adopted a neutral stance, a neutral expression, but then he heard the crowd give a little collective 'Aah' of horror and he registered the baseball bat that had suddenly appeared in the guy's hand out of nowhere and thought, *shit*.

That was the last thought he had for several seconds. When he was able to think again he was sprawled on the street, holding the side of his head where the guy had cracked him. He heard the sound of broken glass – the bastard was putting in every window in his car now. He tried, unsuccessfully, to struggle to his feet but managed only to get to a kneeling position as if he was at prayer and now the guy was advancing with the bat lifted, feeling the heft of it in his hand, ready to swing for a home run on his skull. Ray put an arm up to defend himself, made himself even more dizzy by doing that and, sinking back on to the cobbles, thought, Jesus, is this it? He'd given up, he'd actually given up – something he'd never done before – when someone stepped out of the crowd, wielding some-thing square and black that he threw at the Honda guy, clipping him on the shoulder and sending him reeling.

He blacked out again for a few seconds and when he

came to there were a couple of policewomen hunkered down beside him, one of them saying, 'Just take it easy, sir,' the other one on her radio calling for an ambulance. It was the first time in his life that he'd been glad to see the police.

2

MARTIN HAD NEVER DONE ANYTHING LIKE THAT IN HIS LIFE
before. He didn't even kill flies in the house, instead
he patiently stalked them, trapping them with a glass
and a plate before letting them free. The meek shall
inherit the earth. He was fifty and had never know-
ingly committed an act of violence against another
living creature, although sometimes he thought that
might be more to do with cowardice than pacifism.

He had stood in the queue, waiting for someone else
to intervene in the scene unfolding before them, but
the crowd were in audience mode, like promenaders
at a particularly brutal piece of theatre, and they had
no intention of spoiling the entertainment. Even
Martin had wondered at first if it was another show –
a faux-impromptu piece intended either to shock or to
reveal our immunity to being shocked because we
lived in a global media community where we had
become passive voyeurs of violence (and so on). That
was the line of thought running through the detached,
intellectual part of his brain. His primitive brain, on

the other hand, was thinking, Oh fuck, this is horrible, really horrible, please make the bad man go away. He wasn't surprised to hear his father's voice in his head (*Pull yourself together, Martin*). His father had been dead for many years but Martin often still heard the bellow and yell of his parade-ground tones. When the Honda driver finished breaking the windows of the silver Peugeot and walked towards the driver, brandishing his weapon and preparing himself for a final victory blow, Martin realized that the man on the ground was probably going to die, was probably going to be *killed* by the crazed man with the bat right there in front of them unless someone did something and, instinctively, without thinking about it at all – because if he'd thought about it he might not have done it – he slipped his bag off his shoulder and swung it, hammer-throw fashion, at the head of the insane Honda driver.

He missed the man's head, which didn't surprise him – he'd never been able to aim or catch, he was the kind of person who ducked when a ball was thrown in his direction – but his laptop was in the bag and the hard weighty edge of it caught the Honda driver on the shoulder and sent him spinning.

The nearest Martin had been to a real crime scene previously had been on a Society of Authors' trip around St Leonard's police station. Apart from Martin, the group consisted entirely of women. 'You're our token man,' one of them said to him and he sensed a certain disappointment in the polite laughter of the others, as if the least he could have done as their token man was be a little less like a woman.

They had been offered coffee and biscuits – chocolate bourbons, pink wafer sandwiches, they had all been impressed by the assortment – and a 'senior policeman' had given a pleasant talk in a new conference room that felt as if it had been specially designed for groups like theirs. Then they were shown round various parts of the building, the call centre and the cavernous space of a room where people in plain-clothes ('NCIS') who were sitting at the computers glanced briefly at 'the authors', decided, correctly, they were irrelevant, and returned to their screens.

They had all stood in a line-up, one of their members had her fingerprints taken and then they were locked – briefly – in a cell, where they had shuffled and giggled to take the edge off the claustro-phobia. 'Giggle', it struck Martin, was an almost exclusively female word. Women giggle, men simply laugh. Martin worried that he was a bit of a giggler himself. At the end of the tour, as if it had been staged for their benefit, they witnessed, with a little frisson of fear, a team being hastily assembled in riot gear to remove a 'difficult' prisoner from a cell.

The tour hadn't had much relevance to the kind of books that Martin wrote, in the person of his alter ego, 'Alex Blake'. They were old-fashioned, soft-boiled crime novels featuring a heroine called 'Nina Riley', a gung-ho kind of girl who had inherited a detective agency from her uncle. The books were set in the Forties, just after the war. It was an era in history Martin felt particularly drawn to, the monochrome deprivation of it, the undertow of seedy disappoint-ment in the wake of heroism. The Vienna of the *The*

Third Man, the Home Counties of *Brief Encounter*. What must it have felt like to have pinned your colours to the standard of a just war, to have experienced so many noble feelings (yes, a lot of propaganda, but the kernel of it was true), to have been released from the burden of individualism? To have stood on the edge of destruction and defeat and come through? And thought, *now what?* Of course, Nina Riley didn't feel any of those things, she was only twenty-two and had seen out the war in a Swiss finishing school. And she wasn't real.

Nina Riley had always been a tomboy, though she had no apparent lesbian tendencies and was constantly courted by a great variety of men with whom she was remarkably chaste. (*'It's as if'*, an *'appreciative reader' wrote to him, 'a Chalet School head girl grew up and became a detective.'*) Nina lived in a geographically vague version of Scotland that contained sea and mountains and rolling moorland, all within a fast drive of every major town in Scotland (and, frequently, England, although never Wales, something Martin thought he should perhaps rectify) in her racy open-top Bristol. When he wrote the first Nina Riley book he had conceived it as an affectionate nod in the direction of an earlier time and an earlier form. 'A pastiche, if you will,' he said nervously, when he was introduced to his editor at the publishing house. 'A kind of ironic *homage*.' It had been a surprise to find that he was being published. He had written the book to entertain himself and suddenly he was sitting in a featureless London office feeling he had to justify the nonsense he had created to a young woman who seemed to find it difficult to keep her mind on him.

'Be that as it may,' she said, making a visible effort to look at him, 'what I see is a book I can sell. A sort of jolly murder mystery. People *crave* nostalgia, the past is like a drug. How many books do you envisage in the series?'

'Series?'

'Hi.'

Martin turned round and saw a man leaning against the door jamb in an attitude of almost absurd casualness. He was older than Martin but dressed younger.

'Hi,' the young editor said in return, giving the man her rapt attention. Their minimal exchange seemed to carry almost more meaning than it could bear. 'Neil Winters, our MD,' she said, with a proud smile. 'This is Martin Canning, Neil. He's written a *wonderful* book.'

'Fantastic,' Neil Winters said, shaking Martin's hand. His hand was damp and soft like something dead you might find on the beach. 'The first of many, I hope.'

Within a couple of weeks Neil Winters was transported into more elevated echelons in the European mothership and Martin never met him again, but nevertheless he saw that handshake as the identifiable moment when his life changed.

Martin had recently sold the television rights for the Nina Riley books. 'Like getting into a warm bath. Perfect fodder for the Sunday evening slot,' the BBC producer said, making it sound like an insult, which of course it was.

In the two-dimensional fictional world that she inhabited, Nina Riley had so far solved three murders, a jewel theft, a bank robbery, retrieved a stolen race-horse, prevented the kidnapping of the infant Prince Charles from Balmoral and, on her sixth outing, almost single-handedly foiled a plot to steal the Scottish crown jewels. The seventh, *The Monkey-Puzzle Tree*, was newly in paperback on the 'Three for Two' tables in every bookshop. The seventh was 'darker', everyone seemed to agree (*Blake is finally moving towards a more mature noir style*, 'a reader' had written on Amazon. Everyone's a critic.), but despite this his sales remained 'buoyant', according to his agent, Melanie. 'No end in sight yet, Martin,' she said. Melanie was Irish and it made everything she said sound nice even when it wasn't.

If people asked him – as they frequently did – why he had become a writer, Martin usually answered that as he spent most of his time in his imagination it had seemed like a good idea to get paid for it. He said this jovially, no giggling, and people smiled as if he'd said something amusing. What they didn't understand was that it was the truth – he lived inside his head. Not in an intellectual or philosophical way, in fact his interior life was remarkably banal. He didn't know if it was the same for everyone. Did other people spend their time daydreaming about a better version of the everyday? No one ever talked about the life of the imagination, except in terms of some kind of Keatsian high art. No one mentioned the pleasure of picturing yourself sitting in a deckchair on a lawn, beneath a cloudless midsummer sky, contemplating the spread of a proper, old-fashioned afternoon tea, prepared by a cosy woman with a mature bosom and spotless apron who said things like 'Come on now, eat up, ducks,' because this was how cosy women with mature bosoms spoke in Martin's imagination, an odd kind of sub-Dickensian discourse.

The world inside his head was so much better than the world outside his head. Scones, home-made blackcurrant jam, clotted cream. Overhead, swallows sliced through the blue, blue sky, swooping and diving like Battle of Britain pilots. The distant *thock* of leather on willow. The scent of hot, strong tea and new-mown grass. Surely these things were infinitely preferable to a terrifyingly angry man with a baseball bat?

Martin had been hauling his laptop around with him because the lunchtime comedy showcase he had been queuing for was a detour on today's (very tardy) path to his 'office'. Martin had recently rented the 'office' in a refurbished block in Marchmont. It had once been a licensed grocer but now provided bland, featureless space – plasterboard walls and laminate floors, broadband connections and halogen lighting – to a firm of architects, an IT consultancy, and, now, Martin. He had rented the 'office' in the vain hope that if he left the house to go and write every day and kept normal working hours like other people it would some-how help him to overcome the lethargy that had descended on the book he was currently working on ('Death on the Black Isle'). He suspected it was a bad sign that he thought of the 'office' as a place that existed only in inverted commas, a fictional concept rather than a location where anything was actually achieved.

'Death on the Black Isle' was like a book under an enchantment, no matter how much he wrote, there never seemed to be any more of it. 'You should change the title, it sounds like a Tintin book,' Melanie said. Before being published eight years ago Martin had been a religious studies teacher and for some reason Melanie, at an early stage of their relationship, had got it into her head (and never been able to get it out again) that Martin had once been in a monastery. How she had made this leap he had never understood. True, he had a premature tonsure of thinning hair, but apart from that he didn't think there was anything particularly monastic in his appearance. It didn't matter how much he had tried to disabuse Melanie of her fixation, it was still the thing about him that she found most interesting. It was Melanie who had disseminated this misinformation to his publicist, who had, in turn, broadcast it to the world at large. It was on public record, it was in the cuttings file and on the internet and no matter how many times Martin said to a journalist, 'No, actually I was never a monk, that's a mistake,' they still made it the fulcrum of the interview – *Blake demurs when the priesthood is mentioned*. Or *Alex Blake dismisses his early religious calling but there is still something cloistered about his character*. And so on.

'Death on the Black Isle' felt even more trite and formulaic to Martin than his previous books, something to be read and immediately forgotten in beds and hospitals, on trains, planes, beaches. He had been writing a book a year since he began with Nina Riley and he thought that he had simply run out of steam.

They plodded along together, he and his flimsy creation, stuck on the same tracks. He worried that they would never escape each other, that he would be writing about her inane escapades for ever. He would be an old man and she would still be twenty-two and he would have wrung all the life out of both of them. 'No, no, no, no, no, no, no, *no*,' Melanie said, 'it's called mining a rich seam, Martin.' Milking a cash cow for all it was worth was how someone else, someone not on 15 per cent, might have put it. He wondered if he could change his name – or, even better, use his real name – and write something different, something with real meaning and value.

Martin's father had been a career soldier, a company sergeant-major, but Martin himself had chosen a decidedly non-combatant path in life. He and his brother Christopher had attended a small Church of England boarding school that provided the sons of the armed forces with a spartan environment that was one step up from the workhouse. When he left this atmosphere of cold showers and cross-country running (*We make men out of boys*), Martin had gone to a mediocre university where he had taken an equally mediocre degree in religious studies because it was the only subject he had good exam grades in – thanks to the relentless, compulsory promotion of Bible studies as a way of filling up the dangerous, empty hours available to adolescent boys at boarding school.

University was followed by a postgraduate diploma in teaching to give himself time to think about what he 'really' wanted to do. He had certainly never intended actually to *become* a teacher, certainly not a religious studies teacher, but somehow or other he found that at the age of twenty-two he had already gone full circle in his life and was teaching in a small fee-paying boarding school in the Lake District, full of boys who had failed the entrance exams of the better public schools and whose sole interests in life seemed to be rugby and masturbation.

Although he thought of himself as someone who had been born middle-aged, he was only four years older than the oldest boys and it seemed ridiculous that he should be educating them in anything, but particularly religion. Of course, the boys he taught didn't regard him as a young man, he was an 'old fart' for whom they had no care at all. They were cruel, callous boys who were, likely as not, going to grow up into cruel, callous men. As far as Martin could see, they were being trained up to fill the Tory back benches in the House of Commons and he saw it as his duty to try to introduce them to the concept of morality before it was too late, although unfortunately for most of them it already was. Martin himself was an atheist but he hadn't completely ruled out the possibility that one day he might experience a conversion – a sudden lifting of the veil, an opening of his heart – although he thought it more likely that he was damned to be for ever on the road to Damascus, the road most travelled.

Except for where the syllabus dictated, Martin had tended to ignore Christianity as much as possible and concentrate instead on ethics, comparative religion, philosophy, social studies (anything except Christianity, in fact). It was his remit to 'promote understanding and spirituality', he claimed, if challenged by a rugby-playing, Anglican, *fascista* parent. He spent a lot of time teaching the boys the tenets of Buddhism because he had discovered, through trial and error, that it was the most effective way of messing with their minds.

He thought, I'll just do this for a bit, and then perhaps go travelling or take another qualification or get a more interesting job and a new life will start, but instead the old life had carried on and he had felt it spinning out into nothing, the threads wearing thin, and sensed if he didn't do something he would stay there for ever, growing older than the boys all the time until he retired and died, having spent most of his life in a boarding school. He knew he would have to do something proactive, he was not a person to whom things simply *happened*. His life had been lived in some kind of neutral gear: he had never broken a limb, never been stung by a bee, never been close to love or death. He had never strived for greatness and his reward had been a small life.

Forty approached. He was on an express train hurtling towards death – he had always found refuge in rather febrile metaphor – when he joined a creative writing class, being run as some kind of rural outreach educational programme. The class met in a village hall and was run by a woman called Dorothy who drove from Kendal and whose qualifications to teach the class were unclear. She'd had a couple of stories published in a northern arts magazine, readings and workshops (*work in progress*) and an unsuccessful play performed at the Edinburgh Fringe about the women in Milton's life (*Milton's Women*). The very mention of 'Edinburgh' in the class made Martin feel sick with nostalgia for a place he hardly knew. His mother was a native of the city and Martin had spent the first three years of his life there when his father had been stationed at the Castle. One day, he thought, as Dorothy rattled on about form and content and the necessity of 'finding your own voice', one day he would go back to Edinburgh and live there. 'And read!' she exclaimed, opening her arms wide so that her voluminous velvet cloak spread out like bat wings, 'Read everything that has ever been written.' There were some mutinous murmurs from the class – they had come to learn how to write (or at least some of them had), not to read.

Dorothy seemed dynamic. She wore red lipstick, long skirts and flamboyant scarves and wraps that she pinned with big pewter or silver brooches. She wore ankle boots with heels, black diamond-print stockings, funny crushed-velvet hats. That was at the beginning of the autumn session when the Lake District was decked in its gaudy finery, but by the time it had descended into the drab damp of winter Dorothy herself was wearing less theatrical wellingtons and fleeces. She also had grown less theatrical. She had begun the session with frequent references to her 'partner' who was a writer-in-residence somewhere, but by the time Christmas loomed she wasn't mentioning the partner at all and her red lipstick had been replaced with an unhappy beige that matched her skin.

They had disappointed her too, her motley collection of retirees and farming wives and people wanting to change their lives before it was too late. 'It's never too late!' she declared with the enthusiasm of an evangelist, but most of them understood that sometimes it was. There was a gruff man who seemed to despise them all and who wrote in a Hughesian way about birds of prey and dead sheep on hillsides. Martin had presumed he was something to do with the country – a farmer or a gamekeeper – but it turned out he was a redundant oil geologist who had moved to the Lakes and gone native. There was a girl, a studenty type, who really did despise them all. She wore black lipstick (disturbing in contrast to Dorothy's beige) and wrote about her own death and the effect it would have on the people around her. And there were a couple of nice ladies from the WI who didn't seem to want to write at all.

Dorothy urged them to produce little pieces of autobiographical angst, secrets of the confessional, therapeutic texts about their childhood, their dreams, their depressions. Instead they wrote about the weather, holidays, animals. The gruff man wrote about sex and everyone stared at the floor while he read out loud, only Dorothy listened with bland interest, her head cocked on one side, her lips stretched in encouragement.

'All right then,' she said, sounding defeated, 'write about a visit or a stay in hospital, for your "homework".' Martin wondered when they were going to start writing fiction but the pedagogue in him responded to the word *homework* and he set about the task conscientiously.

The WI women wrote sentimental pieces about visiting old people and children in hospital.

'Charming,' Dorothy said. The gruff man described in gory detail an operation to remove his appendix. 'Vibrant,' Dorothy said. The miserable girl wrote about being in hospital in Barrow-in-Furness after trying to cut her wrists. 'Shame she didn't manage it,' muttered one of the farmers' wives sitting next to Martin.

Martin himself had been in hospital only once in his life, when he was fourteen – Martin had found that each year of his teens brought some fresh hell. He had passed a funfair on his way back from town. His father was stationed in Germany at the time, and Martin and his brother, Christopher, were spending the summer holidays there on leave from the rigours of their boarding school. The fact that it was a German funfair made it an even more terrifying place for Martin. He didn't know where Christopher was that afternoon, probably playing cricket with other boys from the base. Martin had seen the funfair at night when the lights and smells and shouting were a dystopian vision that Bosch would have enjoyed painting. In the daylight it seemed less threatening and his father's voice appeared in his head, as it was wont to do (unfortunately), shouting, 'Face the thing you're afraid of, boy!' So he paid the entrance fee and proceeded to skirt gingerly around the various attractions because it wasn't really the atmosphere of a funfair that scared him, it was the rides. Even playground swings used to make him sick when he was younger.

He searched in his pocket for change and bought a *Kartoffelpuffer* from a food stall. His grasp on the language was slippery but he felt pretty safe with *Kartoffel*. The fritter was greasy and tasted oddly sugary and sat in his stomach like lead so it really was a bad time for his father's voice to make a reappearance in his head, just at the moment when Martin wandered past a huge swing, like a ship. He didn't know the name for it in German, but in English he knew it was a Pirate Boat.

The Pirate Boat was rising and falling in a huge, impossible parabola in the sky, the cries of the occupants following the trajectory in a swoop of terror. The very idea of it, let alone the palpable reality in front of him, struck an absolute kind of horror in Martin's breast and, on that principle, he tossed the remains of his *Kartoffelpuffer* into a waste bin, paid the fare and climbed aboard.

It was his father who came to the civilian *Krankenhaus* to take him home. He had been taken to the hospital after he was found on the floor of the Pirate Boat, limp and semi-conscious. It wasn't a mental thing, it was nothing to do with courage, it turned out that he was particularly sensitive to g-forces. The doctor who discharged him laughed and said, in perfect English, 'If you want my advice, you'll not apply to be a fighter pilot.'

His father had walked right past his hospital bed without recognizing him. Martin tried to wave but he failed to see his son's hand flapping weakly on the covers. Eventually someone at the nurses' station directed him to his son's bed. His father was in uniform and looked out of place in the hospital ward. He loomed over Martin and said, 'You're a fucking fairy. Pull yourself together.'

'There are some things that are nothing to do with

36

character weakness. There are some things that a person is constitutionally incapable of dealing with,' Martin concluded. 'And, of course, that was another country, another life.'

'Very good,' Dorothy said.

'It was a bit *thin*,' the gruff man said.

'My life has been a bit thin so far,' Martin said.

For the last class of the session Dorothy brought in bottles of wine, packets of Ritz crackers and a block of red cheddar. They appropriated paper cups and plates from the kitchen of the village hall. Dorothy raised her cup and said, 'Well, we survived,' which seemed an odd kind of toast to Martin. 'Let's hope,' she continued, 'that we all meet again for the spring session.' Whether it was the imminence of Christmas or the balloons and shiny foil decorations hanging in the village hall, or indeed simply the novel notion of survival, Martin didn't know, but a certain celebratory air washed over them. Even the gruff man and the suicidal girl entered into the jubilee spirit. More bottles of wine emerged from people's backpacks and A4-sized bags, they had been unsure if there was going to be an end-of-term 'do' but had come prepared.

Martin supposed that all of these elements, but particularly the wine, contributed to the surprising fact of his waking up next morning in Dorothy's bed in Kendal.

Her pale face was pouchy and she pulled the covers over her and said, 'Don't look at me, I'm a fright first thing.' It was true she did look a bit of a fright but, of course, Martin would never have said so. He wanted to ask her how old she was but he supposed that would be even worse.

Later, over an expensive dinner in a hotel overlooking Lake Windermere, which Martin reckoned they both deserved for having survived more than just the course, she toasted him in a nice steely Chablis and said, 'You know, Martin, you're the only one in the class who can put one word in front of another and not make me want to fucking puke, excuse my split infinitive. You should be a writer.'

Martin expected the Honda driver to pick himself up off the ground and search the crowd to find the culprit who had thrown a missile at him. Martin tried to make himself an anonymous figure in the queue, tried to pretend he didn't exist. He closed his eyes. He had done that at school when he was bullied, clinging to an ancient, desperate magic – they wouldn't hit him if he couldn't see them. He imagined the Honda driver walking towards him, the baseball bat raised high, the arc of annihilation waiting to happen.

To his amazement, when he opened his eyes, the Honda driver was climbing back into his car. As he drove away a few people in the crowd gave him a slow hand-clap. Martin wasn't sure if they were expressing disapproval of the Honda driver's behaviour or disappointment at his failure to follow through. Whichever, they were a hard crowd to please.

Martin knelt on the ground and said, 'Are you OK?' to the Peugeot driver, but then he was politely but firmly set aside by the two policewomen who arrived and took control of everything.

3

GLORIA HADN'T REALLY SEEN WHAT HAD HAPPENED. BY THE time the rumour of it had rippled down the spine of the queue she suspected it had become a Chinese whisper, *Someone had been murdered*. 'Queue-jumping probably,' she said matter-of-factly to a twittery Pam standing next to her. Gloria was stoical in queues, irritated by people who complained and shuffled as if their impatience was in some way a mark of their individuality. Queuing was like life, you just shut up and got on with it. It seemed a shame she had been born just too late for the Second World War, she possessed exactly the kind of long-suffering spirit that wartime relied on. Stoicism was, in Gloria's opinion, a very underrated virtue in the modern world.

She could understand why someone might want to kill a queue-jumper. If it had been up to her she would have summarily executed a great many people by now – people who dropped litter in the street, for example, they would certainly think twice about the discarded sweet wrapper if it resulted in being strung up from

39

the nearest lamp-post. Gloria used to be opposed to capital punishment – she remembered, during her too-brief time at university, demonstrating against an execution in some faraway country that she couldn't have placed on the map – but now her feelings tended to run in quite the opposite direction.

Gloria liked rules, rules were Good Things. Gloria liked rules that said you couldn't speed or park on double yellow lines, rules that told you not to drop litter or deface buildings. She was sick and tired of hearing people complain about speed cameras and parking wardens as if there was some reason that they should be exempt from them. When she was younger she used to fantasize about sex and love, about keeping chickens and bees, being taller, running through fields with a black-and-white Border collie. Now she daydreamed about being the keeper at the gates, of standing with the ultimate ledger and ticking off the names of the dead as they appeared before her, giving them the nod through or the thumbs down. All those people who parked in bus bays and ran the red light on pedestrian crossings were going to be very sorry when Gloria peered at them over the top of her spectacles and asked them to account for themselves.

Pam wasn't what Gloria would have called a friend, just someone she had known for so long that she had given up trying to get rid of her. Pam was married to Murdo Miller, Gloria's own husband's closest friend. Graham and Murdo had attended the same Edinburgh school, an expensive education that had put a civil polish on their basically loutish characters. They were now both much richer than their fellow alumni, a fact which Murdo said, 'Just goes to show.' Gloria thought that it didn't go to show anything except, possibly, that they were greedier and more ruthless than their former classmates. Graham was the son of a builder ('Hatter Homes') and had started his career carrying hods of bricks on one of his father's small building sites. Now he was a multi-millionaire property developer. Murdo was the son of a man who owned a small security firm ('Haven Security') and had started off as a bouncer on a pub door. Now he ran a huge security operation – clubs, pubs, football matches, concerts. Graham and Murdo had many business interests in common, concerns that spread everywhere and had little to do with building or security and required meetings in Jersey, the Caymans, the Virgin Islands. Graham had his fingers in so many pies that he had run out of fingers long ago. 'Business begets business,' he explained to Gloria, 'money makes money.' The rich get richer and the poor get poorer.

Both Graham and Murdo lived with the trappings of respectability – houses that were too big for them, cars that they exchanged each year for a newer model, wives that they didn't. They wore blindingly white shirts and handmade shoes, they had bad livers and untroubled consciences but beneath their ageing hides they were barbarians.

'Did I tell you we've had the downstairs cloakroom done out?' Pam said. 'Hand-stencilling. I wasn't sure to begin with but I'm coming round to it now.'

'Mm,' Gloria said. 'Fascinating.'

It was Pam who had wanted to come to this lunchtime radio recording (*Edinburgh Fringe Comedy*

Showcase) and Gloria had tagged along in the hope that at least one of the comics might be funny, although her expectations were not high. Unlike some Edinburgh residents who regarded the advent of the annual Festival as something akin to the arrival of the Black Death, Gloria quite enjoyed the atmosphere and liked to attend the odd play or a concert at the Queen's Hall. Comedy, she wasn't so sure about.

'How's Graham?' Pam asked.

'Oh, you know,' Gloria said, 'he's Graham.' That was the truth of it, Graham was Graham, there was nothing more, or less, that Gloria could say about her husband.

'There's a police car,' Pam said, standing on tiptoe to get a better look. 'I can see a man on the ground. He looks dead.' She sounded thrilled.

Gloria had fallen to dwelling a lot on death recently. Her elder sister had died at the beginning of the year and then a few weeks ago she had received a postcard from an old schoolfriend, informing her that one of their group had recently succumbed to cancer. The message 'Jill passed away last week. The first of us to go!' seemed unnecessarily jaunty. Gloria was fifty-nine and wondered who would be the last to go and whether it was a competition.

'Policewomen,' Pam trilled happily.

An ambulance nosed its way cautiously through the crowd. The queue had shuffled on considerably so now they could see the police car. One of the policewomen shouted at the crowd not to go into the venue but to stay where they were because they would be collecting statements from them about the 'incident'. Undeterred, the crowd continued in a slow stream into the venue.

Gloria had been brought up in a northern town. Larry, her father, a morose yet earnest man, sold insurance door-to-door to people who could barely afford it. Gloria didn't think that people did that any more. Gloria's past already seemed an antiquated curiosity — a virtual space recreated by the museum of the future. When he was at home and not lugging his ancient briefcase from one unfriendly doorstep to another, her father had spent his time slumped in front of the fire devouring detective novels and sipping conservatively from a half-pint glass mug of beer. Her mother, Thelma, worked part-time in a local chemist's shop. For work, she wore a knee-length white coat, the medical nature of which she offset with a large pair of pearl and gilt earrings. She claimed that working in a chemist's made her privy to everyone's intimate secrets but as far as the young Gloria could tell she spent her time selling insoles and cotton wool and the most excitement she derived from the job was arranging the Christmas window with tinsel and Yardley gift boxes.

Gloria's parents led drab, listless lives that the wearing of pearl and gilt earrings and the reading of detective novels did little to enliven. Gloria presumed her life would be quite different — that glorious things would happen to her (as her name implied), that she would be illuminated within and without and her path would scorch like a comet's. This did not happen!

Beryl and Jock, Graham's parents, were not that different from Gloria's own parents, they had more money and were further up the social ladder but they had the same low expectations of life. They lived in a pleasant 'Edinburgh bungalow' in Corstorphine and Jock owned a relatively modest building firm from which he had made a decent living. Graham himself had done a year of civil engineering at Napier ('waste of fucking time') before joining his father in the business. Within a decade he was in the boardroom of his own large empire, *Hatter Homes, Real Homes for Real People*. Gloria had thought up that slogan many years ago and now really wished that she hadn't.

Graham and Gloria had married in Edinburgh rather than in Gloria's home town (Gloria had come to Edinburgh as a student) and her parents travelled up on a cheap-day return and were away again as soon as the cake was cut. The cake was Graham's mother's Christmas cake, hastily converted for the wedding. Beryl always made her cake in September and left it swaddled in white cloths in the larder to mature, tenderly unwrapping it every week and adding a baptismal slug of brandy. By the time Christmas came around, the white cloths were stained the colour of mahogany. Beryl fretted over the cake for the wedding as it was still far from its nativity (they were married at the end of October) but she put on a stalwart face and decked it out in marzipan and royal icing as usual, but in place of the centrepiece snowman a plastic bridal couple were caught in the act of an unconvincing waltz. Everyone presumed Gloria was pregnant (she wasn't), as if it was the only reason Graham would have married her.

Perhaps their decision to marry in a register office had thrown the parents off balance. 'But it's not as if we're Christians, Gloria,' Graham had said, which was true. Graham was an aggressive atheist and Gloria — born one quarter Leeds Jewish, one quarter Irish Catholic, and raised a West Yorkshire Baptist — was a passive agnostic, although, for want of anything better, 'Church of Scotland' was what she had put on her hospital admission form when she had to have a bunion removed two years ago, privately at the Murrayfield. If she imagined God at all it was as a vague entity that hung around behind her left shoulder, rather like a nagging parrot.

Long ago, Gloria was sitting on a bar stool in a pub on the George IV Bridge in Edinburgh, wearing (unbelievable though it now seemed) a daringly short mini-skirt, self-consciously smoking an Embassy and drinking a gin-and-orange and hoping she looked pretty while around her raged a heated student conversation about Marxism. Tim, her boyfriend at the time — a gangly youth with a white boy's afro before afros of any kind were fashionable — was one of the most vociferous of the group, waving his hands around every time he said *exchange of commodities* or *the rate of surplus value* while Gloria sipped her gin-and-orange and nodded sagely, hoping that no one would expect her to contribute because she hadn't the faintest idea what they were talking about. She was in the second year of her degree, studying history but in a lackadaisical manner that ignored the political (the Declaration of Arbroath and Tennis-Court Oaths) in favour of the romantic (*Rob Roy*, Marie-Antoinette) and didn't endear her to the teaching staff.

She couldn't remember Tim's surname now, all she

could remember about him was his great cloud of hair, like a dandelion clock. Tim declared to the group that they were all working class now. Gloria frowned because she didn't want to be working class, but everyone around her was murmuring their agreement – although there wasn't one of them who wasn't the offspring of a doctor or a lawyer or a businessman – when a loud voice announced, 'That's shite. You'd be nothing without capitalism, capitalism has saved mankind.' And that was Graham.

He was wearing a sheepskin coat, a second-hand car salesman's kind of coat, and drinking a pint on his own in the corner of the bar. He had seemed like a man but he hadn't even reached his twenty-fifth birthday, which Gloria could see now was nothing. And then he downed his beer and turned to her and said, 'Are you coming?' and she'd slipped off her bar stool and followed him like a little dog because he was so forceful and attractive compared to someone with dandelion-clock hair.

And now it was all coming to an end. Yesterday the Specialist Fraud Unit had made an unexpected but polite appearance at Hatter Homes' headquarters in Queensferry Road and now Graham feared that they were about to throw a light into every murky corner of his business dealings. He had arrived home late, the worse for wear, downed a double of Macallan without even tasting it and had then slumped on the sofa, staring at the television like a blind man. Gloria fried him a lamb chop with leftover potatoes, and said, 'Did they find your secret books then?' and he laughed grimly and said, 'They'll never find my secrets,

Gloria,' but for the first time in the thirty-nine years Gloria had known him he didn't sound cocky. They were coming for him, and he knew it.

It was the field that had done it for him. He had bought a green-belt site that had no planning permission attached to it. He had got the land cheaply – land without planning permission was just a field, after all – but then, hey presto, six months later the planning permission was granted and now a hideous estate of two-, three- and four-bedroom 'family homes' was under construction on the north-eastern outskirts of town.

A tidy little sum to someone in the planning department was all it had taken, the kind of transaction Graham had done a hundred times before, *greasing the wheels*, he called it. For Graham it had been a little thing, his corruption was so much wider and deeper and far-reaching than a green field on the edge of town. But it was the littlest things that often brought big men down.

Once the ambulance containing the Peugeot driver had disappeared, the policewomen started to take statements from the crowd. 'Hopefully we'll get something on the CCTV,' one of them said, indicating a camera that Gloria hadn't noticed, high up on a wall. Gloria liked the idea that there were cameras watching everyone everywhere. Last year Graham had installed a new state-of-the-art security system in the house – cameras and infra-red sensors and panic buttons and goodness knows what else. Gloria was fond of the helpful little robots that patrolled her garden with their spying eyes. Once the eye of God watched people, now it was the camera lens.

'There was a dog,' Pam said, fluffing her apricot-tinted hair self-consciously.

'Everyone remembers the dog.' The policewoman sighed. 'I have several very accurate descriptions of the dog, but the Honda driver is variously described as "dark", "fair", "tall", "short", "skinny", "fat", "mid-twenties", "fiftyish". No one even took down his car's registration number, you would think someone would have managed that.'

'You would,' Gloria agreed. 'You would think that.'

They were too late now for the BBC radio showcase. Pam was delighted that they had been entertained by drama rather than comedy.

'And I've got the Book Festival on Thursday,' she said. 'You're sure you don't want to come?' Pam was a fan of some crime writer who was reading at the Book Festival. Gloria had no enthusiasm for crime writing. It had sucked the life out of her father, and anyway wasn't there enough crime in the world without adding to it, even if it was only fictional?

'It's just a bit of escapism,' Pam said defensively.

If you needed to escape, in Gloria's opinion, you just got in a car and drove away. Gloria's favourite novel still resolutely remained *Anne of Green Gables*, which when she was young had represented a mode of being that, although ideal, hadn't yet become impossible.

'We could go for a nice cup of tea somewhere,' Pam said, but Gloria excused herself, saying, 'Things to do at home,' and Pam said, 'What things?'

'Just things,' Gloria said. She was in an eBay auction for a pair of Staffordshire greyhounds that closed in two hours and she wanted to be in there at the finish.

'My, but you're a woman of secrets, Gloria.'

'No, I'm not,' Gloria said.

4

BRIGHT LIGHTS SUDDENLY ILLUMINATED A WHITE SQUARE, making the surrounding darkness seem even blacker. Six people walked into the square from all directions. They walked fast, criss-crossing each other in a way that made him think of soldiers performing a complex drill display on the parade ground. One of them stopped and began to swing his arms and rotate his shoulders as if getting ready for strenuous physical exercise. All six of them began to speak nonsense. 'Unique New York, unique New York, unique New York,' a man said and a woman answered, 'Rubber baby buggy bumpers, rubber baby buggy bumpers,' while doing some kind of t'ai chi. The man who had been swinging his arms now addressed empty air, speaking rapidly without pausing for breath, 'Thou-sleepst-worse-than-if-a-mouse-should-be-forced-to-take-up-her-lodging-in-a-cat's-ear-a-little-infant-that-breeds-his-teeth-should-lie-with-thee-would-cry-out-as-if-thou-were-the-unquiet-bedfellow.' A woman stopped in the middle of her mad walking and declared,

'Floppy fluffy puppies, floppy fluffy puppies, floppy fluffy puppies.' It was like watching the inmates of an old-fashioned asylum.

A man walked out of the darkness and into the square of light, clapped his hands and said, 'OK, everyone, if you've finished your warm-up can we get on with the dress, please?'

Jackson wondered if this was a good time to make his presence known. The actors – 'the company' – had spent the morning doing the technical run-through. This afternoon they were having the dress rehearsal and Jackson had been hoping that he could take Julia to lunch before then, but the actors were already attired alike in brown and grey shifts that looked like potato sacks. His heart sank at the sight of them. Theatre for Jackson, although of course he would never say this to any of them, was a good pantomime, preferably in the company of an enthusiastic child.

They had arrived yesterday, they had been rehearsing in London for three weeks, and he was finally introduced to them for the first time last night in a pub. They had all gone into raptures, one of them, a woman older than Jackson, had jumped up and down in a parody of a small child and another (already he had forgotten their names) dropped dramatically to her knees with her hands raised up in prayer to him and said, 'Our saviour.' Jackson had squirmed inwardly, he didn't really know how to deal with thespian types, they made him feel staid and grown-up. Julia was standing in the background (for once) and acknowledged his discomfort by winking at him in a way that might have been salacious but he couldn't really tell. He had recently (finally) admitted to himself that he needed spectacles. The beginning of the end, downhill from now on.

The actors were a small ad hoc group, based in London, and Jackson had stepped in when at the eleventh hour they lost their funding to bring their play to the Edinburgh Fringe. Not out of any love of theatre but because Julia had wheedled and cajoled in her usual over-the-top fashion, which was un-necessary – all she had needed to do was ask. It was the first real acting job she'd had in a while and he had begun to wonder to himself (never to her, God forbid) why she called herself an actress when she hardly ever *acted*. When she thought she was about to lose this part at the last moment because of the lack of money she had been plunged into a profound gloom that was so uncharacteristic of her that Jackson felt impelled to cheer her up.

The play, *Looking for the Equator in Greenland*,was Czech (or maybe Slovakian, Jackson hadn't really been listening), an existentialist, abstract, impenetrable thing which was about neither the equator nor Greenland (nor indeed about looking for anything). Julia had brought the script over to France and asked him to read it, watching him while he did so, saying, 'What do you think?' every ten minutes or so as if he knew anything at all about theatre. Which he didn't. 'Seems . . . fine,' he said, helplessly.

'So you think I should take the job?'

'God, yes,' he said, a little too promptly. In retro-spect, he realized there was no question of her *not* taking the job and wondered if she'd known from the beginning that funding was going to be a nightmare and had wanted him to feel involved with the play in some way. She wasn't a manipulative person, quite the opposite, but sometimes she had a way of looking ahead that surprised him. 'And if we're successful you'll get your money back,' she said cheerfully when he offered, 'and you never know, you might make a profit.' In your dreams, Jackson thought, but he didn't say that.

'Our angel', Tobias, the director, had called him last night, embracing him in a queeny hug. Tobias was camper than a Scout jamboree. Jackson had nothing against gays, he just wished that sometimes they wouldn't be quite so *gay*, especially when being introduced to him in what had turned out, unfortunately, to be a good old-fashioned macho Scottish pub. Their 'saviour', their 'angel' – so much religious language from people who weren't in any way religious. Jackson knew himself to be neither saviour nor angel. He was just a guy. A guy who had more money than they did.

Julia spotted him and waved him over. She looked flushed and her left eyelid was twitching, usually a sign she was wound too tightly. Her lipstick had almost worn off and her body was camouflaged by the sackcloth and ashes costume so that she didn't really look like Julia at all. Jackson guessed the morning hadn't gone well. Nonetheless she gave him a big, smiley hug (say what you like about Julia, she was a real trouper) and he wrapped his arms round her and heard her breathing, wet and shallow. The 'venue' where they had their makeshift theatre was below ground level, in the underbelly of a centuries-old building that was a warren of damp stone passages scuttling off in all directions, and he wondered if Julia could survive down here without dying of consumption.

'No lunch then?' he said. She shook her head. 'We haven't even finished tech-ing properly. We're going to have to work through lunch. How was your morning?'

'I took a walk,' Jackson said, 'went to a museum and the Camera Obscura. Had a look at Greyfriars Bobby's grave—'

'Oh.' Julia made a tragic face. The mention of a dog, any dog, always provoked an emotional reflex in Julia but the idea of a dead dog upped the ante on the emotion considerably. The idea of a dead, *faithful* dog was almost more than she could handle.

'Yeah, I paid him your respects,' Jackson said. 'And I saw the new parliament building as well.'

'What was it like?'

'I don't know. New. Odd.'

He could see she wasn't really listening. 'Shall I stay?' he asked. She looked panicked and said quickly, 'I don't want you to see the show until press night, it's still a bit rough around the edges.' Julia was always upbeat about any piece of work so he understood that 'a bit rough around the edges' translated as 'bloody awful'. This fact went unacknowledged between them. He could see wrinkles round her eyes that he didn't remember being there two years ago. She stood on tip-toes to be kissed and said, 'You have my permission to scarper. Go and have a good time.'

Jackson kissed her chastely on the forehead. Last night, after the pub, he'd been expecting to have heroic sex with Julia the moment they got through the door of the rented flat in Marchmont that the promoters had found for her. New locations always tended to make her peppy where sex was concerned but instead she said, 'I'm going to *die*, sweetie, if I don't go to sleep *this very second*.' It wasn't like Julia not to want sex, Julia always wanted sex.

He guessed it was a student flat in term-time – Sellotape marks on the wall and a toilet that Jackson used two bottles of bleach on before it even began to look clean. Julia didn't clean toilets, Julia didn't really do housework, or not so you would notice. 'Life's too short,' she said. There were days when Jackson thought life was too long. He had offered to pay for something nicer, something more expensive, even a hotel for the run if Julia wanted, but she had been uncomfortable with the idea. *Everyone else living a life of penury while I'm in the lap of luxury? I don't think that's right, sweetie, do you? Group solidarity and all that.*

When he woke this morning it was to find Julia's side of the bed as cold and smooth as if she'd never nested restlessly next to him all night. He could tell the air of the Marchmont flat was undisturbed by her presence, she wasn't bathing or breathing or reading, none of which she did silently. His heart had given a little contraction of sorrow at her absence. He tried to remember the last time Julia had woken up before him. He didn't think there ever had been a time. Jackson didn't like change, he liked to think things could stay the same for ever. Change was insidious, creeping up on you as if it was playing a game of statues. From day to day he and Julia seemed to remain the same but if he thought about them two years ago they were like different people. Then they had been clinging to each other, grateful, self-indulgent survivors of wreckage and disaster, now they were just jetsam bobbing on the aftermath. Or was it flotsam? He was never sure of the difference.

'Oh, wait, I've got something for you,' Julia said, raking around in her bag and finally producing a timetable for Lothian buses.

'A bus timetable?' he said when she handed it to him.

'Yes, a bus timetable. So you can catch a bus. And here, take my daysaver ticket.'

Jackson wasn't in the habit of taking buses. Buses, in Jackson's opinion, were for the old and the young and the dispossessed.

'I know what a bus timetable is,' he said, rather churlishly, even to his own ears. 'Thanks,' he added, 'but I'll probably go and look at the Castle.'

'And with one bound he was free,' Jackson heard her say as he walked away.

As Jackson made his way out of the labyrinth he half expected to find stalactites and stalagmites ('Stalactites from the ceiling, stalagmites from the ground,' the voice of his old geography teacher muttered unexpectedly in his brain). The whole place was carved out of the rock, the walls mildewed, the lighting dim, an underground cavern that gave Jackson the creeps. He thought about his father going down the pit every night.

It felt like an incredibly sick building. Jackson suspected he had inhaled bacilli from the plague. And if there was a fire he couldn't imagine anyone getting out alive. Up the road from here there had been a dramatic fire a couple of years ago and Jackson thought it was probably a good thing – plague followed by cleansing fire. He had asked a lethargic girl at the box office if they had a fire certificate and if so could he see it, and she had stared at him as if he'd just grown an extra head in front of her eyes.

Jackson liked things done properly. There was a file in his house in France neatly labelled 'What to do when I die' and inside it there was all the information that anyone would need in order to tidy up his affairs – the name and address of his accountant and his solicitor, a power of attorney for the same solicitor (in case he went gaga before he died), his will, an insurance policy, his bank details . . . He was pretty sure he'd covered all the bases, everything squared away because at heart he was still army. Jackson was forty-seven and in good health but he had seen a lot of people die when they weren't planning to and had no reason to think it wouldn't happen to him. There were some things you could control and some things you couldn't. The paperwork, as they said, you could control.

Jackson was ex-army, ex-police, and now an ex-private detective. Ex everything, except Julia. He had sold up his private investigation business and taken a precipitous and unexpected retirement from the world of work after inheriting money from a client, an old woman called Binky Rain. It was a serious amount of money – two million – more than enough to put some away for his daughter and buy a house in France in the foothills of the Pyrenees, complete with a trout stream, an orchard and a meadow that came all kitted out with two donkeys. His daughter, Marlee, was ten now, and getting to an age where she preferred the donkeys to him. This French life had been his dream, now it was his reality. He had been surprised by the difference between the two.

Julia said two million wasn't that much really, two million was 'barely' a flat in London or New York. 'A Learjet will set you back twenty-five million,' she said airily, 'and you won't get much change out of five million for a good yacht these days.' Julia never had any money and yet she always behaved as if she had (*That's the trick, sweetie*). She had never, as far as he knew, even seen a five-million-pound yacht, let alone stepped on board one. Jackson, on the other hand, had money and behaved as if he hadn't. He was wearing the same battered leather jacket on his back as before, the same trusty Magnum Stealths on his feet. His hair was still badly cut and he was still a pessimist. *Everyone else living a life of penury while I'm in the lap of luxury? I don't think that's right, sweetie, do you?* No, he didn't.

'Gosh, you could spend two million in a day, if you put your mind to it,' Julia had said. She was right, of course, inheriting his two million had been like winning the lottery (*trailer trash money*, Julia called it). Real money was old money, the kind of money you could never get through, no matter how hard you tried. It was passed down from generation to generation and *hoarded*. It came from enclosing your peasants' fields, from getting in on the ground floor of the Industrial Revolution and from buying slaves to cut down your sugar cane. The people with real money ran everything.

'And those are the people we don't like,' Julia said. 'The enemy of the socialist future. Which is just around the corner, isn't it, sweetie? And always will be, for ever and ever, amen – God forbid we should ever achieve some kind of prelapsarian utopia on earth because then you would have to live your life instead of just complaining about it.'

Jackson looked at her doubtfully. He didn't think he'd ever heard the word 'prelapsarian' before but he wasn't about to ask her what it meant. It wasn't so long since he could read her like a book, now sometimes he didn't understand her at all.

'Get over it, Jackson,' Julia said, 'the serfs are free and roaming the land, buying shares in high-risk Asian markets.'

The funny thing was, sometimes she sounded just like his wife. His wife was also an argumentative person. 'I only argue with people I like,' Julia said. 'It means I feel secure with you.' Generally speaking, Jackson only argued with people he *didn't* like. His *ex-*wife, he reminded himself. Yet another 'ex' in his life. They were divorced, she was remarried and pregnant with another man's child and yet he still thought of her – technically rather than emotionally – as his wife. Maybe that was the Catholic in him.

And Julia was wrong. The serfs were all watching reality television, the new opium of the people. He

watched it himself sometimes, he had satellite broadband in France, and couldn't believe the ignorance
and insanity of people's lives. Sometimes when he
turned on the television Jackson got the feeling that
he was living in a terrible version of the future, one he
didn't remember signing up for.

He fought his way past a long queue knotted up in
the doorway. They were queuing for some comedy
thing. He found himself looking at a poster, a photograph of a man making a dementedly comic face,
'Richard Moat – Comic Viagra for the Mind' it said. It
took a lot to make Jackson laugh. In my day, he
thought, comedy was funny. *In my day* – that was
what old people said, their days already behind them.

Back outdoors in what passed for daylight, he was
greeted by ancient, tall tenements staring blankly at
each other from either side of the street, making it feel
more like a tunnel, making it feel as if night had fallen.
If there had been no people around, you might have
mistaken it for a film set of a Dickens novel. You might
have mistaken it for the past itself.

Julia said it was a good venue to be in although they
had been disappointed when they had failed 'to get
into the Traverse'. 'But really this is good,' Julia
insisted, 'central, lots of people.' She was right about
there being a lot of people, the place was crowded,
'hoaching' his father would have said. Jackson's father
was a miner, from Fife originally, and might not have
had much time for this expensive, thriving capital city.
Too chichi. 'Chichi' was something Julia said.
Jackson's vocabulary seemed to be full of other
people's words these days, French people's mainly as

60

that was now his 'place of domicile', which was a different thing from 'home'.

Other than being conceived on holiday in Ayrshire (according to his father anyway) Jackson had never been to Scotland before. He had never given it much thought but now it struck him as odd (and psychologically revealing) that he had never visited the land of his father. When he stepped off the train in Waverley station yesterday he had been expecting the 50 per cent of his genes that were Scottish to recognize their heritage. He thought perhaps he would discover an emotional link with a past he'd never known, walk down a street and the faces would feel familiar, turn a corner or climb a stair and there would be an epiphany of sorts, but in fact Edinburgh felt more foreign to him than Paris did.

As he pushed his way through the crowd he tried to orientate himself towards the Castle. The ancient bird part of his brain that was usually so good at directions seemed to have gone on holiday since his arrival in Edinburgh, probably because he had been reduced to being a pedestrian ('reduced' being the apposite word here, because, let's face it, pedestrians were inferior creatures). To understand the topography of Edinburgh his brain would have had to be connected directly to the compass of a steering wheel. Jackson was a man for whom having a car was an extension of his thinking. Since going to live in France he had abandoned his old love, the BMW, and now had a hundred and fifty thousand euros' worth of brand-new Mercedes tucked away in his French barn.

At the moment, of course, all he had was a daysaver ticket in his pocket. He didn't understand how people managed without cars. 'They walk,' Julia said. Julia didn't walk much, she took the Tube or rode her bike. Jackson couldn't think of anything more dangerous than riding a bike in London. (*Have you always worried this much?* Julia asked him, *or is it just since you met me?*) Julia had a reckless streak a mile wide. Jackson wondered if it was because she didn't think she could die or because she didn't care if she died. Apart from one remaining sister, all of Julia's family were dead, a fact which seemed to make her treat existence with an odd nonchalance (*We all have to die some time.* Yes, but not yet.).

'Let's face it, Jackson, you feel *unmanned* without a car,' Julia said to him on the train journey from London. 'Unmanned' was such a Julia word – archaic and theatrical.

'No, I don't,' Jackson said, 'I feel as if I can't *get* anywhere.'

'You're getting somewhere now,' she pointed out, as they passed through Morpeth station. 'Here we go, up to Scotland,' Jackson had said at the beginning of the journey and now, hours later, in a typically Juliaesque non sequitur she turned to him and said crossly, 'And you don't say "up" from London,' Julia said, 'you say "down" because it's the capital.'

'I know that,' Jackson said, 'I'm not a hick. I just think it's stupid, Edinburgh's a capital city as well, and the whole of the north of England is blatantly geographically *up*.'

'Golly,' Julia said mildly, 'I didn't know you felt so strongly about it.'

Julia was wrong, it wasn't not having a car that had

unmanned him, it was the money. Real men had to earn a hard crust. They had to labour at the coalface, both real and metaphorical. They didn't spend their days filling up their iPods with sad country songs and feeding apples to French donkeys.

He exited Julia's venue just in time to witness a silver Peugeot get shunted by a Honda Civic (a car for losers if ever there was one). The guy who got out of the Honda was spitting mad, quite unnecessarily so, his bumper didn't even look dented. He caught the accent, English like himself. Strangers in a strange land. Honda Man was wearing driving gloves. Jackson had never understood driving gloves. The Peugeot guy wasn't big but he was wiry and tough-looking, the type who looked as if he could take care of himself but his body language was all about conciliation, which made Jackson think he was used to being in hairy situations – army or police. He felt a little tug of empathy with the Peugeot driver.

Honda Man, on the other hand, was a nutter up for a rammy and when he suddenly produced a baseball bat Jackson realized he must have had it with him when he got out of the car. Premeditated, GBH, the ex-policeman in him was thinking. They had different terms for it up here, they probably had different terms for everything up here. There was a dog in the back of the Honda. He could hear the big bass rumble of its bark, could see its snouty face attacking the car window as if it could push its way out and finish off the Peugeot guy. It was true what they said about people resembling their dogs. Julia still lamented the loss of her childhood pet, Rascal, an enthusiastic terrier. That was Julia, an enthusiastic terrier.

At the sight of the baseball bat Jackson was suddenly all instinct. He started weaving his way through the crowd quickly, on the balls of his feet all ready for whatever, but before he got close enough to the scene to do anything someone in the queue had thrown what looked like a briefcase and knocked the Honda driver for six. Jackson held back and watched. He didn't want to get involved if there was no need. Honda Man picked himself up and took off and within minutes a police car was on the scene. The sound of the approaching siren made Jackson's heart beat faster. You didn't hear police sirens in rural France. Two policewomen, both young, one prettier than the other, climbed out of the car, authoritative in their yellow fluorescent jackets and bulky belts.

The guy who had thrown the briefcase was sitting on the kerb, looking as if he was going to pass out. Jackson said, 'Are you OK?' to him. 'Try putting your head between your legs.' An acrobatic, rather sexually charged-sounding suggestion but the guy tried to do as he was told.

'Can I help you?' Jackson said, crouching down next to him. 'What's your name?'

The guy shook his head as if he didn't know. He was as white as milk. 'My name's Jackson Brodie,' Jackson said, 'I used to be a policeman.' He experienced a sudden, unexpected shiver, that was it, that was his whole life summed up in two sentences, *My name's Jackson Brodie, I used to be a policeman.* 'Can I help you?'

'I'll be all right,' the guy said, with an effort. 'Sorry. Martin Canning,' he added.

'No need to apologize to me,' Jackson said. 'I'm not the guy you floored.' That was a mistake, the guy looked horrified. 'I didn't attack him. I was trying to help *him*,' he said, pointing at the Peugeot driver, still in the middle of the street and now being tended by paramedics.

'I know, I know,' Jackson said, 'I saw it. Look, I'll give you my mobile number. Give me a call if you need your story backing up, if the police or the Honda driver give you any trouble. But I'm sure they won't, don't worry.' Jackson wrote down his number on the back of a flyer for some Fringe show that he had stuffed in his pocket and handed it over. He stood up, registering a creak in his knees as he did so. He wanted away from here. He didn't like being at crime scenes and seeing them being run by policewomen only a few years older than his daughter, it made him feel ancient. Surplus to requirements. He felt an un-expected pang of desire for his warrant card.

Jackson had made a mental note of the Honda's number plate but he walked away without giving a statement to the policewomen. Someone else would have caught the registration, there were enough people around to be witnesses, Jackson said to himself, but the truth was he didn't want to get caught up in all that bureaucratic rigmarole. If he wasn't in charge then he didn't want to be part of it. He was just an innocent bystander, after all.

5

ARCHIE AND HAMISH HAD DEVISED A PLAN. IT WAS ACTING really, it was like being in a film. They entered a shop separately, several minutes apart because more than one teenage boy coming into a shop at any one time made assistants *insane* with paranoia (which was ridiculous – how many thousands of times had he gone into a shop with Hamish and *not* committed a crime?). They browsed at different ends of the shop for a while and then, out of sight of the shop assistant, Archie would phone Hamish, Hamish would take the call and then go mental, right in front of the assistant – sometimes it was just rage at the 'caller' on the phone – *What the fucking fuck, you fucking bastard, don't you fucking dare* – that kind of thing, or sometimes he introduced a note of tragedy – the 'caller' apparently telling him about some terrible accident that had befallen a member of his family. Anything really, it didn't matter as long as it engaged the full attention of the shop assistant – *Oh, my God, not my little sister! Oh please Jesus, no.*

Sometimes Hamish could be a *little* over the top.

All this time Archie was still pretending to be looking at things in the shop. The goods. But really he was *stealing* them. Ha ha! To make this work it had to be a small shop – not too many assistants and no alarm on the door that detected security tags and crap like that. He'd learned from his past mistakes. Of course, if places didn't have alarms that usually meant they didn't have anything worth taking (they didn't steal for the sake of it, that was shite, you stole because you *wanted* something). Sometimes Archie took the phone call and Hamish nicked the stuff, but, though he didn't like to admit it, Archie was rubbish at acting.

It was the first day of the new term, their school lunch hour, and Archie hadn't worked out whether their school uniform made them look more or less of a threat. It was the uniform of a 'good school', his mother had lied about where she lived, using a friend's address to get him into the catchment area for Gillespie's. And then she said lying was wrong! She lied all the time. All it meant for Archie was that he had two long bus rides every day.

It was the middle of the Festival, the middle of the summer almost and there were all these wanker foreigners and visitors wandering around town, having a good time, still on holiday and here they were back at school. 'It's enough to make a boy turn to crime, eh, Archie?' Hamish said. He had a funny way of talking and Archie had worried at first that it was effeminate but now he realized it was probably just posh. Hamish had been expelled from Fettes and had only joined Archie's class last year. He was weird but Archie put that down to his being rich.

This place was a find, a little shop in the Grassmarket that sold snowboarding gear. Really nice. Tastee. There was only one assistant, a stuck-up bitch, all make-up and attitude. He'd like to do it to her, that would show her. He hadn't managed to do it with any girl yet but he thought about it 90 per cent of his waking life and 100 per cent of his dreaming life.

He phoned Hamish's number and then rang off and Hamish went into his whole drama-queen thing – *What do you mean, Mum? Which hospital? But Dad was fine this morning*, and so on while Archie stuffed a Quiksilver T-shirt into his bag. Maybe Hamish was too obvious, maybe the stuck-up bitch was more on the ball than she looked, whatever, all of a sudden the pair of them were legging it out of the door, running like fucking *athletes*, Archie thought he was going to have a heart attack. He came to a halt, bent over double, fighting for a breath. Hamish skidded and bumped into him behind. Hamish was pissing himself with laughter. 'The dozy cow, didn't even leave the shop,' he said and then, looking around, 'What's going on here?'

'Dunno, something.'

'A fight,' Hamish said, sticking his arm up in the air in triumph. '*Yes!*'

Archie saw the baseball bat come out, saw the guy cowering on the road, turned to Hamish and said, 'Cool.'

6

ONE OF THE POLICEWOMEN SAID, 'ARE YOU GOING TO RIDE with him in the ambulance?' She seemed to think he was a friend of the injured man and as the injured man was at that moment friendless, Martin dutifully climbed on board the ambulance. *Do unto others as you would have them do unto you.*

It was only when they eventually arrived at the new Royal Infirmary on the outskirts of town that he realized he no longer had his bag. He remembered it clattering and skidding on the wet cobblestones but he didn't know what had happened to it after that. It wasn't a disaster, everything was backed up safely on disk – the tiny lilac flake of a Sony memory stick in his wallet – and that disk was itself replicated, the backup copy in a drawer in the 'office'. He imagined whoever found his laptop turning it on, going into My Documents and reading his work, thinking what a lot of crap it was, reading passages out loud to friends and them all pissing themselves with laughter – because he imagined the kind of person who found his laptop being the kind of person who would 'piss himself' with laughter rather than simply laugh. And they certainly wouldn't giggle. A less bourgeois, less pathetic person than Martin (*You're such an old woman*, his father had said to him on more than one occasion), a person who would think Martin's life and work was worthy of derision. *'Something's up, Bertie,' Nina whispered as she balanced on Bertie's shoulders to get a good view of Lord Carstairs in the palm-filled conservatory of Dunwrath Castle.* Bertie was Nina Riley's seventeen-year-old sidekick, whom she had rescued from a life of poaching.

There was correspondence in Martin's files as well (*Thank you so much for your letter, I'm so glad you like the Nina Riley books, best wishes, Alex Blake*). Perhaps the strangers pissing themselves with laughter would find his address and return the laptop to him. Or perhaps they would come to his house and steal everything else he had. Or perhaps a car would run over the laptop, crush its mysterious motherboard, warp its plasma screen.

The Peugeot driver was conscious and quite lucid now. He had a fierce-looking lump on his temple as if an egg was buried beneath the skin. 'My Good Samaritan,' he said to the female paramedic, nodding in Martin's direction. 'Saved my life.'

'Really?' the paramedic said, unsure whether to believe such hyperbole. The Peugeot driver was wrapped in a large white-cotton cellular blanket like a baby. He struggled to remove his arm from the swaddling and extended it towards Martin. 'Paul Bradley,' he said and Martin shook his hand and said,

'Martin Canning.' He was careful not to squeeze the Peugeot driver's hand too hard in case he caused him more pain but then worried that his handshake might seem wimpish. Martin's father, Harry, was firm on the matter of manly introductions (*You're not a fucking limp-wristed Mary-Ellen – shake hands like a man*). He needn't have worried, Paul Bradley's surprisingly small, smooth hand gripped with the vice-like efficiency of an automaton.

Martin hadn't touched another human being for months, except accidentally, taking change from a cashier in the supermarket, holding Richard Moat over the toilet bowl one night while he vomited up an evening's worth of alcohol. He had helped an old woman on to a bus a week ago and been surprised by how moved he'd been by the touch of her weightless, papery hand.

'You look like you should be lying here, not me,' Paul Bradley said. 'You're white as a sheet.'

'Am I?' He did feel distinctly weak.

'It was a nasty incident by the sound of it,' the paramedic said. 'Incident', that was what one of the policewomen had called the road rage. *We'll need to take a statement about the incident, sir.* A nice neutral word, almost like 'innocent'. Perhaps he could use it for what had happened to him. *Oh yes, well, when I was in Russia there was this unfortunate incident . . .*

When they entered the A and E, a receptionist asked Martin for the Peugeot driver's details and Martin realized he had already forgotten the man's name. The Peugeot driver had been wheeled off into the hinterland of the ward and the receptionist gave Martin a

71

teacher's look and said, 'Well, could you find out? And get an address and a next of kin as well.'

Martin went looking for the Peugeot driver and found him in a curtained cubicle where a nurse was taking his blood pressure. 'Sorry,' Martin whispered, 'just need his details.' The Peugeot driver tried to sit up and was pushed gently down by the nurse.

'Take my wallet out of my jacket, mate,' the Peugeot driver said from his prone position. A black leather jacket was hanging on a metal-framed chair in the corner and Martin reached gingerly into the inside pocket and retrieved a wallet. It felt oddly intimate to be searching through someone else's pockets, like a reluctant thief. The jacket was an expensive, buttery leather, lambskin, Martin guessed, and he had to stifle a desire to slip it on and feel what it would be like to be someone else. He waved the wallet at the nurse to show that he had it, that he was innocent of all trickery, and she gave him a nice smile. 'Shall I look after your bag?' he asked the Peugeot driver. The bag, a holdall, had travelled with them in the ambulance and the Peugeot driver said, 'Cheers,' which Martin took to be acquiescence. The holdall looked almost empty but was surprisingly heavy.

The receptionist rifled efficiently through the Peugeot driver's wallet. Paul Bradley was thirty-seven years old and he lived in north London, he had a driver's licence, a wad of twenty-pound notes and a rental agreement with Avis for the Peugeot. Nothing else, no credit card, no photographs, no scraps of paper with phone numbers scrawled on them, no receipts or ticket stubs. No sign of a next of kin. Martin offered himself for the role and the receptionist said, 'You didn't even know his name,' but nonetheless wrote down 'Martin Canning' on the form.

'Church of Scotland?' she asked and Martin said, 'He's English, better put Church of England.' He wondered if there was a Church of Wales. He'd never heard of one.

The hospital was more like a station or an airport than a hospital, people stopping off on their way somewhere rather than being there for a reason. There was a café and a shop that was like a small supermarket. There was no indication that there might be sick people anywhere.

He took a seat in a waiting room. He supposed he would have to see it through now. He read the whole of a *Period Homes* magazine and a copy of *Hello!* that dated from three years ago. He remembered reading somewhere how hepatitis C could live outside the body for a long time. You could pick it up just by touching something – a door handle, a cup, a magazine. The magazines were older than the hospital. Someone must have boxed them up and brought them from the old Royal in Lauriston Place. Martin remembered being in the A and E there when his mother had scalded her hand while on a rare visit to him. That was the only thing she remembered about the visit, not the drive out to Hopetoun House where they had a lovely walk in the grounds, followed by afternoon tea, not lunch in the Pompadour in the Caledonian Hotel, nor the visit to Holyrood Palace, only the way she had managed to pour water from the kettle on to her hand.

Your kettle, she said, as if Martin was directly responsible for the boiling point of water.

The waiting room had been like something from the Third World, filthy, with old chairs that smelt of urine. She had been taken into a cubicle with pale green curtains that were stained with dried blood. Now the old hospital was being converted into flats, amongst other things. Martin thought it was odd that people would want to live where other people had died and been in pain or simply been bored to tears sitting in Outpatients waiting for an appointment. Martin himself lived in a Victorian house in the Merchiston area and before it was a house there had, presumably, been a field there. Living somewhere that had once been a field seemed preferable to living somewhere that had once been an operating theatre or a morgue. People didn't care, there was a hunger for housing in Edinburgh that was almost primitive. A report in the paper last week recorded a garage selling for a hundred thousand pounds. Martin wondered if people were going to live in it.

He had bought his own house three years ago. When he moved to Edinburgh – after signing his first publishing deal – he lived in a small rented flat off the Ferry Road while he saved for something better. He had been as obsessive and crazed as every other house-hunter in the city, poring over the property listings, off the starting blocks like a sprinter for the viewings on Thursday evenings and Sunday afternoons.

He fell in love with the Merchiston house as soon as he walked in the door to view it one misty October day. The rooms seemed as if they were full of secrets and shadows and the fading afternoon light had shone dully through the stained glass. *Opulent*, he had thought. He had a vision of how it must have been once, heard it echoing with the laughter of old-fashioned children, the boys wearing striped school caps, the girls in smocked dresses and white ankle socks. The children were conspirators, thinking up merry japes in front of the nursery fire. Everywhere the house was busy with life – a maid who washed and scrubbed willingly – no class resentment – and who sometimes aided and abetted the children in their japes. There was a gardener and a cook who prepared old-fashioned meals (kippers, blancmanges, cottage pies). And overseeing everything a loving pair of parents, gracious and good-tempered, except when the japes got out of hand when they became stern and solemn arbiters. Father commuted every day and did something mysterious 'at the office' while Mother threw bridge parties and wrote letters. On darker days Father was mistaken for a criminal or a spy and the family was forced into temporary hardship and poverty (Mother pulled it all off magnificently) before everything was explained and restored.

'I want it,' he said to the woman from the solicitor's office who was showing him round.

'You and ten other people who've put in notes of interest,' she said.

She didn't understand that when he said, 'I want it,' it wasn't a simple statement about house-buying, about surveying and bidding and paying, it was a cry from the heart for a home. After an itinerant army childhood, a boarding-school adolescence and a staff cottage in the grounds of the Lake District school, he craved his own hearth. At university he had once done one of those word-association tests for a fellow student's psychology module and when he was presented with the word 'home' Martin had drawn a complete blank, a verbal space where an emotion should have been.

When Harry, his father, retired from the army, their mother had tried to persuade him to return to her native Edinburgh. She failed miserably, and instead they had gone to live in Eastbourne. It turned out (no surprise really) that Harry was temperamentally unsuited to retirement, temperamentally unsuited to living in one place in a solid three-bedroom terrace with a nice white-wood trim, in a quiet street five minutes from the English Channel. The sea held no attraction for him, he took a brisk walk along the beach every morning but its purpose was exercise rather than pleasure. It was a relief to everyone, especially his wife, when, three years after he retired, he dropped dead of a heart attack in the middle of an argument with a neighbour who had parked his car in front of their house. 'He never accepted that it was a public highway,' their mother explained to Martin and Christopher at the funeral, as if that was somehow the cause of his death.

Their mother lacked the will to leave Eastbourne – she had never been someone with any sap – but both Martin and Christopher gravitated back to Scotland (like eel or salmon), and lived about as far as they could get from her.

Christopher was a quantity surveyor, living beyond

his income in the Borders, with his neurotic, bitchy wife, Sheena, and their two surprisingly pleasant teenage children. The geographical distance between Martin and his brother was small yet they hardly ever saw each other. Christopher was uneasy company, there was something stilted and artificial about the way he navigated his route through the world, as if he'd observed other people and thought by copying them he would be more acceptable, more authentic. Martin had long ago given up hope of being like other people.

Neither Martin nor Christopher had ever referred to the Eastbourne house as home, their mother didn't have enough personality to infuse a house with the sense of home. They always said to each other, *When are you next going down to the house?* as if the house had more character than their mother, and yet it had hardly any identity at all, repainted in the same inoffensive shade of biscuit every couple of years, after which it never took long for the walls to acquire their customary stain of nicotine yellow. His mother was a heavy smoker, it was perhaps her defining trait. Martin believed that hell would be to endure for ever a wet Sunday in his mother's house – always four o'clock in the afternoon in January with the smell of a shin of beef stew cooking in the unventilated kitchen. Tobacco fumes, weak tea, the jaw-clenching sweetness of a fondant fancy. A rerun of *Midsomer Murders* on the video.

Their mother was tremulously old now, yet showed no sign of dying. Christopher, teetering on the edge of his income, complained that she was going to outlive him at this rate and he would never inherit the half of the Eastbourne house that his bank account needed so badly.

Martin had visited his mother not long after he had first made an appearance in the bestseller lists. He showed her the week's top fifty in the *Bookseller*, explaining, 'Alex Blake – that's me, nom de plume.' He laughed, and she sighed, 'Oh, *Martin*,' as if he'd done something particularly irksome. When he bought his house in Merchiston he might not have been sure what it was that made a house a home but he knew what didn't.

Christopher had visited Martin's house only once, just after he bought it – a difficult visit made more difficult by Sheena, a woman who ran with hyenas.

'What the fuck do you need such a big house for, Martin?' Christopher asked. 'There's only you.'

'I might get married, have children,' Martin said defensively and Sheena yelped, 'You?'

There was a small room at the top of the house, overlooking the garden, that Martin earmarked as a study. He felt it was the kind of room where he would be able to write something with strength and character, not the trite and formulaic Nina Riley but a text where every page was a creative dialectic between passion and reason, a thing of life-changing artistry. Disappointingly, not only did this not happen but all the life he had sensed in the house disappeared after he purchased it. Now, when Martin walked through the front door it often felt as if no one had ever lived there, including himself. There was no sign of any merry japes. 'Merry' was a word Martin particularly liked. He had always thought that if he had children he would give them names like Sonny and Merry. The name maketh the man. There was something to be said for all those religiously influenced names – Patience, Grace, Chastity, Faith. Better to be named for a virtue than to be landed with a forgettable 'Martin'. Jackson Brodie, that was a fine name. He had been unruffled by events (*I used to be a policeman*) whereas Martin had felt sick with the excitement of it all. Not the good sort of excitement, not the merry jape sort, but the *incident* sort.

At university he had briefly gone out with a girl called Storm (because he *had* had girlfriends, despite what most people thought). It had been an experience – an experience rather than a relationship – that led him to believe that people lived up to their names. Martin was pretty dull as names went but 'Alex Blake' had a certain dash to it. His publishers hadn't considered Martin's own name to be 'punchy' enough. The pseudonym Alex Blake was chosen after much deliberation, most of which excluded Martin. 'A strong, no-nonsense sort of name,' his editor said, 'to compensate.' For what, she didn't say.

He accidentally kicked Paul Bradley's overnight bag with his foot, and felt something hard and unyielding where he had expected the softness of clothes. He wondered what a man like that – admirably competent even when injured – carried with him. Where had he come from? Where was he going? Paul Bradley didn't seem like someone who had come up for the Festival, he seemed like someone with more purpose than that.

Martin looked for his watch on his wrist and

remembered that he hadn't been able to find it this morning. He suspected that Richard Moat had 'borrowed' it. He borrowed things all the time, as if being in someone's house gave you rights to all of their possessions as well. Martin's books, shirts, his iPod (*You listen to some real shit, Martin*), had all been appropriated at one time or another by his house guest. He had even found the spare keys to Martin's car and seemed to think he could drive it whenever he wanted.

The watch was a Rolex Yacht-Master that Martin had bought himself to celebrate selling his first book to a publisher. It was an extravagance that had made him feel guilty and he had felt compelled to give an equivalent amount to charity to salve his conscience. Prosthetics Outreach, supplying artificial limbs for the victims of landmines. The cost of his Rolex was equivalent to nearly a hundred arms and legs somewhere in the unimaginable nether world of so-called civilization. Of course, if he hadn't bought the Rolex he could have bought two hundred arms and legs so his guilt was doubled rather than assuaged. The price of the watch was puny compared to the price of his house in Merchiston. For the cost of his house he could probably have fitted artificial limbs on every amputee in the world. He still wore the watch, even though it reminded him every day of the *incident* in Russia. That was his punishment, never to forget.

Richard Moat would probably have finished his show now. Afterwards, Martin supposed, Richard would be at a bar somewhere drinking and socializing – networking. It was a one-off thing that the BBC was recording, a 'showcase' for several comics. Richard's usual show was at ten. 'Comedy always happens at night,' he explained to Martin, which Martin thought was, as a statement, quite amusing and pointed it out to Richard. 'Yeah,' Richard said, in that strange laconic London way he had. He was a gag man, not a naturally funny person, and in the two weeks of knowing him he hadn't made Martin laugh once, at least not intentionally. Perhaps he saved it all for the ten o'clock show. His glory days had been in the Eighties when it was easy to pretend to be political. After Thatcher was booted out Richard Moat's star began to descend, although he had never gone far enough away to make a comeback, keeping his profile up with appearances on 'alternative' quiz shows, providing a reliable filler on chat shows and even doing a bit of (bad) acting.

On the whole, Martin thought he would rather be reading old, germ-laden magazines in a hospital, waiting for news of a stranger, than socializing at a Festival bar somewhere with Richard Moat.

Richard was a friend of a friend of an acquaintance. He had phoned up out of the blue a couple of months ago and said he was 'doing a gig at the Fringe' and was there any chance he could rent a room off Martin? Martin quietly cursed the acquaintance for giving his phone number. He had always found it difficult to say No. There had been a time, several years ago, when he had been desperately trying to finish a book but was continually interrupted by people turning up at his door, a succession of day-trippers from Porlock (as he thought of them), and he had taken to keeping a coat and an empty briefcase in the hall so that whenever the doorbell rang he could slip the coat on, pick up the briefcase and say, 'Oh, sorry, just going out.'

This was during the period in his life when he had just moved to Edinburgh from the Lakes and was making an attempt to get to know people, to start afresh with an active social life, no longer 'Mr Canning', the old fart, but *Martin Canning, how d'you do? Me, oh, I'm a writer. Crime novels. It's called* Highland Fling. *In the bestseller lists actually. Where do I get my ideas from? Oh, I don't know, always had a lively imagination, felt the urge to be creative. You know how it is.* Of course, all that happened was that, instead of an active social life, he became saddled with all kinds of unwanted people that he then had to spend the next several months (and in some cases years) trying to get rid of. Nearly all of these unwanted people seemed to have nothing better to do than drop in on Martin at all times of day and night. One in particular – a man called Bryan Legat – haunted him for years.

Bryan was a fortyish loser with an unpublished manuscript and a bitter resentment against every agent in Britain, all of whom had been incapable of recognizing his genius. Martin had seen some of the letters that Bryan had written in reply to the many letters of rejection he had received. *You stupid, stupid, stupid, arrogant English bitch* and *I know where you live, you ignorant prick* kind of letters that scared Martin with their madness. Bryan had shown him his manuscript, 'the magnum opus', entitled 'The Last Bus Driver'. 'Well,' Martin murmured politely when he returned it to Bryan, 'it's certainly *different*. And you can write, there's no doubt about that.' And he wasn't lying, Bryan *could* write, he could take a pen with turquoise ink in it and make big, loopy joined-up handwriting with verbs scattered randomly throughout sentences, sentences that in every comma and exclamation mark screamed *crazy*. But Bryan knew where Martin lived and so he wasn't about to antagonize him.

When the doorbell rang this particular day, Martin threw his overcoat on, picked up the briefcase and yanked open the door to find Bryan hovering hopefully on the doorstep. 'Bryan!' Martin said with a jauntiness he didn't feel. 'What a surprise. Sorry, but I'm just going out unfortunately.'

'Where are you going?'

'I have a train to catch.'

'I'll come with you to the station,' Bryan offered cheerfully.

'No need to do that.'

'No trouble, Martin.'

They had ended up going to Newcastle together on an eleven-thirty King's Cross GNER. In Newcastle, Martin had chosen an office block in the town centre at random and said, 'Well, this is me,' and plunged into a lift. He ended up on the eighth floor in the offices of a time-share company where it was a relief to discuss the purchase of a luxury property in Florida, 'adjacent to golf course and leisure facilities'. He took the unsigned papers away with him 'to look over' and threw them in the nearest bin on the way out. Needless to say, Bryan was waiting for him down in the foyer. 'Good meeting?' he enquired genially when he caught sight of Martin. They returned together on the four-thirty train to Edinburgh and somehow or other Bryan ended up with him in a taxi at Waverley. Martin couldn't think of anything to say to him short of *Fuck off out of my life for ever, you crazy madman*, and anyway by the time he'd paid off the taxi Bryan was already halfway up the path, saying, 'Shall I put the kettle on? I wanted to have a word with you about my novel. I've been thinking about putting it all into the present tense.'

The following year Bryan Legat fell to his death off Salisbury Crags. It was unclear whether he had jumped or fallen (or, indeed, been pushed). Martin had felt relief and guilt in equal measures when he heard of Bryan's demise. Something should have been done to help a person who was clearly so deluded but all Martin had been able to say to him was, 'The way you use the vernacular is quite startling.'

So, when put on the spot, he had found it hard to refuse Richard Moat. When Richard said, 'How much shall we say?' Martin said, 'Oh no – don't be silly, I couldn't take money off you.' As a gift, Richard had brought with him a DVD of his last tour and in the few days since then he had bought one bottle of wine, most of which he drank himself, and, as a contribution to the housework, he had loaded the dishwasher once – attempting to make a comic performance out of the mundane task. Martin had to reposition all the crockery in the machine when Richard left the kitchen. He had also bought an expensive steak that he fried for himself, splattering the whole cooker with grease, the rest of the time he seemed to eat out.

Two days ago, on his opening night (which Martin

had managed to avoid), Richard had invited Martin for 'a curry' with 'some people' here from London for his show. Martin had suggested the Kalpna in St Patrick Square because he was a vegetarian (*Nothing with a face actually*) but somehow or other they had ended up at a rabidly carnivorous place that some other 'people' in London had recommended to Richard. When it came to the bill, Martin found himself insisting on picking the whole thing up. 'Thanks, Martin, thanks a lot,' one of the London people said, 'although I could have put it on expenses, you know.'

'How do you feel about smoking in the house?' Richard had asked ten minutes after he arrived, and Martin had been caught between wanting to be a warm, welcoming host and wanting to say that he loathed everything to do with cigarettes. 'Well . . .' he began, and Richard said, 'Just in my room, of course, I wouldn't make you breathe my filthy, carcinogenic smoke,' but every morning when Martin came downstairs there was a little pile of butts in the living room in whatever saucer or plate (and once a tureen) he had foraged from the Wedgwood service Martin had bought when he moved into the house.

Richard came in very late and then didn't surface until midday, which was something to be thankful for. Once he was up he spent his time on the phone. He had a new video phone that Martin admired politely ('Yeah, she's a sexy mother, isn't she?' Richard agreed) even though he thought it was odd and rather dumpy and reminded him of a *Star Trek* communicator. Richard had downloaded the theme tune from *Robin Hood*, the old Fifties television programme, as his ringtone and the sound of it, rendered tinnily tiny and stupid, was slowly driving Martin crazy. As an antidote Martin himself had recently downloaded 'Birdsong' and had been pleasantly surprised by how authentic the birds sounded.

Looking around him in A and E, he found a clock on the wall that said it was half-past one. It felt much later, the day had lost its shape, distorted under the weight of unexpected reality.

Martin had read a spiteful review of Richard Moat's show in the *Scotsman*. It said, amongst other things, 'Richard Moat's humour creaks with banality these days. He hashes up the same old tired material he was using ten years ago. The world has moved on but Richard Moat hasn't.' Martin felt embarrassed just reading it. He couldn't mention to Richard that he'd seen it because that would mean they would both have to face the awfulness of it all, and Martin had acquired enough bad reviews himself to know the abysmal feelings they generated.

'I never read my reviews,' Richard volunteered morosely after his opening night. Martin didn't believe him. Everyone read their own reviews. It was some years since Richard had 'done the Festival', and whatever feelings he had once had about Edinburgh (he had been gloriously successful here at the beginning of his career) had now turned mostly to antipathy. 'You see, it's a great city,' he said to one of the 'people from London' during their flesh-feeding frenzy in the phobia-inducing crowded Indian restaurant, 'fantastic to look at and all that, but it has no *libido*. And obviously you have to blame Knox for that.' Martin hated the way Richard said 'Knox' with such offhand familiarity. He felt like saying, Knox might have been a dour, tight-arsed, puritanical bastard, but he was *our* dour, tight-arsed, puritanical bastard, not yours.

'Exactly!' another one of them said. He was wearing narrow spectacles with thick black rims and smoked even more than Richard. Martin, a spectacle wearer since the age of eight, wore rimless lightweight glasses in an attempt to disguise the fact he had defective eyesight, rather than making a feature of it. 'No libido – very good, Richard.' The man with the black-framed spectacles jabbed the air with his cigarette to emphasize his agreement. 'That's Edinburgh *exactly*.' Martin wanted to defend his home city but couldn't quite work out how. It was true, Edinburgh didn't have a libido, but why would you want to live in a city that did?

'Barcelona!' another of Richard's friends shouted across the table (they were loud and not a little drunk) and the man with the old-fashioned but trendy spectacles barked back, 'Rio de Janeiro!' And so the shouting of cities went on ('Marseilles!' 'New York!') until they got to 'Amsterdam!' and a row broke out over whether Amsterdam possessed its own libido or was 'merely a locus for the exploitative commercial transactions of other people's libidos'.

'Sex and capitalism,' Richard intervened languidly, 'what's the difference?' Martin waited for a punchline but apparently there wasn't one. Personally he thought there was a lot of difference between the two, but then he remembered undressing in front of Irina in that awful hotel room with its view of the Neva and the cockroaches scuttling along the skirting boards. 'Well-upholstered. Built for comfort, not for speed,' he'd joked, cringing with embarrassment. '*Da?*' She laughed accommodatingly, apparently not understanding a word. The very remembrance of it made him double up as if he'd been hit by an invisible fist.

'Girls,' one of them said suddenly, 'we should go and find some girls after this.' The idea was greeted with frightening enthusiasm.

'Pole-dancing!' Richard sniggered like an adolescent boy.

'Oh, sorry, Martin,' another of them said, 'sorry to be so rampantly hetero.'

'Do you think I'm gay?' Martin asked, surprised. They all turned to look at him as if he'd said something interesting for the first time.

'There's nothing wrong with that, Martin,' Richard said. 'Everyone's gay.'

Martin would have argued with this ridiculous statement but he had just discovered that he was chewing on a piece of chicken from his 'vegetable biryani'. He removed it from his mouth as discreetly as he could and put it on the side of his plate. The last gristly remnant of some poor, abused bird that had been pumped full of hormones and antibiotics and water in a foreign country. He could have wept for it.

'It's OK, Martin,' Richard Moat said, slapping him on the back, 'you're with friends.'

Without asking him whether he wanted to go or not, Richard informed him that he had left a ticket for the radio showcase for Martin at the box office, but when Martin got to the venue the indifferent girl behind the counter said to another indifferent girl, 'Are there any comps in Richard Moat's name?' The other girl made a face and glanced around while the first girl returned to glaring at her computer screen.

Martin found himself staring at a poster for Richard's show. It was a close-up of Richard making a quirky face. A strap-line running under it said, 'Comic Viagra for the Mind'. Martin thought that sounded off-putting rather than inviting.

When nothing more was forthcoming from either of the girls, Martin pointed out a rickety wooden dove-cote on the wall at the back with names sellotaped beneath each individual pigeon hole. The one that said 'Richard Moat' contained a white envelope. The second indifferent girl read the name written on the envelope. 'Martin Canning?' she asked suspiciously and then gave it to him without waiting for confirmation. He checked the tickets and found a scribbled note on one of them. 'Your car's parked in front of Macbet in Leith Walk, cheers, R.'

'Can I go straight in?' he asked and the first girl, without removing her eyes from her computer screen, said, 'No, you have to join the queue.'

'Thanks,' he said, unacknowledged and invisible. And then he had joined the queue. And then the man with the baseball bat stepped out of the Honda.

7

JACKSON FOUGHT HIS WAY UP THE ROYAL MILE, THROUGH THE
crowds and the tartan tat, until he finally gained the
Castle, soaring almost Cathar-like on top of the
volcanic rock. He paid the entrance fee and walked
along the Esplanade, past the towering scaffolded
stands built for the Edinburgh Tattoo – 'The Tattoo has
a hundred per cent box office,' Julia had told him
enviously and tickets were 'like gold dust' and yet
within minutes of arriving in Edinburgh she had been
given comps for the Tattoo by a complete stranger
(claiming to be a piper, although Jackson saw no
evidence of bagpipes). She tried to palm them off on
Jackson but he couldn't think of anything worse than
being trapped for two hours in the dark and the
summer damp watching a camp spectacle that had
nothing to do with the reality of being in the military.
'Don't think of it as military, think of it as theatrical.
Massed pipes and drums,' Julia said, reading from a
programme the so-called piper had given her, 'and an
army motorcycle stunt team. Highland dancers? And,

oh look, "Russian Cossack Dancers". That sounds like fun, doesn't it?'

'No.'

Jackson couldn't imagine Julia's play having any kind of box office, couldn't believe anyone would actually pay good folding money to see *Looking for the Equator in Greenland*.

The Castle was a brute of a building, all fairy-tale Scottish from below but once you were within its glowering walls it was dank and doom-laden. (This bit of Edinburgh his father might have liked.) The Castle seemed not so much a product of engineering as of organic growth, the dressed stone fused with the rough black basalt of the rock and its own bloody history. Jackson bought a guidebook but didn't pick up an audio, he hated those things, the unruffled tones of some woman (always a woman) regurgitating pre-digested bits of information. It reminded him of the voice on his GPS ('Jane'). He had tried other voices on the GPS but they hadn't worked for him: the French was too sexy, the American too American and even if he had understood the language he didn't think he could have trusted an Italian voice telling him how to drive, so in the end he always came back to the quietly insistent tones of Jane, a woman who believed she was always right. It was rather like being in a car with his wife. His ex-wife.

He had Julia's camera with him so he took a few snaps of the view from the ramparts. Julia never took photographs of views, she said pictures were meaningless unless they had people in them, so he asked one of a group of Japanese to take a photo of him next to the One O'Clock Gun. The Japanese seemed to think this was hilarious and insisted on posing with him before moving off like a school of fish after their guide.

Julia always grinned at the camera as if it was the happiest day of her life. Some people had it and some didn't. Jackson himself tended to look surly. Perhaps it wasn't just in photographs. Julia had once told him that he had a 'somewhat threatening demeanour', a perception of himself that he found alarming. He had tried to take on a more benign aura for his photograph with the Japanese. For a moment Jackson envied them. He imagined it must be nice to belong to a group. Most people thought of him as a loner but he suspected he had been at his most comfortable when institution-alized, in the army and then the police. The individual was overrated in Jackson's opinion.

He found a table outside the café and had a cup of tea and a cake, a lemon poppy-seed thing. The poppy seeds made the cake look as if it was speckled with insect eggs and he left most of it. Julia believed no out-ing was worth its while unless it ended up with tea and cake. He knew everything Julia believed. He could have gone on one of those *Mr and Mrs* quizzes and answered everything about her likes and dislikes. He wondered if she would be able to do the same for him. He honestly didn't know.

A rustle of excitement preceded the firing of the One O'Clock Gun. The story went that the citizens of Edinburgh had been too mean to pay for twelve cannon shots for midday and so had settled for a gun at one o'clock. Jackson wondered if that was true. Was the Scots' reputation for meanness really justified?

Half-Scottish himself (although he didn't feel it), he liked to think he had been generous with money even when he didn't have any. Now he had it he tried to distribute his wealth far and wide – diamond earrings for Julia, a herd of cows for a village somewhere in Africa. Nowadays you could shop for charity on the internet as easily as trawling the cyber shelves of Tesco.com, adding goats and chickens to your 'shopping basket' as if they were bags of sugar, tins of beans.

Jackson knew that ever since he'd inherited the money he'd been looking for ways to get it off his conscience – it was the Puritan in him, the little voice that said if you didn't suffer for something then it wasn't worth having. That was what he admired in Julia – she was a total and complete hedonist. And it wasn't that Julia hadn't suffered in her life, because she had, more than Jackson. They both had a sister who had been murdered, they had both been motherless children, Jackson's elder brother and Julia's eldest sister had both killed themselves. Bad luck on bad luck. The kind of stuff you tended not to talk about because it wasn't usually a good idea to reveal so much disrepair to other people. That was the good thing about Julia, her family background was even more fucked up than his. They were a pair of freakishly bereaved people.

Jackson and Julia had stood side by side in a police mortuary, gazing at the fragile bird-bones of Julia's long-lost sister, Olivia. Such things cast a long shadow on the soul and Jackson feared that it was their understanding of loss that made them true companions of the heart. He suspected that it might not be a healthy thing – yet wasn't the shared twist of grief in them stronger than, say, a mutual love of skiing or Thai food or all the other things couples based their lives on?

'A couple?' Julia had said ruminatively, when he mentioned something to this effect. 'Is that how you think of us?'

'Don't you?' he said, suddenly alarmed, and she laughed and said, 'Of course I do,' tossing her head so that the curls piled upon it bounced around like springs. He knew that gesture well, it nearly always accompanied dissimulation on Julia's part.

'You don't think of us as a couple?'

'I think of us as you and me,' Julia said, 'two people, not an entity.'

One of the things Jackson liked about Julia was her independence, one of the things he didn't like about Julia was her independence. She had her own life in London, Jackson visited her there, and she came to stay in his house in the Pyrenees where they built log fires in the huge stone hearths and drank a lot of wine and had a lot of sex and talked about getting a Pyrenean Mountain Dog (or Julia did). Sometimes they went to Paris together, they liked Paris a lot, but she always went back to London. 'I'm like a holiday romance for you,' Jackson complained and Julia said, 'But that's rather wonderful, isn't it?'

For her birthday in April, Jackson took Julia to Venice, to the Cipriani, although both of them discovered that an entire week of either, let alone both, was a little too much. Julia said it was like finding the best cake in the world and then eating nothing else, so that you 'sickened on the very thing you craved the most'. Jackson wondered if she was quoting from a play, she often did and he hardly ever got the reference. 'I don't have a sweet tooth to begin with,' he said, rather grumpily.

'Just as well that life isn't really like a box of chocolates then, isn't it?' she said. He got that reference. He'd hated that film. They were on the water bus at the time, making their way up the Grand Canal, and Jackson snapped her as they passed Santa Maria della Salute. Wherever you went, it was like being on a stage set. It suited Julia perfectly.

On her birthday, Jackson took Julia for an evening gondola 'excursion' – along with just about every other tourist in Venice. 'He's not going to sing, is he?' Julia whispered as they settled themselves on to the red velvet seat. 'I hope not,' Jackson said, 'I think you pay extra for singing.' The gondolier in his striped vest and straw boater seemed like a dreadful tourist cliché, reminding Jackson of the punts on the river in Cambridge. Cambridge was where he had lived in the 'before' time, it was where Julia grew up, it was where his own daughter was growing up now. Before, Jackson never really thought of Cambridge as home, home was (strangely) the army, or the dark place where he himself had grown up, a place where it was always raining in his memory, and possibly in reality too. Now, with the curse of hindsight, he could see that perhaps Cambridge had been a real home – a place of safety with a wife and a house and a child. Another kind of institution. Before and after – that was how he classified his life. Before and after the money.

The gondolier didn't sing and it turned out to be not such a cliché after all. Venice was even more gorgeous at night, the lamps glittering on the black water, like soft jewels, and something unsuspected and beautiful to marvel at around every turn in the narrow canal – Jackson felt the poetry in his soul rising until Julia hissed in his ear, 'You're not going to propose, are you?' The thought hadn't been in his head at all but once she said that – in exactly the same tone as she had voiced her anxieties about the singing gondolier – he felt irritated with her. Why shouldn't he propose to her, would it be such a dreadful thing? He knew that these weren't the circumstances in which you should kick off an argument (Venice, birthday, gondola, etc.) but he couldn't stop himself. 'So you wouldn't marry me if I asked you?' he said defensively.

'Is that a proposal, Jackson?'

'No. I'm just saying, if I asked you, would you say no?'

'Yes, of course, I would.' They'd hit some kind of traffic jam on the canal, squeezing past a large gondola containing a cargo of Americans. 'Be reasonable, Jackson, neither of us are the marrying kind.'

'*I* am,' Jackson said, 'and you've never been married so how can you know?'

'That's a specious argument,' Julia said, turning her face away from him and making a show of looking up at the windows of some palazzo or other. The gondola rocked on the water as the gondolier finally manoeuvred it past the Americans.

'So how *do* you see our relationship?' he persisted. He knew he shouldn't. 'Do we just see each other now and then, whenever you feel like it, fuck each other's brains out and after a few years you grow bored and it all peters out? Is that how you see it? I mean, goodness, Julia,' he said sarcastically, 'this is the longest you've ever been with anyone. What was the record before – a week?'

'Crikey, you've really been giving this some thought, haven't you, Jackson?'

'Of course I've been giving it some thought. Jesus, haven't you?'

'Not in such lurid detail apparently,' Julia said mildly. 'Do you honestly think, sweetie, that being married would stop us getting bored with each other?'

'No, but that's not the point.'

'Yes it is. Stop it, Jackson, don't be so curmudgeonly, you're going to spoil a lovely evening.'

But the evening was clearly spoiled already.

He wasn't sure that he did actually want to marry Julia but he found her absolute negativity on the subject disturbing. He knew the topic couldn't be introduced again, not without a huge row, a fact that festered in a way that he found surprising.

The One O'Clock Gun boomed over the town and the tourists dutifully flinched and laughed. It seemed to have more to do with theatre than timekeeping, a show for the Japs and Yanks. And nothing to do with real gunfire. Real gunfire cracked and popped mysteriously in the distance or exploded so loudly near you that it blew your eardrums out.

He had a look in the building at the heart of the Castle that housed the Scottish National War Memorial. He was surprised by how beautiful it was inside – Arts and Crafts style, he knew that from Julia. The names of the dead, so many dead, were written in big red books. He knew he had three great-uncles (three brothers, God help their mother) in those books somewhere but he didn't look for them. Scotsmen all over the globe building the British Empire and then dying for it. His own father hadn't fought in the Second World War because mining was a protected occupation. 'As if it was a soft option,' his father scoffed, 'working a double shift in the bowels of the earth.' When he'd left school at sixteen Jackson had gone to sign on at the pit, but his father said that he hadn't worked all his life 'in this filthy hell-hole' just so that his son would have to as well. So Jackson joined the army, a Yorkshire regiment because Yorkshire was his home, not this place of grey stone and blasting wind. Francis, his brother, had worked as a welder at the pit and his father had made no effort to stop him. But Francis was dead by the time Jackson was sixteen and Jackson had become the only one of three children left to his father and he supposed that had made him more precious in some way, not that the old bastard had ever shown it.

Jackson was left relatively unmoved by the ranks of the dead (death was so commonplace), by the plaques for the fallen, for the women, for the merchant seamen. Not even the verse from the Binyon poem, *At the going down of the sun and in the morning/We will remember them*, on the Women's Services Memorial was able to touch him as it usually did; it was something else entirely that set off the emotion – a small relief carved into the stone at knee height, depicting a cage of canaries and a little gathering of mice. 'The Tunnellers' Friends', the inscription read. He blinked back the tears, coughed and did some manly throat-clearing to cover his emotion. Julia would have been on her knees next to it, stroking the stone as if it was an animal. Kissing it probably. He could bring her to see it once her show opened. She would like that.

Outside, he stood across the courtyard and took a photograph of the building that housed the memorial, but he knew already that when he showed it to Julia it would just look like a building.

The camera had been his present to Julia last Christmas, a nice chunky Canon digital that had appealed to him as a piece of equipment. Their photos from Venice were still on the memory card, and while he drank his tea in the Castle's café he scrolled through the little coloured pictures that looked like miniature paintings. There had been a perfect blue spring sky for the whole week so that through the viewer the photographs looked like tiny Canaletto backdrops with Julia or Jackson inserted into them. There were only two of them together, one on the Rialto, taken by a helpful German tourist, and a second one taken with the camera's timer – both of them sitting up on their king-size bed in the Cipriani, toasting each other with champagne. It was taken just before they left for the gondola ride.

Julia was very photogenic, every time turning on the full beam of her lipsticky smile. She had a great smile. Jackson sighed, paid the bill for his tea and cake, put a big tip on the table and left the Castle.

Crowds flowed down the Royal Mile like the lava that had once moulded landscape out of fire, moving around obstacles in the way – the statue of David Hume, a mime artist, a piper, several student theatre groups, people handing out flyers (lots of them), another piper, a man eating fire, a man juggling fire, a woman dressed as Mary Queen of Scots, a man dressed as Sherlock Holmes. Another piper. It certainly was a city *en fête*. It was strange to think that somewhere – far away in a country about which people knew nothing – there was a war going on. But then there was always a war going on somewhere. War was the human condition. War had fed, clothed and paid Jackson in its time so perhaps he shouldn't be the one to complain. (Although someone should.)

He walked down to Holyrood Palace, bought a poke of chips and walked back up the Royal Mile. Another day where nothing had happened, he thought. That was a good thing, he reminded himself – what was the Chinese curse? *May you live in interesting times*. Still, a *little* bit more interesting wouldn't be such a dreadful thing to ask for. He remembered Honda Man and Peugeot Guy, it had been an interesting day for them. He felt a pang of guilt for not acting like a concerned citizen and reporting the Honda's registration. He could still reel it off, he'd always had a good memory for numbers even though he had no feel for maths – one of the brain's many baffling anomalies.

He must have looked as if he belonged because someone, Swedish or Norwegian, asked him for directions and Jackson said, 'Sorry, I'm a stranger here.' That wasn't what you said, was it? *Stranger* – 'visitor' was the correct word. 'Stranger' implied an outsider, a threat. 'A tourist,' he added for clarification. 'I'm a tourist too.'

8

GLORIA OPENED HER FRONT DOOR AND FOUND HERSELF FACE
to face with another pair of policewomen. They looked
very like the two from earlier in the day, as if they had
all come out of the same box.

'Mrs Hatter?' one of them said, her face already
adjusted to bad news, 'Mrs Gloria Hatter?'

Graham was not, as Gloria had thought, in a crisis
meeting with his accountants in Charlotte Square,
instead he was in Accident and Emergency at the new
Royal Infirmary, having succumbed to a heart attack in
an Apex hotel room in the company of someone who
apparently went by the name of 'Jojo'. Jojo was the
name of a clown in Gloria's opinion, although it
turned out that she was actually a call-girl, which was
simply another word for a whore.

'Call a spade a spade,' Gloria sighed.

The policewomen ('PC Clare Deponio and this is PC
Gemma Nash') looked like teenagers who had hired
police uniforms for a fancy-dress party. 'A simple

phone call would have done,' Gloria said to them. She made them all tea and they sat on the peach-damask sofa in her peach-themed living room balancing the Royal Doulton cups and saucers primly on their knees, politely nibbling on Gloria's home-made shortbread. Gloria was sure they had much better things to do and yet they seemed grateful for the space. 'It makes a change,' one of them (Clare) said. They were very busy, Gemma said, because of a bout of 'summer flu' that was 'knocking down' the Lothian and Borders Police 'like ninepins'.

'You have a nice house,' Clare said appreciatively. Gloria looked around the peach-themed living room and tried to see it through a stranger's eyes. She wondered what she would miss if it was all taken away from her. The Moorcroft? The Chinese carpets? The Staffordshire ornaments? She was fond of her collection of Staffordshire. She wouldn't miss the picture above the fireplace, a nineteenth-century painting of the stag at bay variety, depicting a terrified stag cornered by a pack of crazed hounds – a sixtieth birthday present to Graham from Murdo Miller. And she certainly wouldn't miss the ugly Scottish Businessman of the Year award which took pride of place on the mantelpiece. It sat next to a photograph of Graham and Gloria on their wedding day, which, as it happened, was the only photograph they had from that day. If there was a fire and Graham had to choose between saving his wedding photograph and his Scottish Businessman of the Year award, Gloria had no doubt that he would save the unattractive resin sculpture. In fact, if it came to a choice between saving the award and saving Gloria, she was pretty sure he would choose it over her.

The policewoman called Clare picked up the wedding photograph and said, with a sympathetic tilt of the head as if Graham was already written off, 'Is this your man?' Gloria wondered if it was odd that she was drinking tea from a delicate Doulton cup when she should have been rushing dramatically to the A and E to fulfil her spousal duties. The unavoidable fact of Jojo seemed to have hobbled the imperative. A stain on the triumphant possibility of Graham's death.

Gloria took the photograph from Clare and scrutinized it. 'Thirty-nine years ago,' Gloria said. Gemma said, 'You should get a long-service medal,' and Clare said, 'Christ, that's a long time, excuse my French. It's a shame,' she added, 'what's happened, the way he was found and everything. Not nice for you.'

'They're all tossers,' Gemma, the plain one of the two, murmured.

The heavy silver frame of the wedding-day photograph couldn't disguise the fact that it hadn't been shot by a professional. It had yellowed with age and looked like a snap taken by a rather incompetent relative (which it was). Gloria wondered at the inertia on the part of both sets of parents that had resulted in no true record of the day.

Gloria regretted not having had a white wedding with all the trimmings because now she would be in possession of a big, white, leather-bound album of photographs to look back on, photographs that showed she'd once had family who cared about her more than she realized at the time, and in the album everyone would be looking their best for ever. And Gloria herself would be at the centre of it all, radiant and thin and unaware of how her life was already slipping out from under her feet. Gloria was surprised Graham had been in an Apex, that wasn't his style at all.

It had, in fact, been more of a brown wedding. Graham was dressed in an up-to-the-minute suit in a colour that, when Gloria was a child, everyone had blithely referred to as 'nigger-brown'. Gloria wore a fur coat that she had bought in a second-hand shop in the Grassmarket. The coat was Forties-style, made from Canadian beaver at a time when people didn't think about whether or not it was wrong to wear fur. Although Gloria would no longer wish to wear the skin of another animal on top of her own, the way she looked at it now, the beavers were already long dead and had lived the happy, uncomplicated life of Canadian beavers before the war.

If Gloria had had the white leather-bound album of photographs, her mother, father and elder sister would all have been preserved within its pages. As well as 'first to go' Jill, of course, who had travelled up with the posse of schoolfriends and drunk into the night, long after everyone else had gone to bed. Gloria's brother, Jonathan, would not have been in the photographs because he died when he was eighteen. Gloria was only fourteen when Jonathan died and the child in her had presumed he would come back eventually. Now that she was older and understood that he was never coming back she missed him more than when he died.

As she watched the young policewomen climb back

into their patrol car, Gloria thought about Graham in a hotel room, lying on a double bed with a veneer headboard, flicking through the TV channels while he ate steak and chips, a pathetic little garnish of a salad, half a bottle of claret, while he waited for a woman to come and perform professional sex. How many times had he betrayed her in this sleazy fashion while she sat at home with only the Bang & Olufsen Avant widescreen for company? Hadn't she known it in some way, in her heart of hearts? Innocence was no excuse for ignorance.

Gloria had happened to glance down at that moment and notice that she was wearing a boxy cashmere camel cardigan from Jenners that had brass buttons that could only be described as tedious. She realized she was wearing the kind of clothes that her mother would have worn if she'd had more money. The matronly cashmere seemed to confirm something that Gloria had suspected for some time, that she had gone straight from youth to old age and had somehow managed to omit the good bit in between.

It was not an unfamiliar feeling. Gloria often had the impression that her life was a series of rooms she walked into that everyone else had just left. The war had been over for only a year when she was born and it still loomed large in their household. Her father had fought 'with Monty' – as if they had stood side by side in battle, while her mother had been engaged on the home front, heroically growing vegetables and keeping chickens. Gloria grew up feeling she had just missed something momentous that would never come again (which was true, of course) and that her life was thereby diminished. She felt much the same about the Sixties. Her formative years had taken place in a no-man's-land between two revolutionary epochs. By the time the Sixties were in full swing, Gloria was married and writing grocery lists on wipe-clean 'memo-boards'.

If Gloria could have gone back she would not have slipped off that bar stool in the pub on George IV Bridge and followed Graham. Instead she would have finished her degree, moved down to London and worn heels and little business suits (kept her figure), drunk a lot at the weekends, had sex with so many different men that she would never be able to remember their names, let alone their faces. She noticed the time and realized that the eBay auction had closed. She wondered if she had been outbid on her Staffordshire greyhounds. Trust Graham to spoil things even when he was at death's door.

On the drive to the new infirmary out at Little France, Gloria had practised the kind of conversation she would have with Graham. Despite the fact that Gemma and Clare had told her he was unconscious, Gloria hadn't really foreseen that this would be a hindrance to his talking. Graham *talked*, it was what made him Graham, so when she saw him in A and E, linked up to an array of blinking, beeping monitors, she was still expecting him to open his eyes and say something typically Grahamesque ('You took your fucking time, Gloria'). So his absolute passivity was puzzling.

The A and E consultant explained that Graham's heart had gone into 'overload' and stopped. His

106

'system' had been 'down' a long time, resulting in his current state of suspended animation, which he might or might not recover from. 'We reckon,' the consultant said to Gloria, 'that roughly one in a hundred men die during sexual intercourse. The pulse of a man having sex with his wife is ninety beats a minute, with a mistress it rises to one hundred and sixty.'

'And with a call-girl?' Gloria asked.

'Oh, through the roof, I imagine,' the consultant said cheerfully. 'Of course, he might have been revived quicker if he hadn't been tied up.'

'Tied up?'

'The girl with him attempted to resuscitate him, she seems quite the inventive sort.'

'Tied up?'

Gloria discovered the inventive call-girl in question, the clown-aliased Jojo, still hanging around in the A and E waiting room. Her real name was Tatiana apparently.

'I'm Gloria,' Gloria said.

'Hello, Gloria,' Tatiana said, her overripe l's making the greeting seem slightly sinister, like a James Bond villainess.

'His wife,' Gloria added, for clarification.

'I know. Graham talks about you.'

Gloria wondered at what point in the transaction between Graham and a call-girl her name would crop up. Before, after – during?

'Not during,' Tatiana said. 'He can't speak during.' She raised expressive eyebrows in response to Gloria's unspoken query. 'Gag,' she said finally.

* * *

'Gag?' Gloria murmured, over a coffee and a Danish in the hospital's café. It was the first time she had been in the new Royal and she felt slightly disorientated by the fact that it was just like a shopping mall.

'Stops the screaming,' Tatiana said matter-of-factly, unrolling the pinwheel of a *pain aux raisins* before delicately chewing on it in a way that reminded Gloria of the squirrels in her garden. Gloria frowned, trying to imagine how you could be tied down on an Apex bed. Impossible, surely? (No bedposts.) 'What does he say?' she asked. 'When he can speak.'

Tatiana shrugged. 'This and that.'

Gloria said, 'Where are you from?' and Tatiana said, 'Tollcross,' and Gloria said, 'No, I mean originally,' and the girl looked at her with her catty green eyes and said, 'From Russia, I am Russian,' and for a moment Gloria had a glimpse of endless forests of thin birch trees and the insides of smoky foreign coffee houses, although she supposed the girl was more likely to have lived in a concrete high-rise in some horrendously bleak suburb.

She was dressed in jeans and a vest top, not working clothes, surely. 'No,' she said, 'here is costume,' indicating the contents of the large bag she had with her. Gloria caught a glimpse of buckles and leather and some kind of corset that, for a surreal moment, brought to Gloria's mind an image of her mother's flesh-pink surgical Camp corset. 'He likes to be submissive.' Tatiana yawned. 'Powerful men, they're all the same. Graham and his friends. *Idyots*.'

His *friends*? 'Oh lord.' She thought of Pam's

husband Murdo. She thought of Pam tootling around town in her split-new Audi 8, going to her bridge club, her health club, Plaisir du Chocolat for afternoon tea. While Murdo was doing – what? Gloria shuddered to think.

Gloria sighed. Was this what Graham really wanted, not Windsmoor and Country Casuals, not tedious brass buttons, but a woman young enough to be his own daughter trussing him up like a turkey? It was strange how something you weren't expecting could, nonetheless, turn out to be no surprise at all.

Gloria noticed Tatiana was wearing a tiny gold crucifix in each ear. Was she religious? Were Russians religious now they weren't communists? You couldn't ask, people never did. Not in Britain. On holiday in Mauritius, the driver taking them from the airport to the hotel asked Gloria, 'Do you pray?' just like that, five minutes after picking them up and loading their suitcases in the boot. 'Sometimes,' she replied, which wasn't really true but she sensed he would be disappointed to learn she was godless.

Gloria had never understood why you would want to wear an instrument of torture and death as an ornament. You might as well wear a noose or a guillotine. At least Tatiana's earrings were plain, no twin dying bodies of Christ writhing on them. Did the crucifixes ever put the clients off? Jews, Muslims, atheists, vampires, how did they feel?

Her father, Tatiana volunteered suddenly, had been a 'great clown'. (So perhaps it did explain her *nom de guerre* in some way.) In the West, she explained, they thought clowns were 'slapstick fools' but in Russia they were 'existential artists'. She drooped with a sudden Slavic melancholy and offered Gloria a piece of gum, which Gloria declined.

'So not funny then?' Gloria said, taking five hundred pounds from a cashline in the hospital corridor. Gloria had been removing five hundred pounds a day from a cashline for the last six months. She kept the money in a black plastic binbag in her wardrobe. Seventy-two thousand so far in twenty-pound notes. It took up a surprisingly small amount of room. Gloria wondered how much space a million would occupy. Gloria liked cash, it was tangible, it didn't pretend to be something else. Graham also liked cash. Graham liked cash a little too much, vast amounts of it swilled around in the Hatter Homes accounts and came out as clean as new white linen. Graham had eschewed the old-fashioned way – launderettes and sunbed shops – that his friend Murdo still adhered to. Pam seemed blissfully unaware that the Jean Muir and Ballantyne cashmere that clothed her back was bought with funny money. Ignorance was not innocence.

Gloria divided the money from the cashline between herself and Tatiana. They had, after all, both earned Graham's money in their own ways. In the Seventies, women had marched for 'Wages for Housework'. Wages for sex seemed to make more sense. Housework had to be done whether you liked it or not, but sex was optional.

'Oh no, I don't have *sex* with them,' Tatiana said. She laughed as if this was the most ridiculous thing she had ever heard. 'I'm not *idyot*, Gloria.'

'But you charge money?'

'Sure. It's business. Everything is business.' Tatiana rubbed her thumb and forefinger together in the universal language of money.

'So, what do they pay you for . . . exactly?'

'Slapped around. Tied up. Beaten. Given orders, made to do things.'

'What kind of things?'

'You know.'

'No, I can't even begin to imagine.'

'Lick my boots, crawl on floor, eat like dog.'

'Nothing useful then, like hoovering?'

Who knew – all these years and Gloria could have been spanking Graham and making him eat like a dog? *And have been paid for it!*

'In Russia I worked in *bank*,' Tatiana said darkly, as if a bank was the most dangerous place in the world to work. 'In Russia I was hungry.' She had very mobile features, Gloria noticed and wondered if it had anything to do with her clowning father.

In exchange for the cash, from somewhere inside the confines of her bra Tatiana produced a little pink card and wrote on the back of it a mobile number and 'Ask for Jojo'. She handed the card to Gloria. On the front, it was engraved in black lettering with 'Favours – We Do What You Want Us To Do!' The exclamation mark gave the impression that Favours would provide entertainers and balloons for a child's party. Again with the clowns, Gloria thought. She had seen that logo somewhere surely, wasn't Favours a cleaning agency? Gloria had noticed their pink vans around her neighbourhood and Pam had used them when her own cleaner had a bladder prolapse last year. Gloria had always done her own cleaning, she liked cleaning. It filled in the hours in a useful way.

'Yeah, sure.' Tatiana shrugged. 'They'll do cleaning if that's what you want.' 'Cleaning' seemed to take on a whole new meaning in Tatiana's lugubrious accent, as if it were, paradoxically, a filthy (if not slightly macabre) activity.

The card was still warm from nestling next to Tatiana's breasts. Gloria was reminded of collecting eggs from beneath the chickens her mother kept in the back garden, long after war and necessity were done with. Tatiana tucked the money inside her bra. Gloria also frequently carried valuables within the armour of her underwear in the belief that even the boldest mugger was unlikely to brave the rampart of her post-menopausal 42EE Triumph 'Doreen'.

They walked together to the entrance of the shopping mall/hospital and on the way Gloria bought a pint of milk, a book of stamps and a magazine from a shop. She wouldn't have been surprised to find a car-wash out the back somewhere.

The entrance was a huge airlock at the front of the building where people hung around, using their mobiles, waiting for taxis and lifts, or getting a break from whatever birth or death or routine treatment had brought them here. A couple of patients in dressing gown and slippers stared glumly through the rain-spotted glass at the outside world. On the other side of the glass the smokers stared back inside, equally glum.

It felt cold outside after the hothouse atmosphere of the hospital. Tatiana shivered and Gloria offered the girl her own three-quarter-length green Dannimac. It made Gloria look like the clone of every other middle-aged woman, but on Tatiana the coat gained a strange unDannimac-like glamour. She snapped gum and smoked a cigarette while she made a call on her mobile, speaking in Russian, very quickly. Gloria felt a little tug of admiration. Tatiana was so much more interesting than her own daughter.

'This was a surprise for you,' Tatiana said when she finished the call.

'Well, yes,' Gloria agreed, 'you could say that. I always imagined him going on the golf course. Not that he's actually gone yet, of course.'

Tatiana patted her on the shoulder and said, 'Don't worry, Gloria, he will soon.'

'You think?'

Tatiana gazed off into the distance like a soothsayer and said, 'Trust me.' Then she gave another little shiver that seemed to have nothing to do with the weather and said, 'Now I have to go.' She slipped off Gloria's Dannimac in an elegant, if rather theatrical way that made Gloria wonder if she had trained as a ballet dancer but she shook her head and, handing back the coat, said, 'Trapeze.'

The last Gloria saw of Tatiana, she was getting into a car with blacked-out windows that had pulled up stealthily at the kerb. For a moment Gloria thought it was Graham's car, but then she remembered where he was.

9

THE NURSE WITH THE NICE SMILE SOUGHT MARTIN OUT IN THE waiting room. She sat down next to him and for a moment Martin thought she was going to tell him that Paul Bradley had died. Would he have to arrange the funeral now that he was somehow responsible for him?

'He's going to be a little while yet,' she said. 'We're just waiting on the doctor coming back, then he'll probably be discharged.'

'Discharged?' Martin was astonished, he remembered Paul Bradley in the ambulance, blood from his head staining the baby-blanket shroud he was wrapped in. He still thought of him as someone who was wrestling with oblivion.

'The head wound's only superficial, there's no fracture. There's no reason he can't go home as long as you can be there to keep an eye on him for the rest of the night. We ask that when people have been unconscious, no matter how briefly.'

She was still smiling at him, so he said, 'Right. OK. No problem. Thank you—?'

'Sarah.'

'Sarah. Thank you, Sarah.' She seemed very young and small, the epitome of neatness, her blond hair smoothed into the kind of tight bun that ballerinas wore.

'He said you were a hero,' she said.

'He was wrong.'

Sarah smiled but he wasn't sure at what. She cocked her head to one side, a sparrow of a girl. 'You look familiar,' she said.

'Do I?' He knew he had a forgettable face. He was a forgettable person, a perpetual disappointment to people when he met them in the flesh. 'Oh, you're so *short*!' one woman declared during question time after a reading last year. 'Isn't he?' she said, turning to the rest of the audience for validation, which was quick in forthcoming, everyone nodding and smiling at him as if he had just turned from a man to a boy in front of their eyes. He was five foot eight, hardly a midget.

Did he write like a short man? How did short men write? He had never had a photograph on his jackets and he suspected it was because his publishers didn't think it would help sell the books. 'Oh no,' Melanie said, 'it's to make you more mysterious.' For his most recent book they had changed their minds, sending up a celebrated photographer to try and capture something 'more atmospheric'. ('Sex him up' was the actual phrase, used on an email that had been mistakenly forwarded to Martin. Or at least he hoped it was a mistake.) The photographer, a woman, had suggested Blackford Pond to him with the aim of taking moody black-and-white shots beneath winter trees. 'Think of

115

something really sad,' she instructed him, while mothers with small children in tow, there to feed the ducks and swans, regarded them with open curiosity. Martin couldn't do sad to order, sadness was a random visual spring tapped by accident – RSPCA adverts showing dead kittens, old documentary shots of piles of spectacles and suitcases, Haydn's Second Cello Concerto. The maudlin, the terrible and the sublime all produced the same watery reaction in him.

'Something in your own life,' the celebrity photographer cajoled. 'How did it feel when you left the priesthood, for example, that must have been difficult?' and Martin, uncharacteristically rebellious, said, 'I'm not doing this.'

'Too difficult for you?' the photographer said, nodding and making a tortuously sympathetic face. In the end the photograph made him look like a polite suburban serial killer and the book was published, as usual, without his picture on the jacket.

'You need more *presence*, Martin,' Melanie said. 'It's my job to tell you these things,' she added. He frowned and said, 'Is it?' The opposite of presence was absence. A forgettable man with a forgettable name. An absence rather than a presence in the world.

'No, really,' Sarah insisted, 'I'm sure I've seen you somewhere. What do you do for a living?'

'I'm a writer.' He immediately regretted saying it. For one thing it always sounded as if he was showing off (and yet there was nothing about being a writer per se that was cause for hubris). And it was a dead-end conversation that always followed the same inevitable path. *Really? You're a writer? What do you write?*

'Novels.' 'What kind of novels?' 'Crime novels.' 'Really? Where do you get your ideas from?' The last one seemed to Martin to be a huge, neuro-scientific and existential question quite beyond his competency to answer, and yet he was asked it all the time. 'Oh, you know,' he said vaguely these days, 'here and there.' ('You think too much, Martin,' his Chinese acupuncturist, Ming Chen, said, 'but not in a good way.')

'Really?' Sarah said, her untainted features struggling to imagine what it meant to be 'a writer'. For some reason people thought it was a glamorous profession but Martin couldn't find anything glamorous about sitting in a room on your own, day after day, trying not to go mad.

'Soft-boiled crime,' Martin said, 'you know, nothing too nasty or gory. Sort of Miss Marple meets Dr Finlay,' he added, conscious of how apologetic he sounded. He wondered if she'd heard of either, probably not. 'The central character is called Nina Riley,' he felt compelled to continue. 'She inherited a detective agency from her uncle.' How stupid it sounded. Stupid and crass.

The policewomen from earlier appeared in the waiting room. When they saw Martin the first one exclaimed, 'There you are, we need to take a statement. We've been looking everywhere for you.'

'I've been here all the time,' Martin said.

'I bet you can't tell what he does for a living?' Sarah said to the policewomen. Both women stared at him gravely for a moment before the second one said, 'Don't know. Give up.'

'He's a writer,' Sarah declared triumphantly.

'Never,' the first one said.

The second policewoman shook her head in amazement. 'I've always wondered about writers. *Where* do you get your ideas from?'

Martin went for a walk around the hospital, taking Paul Bradley's bag with him. It was beginning to feel like his own. He went to the shop and looked at the newspapers. He went to the café and had a cup of tea, working his way through the loose change in his pocket. He wondered if it was possible to live in the hospital without anyone noticing you were there. The place had everything you needed really, food, warmth, bathrooms, beds, reading material. Someone had left a *Scotsman* on the table. He made a listless start on the Derek Allen crossword. *First Scotsman on the road*. Six letters. *Tarmac*.

While he was drinking his tea he heard an accent – a girl or a woman – drifting across the clatter and chatter of the café. Russian, but when he looked around he couldn't identify who it belonged to. A Russian woman manifesting unexpectedly in the Royal Infirmary to castigate him, to bring him to justice. Maybe he was hallucinating. He tried to concentrate on the black and white squares. He wasn't very good at crosswords. *Grebe reared in Northern Scandinavian city*, six letters. He liked anagrams best. Little rearrangements. *Bergen*.

Idyot, he was sure he heard the invisible Russian girl say. There was a café in St Petersburg called the Idiot. He had been there with Irina and eaten bortsch

118

that was the exact colour of the blazer he'd had to wear every day as a schoolboy. For a man wrestling with an immoral, uncaring universe Dostoevsky must have spent a lot of time in cafés, every other one in St Petersburg seemed to claim him as a customer. *Jack, say, and little Arthur going to a capital city.* Seven letters. *Jakarta.* He took his spectacles off and rubbed the bridge of his nose.

It had been on one of those packages they advertised in the travel pages of the papers on a Saturday: 'See the Northern Lights – Five-day cruise off the coast of Norway', 'The Wonders of Prague', 'Beautiful Bordeaux – Wine-Tasting for the Beginner', 'Autumn on Lake Como'. It offered a safe way to travel (the coward's way), everything organized for you so that all you had to do was turn up with your passport. Middle-class, middle-aged, middle England. And middle Scotland, of course. Safety in numbers, in the herd.

Last year it had been 'The Magic of Russia – Five Nights in St Petersburg', a city Martin had always wanted to visit. The city of Peter the Great, of Dostoevsky and Diaghilev, the setting for Tchaikovsky's last years and for Nabokov's first. The storming of the Winter Palace, Lenin arriving at the Finland Station, Shostakovich broadcasting his Seventh Symphony live in August 1942 in the middle of the siege – it was hard to believe one place could be so heady with history. (Why hadn't he done history at university? Instead of religious studies? There was more passion in history, more spiritual truth in human actions than in faith.) He thought how much he would like to write a novel set in St Petersburg, a real novel, not a Nina Riley. And anyway, in the late Forties Nina would have found it difficult to travel to St Petersburg – Leningrad as it was then. Perhaps she could have crossed secretly from Sweden, into Finland and then smuggled herself over the border, or crossed the Baltic on a small craft (she was handy with a skiff).

Martin had, as usual, effortlessly acquired an unwanted holiday companion – a man who had latched on to him in the departure lounge and had hardly left his side from then on. He was a retired grocer from Cirencester who introduced himself to Martin by telling him that he had terminal cancer and St Petersburg was on his list of 'things to do before I die'.

Their hotel had been advertised as 'one of the best tourist hotels' and Martin wondered if 'tourist hotel' was Russian for a featureless concrete block from the Soviet era, containing endless identical corridors and serving up execrable food. In the guidebook he had been studying prior to departure, there were photographs of the interiors of the Astoria and the Grand Hotel Europe, places that seemed redolent with luxury and pre-Bolshevik decadence. His own hotel, on the other hand, had rooms that were like shoeboxes. He was not alone in his shoebox cell, however. The first night he was there he got up to go to the bathroom and almost stood on a cockroach pasturing on his bedroom carpet. And there was construction going on, the hotel seemed to be simultaneously undergoing demolition and rebuilding. Men and women on scaffolding – no safety gear apparent anywhere, he noticed. A fine layer of concrete dust everywhere. The room was on the seventh floor and the first morning Martin had opened the curtains and found two middle-aged women standing on scaffolding outside the window, headscarves on their heads and tools in their hands.

The room was made bearable by the view – the sweep of the Neva ornamented by the scroll of the Winter Palace, as iconic a view as Venice approached across the lagoon. From his window he could see the *Aurora* berthed opposite – 'The *Aurora*!' he exclaimed excitedly, next morning at breakfast, to the dying grocer. 'Fired the opening shot in the revolution,' he added, when the dying grocer looked at him blankly.

The first day it was all churches and they had trailed dutifully at the heels of their guide, Mariya, around the Kazan Cathedral, St Isaac's Cathedral, the Church of Our Saviour on the Spilled Blood, the Peter and Paul Cathedral ('Where our Tsars are buried,' Mariya announced proudly as if Communism had never happened).

'You must be enjoying this,' the grocer said to Martin during a brief break for lunch in a place that reminded Martin of a school cafeteria, except that smoking was encouraged. 'You being a religious man and everything.'

'No,' Martin said, not for the first time, 'religious studies *teacher*, that doesn't necessarily make me *religious*.'

'So you teach something you don't believe in?' the dying grocer said, becoming suddenly quite belligerent. Dying seemed to have made the man rectitudinous. Or perhaps he had always been that way.

'No, yes, no,' Martin said. This conversation was

made awkward by the fact that Martin was still pretending to be a religious studies teacher, even though it was more than seven years since he had been inside a school. He was reluctant to say he was a writer and be stuck with that delimitation for the whole five days, knowing the questions it would provoke and knowing there would be nowhere to hide. One of their party, sitting across the aisle from Martin on the plane out, had been reading *The Forbidden Stag*, the second Nina Riley mystery. Martin wanted to say – casually – 'Good book?' but couldn't countenance the response, more likely to be 'Load of crap' than 'This is a fantastic book, you should read it!'

Martin gave up protesting his lack of religion to the grocer because the man was dying, after all, and for all Martin knew faith might be the only thing that was keeping him going, that and ticking off things on his list. Martin didn't think it was a good idea to have a list, it meant that when you got to the last item the only thing left to do was die. Or perhaps that *was* the last item.

On the way back from lunch, walking along a canal on a side street towards yet another church, they passed a sign, a wooden advertising board on the pavement, announcing, 'St Petersburg Brides – come inside'. Some of the party sniggered when they noticed it and the grocer, who was clearly stuck to Martin's side until he actually *died*, said, 'We all know what that means.'

Met horrid accident with lobster dish, nine letters. *Thermidor*.

Martin felt a little flush of guilt. He had been on the

internet. He had considered buying a bride (because, let's face it, he was incapable of getting one for free). When he first became successful he thought that it might make him more attractive to women, that he would be able to borrow some charisma from his more interesting alter ego, Alex Blake. It had made no difference, he obviously carried an aura of untouchability with him. He was the kind of person who, at parties, ended up in the kitchen washing glasses. 'It's as if you're asexual, Martin,' one girl had told him, thinking she was being helpful in some way.

If there'd been a site that advertised 'Old-Fashioned British Brides (but not like your mother)' he might have signed up but there wasn't, so first he had looked at the Thai brides ('petite, sexy, attentive, affectionate, compliant') but the very idea had seemed so *sleazy*. He'd seen one a couple of months before, in John Lewis – an ugly, overweight middle-aged man and on his arm this beautiful, *tiny* girl, smiling and laughing at him as if he was some kind of god. People looking at them, *knowing*. She was just like the ones on the internet sites – vulnerable and small, like children. He'd felt sick, as if he was on a pornography site. He would rather die than go on one of those – for one thing he was terrified they were monitored and that he would take one quick curious peek at 'Cum Inside' or 'Sexy Pics' and the next moment there would be a hammering on the door and the police would break it down and rush in and arrest him. He would have been similarly mortified to buy anything off the top shelf in a newsagent's. He knew (because this was part of his karma too) that he would take a magazine to the counter and the girl (because it would be a girl) would shout out to the manager, 'How much is *Big Tits*?' Or if he had something sent in the post it would fall out of its wrapper just as the postman handed it to him on the doorstep – undoubtedly at the moment when a vicar, an old lady and a small child passed by. *Whinge may have upset novelist*, nine letters. *Hemingway*.

The Russian brides on the internet didn't look child-like, however, and they didn't even look particularly compliant. The Lyudmilas and Svetlanas and Lenas looked like women, women who knew what they were doing (selling themselves, let's face it). They had a startling range of attributes and talents, they liked 'disco' as well as 'classical', they went to museums and parks, they read newspapers and novels, they kept fit and were fluent in several languages, they were accountants and economists, they were 'serious', 'kind', 'purposeful' and 'elegant', they were looking for a 'decent man', 'pleasant dialogue' or 'romanticism'. It was hard to believe that their poignant CVs could translate into living, breathing women and yet here they were – the Lyudmilas and Svetlanas and Lenas, or their equivalent, behind a large wooden door on the (somewhat frightening) streets of St Petersburg rather than simply floating in virtual space. The idea made his insides flutter with terror. He recognized the feeling: it wasn't desire, it was temptation. He could have the thing he wanted, he could buy a wife. He didn't think they were actually *in* the building, of course, corralled inside its peeling walls. But they were close. In the city. Waiting.

Martin had an ideal woman. Not Nina Riley, not a

bought bride looking for economic security or a passport, no, his ideal woman came from the past – an old-fashioned Home Counties type of wife, a young widow who had lost her fighter-pilot husband to the Battle of Britain and who now struggled bravely on, bringing up her child alone. *Daddy died, darling, he was handsome and brave and fought to stay alive for you but in the end he had to leave us.* This child, a rather serious boy called Peter or David, wore sleeveless Fair Isle jerseys over grey shirts. He had brilliantined hair and scraped knees and liked nothing better than to sit in the evening making aircraft kits with Martin. (*This is like the one Daddy flew in, isn't it?*) Martin didn't mind being second-best to the Spitfire pilot ('Roly' or 'Jim'), a man who had sliced through the blue, blue skies above England like a swallow. Martin knew that the woman was grateful to him for picking up the pieces of a bereaved life and she would never leave him.

Occasionally she was called Martha, and very infrequently she went by the name Abigail (in the imaginary life identities were less fixed), but usually she was nameless. To assign a name was to make her real. To make her real was to render her impossible.

It was best to keep women locked inside your imagination. When they escaped into the chaotic mess that was the real world they became unstable, unfriendly, ultimately terrifying. They created *incidents.* He felt suddenly queasy. *Something used in carrying out suspended sentences.* Five letters.

10

JACKSON CLIMBED ON BOARD THE 41 BUS ON THE MOUND AND thought, OK, if she wanted him to take a bus he would take a bus. The 41 covered a long route that ended up at Cramond. He knew Cramond as a hymn tune, not a place. Or was it 'Crimond'? So many things he didn't know. 'The Lord is my Shepherd'. Was he? It seemed unlikely somehow.

An old woman waiting at the bus stop with him said, 'Oh, it's very nice out at Cramond, you can go to Cramond Island from there. You'll like it.' He believed her; years of experience had taught Jackson that old women tended to tell the truth.

He sat on the top deck, at the front, and felt for a moment like a child again – some boyhood memory of sitting up there next to his big sister as a treat. Those were the days when the top deck was for smokers. And a time when life was painfully simple. He often thought about his dead sister but she was usually an image in isolation (the *idea* of his sister), he rarely had a sharply focused picture of something that had actually occurred and this sudden, unexpected memory of sitting next to Niamh on the bus – the smell of her violet cologne, the rustle of her petticoat, the feel of his arm resting next to hers – tied a tight knot in his heart.

The old woman was right, it *was* nice out at Cramond. It was a satellite of Edinburgh but it seemed like a village. He walked past expensive houses, past a nice old church, down to the harbour where swans were swimming idly. The smell of coffee and fried food wafting from the extractor of the Cramond Inn mixed with the salty scents of the estuary. He had been expecting to catch some kind of ferry out to the island but now he could see that it was easily reachable along a short causeway of rocks. He didn't need a tide table to tell that the sea was shrinking away from the rocky spine of this causeway. The air was still damp from this morning's rain but the sun had put in an unexpected and welcome appearance, making the newly washed sand and shingle glitter. A host of different types of wader and gull were busy beachcombing amongst the rocks. Exercise and fresh air would be just the ticket, as Julia would have said. He needed to blow away the stale thoughts that had accumulated in his brain, find the old Jackson that he seemed to have lost sight of. He set out along the causeway.

He passed a couple on their way back, retired middle-class types in Peter Storm jackets, binoculars slung around their necks, yomping briskly back to shore, their breezy 'Good afternoons' ringing in Jackson's ears. 'Tide turning!' the female half of the pair added cheerfully. Jackson nodded agreement.

Birdwatchers, he supposed. What were they called? Twitchers. God knows why. He'd never really seen the attraction of watching birds, they were nice enough things in themselves but *watching* them was a bit like train-spotting. Jackson had never felt that autistic (mainly) male urge to collect and collate.

The sun disappeared almost as soon as he reached the island, rendering the atmosphere of the place oddly oppressive. Occasionally he stumbled across the relics of wartime fortifications, ugly pieces of concrete that gave the place a bleak, besieged air. Seagulls swooped and screeched threateningly overhead, defending their territory. It was much smaller than he had expected, it took him hardly any time to walk round the whole island. He encountered no one else, something he was rather glad of. He didn't like to think what kind of weirdos might be lurking in a place like this. Obviously he didn't include himself in the weirdo category. Despite not seeing anyone, he had an odd feeling – not one he was willing to give any daylight credence to – of being watched. A little frisson of paranoia, nothing more. He wasn't about to start getting fanciful, but when a swollen purple cloud appeared from the direction of the sea and made an inexorable progress up the Forth, it seemed like a welcome sign that it was time to go back.

He checked his watch. Four o'clock – teatime on Planet Julia. He remembered a warm, lazy afternoon they had spent together last summer in the Orchard Tea Rooms at Grantchester, the two of them stretched out on deckchairs beneath the trees, replete with afternoon tea. They had been on a brief, rather uncomfortable visit to Julia's sister who still lived in Cambridge, and who had declined to join them on their 'jaunt'. Julia's word. Julia's vocabulary was 'chock full' of strangely archaic words – 'spiffing', 'crumbs', 'jeepers' – that seemed to have originated in some pre-war girls' annual rather than Julia's own life. For Jackson, words were functional, they helped you get to places and to explain things. For Julia they were freighted with inexplicable emotion.

'Afternoon tea' itself, of course, was one of Julia's all-time favourite phrases ('Good enough words on their own, but together perfect'). Afternoon tea usually trailed a few excessive adjectives in its wake – 'scrumptious', 'yummy', 'heavenly'.

'Warm Bakery Basket' was another of her favourites, as were (mysteriously) 'autumn equinox' and 'lamp black'. Certain words, she said, made her toes 'positively curl with happiness' – 'rum', 'vulgar', '*blanchisserie*', 'hazard', 'perfidious', 'treasure', '*divertimenti*'. Certain scraps and lines of poetry – *Of his bones are coral made* and *They flee from me that sometime did me seek* sent her into sentimental rapture. The 'Hallelujah Chorus' made her sob, as did *Lassie Come Home* (the whole film, title to closing credits). Jackson sighed. Jackson Brodie, the all-time winner of *Mr and Mrs*.

His phone buzzed like a trapped bee in his pocket. He peered at the screen – having an eye-test would be something useful he could do while he was up here. A text message from Julia read, *How r u? comp 4 r moat 2nite at our box! Luv Julia xxxxxxxxxxxx*. Jackson had no idea what the text meant but he felt a surge of affection when he thought of Julia laboriously tapping in all those x's.

He was about to set off back when his eye was caught by something on the rocks, below the remains of a concrete lookout. For a second he thought it was a bundle of clothing that had been dropped there, hoped it was a bundle of clothing, but it didn't take him more than a skipped heartbeat to know it was a body that had been cast up by the tide. Jetsam, or was it flotsam?

A young woman, jeans and a vest top, bare feet, long hair. The policeman in him automatically thought, hundred and twenty pounds, five foot six – although the height was a guess as she was lying in a foetal position with her legs drawn up as if she'd gone to sleep on the rocks. If she'd been alive he would have automatically thought, what a great body, but in death this judgement was translated into a lovely figure – aesthetic and asexual as if he was contemplating the cold, marble limbs of a statue in the Louvre.

Drowned? Fresh, not a 'floater' who had gone down and come back up again as a nightmare of slippery, bloated flesh. He was glad she wasn't naked, naked would immediately have meant something different. Jackson scrambled down the grass and on to rocks that were treacherous with barnacles and slick with sea-weed. Nothing on the body that he could see, no ligature marks around the neck, her skull looked intact. No needle tracks, no tattoos, no birthmarks, no scars, she was a blank canvas, just tiny gold crucifixes in her ears. Her green eyes – half open – were filmy with death and as blank as the aforesaid statue.

He could see some kind of card, like a business card, poking out from the cup of her bra. It was pale pink, an extra patch of wrinkled wet skin. He tweezered it out with his fingers. In black letters it said 'Favours – We Do What You Want Us To Do!' and a phone number, a mobile. A prostitute? A lap dancer? Or maybe Favours was just a helpful charity that went around doing old ladies' shopping. Yeah, that would be right, Jackson thought cynically.

He touched her cheek, he wasn't sure why, she was clearly dead. Perhaps he wanted her to feel a friendly touch. Between dying before her time and being sliced open by the pathologist's scalpel, he wanted her to know that someone had felt for her predicament. A wave washed over both the girl and Jackson's boots. She was beached below the tidemark and he was going to have to haul her to higher ground. Another wave. The rising waters were going to take her back out to sea if he didn't do something fast. The rising waters? When he stood up and looked back towards the causeway he realized that the rock pools were filling up with seawater and the sand and shingle were almost obliterated. *Tide turning*, the twitcher woman had said. Not going out, as he had thought, but coming in. Shit.

Another wave came, lapping at Jackson's boots. He was going to be trapped in this place if he didn't get a move on. He took out his mobile and dialled 999 but there was only the squeaky electronic noise that indicated no signal. He remembered the camera in his pocket, at least he'd be able to give the police a record of her *in situ* before he moved her. He took a quick shot, not the usual holiday snap of a tourist, but then he had to abandon photography because the water was rising so fast now that he had to wade into the water to grab hold of her. Just as he did, however, a wave bigger than all the ones that had gone before caught her, lifted her up and rolled her away. Oh bugger, Jackson thought. He flung the camera down, threw off his jacket and launched himself into the freezing grey water. The cold of the water was astonishing, the swell more powerful than it looked. Jackson didn't think that any of his Celtic ancestors had been the seafaring sort. He was a good swimmer but water wasn't his element, he liked earth, the ground under his feet.

He had put a swimming pool in the garden of his house in France. It was tiled with little azure mosaics and in summer the sun on the water was so dazzling you could barely look at it. When he lived in Cambridge he used to go for a run every morning but since moving to France it had seemed a ridiculous thing to do. No one ran in rural France. They drank, if you didn't drink you weren't part of the social fabric. The French seemed able to down litres of alcohol without facing any consequence, whereas Jackson felt the consequences almost every morning. So he swam in his turquoise-mosaic swimming pool, up and down, up and down, lap after lap, to swim off the alcohol, the boredom.

His swimming pool bore no relation to the hostile environment of the Forth in August. 'Sagittarius,' Julia said, 'you're a fire sign, water is your enemy.' Did she believe crap like that? 'Watch out for Pisceans,' she told him. Pisces was the Latin for fish. At home in

France his swimming pool was a *piscine*. Julia was Aries, another fire sign, not ideal, she said. Fighting fire with fire. What would happen to them, would they just burn up? Become cold ashes?

He managed to grab the dead woman beneath the shoulders, life-saving style, but she was a dead-weight, in all ways. A relentless succession of waves began to batter them both. Jackson took in a mouthful of brackish seawater that left him choking. He tried to tread water while he worked out the best way of getting them both out of the sea, but the waves kept coming. Jackson had saved people from drowning, once on duty, once off. And once, on a holiday week-end in Whitby, with Josie and Marlee, he had watched as a man jumped into the sea off the pier after his dog – a bouncy little terrier that had been so excited it had simply raced off the edge and into the sea below while all around people screamed in horror. The man got into difficulties immediately and another two men dived in after him. They were brothers, both in their thirties, married with five children between them. Only the dog came out of the water alive. Jackson would have jumped in too, tried to rescue the lot of them, but the anchor of an hysterical four-year-old Marlee around his leg had prevented him. The inshore lifeboat was on its way by then, he told himself after-wards, but to this day he hadn't forgiven himself and if he could have put the clock back he would have shaken Marlee off and jumped in. It wasn't heroism, it was a kind of necessity. Maybe that was a Catholic thing too.

He went under, still hanging on to the leaden girl.

Somewhere in his head he could hear Marlee screaming, *Daddeee*, and the old woman at the bus stop saying, *It's very nice out at Cramond, you'll like it*, and for a glorious second he was back in his swimming pool in France, the warm sun reflecting off the turquoise mosaics. He knew he was being pulled further away from land all the time, knew that the dead woman was going to drag him under like some lovesick mermaid. Half-woman, half-fish, a Piscean. The words from Binyon's poem came back to him, *They shall not grow old, as we that are left grow old*. He thought how ironic it would be if he drowned trying to save a corpse. He wondered if part of him believed he *could* still save her. (That would be the pesky Catholicism again.) He wondered if he was still trying to save the three men who drowned off the Whitby pier. If he wanted to save himself he was going to have to let her go. But he couldn't.

The Little Mermaid, Marlee had loved that when she was little. She would never be little again, she was poised, right on the cusp of her future. If he drowned he would never see her in that future. *The briny deep*. He didn't know why those words came into his head, they must belong to someone else. *Of his bones are coral made*. No coral in the Forth. Julia, as brown as a nut, swimming in his pool in France, Julia punting him down the river in Cambridge, Julia the ferrywoman rowing him over the Styx. Marlee had a book called *Greek Myths for Children* that she had made him read to her. He had learned a lot from that book, his introduction to classicism.

He sent up a prayer to whatever god was on duty

that afternoon, sent another one up to Mary, Mother of God, a recessive instinct, the knee-jerk reaction of a lapsed Catholic staring death in the face. Was this how it was going to be? No last rites, no extreme unction? He always imagined he would come round at the end, fall back into the fold, embrace the mother of all churches and have his slate wiped clean, but it looked like that wasn't going to happen now.

He remembered seeing his sister's body being pulled out of the canal. Of course – *that* was why it wasn't his element, why hadn't he realized that before? Nothing to do with star signs. *Stella maris.* Our Lady of Sorrows with a starry crown upon her head. Water, water everywhere. He was going down, down to Poseidon's watery realm, the mermaid was taking him home with her.

11

GRAHAM HAD BEEN TRANSFERRED FROM THE A AND E TO THE ICU. According to the staff in the ICU there had been no change in his condition. Gloria wondered if he would stay like this for ever, as passive as a stone effigy on a sarcophagus. Perhaps he would be moved into some long-term care facility where he would use up valuable resources for several more decades, depriving more worthy people of kidneys and hips. If he were to die now there might be bits of him that could be recycled in a more useful person.

It was quiet in the ICU, the pace of life slower and denser than in the outside world. You could feel how the hospital was a big humming machine, sucking air in and pushing it out, leaking an invisible life – chemicals, static, bugs – through its pores.

Gloria regretted she wasn't a knitter, she could be producing handy garments while waiting for Graham to die. The tricoteuse of the ICU. Beryl, Graham's mother, had been a knitter, producing endless matinee sets when Emily and Ewan were babies – hats, jackets,

136

mittens, bootees, leggings – threaded with fiddly ribbons and full of holes for tiny fingers to get caught in. Gloria had dressed her children up like dolls. Emily put the oddly named Xanthia into sensible stretchy white suits and little beanie hats. Gloria hardly ever saw her grandchild. When Emily announced she was pregnant you would have thought she was the first woman on the planet ever to have a baby. To be honest, Gloria would have been more excited if her daughter had given birth to a puppy rather than the permanently angry Xanthia, who seemed to have inherited Emily's worst traits.

She regarded the steady rise and fall of Graham's chest, the lack of expression on his face. He looked smaller. He was losing his power, shrinking, no longer a demi-god. How are the mighty fallen. Graham made a little noise, a susurration as if he was speaking in a dream. His features remained unmoved, however. Gloria stroked his hand with the back of her fingers and felt a twinge of sorrow. Not for Graham the man so much as Graham the boy she had never known, a boy in long flannel shorts and grey shirt and school tie and cap, a boy who knew nothing about ambition and acquisition and call-girls. 'You stupid bugger, Graham,' she said, not entirely without affection.

Where would he go if the machines were turned off? Drift off into some inner space, a lonely astronaut, abandoned by his ship. It would be funny (well, not funny, astounding) if there was an afterlife. If there was a heaven. Gloria didn't believe in heaven although she did occasionally worry that it was a place that existed only if you *did* believe in it. She wondered if people would be so keen on the idea of the next life if it was, say, underground. Or full of people like Pam. And relentlessly, tediously boring, like an everlasting Baptist service but without the occasional excitement of a full immersion. For Graham, presumably, heaven would be a thirty-year-old Macallan, a Montechristo and, apparently, Miss Whiplash.

He thought he was invincible but he'd been tagged by death. Graham thought he could buy his way out of anything but the grim reaper wasn't going to be paid off with Graham's baksheesh. The Grim Reaper, Gloria corrected herself – if anyone deserved capital letters it was surely Death. Gloria would rather like to be the Grim Reaper. She wouldn't necessarily be grim, she suspected she would be quite cheerful (*Come along now, don't make such a fuss*).

They'll never get me, that's what Graham said. Graham who always behaved as if he were untouchable, some kind of maverick, an outlaw not subject to the normal rules, crowing with triumph when he fooled the Inland Revenue or Customs and Excise, bypassing health and safety and building regulations, pushing his way through planning, sweetening his path with bribes and backhanders, cruising along in the outside lane at a hundred miles an hour in that bloody great car of his with its blacked-out windows. Why would you need blacked-out windows unless you were up to something nefarious? Gloria didn't like the drawn curtain, the closed door, everything should be on show in broad daylight. If you were doing something you were ashamed of then you shouldn't be doing it.

Twice he'd managed to wriggle out of being prosecuted for speeding, once for reckless driving, once for being over the limit – thanks to a brother Mason in the courts, no doubt. A few months ago he had been stopped on the A9 going at 120 miles an hour, while talking on his mobile at the same time as eating a double cheeseburger. Not only that! When he was breathalysed he was found to be over the limit, yet the case never even got to court, being conveniently dropped on a technicality because Graham hadn't been sent the correct papers. Gloria could imagine him only too well, one hand on the wheel, his phone tucked into the crook of his neck, the grease from the meat dripping down his chin, his breath rank with whisky. At the time Gloria had thought that the only thing lacking in this sordid scenario was a woman in the passenger seat fellating him. Now, she thought that had probably been going on as well. Gloria hated the term 'blow-job' but she rather liked the word 'fellatio', it sounded like an Italian musical term – contralto, alto, fellatio – although she found the act itself to be distasteful, in all senses of the word.

When he had got off the latest charge he celebrated with a noisy, bloated dinner at Prestonfield House with Gloria, Pam, Murdo and Sheriff Alistair Crichton. It undoubtedly helped if your big golfing pal was a sheriff. Despite having lived in Scotland for four decades the word 'sheriff' did not immediately conjure up the Scottish judiciary for Gloria, instead she tended to see tin stars at high noon and Alan Wheatley as the evil Sheriff of Nottingham in the old children's television programme *Robin Hood*. She started to hum the theme tune. Why was he riding through a glen? Did they have glens in Nottingham?

Gloria liked *Robin Hood* and its simple message – wrong punished, right rewarded, justice restored. Stealing from the rich, giving to the poor, they were basic communist tenets. Instead of slipping off the bar stool and following Graham she should have donned a duffle coat and sold the *Socialist Worker* on wet and windy street corners on Saturday mornings (and still have had sex with so many different men that she would never be able to remember their names, let alone their faces).

They'll never get me. But they would. She thought of the stag at bay on the living-room wall, its lips curled back from its teeth in horror as the dogs closed in. No escape. Of course a deer was far too nice an animal for Graham to be compared with. He was more of a magpie, jabbering, yobbish birds who stole from other birds' nests.

'Needles and camels,' Gloria said to Graham. He had nothing to say on either topic, the only noise came from the machines that were keeping him alive. 'What profiteth it a man if he gaineth the whole world but loseth his soul? Answer that one, Graham.'

A Church of Scotland minister entered the ICU at that moment, dutifully visiting the lost lamb of his flock. Gloria had put 'Church of Scotland' on Graham's admission form just to annoy him if he lived. Now she rather regretted not putting 'Jain Buddhist' or 'Druid' as it might have led to an interesting and informative discussion with whatever hierophant represented their religion in the Royal Infirmary. As it was, the

Church of Scotland minister, apart from being surprised at finding Gloria quoting scripture ('No one does any more') proved harmless company, chatting to her about global warming and the problem of slugs. 'If only they could be persuaded to eat just the *weeds*,' he said, wringing his hands.

'From your mouth to God's ear,' Gloria said.

'Well, no rest for the wicked,' the minister said eventually, standing up and holding one of her hands in both of his for an intense moment. 'Always a difficult time when a loved one is in hospital,' he said, glancing vaguely at Graham. Even supine and comatose Graham failed to look like a loved one. 'I hope it all goes well for you,' the minister murmured.

'So do I,' Gloria said.

12

LOUISE WAS RUNNING. LOUISE HATED RUNNING BUT IT WAS marginally preferable to going to the gym. The gym involved regular commitment and, outwith her job, she was crap at regular commitment. Go ask Archie. So, all in all, it was easier to grit her teeth and throw on her sweats, then jog sedately around the estate to warm up before heading off over the fields and, if she was feeling virtuous, or guilty (the other side of the coin), then up the hill and back again. The one good thing about running was that it gave you the space to think. That was the downside as well, of course. Dualism, the Edinburgh disease, Jekyll and Hyde, dark and light, hill and valley, New Town, Old Town. Catholics and Protestants. A game of two halves. An eternal Manichean dichotomy. It was her day off and she could have had a swim, read a book, caught up with laundry but, no, she had chosen to run up a bloody big hill. Confessions of a justified sinner. 'Antisyzygy and the Scottish Psyche'. She had done Hogg for her under-graduate dissertation, but then who hadn't?

She had drunk what she thought of as a moderate three glasses of wine last night but it was taking its toll on her. Her mouth felt like an old boot and the Peking duck that had accompanied the wine still lived on like a game old bird. A rare and belated girls' night out in the Jasmine, to celebrate Louise's promotion two weeks ago. Afterwards, they had gone to 'see something in the Festival', a vague, unplanned mission that hadn't taken into account the fact that anything good was going to be sold out by the time they arrived. They had ended up in a dive, near the police mortuary appropriately, and had gone to see some dreadful has-been comic. Three glasses of wine and Louise found herself heckling. They had made their rowdy way back through the Old Town, belting out 'You Make Me Feel Like A Natural Woman', like the worst of hen parties. Louise liked to think it was Carole King's own version rather than anything more unbridled but she might have been kidding herself. They were lucky they weren't lifted by the police. Shameful.

But there you go, she was paying for it now, because no good member of the narrow church that was Scotland got away without punishment. Scot-free.

By the time she was halfway up the hill her breathing had started to become laboured. She was thirty-eight and worried she wasn't as fit as she would like to be, as fit as she should be. She had a pain exactly where her appendix would be if she still had one – she imagined an empty space where it had nestled like a fat worm. It had come out last year ('whipped out' seemed to be the cliché that hospital staff adhered to). Both her mother and her grandmother had to have appendectomies and she wondered if that meant Archie would lose his too.

Archie talked vaguely about travelling in his gap year although, at fourteen, both concepts – travelling and gap year – were still too far away to seem more than part of a nebulous, improbable future to him. She wondered if she could persuade him into having elective surgery on unnecessary organs before he set off (*if* he set off, she couldn't imagine him having the energy, he was so lazy) so that he wouldn't find himself halfway up a mountain in New Zealand with peritonitis. A hundred or so years ago and Louise would be dead now. Or teeth – teeth must have killed a lot of people, abscesses that led to blood poisoning. A scratch, a cold. The littlest thing. Her own mother died of liver failure, her flesh the colour of ancient vellum, her organs pickled. Served her right. When Louise went to look at her in the Co-op undertaker's last week she had to resist the urge to take a needle with her, the old sailor's trick for death at sea, and push it through the yellow flesh (like rancid cheese) of her nose. Just to make sure she was really dead.

Her funeral was three days ago, at Mortonhall Crematorium, a service as torpid as her life. Though her name was Aileen the minister drafted in continually referred to her as Eileen, but neither Louise nor the ramshackle bunch of people who regarded themselves as her mother's friends had bothered to correct him. Louise liked the way 'Eileen' made her mother seem like someone else altogether, a stranger and not her mother.

When she was doing her cool-down stretches on the

front path she noticed the thing on the doorstep, where the milk would have been if they delivered milk in this area. A nondescript brown canister. She felt a sudden irrational fear. A bomb? Some weird practical joke? Would she open it and find faeces or worms or something poisonous? It took her a couple of seconds of panic before she realized it was an urn, and that inside the urn was what was left of her mother. For some reason she had expected something tasteful and classical – an amphora made from alabaster, with a lid and a finial, not something made from a kind of plastic material that looked for all the world like a tea caddy. She remembered her mother's cousin saying he would collect the ashes from the crematorium for her. If it had been left up to her she wouldn't have bothered.

Now she was left with the problem of what to do with the remains. Could she just put them in the bin? She had the feeling that might be illegal.

She turned her key in the lock but had to give the front door a hefty shove to get it to open. It had been a wet summer and all the wood in the house had swelled, although the door had fitted badly to begin with. The house was only three years old but had all kinds of small annoying things wrong with it – snagging that had never got done no matter how many times she had complained – cracked plaster, sockets that were attached crookedly, a kitchen sink that wasn't earthed. Thank you, Graham Hatter. The Kinloch model was the smallest detached you could buy, but it was a house, a proper house, the two eyes and a mouth kind that she used to draw when she was a child. Houses that contained an ideal family, she had drawn those too – mother, father, two children and a dog. All she'd had in reality was the mother, a pretty piss-poor one at that. Poor Louise. When she thought of herself as a child she usually put herself in the third person. She was sure a psychiatrist would have a field day with this fact but no psychiatrist was ever going to get anywhere near her head.

Modern houses were shit, but the estate (Glencrest) was safe, in as much as anything ever was. Most of the neighbours in her little enclave knew each other, if only by sight. There were no pubs anywhere near, there was a Neighbourhood Watch, there were young women with pushchairs who went to Mother and Baby groups, there were guys who washed their cars at the weekend. It was as near as you got to normal.

She took the urn inside with her and placed it on the kitchen draining board. She unscrewed the lid and poured some of the contents into a saucer and examined them, poking them around with a knife, like a forensic technician. It was gritty, more like clinker than ash, and Louise half expected to see a bit of tooth, a recognizable bone. Toxic waste. Perhaps if she added water to the saucer her mother would be resurrected, the clay reformed from the dust. Her moth-wing lungs might reinflate and she would rise like a genie from the urn and sit opposite Louise at the too-small kitchen table in the too-small kitchen and tell Louise how sorry she was for all the bad things she'd done. And Louise would say, 'Too fucking late, get back in your urn.'

The cat, old and arthritic, jumped awkwardly on to the draining board and sniffed hopefully at the contents of the saucer. Jellybean's health was failing, he had a tumour growing inside him, the vet said 'the time was coming very soon' when Louise was going to have to make a 'decision'.

Jellybean was once a tiny, hurtling ball of fur as light as a shuttlecock, now he was a slack sack of bones. He was older than Archie, in fact Louise had known the cat longer than she'd known anyone else, except for her mother and she didn't count. She had found him when he was a kitten, abandoned in an empty house. She'd never had a pet, didn't like cats, still didn't like cats but she loved Jellybean. It was the same with kids, she didn't like babies, didn't like children, but she loved Archie. She couldn't say it to anyone (especially not Archie) because they would think she was mad but she thought she might love Jellybean as much as she loved Archie. Possibly more. They were her pair of Achilles heels. They said love made you strong but in Louise's opinion it made you weak. It corkscrewed into your heart and you couldn't get it out again, not without ripping your heart to pieces. She kissed the top of Jellybean's wobbly head and felt a sob catch in her chest. Jeez, Louise, pull yourself together, for fuck's sake.

The front door crashed open and was slammed shut again. Archie's passage through the house was marked by the noise of things thrown and dropped and walked into. He was like the ball in a pinball machine. He exploded into the kitchen, nearly falling over his own feet. After he was born the midwife said, 'Boys wreck your house, girls wreck your head.' Archie seemed intent on doing both.

He looked hot and bothered. She remembered that feeling, suddenly having to don a school uniform in what still felt like the middle of summer. English schools went back in September but Scottish schools had always thought it a good idea to make kids go back in the dog days of heat. It would be a Presbyterian thing. No doubt John Knox looked out of his window one fine August morning and saw a kid bowling along the street with a hoop, or whatever kids did in the sixteenth century, and he thought, That child should be suffering in a hot, airless classroom in a uniform that makes him ridiculous. Yeah, that would be Knox, Louise thought. Hey, Knox, leave that kid alone.

What had happened to her little boy, had he been eaten by this monster? Not long ago Archie had been a handsome child – silky blond hair, round, kissable arms. Looking at him now, in his badly fitting body that seemed to have been put together from the salvage of other people's limbs, it was hard to believe that women would ever find him attractive, that he would have sex with them, that he would fumble and wrestle and convulse, that he would do it with virgins and married women, with college students and girls who worked in shops. Her heart ached for him in his new ugliness, made even more poignant somehow by the fact that he seemed unaware of it.

'What's that?' Archie asked, glancing at the saucer of ash. No 'Hello, Mum,' no 'How was your day?'

'My mother, what's left of her.'

He grunted incomprehension.

'She was cremated last week,' Louise reminded him. A public burning. She hadn't allowed Archie to go to the crematorium, she'd kept him away from his grand-mother when she was alive so she wasn't going to waste his time on her when she was dead. Louise took the morning off work, said she had a hospital appointment. It was amazing the lies you could tell that were believed without question. If anyone had looked back through her employment records they would have seen that they showed her mother was already dead. Everyone she knew believed her mother died long ago. 'She's dead to me,' she would have said, if challenged over her veracity.

Archie lifted up the saucer and scrutinized the contents. 'Cool,' he said, 'can I have it?'

It wasn't his fault (she had to remind herself on a daily basis) that some unkind biological imperative had turned him into a hormone factory on overtime, producing torrents of the stuff on double shift. He should be out playing football, pool in a church youth club, on parade with the army cadets, anything that would channel the glut of chemicals in his body, but no, he spent his time lying around in the smelly lair of his bedroom, hooked up to his iPod, his PlayStation, his computer, the TV, like some kind of half-human, half-robot hybrid that needed electricity to maintain life. Bionic boy.

At least he wasn't on drugs (not yet anyway). She was pretty sure she'd be able to tell. Some porn in the form of magazines – she doubted there was anything he could hide from her, she was ruthless, she was an expert at that kind of thing, she was a mother. A few fairly tame porn mags, that was all, par for the course for a fourteen-year-old, wasn't it? Better to be realistic than draconian. No online porn as far as she knew, unless he'd got himself a credit card, although it would hardly be difficult and he was good with computers, but not as good as his friend Hamish Sanders. Hamish was scarily good for a fourteen-year-old. Boys were definitely hard-wired for that sort of stuff. Hamish set up Louise's wireless broadband, and he was a hacker, she was pretty sure of it. She didn't like Hamish, he was a natural-born liar and full of shit. Louise was a natural-born liar too, but her lies had always tended to be utilitarian rather than malicious. That was her excuse, anyway.

The first time Archie brought him back to the house, Hamish said, 'Hello, Ms Monroe, is it all right if I call you Louise?' and she'd been so surprised she hadn't said, 'No, it's not, you little wanker.' Hamish was a new friend, who had been expelled from his posh school and wheedled into Gillespie's by his parents. Louise was still trying to find out what he had been expelled for. 'Stuff,' Archie said. 'Oo, your mum's such a cop, Archie,' she had overheard Hamish saying, 'she's so powerful, I love it.'

She wasn't sure how much Archie himself knew about hacking. She wouldn't mind so much if they were trying to get into the Pentagon or bring down a multinational but they were probably just crashing some poor schmuck's email in Singapore or Düsseldorf.

The shoplifting was probably a one-off. All kids shoplifted. Louise had shoplifted. Woolworth's was begging you to slip their merchandise into your pocket – sweets, pencils, keyrings, lipstick – and Louise wouldn't have had any of that stuff if she hadn't taken it. When she was older she got a Saturday job in Woolworth's and always turned a blind eye to the thieving kids. But her own son, that was something different. Do as I say, not what I did.

Still, look on the bright side – he had friends (would-be gothic slackers like himself, but friends were friends) and he wasn't dead. That was always the bottom line with kids. Dead was the unthinkable. Never think it in case you make it come true, like some kind of bad voodoo.

'How was school?' The daily litany since he was five. 'What did you do?' No satisfactory answer had ever been forthcoming. *We drew a tree, we had custard for lunch, a boy fell and hurt himself.* No information about the curriculum, Louise used to wonder if they ever taught them anything. Now she didn't even get these little daily titbits.

Archie mumbled something.

'What?'

'Stuff,' he said, looking at the floor. She couldn't remember the last time he had made eye contact with her.

'You did "stuff" at school?'

'Yeah.'

'Can you be more specific?'

'Mm.' He gave the impression he was thinking but he looked vague, disassociated. Had he taken something? 'What the Nazis did for us,' he said finally.

'I think you might have got that slightly wrong.'

She would have liked a good argument with him, a rumbustious set-to, but he couldn't do that, if she

151

started in on him he just went quiet, waited it out patiently until she'd finished and then said, 'Can I go now?'

The phone rang. She knew without answering it that it would be work. It was her day off but they were short-staffed, everyone down with a bug, she'd been expecting all day to be called in. She watched Archie while she was talking on the phone. He was having a staring competition with the cat, not much of a competition probably as Jellybean had cataracts and had started bumping into walls and furniture in much the same way that Archie did. Archie didn't seem to have any fond feelings for animals but she'd never seen him be actively cruel to one. He wasn't a potential psychopath, she reminded herself, just a fourteen-year-old boy. Her baby. She put the phone down. 'I have to go,' she said. 'There's been an incident out at Cramond.'

'I know what incident means,' he said, 'it means somebody's dead.' Louise wished he didn't look quite so excited by the idea.

'Probably,' she agreed.

13

MARTIN WAS BEGINNING TO FEEL SICK. HE HAD EATEN TOO many mints and nothing else, still living off the modest piece of toast he'd breakfasted on this morning, in another lifetime.

He went outside for some air and read the bus timetables. He sat on a wall until it started to rain and then he came back inside and found the hospital chapel. It was pleasantly nondescript, a relief from the continual to-ing and fro-ing that seemed to form the bedrock of hospital life. All this time he had Paul Bradley's holdall with him. It was black, made from a cheap imitation leather that seemed unaccountably masculine. The bag had a collapsed look about it, like a mouth with no teeth, and its strange gravity suggested it contained a brick or a Bible. He placed it on the seat next to him.

Martin had grown more and more curious about the stranger he was waiting so stoically for, and the longer he waited the more the intrigue scratched away at him. He had begun to think there was a short story in there somewhere, a novel even, a serious one, not a Nina Riley. A piece plotted around the mysterious stranger who comes into town. No, that sounded like *A Fistful of Dollars*. A man whose day is changed, who goes from being anonymous and unrecognized to being the centre of an unlooked-for drama. It would be existential and yet gripping (the two rarely went hand in hand, in Martin's experience). Where had Paul Bradley been going before his destiny was changed? The littlest thing. A man stepping off the pavement in front of your car. A girl saying, *You want coffee?* The littlest thing could change your life for ever.

Martin wondered if it was really his meanderings that had brought him to the chapel. Wasn't it because he knew it would be the least busy place in the hospital? Hadn't temptation lured him like something vaguely obscene so that he could look in the holdall? Wasn't knowledge the reward of temptation? Eve, Adam's disobedient wife, knew that. So did Bluebeard's disobedient wife, nameless like his own imaginary spouse.

He was dissembling. Didn't he know better? He had been tempted in St Petersburg and look what had happened. Knowledge was not necessarily a good thing. Go ask Eve. It was wrong to look in the bag, there was no way round that fact, it was a moral absolute and yet once the idea had lodged itself in his mind it wouldn't go away. He had a bond with Paul Bradley, he had saved his life, for all he knew it might be the best thing he was fated to do in his own life. Didn't that bond give him permission to know more? You could find your way round temptation, you could say no, I'm not going to go behind the wooden door and buy a Lyudmila or a Svetlana, but then you ended up picking up a girl on a matryoshka stall. *You're a weak-willed, lily-livered little pansy, Martin.* Flowery language from his father, on the occasion of what? He couldn't remember, probably when he left the army cadets because he couldn't complete the assault course. A girl called Irina who had the palest skin, who called him Marty.

Of course, it could be a story about a man like Martin, a man to whom nothing ever happens. 'The Man To Whom Nothing Happened'. How he got unexpectedly caught up in someone else's life, how he discovered something in a bag that changed his world for ever. It was a lie. He lied to himself, all the time. Something had happened to him. Once. The *incident*. The girl from the matryoshka stall happened. Once. But once was enough.

The chapel was deserted. He checked this fact several times. This was how he would feel if he was about to masturbate in public – not that he would ever do that. The horror of being caught! Then, casually, as if it was his own bag that he needed something from, pulling on the zip and peeling the bag open. A sponge bag, a change of underwear and a box, that was all. The box was unremarkable and black, like the holdall, but made of some rigid plastic material, pitted like orange peel and with steel clasps. That was that then, he had seen inside the bag and there was nothing that revealed anything about Paul Bradley, just a black plastic box, a mystery within a mystery. Perhaps the box would contain another box, and inside that box another box, and so on, like the Russian dolls. Like his own Russian dolls, the prelude to his brief courtship and consummation with the girl from the matryoshka stall. Wasn't that a lesson? A lesson not to go somewhere that you shouldn't?

Someone entered the chapel and Martin clamped his hand on the bag as if it was about to shout out his guilty name. He thought it was a patient or a patient's relative but it was some sort of church minister who was smiling encouragingly at him, saying, 'Everything all right?' Martin said, yes, everything was fine, and the minister nodded and smiled and said, 'Good, good, always a difficult time when a loved one's in hospital,' and wandered out again.

Paul Bradley might be a rep of some kind, a travelling salesman, the black box containing samples. Samples of what? Or maybe it held jewellery? A gift. Something he was delivering. Would it really hurt to look? Could he *not* look now? It was only after he'd unhinged the metal clasps and started to lift the lid that he wondered if it might be a bomb.

'There you are, Martin!' He snapped the black box shut again. His heart had gone up several floors and then shot down to the bottom of the shaft. 'We've been looking everywhere for you,' Sarah, the nurse with the nice smile, said. She was standing in the doorway of the chapel, grinning at him. 'Your friend's been discharged, he's ready to go.'

'Right, I'm just coming,' Martin said too loudly, grinning inanely back at her while surreptitiously tugging on the zip. He stood up and Sarah asked, 'Are you all right, Martin?' touching his elbow. She looked concerned, yet tomorrow he knew she would have forgotten his name.

'Hello, Martin,' Paul Bradley said. He was waiting in the corridor, a bandage on his head but otherwise he looked fine. He took the bag off Martin and said, 'Thanks for taking care of that.' Martin was sure that just by looking at the bag he would be able to tell that Martin had been searching inside it.

'Saying your prayers in there, Martin?' Paul Bradley asked, indicating the chapel with a nod of his head.

'Not really,' Martin said.

'Not a religious man then?'

'No. Not at all.' It felt odd to hear Paul Bradley say 'Martin', as if they were friends.

There was one forlorn taxi standing at the rank outside the hospital.

Martin suddenly remembered the silver Peugeot and wondered what had happened to it. The police must have seen to it presumably, but Paul Bradley seemed unconcerned. 'It was rented,' he said, offhandedly. Martin's own car was parked where Richard Moat had left it earlier in the day, in the car park at the St James Centre. Too late to retrieve it now, he couldn't begin to imagine how much it was going to cost him to liberate it in the morning.

Martin hadn't really thought about where they were going until they climbed into the taxi and the driver said, 'Where to?' and before he could speak, Paul Bradley said, 'The Four Clans Hotel.' Martin protested, offered his own home (as if he hadn't learned his lesson with Richard Moat) but Paul Bradley just laughed, said he had agreed to Martin 'watching over' him in order to get out of the hospital and that Martin was now 'discharged of his duty'. He asked Martin's address and said to the taxi driver, 'Did you get that?' peeling a twenty-pound note from the wad in his wallet and handing it through the window. 'Take him on after you've dropped me, OK, mate?' You had to admire his sangfroid, Martin thought, he could have died today and yet here he was, quite the man, only the professional dressing on his head indicating the day might have deviated from its intended course. Martin had returned the wallet to Paul Bradley with a strange reluctance that he couldn't explain to himself.

The taxi eventually drew up outside a small tourist hotel in the West End that announced itself to be the Four Clans. An illuminated red sign saying 'Vacancies' hung in one of the windows. Martin thought the sign made the hotel look like a brothel. He had no idea who or what the 'four clans' were. Scottish by birth and inclination, Edinburgh born but not bred, Martin knew there were certain things about his native culture and history that he would never understand.

'It was all I could get,' Paul Bradley said, peering at the unpromising frontage of the hotel through the taxi window. 'The town's booked out.'

'The Festival,' Martin said gloomily.

Paul Bradley climbed out of the taxi and Martin sighed but followed resolutely. It was no good, much as he wanted to go home and fall into his own comfortable bed, he just couldn't let Paul Bradley go like that. He had made a contract with a nice nurse called Sarah.

'Really,' Paul Bradley said, 'get on home, mate.'

Martin shook his head stubbornly, rooting himself on to the pavement as if Paul Bradley might try to place him physically back inside the taxi. 'I can't,' he said, 'I couldn't forgive myself if you died in the night, in a strange hotel room, away from home, family, friends.' Martin heard himself talking like an agony aunt and didn't imagine it was going to have much persuasive effect on a man like Paul Bradley.

'I'm not going to die, Martin,' he said.

'I hope not,' Martin said, 'but I'd like to make sure. You can go,' he said, turning suddenly to the taxi driver, slamming shut the passenger door of the taxi and slapping it twice with his palm as if it were a horse's flank, an uncharacteristically emphatic gesture that took him by surprise. He picked up Paul Bradley's bag and strode up the stone steps and windmilled his way through the revolving door of the Four Clans before Paul Bradley could raise any further objections.

Paul Bradley followed him into the empty reception area and, making a gesture of helplessness, laughed and said, 'OK, Martin, mate, have it your way.'

The hotel smelt of fried bacon, despite the time of day, and made Martin salivate although he hadn't eaten pig in twenty years and had no desire to start now. The hotel was surprisingly cheap and un-surprisingly awful. Anything that could be decorated with tartan was, even the ceiling had been papered in a funereal Black Watch. On the walls were hung framed prints of old Edinburgh and heraldic clan insignia mounted on wooden shields.

Martin had a book about tartans, bought when he was looking for one for himself for a kilt, in the expectation that as a writer he would have a glamorous life attending black-tie dinners and celebrity launches, perhaps a reception at Holyrood Palace. Alex Blake had received a great many invitations in the past but Martin always felt he was an inadequate substitute for his more exciting counterpart. People always seemed to be looking over his shoulder for the real Alex Blake, and nowadays he rarely attended anything.

His mother was a MacPherson before her marriage and so he had eventually decided on a kilt made up in a MacPherson dress green, but he had never had the nerve to wear it in public and it hung neglected in his wardrobe. Occasionally he tried it on and wore it around the house but it was an odd, closeted act, as if he were a secretive transvestite rather than a swaggering Scot.

Paul Bradley banged authoritatively on the old-fashioned brass bell on the reception desk. It sounded very loud in the muffled atmosphere.

'You don't think it's a bit late for checking in?' Martin said and Paul Bradley frowned at him and said, 'It's me that's paying *them*, Martin, they're not doing me a favour.'

An unfriendly night porter appeared and made a performance of searching for Paul Bradley's reservation. He looked them both up and down and said, 'It says a single here.' Martin wanted to say, 'We're not gay,' but then perhaps Paul Bradley *was* gay and would find his protestations insulting. (Perhaps the night porter was gay.) Martin thought that if he was gay Paul Bradley would probably be out of his league as a partner, even for a night.

'I'm not staying,' Martin said to the night porter, 'not really. I'm not *sleeping*.'

'I don't give a monkey's nut what you do,' the night porter said in a long-suffering way, barely glancing at the dressing on Paul Bradley's temple, 'but you have to pay for a double if there's two of you in the room.'

'No problem,' Paul Bradley said pleasantly, taking more twenties from his wallet and placing them on the counter.

Martin tried to take the holdall again but Paul Bradley said, 'Give us a break, Martin, you're not my manservant,' and swung the heavy bag over his shoulder as if it weighed nothing and set off up the stairs, Martin in his wake, following the path of a dress-Stewart stair carpet. He avoided meeting the wretched gaze of the large, moth-eaten stag whose decapitated head had been hung above the stairs. He wouldn't have been surprised if it had suddenly opened its mouth and spoken to him. He wondered why it was all right to mount stags' heads but not, say, horses' heads or dogs' heads.

The room had a double bed, despite it being nominally a single, and Paul Bradley threw his bag down on the brown and orange bedspread and said, 'I'll take the left side, you take the right,' in an easy manner that made Martin think he was used to sleeping anywhere, used to sleeping with other men in a non-sexual way. He had known a lot of Paul Bradleys when he was younger. Army.

'Were you in the army?' he asked. He realized it was the first personal question he had asked him. Paul Bradley gave him a quizzical look but held it a little longer than most people would have done so that Martin said, 'Sorry, didn't mean to pry.' Paul Bradley shrugged it off, said, 'That's OK, I'm not hiding anything. I was in the navy actually. SBS. We don't seek out attention like the SAS do. Now I'm just a desk jockey pushing pieces of paper around. Very boring. Have you served in the forces then?'

'Not exactly,' Martin said. 'My father was a CSM, he brought us up in a domestic boot camp.'

'Us?'

'My brother and me. Christopher.'

'Are you close?'

'No,' Martin said. 'Not really.' He could see what Paul Bradley was doing, turning the tables, questioning Martin to avoid answering anything about himself. 'I'll just sit in this chair here,' he said. 'I'm supposed to be watching you, not sleeping.'

'Up to you,' Paul Bradley said, taking the holdall into the tiny en-suite and shutting the door. Martin tried to close his ears to the noise of another man washing, brushing, peeing. He switched on the television in an effort to mask the sounds but it was showing snow on all channels. He leafed idly through the only reading matter in the room, a brochure advertising Scottish tourist attractions, a mish-mash of whisky distilleries, woollen mills and heritage trails.

'The bathroom's free,' Paul Bradley said when he emerged, smelling of cheap soap and toothpaste. Martin felt like the shy bride on a virgin honeymoon, the groom oblivious to his blushing reticence.

Paul Bradley opened the mini-bar and said, 'Have a drink.'

'Maybe just a mineral water,' Martin said but when he inspected the mini-bar he saw that water was too sophisticated a request. Its contents were basic, no water or mixers, no Toblerone, no unpalatable Japanese crackers or quarter bottles of champagne, not even any salted peanuts – just cans of lager, spirit miniatures and Irn-Bru. The sight of the miniatures triggered a sudden desire for alcohol, something to wash away the turmoil of the day.

'Let me fix you something,' Paul Bradley said, retrieving a tiny bottle of whisky and a can of Irn-Bru. 'Hang on, I'll get a glass from the bathroom.'

Martin looked in horror at the glass of orange liquid that Paul Bradley came back with but felt obliged to say, 'Thanks,' and take a drink. He was sure there were cells in his liver that were committing suicide rather than deal with Scotland's two national drinks together in one vile cocktail. The copper tones of the room's décor, the fluorescent orange of the Irn-Bru and the marmalade tint of the sodium street lamp outside the window all contributed to Martin's sense of alienation, as if he had stepped into a sickly science-fiction world, tainted by some ecological catastrophe.

'All right?' Paul Bradley said.

'Yes, fine,' Martin said. He took another drink of the orange liquid. It was deeply unpleasant and yet strangely compelling. Swiftly, without a sign of any self-consciousness, Paul Bradley stripped down to grey T-shirt and grey boxers. Expensive, nice cotton jersey fabric, Martin noticed, although he averted his eyes almost immediately and stared instead at a surprisingly graphic print of Culloden that was hanging above the bed – bodies being pierced by bayonets and swords, open mouths, heads tumbling. When he next looked Paul Bradley was on the bed, on top of the orange and brown coverlet. Martin wondered when it had last been washed. Within seconds, Paul Bradley's features softened into sleep.

Martin went to the bathroom and locked the door. He tried to urinate quietly. He washed his hands and dried them on the thin towel that was damp from Paul Bradley's ablutions. Paul Bradley's toothbrush stood at ease in a glass next to the taps. It was old, the bristles worn and splayed, proof of a life that preceded their strange encounter. Martin always found something poignant in the sight of a singular toothbrush. He had never once walked into his own bathroom and seen two toothbrushes standing companionably together.

The holdall was on the floor, its mouth gaping wide. Martin could see the black box inside. Surely Paul Bradley wouldn't have left it lying there if it contained something private or illegal? Adam's wife whispered in one ear, Bluebeard's wife in the other, urging him, *Just one look.* And Pandora, of course, not to forget Pandora, standing behind him saying, *Open the box, Martin, what harm can there be?* He had a vague memory of watching *Take Your Pick* on television when he was a child, the audience shouting at the contestant, *Open the box!* The sensible ones took the money, the gamblers opened the box. Martin opened the box.

Inside was a charcoal-coloured sponge material that had moulded itself to the contents – a golfing trophy, a figure eight inches or so high, in a chrome finish that reflected the light in the bathroom like a mirror. Dressed in plus-fours and diamond-patterned sweater with a tammy on the head, he was caught at the height of his swing, the little pitted ball waiting for ever at his feet. The plinth he stood on was engraved with the name 'R. J. Benson – 1938', but there was no indication of what tournament it had been awarded for. It looked cheap, a generic kind of thing that ended its life in a charity shop following a house clearance after an old man died. The kind of old man who had lived alone with one toothbrush.

The trophy didn't look valuable enough to merit a padded box and the box itself was all wrong, the size of it indicating a void. Nina Riley would have discovered the false bottom immediately, but it took Martin a few moments longer. He placed the golfing trophy on the sink, next to the glass containing Paul Bradley's lone toothbrush, and wrestled with the charcoal sponge. It felt clammy to the touch, like the ancient green oasis that his mother used to stab with flower stems in her less than half-hearted attempts at artistic arrangements. Pandora, Eve, Bluebeard's anonymous wife and the entire ghostly audience of *Take Your Pick* were at his back urging him on. Finally, he managed to remove the sponge.

A gun.

He hadn't been expecting that somehow and yet, when he saw it, there seemed a perfect logic about it.

The fact of the gun was overwhelming, eliminating any thought about the reason for it. It took his breath away, literally, and he had to hold on to the sink for a few seconds before he recovered.

Not any old gun. A Welrod. Of course, that figured, an ex-SBS man would have a Welrod. His father had owned an old one, illegally. He kept it in a shoebox on top of the wardrobe, the same place that Martin's mother kept her 'party shoes' – uncharacteristically frivolous footwear in gold or silver leather. Although Martin was born more than a decade after the war ended, he and Christopher were nonetheless brought up on tales of their father's best years – parachuting behind enemy lines, hand-to-hand combat, daring escapes – like one of their boys' comics come to life. Were those tales of Harry's all true? From this distance in time it seemed less likely. After the war, life was, necessarily, a disappointment for Harry. Martin himself knew, from a young age, that any chances he might have had in life to be a hero had already been used up by his father.

Martin wasn't a stranger to handling guns, his father's casualness around them had extended to teaching his sons to shoot. Christopher was a rotten shot but Martin, to his father's perpetual astonishment, wasn't too bad. He might not be able to bowl a cricket ball but he could line up a sight and hit a bull's-eye. He had never shot at a living thing (to his father's disgust), limiting himself to inanimate targets in junior competition.

Harry liked to take them out into the woods with shotguns to shoot rabbits. Martin had an unfortunate flashback to an image of his father stripping the pelt off a rabbit as easily as peeling a banana. The memory of the glistening candy-pink carcase hidden beneath the fur was still enough to make Martin nauseous, even now.

Once when Martin and Christopher were children they came home from school and found their father holding a gun – the Welrod, in fact – to their mother's head. 'What do you say, boys,' his father said, pressing the barrel harder against his wife's temple, 'shall I shoot her?' He was drunk, of course. Martin couldn't remember what he had said or done, he was only eight at the time and he seemed to have blocked out the rest of the 'incident'. He hoped he had stood up for his mother, although God knows there were enough times when she didn't stand up for him. He always expected that, at the end, his father would blow his own brains out and was surprised by the tameness of his exit.

There was no way he could look at a gun these days and think it was a good thing. He touched it, noticed the slight tremor in his hand. He stroked the metallic smoothness, expecting it to be cold, but it was almost the temperature of his hand. The Welrod, beloved of special forces everywhere, developed in Britain during the war. The only truly silenced gun. 9mm, single shot. Not a great range, best close up. There was only one thing really that you would use a Welrod for and that was shooting a single target at close range as covertly as possible. In other words, it was an assassin's gun.

He took a deep breath. He was going to walk out of the bathroom, out of the hotel room, quietly. He was going to tiptoe down the stairs, past reception and out of the building, then he would jump in the first taxi he found and ask to be taken to the nearest police station.

He opened the bathroom door. Paul Bradley was sleeping soundly, snoring gently, his arms flung out

167

innocently, like a child. Martin began to cross the room towards the door but his legs were starting to melt. When he looked down, the carpet was swimming in front of his eyes. A spasm of dizziness seemed to pass through his brain. He was suddenly extraordinarily tired, he had never been this tired in his life, he hadn't known it was possible to be this tired. He had to lie down and sleep for a little while, right here on this unpleasant tartan carpet.

14

GLORIA MADE SURE ALL THE DOORS AND WINDOWS WERE locked, set the burglar alarm and then went down to the basement to check the security cameras.

All quiet on the garden front, except for a vixen trotting briskly across the lawn. Gloria put out food for the foxes most nights. She'd started by just giving them leftovers but now she often bought them food specially, packets of pork sausages, a little piece of stewing steak. For the hedgehog (there might have been more than one but how could you tell?) she put out cat food and bread and milk. The fox ate that as well, of course. Sometimes rabbits romped on the lawn (the fox ate them too) and Gloria had seen countless neighbourhood cats, as well as the small, shy rodents that only come out at night. The fox particularly liked the small, shy rodents. Sometimes, down in the basement, it was like watching a nature programme on television.

The night-vision cameras showed everything in strange greens and greys, so that it seemed like a different garden altogether, a shadowy place seen through ghostly eyes. Something moved in the chaos of leaves that formed the big rhododendron bushes along the drive. Something glinting, diamonds set in jet. Eyes. Gloria tried to think what animal could be that tall. A bear? A horse? Both unlikely. She blinked and it was gone. A creature of the night.

For all their technology, the cameras couldn't go out there and snuffle amongst the leaves, couldn't howl and bark at an intruder. If Graham died, the first thing Gloria would do would be to go to the dogs' home at Seafield and bring home a soft-eyed lurcher or a springy little terrier. Graham didn't like animals, there had never been a pet in the house because he claimed to have a serious allergy to fur and feathers. Gloria had never witnessed any manifestation of this or any other allergy in Graham. Once, she had taken some fur from a neighbour's cat – the poor thing had some kind of alopecia so all you had to do was stroke it and you came away with a handful of its coat – and she had placed the fur beneath Graham's pillow and stayed awake half the night watching him to see what happened, but he woke in the morning just the same as usual, fancying 'a couple of poached eggs'. Gloria suspected her children would have turned out to be nicer people if they had been brought up with a dog.

She thought of Graham occupying the limbo of the ICU, a dim no-man's-land between life and death, waiting for the Great Architect in the sky to reveal his plans. Gloria was hugging to herself the secret of this occurrence, preparing herself for the consequences of it. She hadn't phoned either Ewan or Emily to tell them that their father was hanging around at death's door, waiting to see if it was going to open for him. She hadn't, in fact, told anyone. She knew she was supposed to tell people, she just couldn't be bothered somehow. They would make such a drama of it and it seemed to Gloria that it was a thing that went off better if you were quiet about it. And anyway, there were things to do before he died, before people knew. So she would just leave him there in his hospital bed, hidden in plain sight, while she got on with preparing for widowhood. His sudden pitch towards mortality had taken her by surprise. Graham didn't often catch her on the hop like that.

Gloria climbed into bed with a mug of Horlicks, a plate of oatcakes with Wensleydale cheese and a fat Maeve Binchy. She always ate Wensleydale, never Lancashire, her sense of county loyalty was bred in the bone. It was in the same spirit of observance that she watched *Emmerdale* rather than *Coronation Street*, simply because *Emmerdale* was set in Yorkshire, although not, it was true, any part of Yorkshire that she recognized.

How vast and wonderful the marital bed suddenly seemed. She had already washed all the sheets, turned and aired the mattress, hoovered out Graham's dead skin from the pillows. As soon as she was settled nicely, sod's law, she heard the patient ringing of the phone. Gloria, who thought Alexander Graham Bell had a lot to answer for, had refused to install a phone by the bed. She failed to see the need, when she was in bed she wanted to sleep, not to talk. Graham's mobile was surgically attached to his ear so he didn't need a phone in the bedroom and there was a panic button by the bed 'for emergencies', although Gloria hesitated to imagine what kind of emergency might take place in the bedroom that would require her to hit a panic button. Graham wanting sex maybe. She hauled herself reluctantly out of bed and went downstairs. It would be best, she supposed, to head off any queries at the pass.

The caller ID proclaimed 'Pam'. Gloria sighed and picked up the receiver but it wasn't Pam, it was her husband, Murdo. 'Gloria! Sorry to bother you so late, I've been trying to raise Graham on his mobile.' She could hear him attempting to sound amiable but Murdo was not an amiable man and the strain of pretending to be one made him seem mildly delirious. 'We were supposed to be having a meeting this afternoon but he didn't turn up. Is he there? Is he in his bed?'

'No, he's in Thurso.'

The word seemed to send Murdo into an hysterical spin. 'Thurso? You're joking. What do you mean, Thurso? What's he doing in Thurso, for fuck's sake, Gloria?'

Why had she chosen Thurso? Perhaps because it rhymed with Murdo. Or because it was the furthest away place she could think of. 'He's building an estate up there.'

'Since when?'

'Since now.'

'That doesn't explain why he's not answering his phone.'

172

'He forgot it,' Gloria said stoutly.

'*Graham* forgot his *phone*?'

'I know, it's hard to believe, but there you go. Astonishing things happen all the time.' (It was true, they did.)

Murdo made an agitated kind of noise, frustration and panic in equal measures. Fortunately, Graham's mobile began to ring at that moment somewhere in the further depths of the house, identified by its irritating 'Ride of the Valkyries' ringtone. Gloria followed the thread of Wagner through the house, like a rat following the Pied Piper, until eventually she ended up in the utility room where she had placed the plastic bag of Graham's belongings that she had brought back from the hospital. He would have been very annoyed to know that his bespoke summer-weight wool suit and his handmade shoes were stuffed in a hospital rubbish bag.

Delving into the bag, she finally recovered the phone from the inside pocket of Graham's jacket and held it up so that Murdo could hear it ringing.

'Hear that?' she said. ' "Ride of the Valkyries". I told you he forgot it.' Murdo made some kind of snorting noise and rang off. 'Good riddance to bad rubbish,' Gloria said. Some people had no manners.

She answered Graham's mobile and heard an urgent voice saying, 'Graham, it's me, Maggie. Where are you? I've been ringing you all afternoon.'

'Maggie Louden,' Gloria murmured to herself, trying to conjure up a mental picture of her. She was a new member of Graham's sales force, a thin-faced woman in her late forties, with a helmet of dyed black hair lacquered to her head like a beetle's shell. The last time Gloria had seen her was at Christmas. Once a year, everyone from judges and chief constables to brick suppliers and roofing contractors, as well as the more privileged members of the Hatter Homes office staff, was invited to drink champagne and eat mince pies under the Hatter roof in the Grange. She remembered Maggie clattering like a cockroach across the tiles in the hall in her badly fitting Kurt Geiger heels. Gloria didn't remember any of the sales force being invited to their Christmas party before.

Gloria was on the point of answering, of saying, 'Hello, Maggie, it's Gloria here,' when Maggie said, 'Graham, darling, are you there?'

Darling? Gloria frowned. She remembered Graham standing in front of the Christmas tree, with Maggie Louden, Murdo Miller and Sheriff Crichton, one hand round a glass of malt, the other placed blatantly on Maggie's back, at the tidemark where the black crêpe of her cocktail dress met the white crêpe of her skin. One of the waitresses employed for the evening offered them a plate of mince pies and Graham had taken two, managing to get them both in his mouth at the same time. Maggie Louden had waved them away as if they were radioactive. Gloria felt suspicious of people who had no time for sugar, it was a personality flaw, like preferring weak tea. Tea and sugar were a test of character. She should have known then.

Graham had leaned towards Maggie, his jowly jaw almost brushing the shellac of her hair as he murmured something in her ear. It had seemed unlikely to Gloria that he was commenting on the new tree lights that she'd recently bought from Dobbies, but she had thought he was just being Graham. She often thought that if he'd been a binman or a newsagent he might not have been so attractive to women. If he hadn't possessed money and power and charisma he would – let's face it – have just been *an old man*.

The phone felt suddenly hot in her hand. 'Is it done yet, is it over?' Maggie said. 'Have you got rid of Gloria? Have you got rid of the old bag?'

Gloria almost dropped the phone in surprise. Graham was planning to *divorce* her? Graham was having an affair with one of his sales team and the pair of them were talking about *getting rid of* her? Gloria slipped the phone back in Graham's pocket and left Maggie Louden speaking to his summer-weight wool. She could still hear her muffled voice, 'Graham? Are you there, Graham?' like a persistent clairvoyant at a seance. In the distance Gloria heard the soft explosion of the fireworks that signalled the end of the Tattoo. Had capitalism really saved mankind? It seemed unlikely but it looked like it might be too late to argue with Graham about it now.

15

HE HAD LET HER GO. HE HAD HEARD MARLEE'S VOICE IN HIS ear saying, *Daddy*, quietly as if she was treading water next to him, and he had relinquished his dead mermaid and kicked for shore. Helping hands had hooked him out of the harbour and taken him into the Cramond Inn, where a malt whisky and a bowl of hot soup had brought him back to life. By the time the police arrived he was wrapped in blankets and his clothes were being washed and dried in industrial machines somewhere in the recesses of the building.

Then he had begun the seemingly never-ending process of telling and retelling his story to a succession of people. 'Have you been drinking, sir?' the first uniformed constable on the scene asked him, looking pointedly at the glass in his hand that had just been refilled. Jackson would have considered hitting him if he could have summoned up the energy. Another, reluctant part of him acknowledged that the guy was just doing his job.

The final person to arrive ('This is actually my day off,' he heard her say to someone) was a detective, a woman, with more attitude than manners. She gave him her card which had printed on it, 'Detective Sergeant Louise Monroe', the 'Sergeant' crossed out in biro and replaced with a handwritten 'Inspector'. He thought that was quite funny. A newly minted inspector. He hoped she didn't have anything to prove. She also asked if he had been drinking.

'Yes, I have been drinking,' he said, showing her the now half-empty glass. 'So would you in the circumstances.'

'Don't make assumptions,' she said sharply. She was pretty, sort of. Her mouth was a little too big for her face and her nose a little too small and she had a crooked front tooth but she was still pretty. Sort of. Late thirties, dark hair, dark eyes, Jackson had never had much luck with blondes. Her hair was in a bob, neat and practical, and she tucked it behind her ears every so often in a gesture that Jackson always found appealing. In women anyway. It was a far-flung outpost of his brain that was making this appraisal. For the most part he was just trying to stop himself falling asleep from exhaustion.

She liked asking questions: what was he doing on Cramond Island, had he realized the tide was coming in when he set out, how had he got here?

'Bus,' he said reluctantly. He felt like he was owning up to being a lower life form. He was naked beneath the blankets and he felt absurdly vulnerable. A naked man who took buses and had nothing better to do with his time than lurk around suspiciously on deserted islands. With the tide coming in. How stupid was he? Very, obviously.

What was he doing in Edinburgh? He shrugged and said he was here for the Festival. She gave him a sceptical look that made him feel as if he was lying, he obviously didn't fit the Festival type. He thought about saying, 'My girlfriend's in a play, she's an actress,' but really that was nobody's business but his own and 'girlfriend' sounded stupid, girlfriends were what young guys had. Jackson tried to think what he would have been doing if he'd been in charge of the investigation. Would he be as suspicious of his own credentials as Louise Monroe was or would he already have divers out on police launches, uniforms combing the coastline?

'Most people are upset when they find a dead body,' Louise Monroe remarked. ' "Shock" and "horror" are the usual reactions, yet you seem remarkably phlegmatic, Mr Brodie. Have you seen a dead body before?' What did she think – that he'd mistaken a seal for a woman, a lump of driftwood for a body?

'Yes,' he said, weariness finally making him snap, 'I've seen hundreds of dead bodies. I know exactly what a dead body looks like, I know what a body looks like when it's been blown up, burnt, hung, drowned, shot, stabbed, beaten to death and hacked to pieces. I know what people look like when they've stood in front of a train going at a hundred miles an hour, when they've been decomposing inside a flat for the whole of a summer and when they're three months old and they've died in their sleep for no apparent reason. I know what a dead body looks like, OK?'

The butch DC accompanying Louise Monroe looked as if she was getting ready to handcuff him but Louise Monroe nodded and said, 'OK,' and he liked her for that. 'Police?' she said and he said, 'Ex. Military and civil – Cambridge.' Name, rank and number, tell the enemy nothing else.

Somewhere back at Force Command, she told him, someone must have decided there was a chance the woman was still alive and the Coastguard had sent out an RNLI launch as well as alerting an RAF helicopter. 'So you can stop fretting, Mr Brodie.' 'Fretting' wasn't exactly the word he would have used himself. 'It's pointless,' he said, 'she was dead.' Every time he said it she seemed to slip further away.

'Has anyone reported a girl missing?' he asked. There were always girls missing, always had been, always would be. There were no women or girls reported missing who fitted the description he had given, Louise Monroe said.

'Well, she probably hasn't been reported yet,' Jackson said. 'She hadn't been in the water long. And sometimes it takes a while for people to realize that someone isn't where they should be. And sometimes people are never missed. Not everyone has someone who'll notice they've gone.' Who would miss him? Julia, Marlee, that was it. Without Julia there would just be Marlee.

'Have you got the egg with you? In your pocket maybe?' she said.

Jackson frowned. 'What do you mean?'

'I just wondered if you had it with you – the egg you're going to teach me to suck.' She was a spiky

179

little thing. Not that little, taller than Julia, but then everyone was taller than Julia.

Jackson wondered if she had someone at home who would notice if she was gone. No wedding ring, he saw, but that didn't mean anything. His own wife (ex-wife) had never worn a ring, never even changed her name to his, yet, interestingly, on the back of her Christmas card last year there had been one of those little address labels which unequivocally declared 'Mr and Mrs D. Lastingham'. Jackson had faithfully worn his wedding ring. He had only taken it off at the end of last year, throwing it into the Seine from the Pont Neuf on a weekend visit to Paris. He had meant it to be a dramatic gesture of some kind but in the end he had let it fall quietly, a brief glint of gold in the winter sun, embarrassed at what people might think (*sad middle-aged loser whose divorce has finally come through*).

'Could be suicide,' he speculated. (Yes, apparently he did have the egg with him, although she was no grandmother.) 'Not many girls drown themselves though, women aren't noted for drowning. Maybe she simply fell into the water, perhaps while she was drunk. A lot of drunk girls around these days.'

One day, undoubtedly, his daughter Marlee would be drunk. Statistically she would smoke cigarettes in her adolescence. Take drugs at least once, have a near miss in a car. Suffer a broken heart (or several), give birth twice, get divorced once, have an illness, need an operation, grow old. If she grew old she would have osteoporosis and arthritis, shuffle along with a walking stick or a shopper, need a hip replaced, watch her friends die one by one, move to a nursing home. Die herself.

'Mr Brodie?'

'Yes.'

By the end of the afternoon a lot of hardware had buzzed around the area, the RAF, the RNLI, a police launch, a Ports Authority pilot vessel, plus a lot of manpower – all to no avail. They found zilch, not even the camera he'd left behind when he went into the water, although they had recovered his jacket (thank you) which at least proved he had been on the island because even that seemed to be in question.

'Well, at least you didn't imagine that,' Louise Monroe said. She smiled, a crooked smile which took the edge off any congeniality.

'I didn't imagine any of it,' Jackson said.

Consider the first person on the scene as a suspect. That was what she was doing. It was what he would do. *What was the purpose of your visit to Cramond, sir?* What could he say – loafing? That he was at a permanently loose end? He thought about saying, 'I understand, I'm one of you,' but he wasn't, not any more, he wasn't part of the coterie any more. The club. And part of him – a perverse part, undoubtedly – was curious to know what it was like on the other side. It was a long time since he'd visited that other side: Jackson's criminal career started and ended when he was fifteen and was caught breaking into the local shop with a friend to nick cigarettes. The police caught them and hauled them off to the station and frightened the life out of them.

'There was a card,' he said suddenly to Louise Monroe. 'I'd forgotten. It was a business card. Pink, black lettering, it said—' What did it say? He could see the card, he could see the word, but he couldn't read it, as if he was trying to decipher something in a foreign language or a dream. Feathers? Fantasia? And a phone number. His good memory for numbers, just about all he had a good memory for nowadays, seemed to have deserted him. 'The name began with an "F",' he said. He couldn't remember what he'd done with the card, you would have thought he would have put it in his jacket pocket but there was no sign of it.

'We didn't find a pink card when we were on the island,' Louise Monroe said.

'Well, you weren't looking for one, were you?' Jackson said. 'It wasn't exactly big.'

'You photographed a dead body?' the butch DC said suddenly, giving him a *you crazy psycho* look.

He thought of the pictures inside the camera, the little jewel-like compositions of Venice with Julia in all her loveliness, nestling next to pictures of an unknown corpse. 'Of course I did,' he said.

The butch DC was called Jessica something, he'd missed her surname when she introduced herself. 'Jessica' was a girly name for a girl who wasn't girly. 'Sure this wasn't a bit of a prank, Mr Brodie?' Jessica something said. He ignored her, the name was on the tip of his tongue, feathers fantasia fandango – 'Favours!' he said suddenly, that was it, that was what had been written on the missing card.

As he was leaving, he heard Louise Monroe requesting

the assistance of police divers. He wondered how pissed she was going to be at him if she found nothing. A lot probably. A uniformed constable gave him a lift back into town, to Julia's venue, where he discovered the actors taking a break from the dress rehearsal.

Julia, now wan rather than flushed, came outside with him where she smoked a cigarette with a frightening kind of purpose, her inhalations punctuated by rasping breaths. 'Tobias is a pillock,' she said angrily. She was nervy and talkative, where earlier she had been quiet and subdued. 'And you know Molly?'

'Mm,' Jackson said. Of course he didn't.

'The neurotic one,' Julia said (not very helpfully, they were all neurotic as far as Jackson could make out). 'Doesn't know her lines. She's still on the book.'

'Really?' Jackson said, trying to strike a note of mild outrage. He wasn't entirely sure what being 'on the book' meant but he could take an educated guess.

'It was all over the place today, thank God we've got previews tomorrow. Did you get my text about the ticket for Richard Moat?'

So that was what her text had said. The name Richard Moat was vaguely familiar but he couldn't put a face to it. 'How come you had a free ticket?' he asked.

'I had a drink with him at lunchtime. He gave me one.'

'Just you?'

'Yes. Just me.' He clearly remembered her having no time for lunch. *We're going to have to work through lunch.* Jackson frowned.

'Don't worry,' Julia said, 'Richard Moat's not my type.'

'I'm not worried.'

'You're always worried, Jackson. It's your default setting. You could meet up with me afterwards. We're going to be *hours* yet.' Julia sighed and stubbed her cigarette out and as an afterthought said, 'How was your afternoon?'

Jackson considered all the things he could say (*I nearly drowned today, I found a corpse, I sparked a huge, futile air-sea search, oh, and the police think I'm a paranoid delusional nutter*) and chose, 'I went to Cramond.'

'That's nice, did you take photos?'

'I lost the camera.'

'No! Our camera? Oh Jackson, that's awful.' He felt an unexpected swell of emotion when she said 'our camera' rather than 'my camera'.

He supposed from Julia's point of view it was awful but compared with everything else that had happened to him this afternoon he found it hard to get worked up about it. 'Yeah,' he said. 'Sorry.'

He accompanied her back down to her inner circle of hell and watched her walk on stage and take her place in an angst-strewn scene where she had to spend ten minutes staring at a black square which at that moment (it was a multi-functional piece of scenery) was representing a window opening on to a raging Arctic storm – a fact that Jackson knew only because he had spent some time in London doing lines with Julia. He reckoned he could have understudied for her if necessary (now *that* would be a nightmare). There was something noble and tragic in the mute pose she adopted, with her sackcloth and disordered hair she

184

looked like the survivor of something terrible and unspeakable. He wondered if, when she was doing scenes like that, she was thinking about her own past.

He turned abruptly on his heel and potholed his way out of the building. The sound of a police siren somewhere in the distance made his heart leap with the old familiar thrill. When the helicopter and launches had arrived at Cramond he had badly wanted to take control and it had been surprisingly hard watching Louise Monroe being the one with all the power. Twice in one day he had observed women younger than himself wielding more authority. Nothing to do with them being women (his only precious child was a girl, after all), more to do with Jackson not being a man. A real man. Real men didn't accept money off dead old ladies and live in France. He missed his warrant card, he missed his child, he missed his iPod which he had accidentally left behind. He missed the sad-voiced women who let him share their pain. Lucinda, Trisha, Eliza, Kathryn, Gillian, Emmylou. Most of all he missed Julia and yet she was the one he had with him.

Without anything better to do than lie in an empty bed and think about what he didn't have, he went and picked up his ticket for Richard Moat.

Jackson remembered Richard Moat from the Eighties, he hadn't found him funny then and he didn't find him funny now. Neither did most of the audience apparently – Jackson was shocked by how vicious some of the jeering and cat-calling was. He dropped off a couple of times but the circumstances were hardly conducive to sleep. When Richard Moat finished to grudging applause, Jackson thought, there goes another couple of hours of my life. He was too old now, too aware of the finite nature of what was left, to squander precious time on crap comedy.

He slipped away as quickly as possible and made his way down to the subterranean depths of Julia's venue, only to find it dark and empty. One day he would find a Minotaur in there. Julia had said they would be hours but there was no sign of anyone. He turned his phone back on and found a text from Julia, saying, *All done, see you back at the flat.*

He discovered a fire exit and made the mistake of leaving the building through it, so that when he hit the street he had no idea where he was. He had read in the *National Geographic* (he had recently taken out a subscription, thereby incontrovertibly confirming his middle-aged status) that it had been proved by geneticists that women navigated by landmarks, men by spatial indicators. It was dark and, lacking any spatial indicators, he tried looking for landmarks, searching for the shape of the Royal Mile, for the skyline of spires and crow-stepped gables culminating in the pomp and circumstance of the Castle. He looked for the massy bulk of the museum on Chambers Street. He looked for the spans of the landlocked bridges, but all he found was the mouth of a dark alley, a narrow close that led to an endless flight of stone steps. He could see lights at the top, and a street still humming with Festival-goers, and he set off without thinking much beyond, this looks like a shortcut. A 'snicket', that's what he would have called it when he was a boy. Different language, different times.

Jackson was forever warning Marlee (and Julia, come to that, but she never listened) about the foolishness of going down dark alleys. *Daddy, I'm not even allowed out in the dark*, Marlee said reasonably. Of course, if you were a girl, if you were a woman, you didn't need to go down a dark alley in order to be attacked. You could be sitting on a train, stepping off a bus, feeding a photocopier, and still be plucked from your life too soon by some crazy guy. Not even crazy, that was the thing, most of them weren't crazy, they were just guys, period. Jackson would have been happier if the women in his life never left the house. But he knew even that wasn't enough to keep them safe. *You're like a sheepdog*, Julia told him, *every last lamb has to be accounted for.*

Jackson himself wasn't afraid of dark alleys, he thought he probably posed more of a threat himself in a dark alley than anyone he was likely to encounter, but obviously he hadn't reckoned on Honda Man. The Incredible Hulk on steroids in all his pumped-up glory, barrelling out of nowhere and staggering into Jackson with all the grace of a rugby prop. Jesus Christ, Jackson thought, as he hit the ground, this was some kind of town. The Minotaur was out of the labyrinth.

He got to his feet instinctively, never stay down, down means kicked, down means dead, but before Jackson could even get a rational thought up and running – *why?* would have been a good one to start with – Honda Man had slammed him with a punch like a battering ram. Jackson heard the air leaving his own body with a kind of *Ouf!* sound before he slumped to the ground. His diaphragm turned to stone and he immediately lost interest in rational thought, his only concern the mechanics of his breathing – why it had stopped, how to start it again. He managed to get on all fours, like a dog, and was rewarded by Honda Man stamping on one of his hands, a bitchy kind of move, in Jackson's opinion, but it hurt so much he wanted to cry.

'You're going to forget about what you saw,' Honda Man said.

'Forget what? What did I see?' Jackson gasped. Full marks for trying to have a conversation, Jackson, he thought. On all fours and still talking, give this man a medal. He blew out air and sucked it in again.

'Don't try to be fucking clever, you know what you saw.'

'Do I?' In reply, Honda Man gave him a casual kick in the ribs that made him recoil in agony. The guy was right, he should stop trying to be clever.

'I'm told that you've been causing a fuss, Mr Brodie.' (The guy knew his *name*?) Jackson thought about saying that he hadn't been doing any such thing, that, indeed, he had actively refrained from saying anything about the road rage to the police and had no interest at all in being a witness, but all he managed to say was 'Uh,' because one of Honda Man's heavy-duty boots gave him another hefty nudge in the ribs. He had to get up off the ground. You had to keep getting to your feet. All the *Rocky* films seemed to pass before his eyes in one go. Stallone shouting his wife's name at the end like he was dying. *Adrian!* The *Rockies*, I–V, contained important moral lessons that men could learn to live by but what did they teach you about fighting impossible enemies? Keep going, against the odds. When there was nothing else to do, all that was left was seeing it through to the end.

Honda Man was squatting like a Sumo and taunting Jackson by making gestures with his hands as if he was helping him reverse into a parking space, the universal machismo mime for *bring it on*.

The guy was twice his size, more like an unstoppable force of nature than a human being. Jackson knew there was no way he could fight him and win, no way he could fight him and *live*. He suddenly remembered the baseball bat. Where was it? Up his sleeve? No, that would be ridiculous, a magician's trick. They circled round like street-fighting gladiators, keeping their weight low. Honda Man obviously had no sense of humour because if he had he would have been laughing at Jackson for behaving as if he had a chance against him. *Where was the baseball bat?*

The other thing Jackson always tried to impress on Marlee – and Julia – was what you had to do if you were attacked because you'd been foolish enough to ignore his advice in the first place and go down the dark alley.

'You're at a disadvantage,' he tutored them. 'Height, weight, strength, they're all against you, so you have to fight dirty. Thumbs in the eyes, fingers up the nostrils, knee to the groin. And shout, don't forget to shout. Lots of noise. If the worst comes to the worst, bite wherever you can – nose, lips and hold on. But then shout again. Keep shouting.'

He was going to have to forget fighting like a man and fight like a girl. Navigating like the fairer sex hadn't worked for him but nonetheless he went for Honda Man's eyes with his thumbs – and missed, it was like jumping for a basketball hoop. He made it to the nose somehow and bit down and held on. Not the most disgusting thing he'd ever done, but close. Honda Man screamed – an unearthly storybook-giant kind of sound.

Jackson let go. Honda Man's face was covered in blood, the same blood that Jackson could taste in his own mouth, coppery and foul. He took his own advice and shouted. He wanted the police to come, he wanted concerned citizens and innocent bystanders to come, he wanted anyone to come who could stop the mad man mountain. Unfortunately, the shout attracted the dog and Jackson remembered – it wasn't the baseball bat he needed to worry about, it was the dog. The dog that was making a beeline for him, its teeth bared like a hound from hell.

He knew how to kill a dog, in theory anyway – you got hold of its front legs and basically just pulled it apart – but a theoretical dog was different from a real dog, an enraged real dog packed with muscle and teeth whose only ambition was to tear your throat out.

Honda Man stopped screaming long enough to give the dog its orders. He pointed at Jackson and yelled, 'Get him! Kill him!'

Jackson watched in mute, paralysed horror as the dog leaped in the air towards him.

Wednesday

16

RICHARD MOAT WOKE WITH A START. HE FELT AS IF AN ALARM bell had gone off in his head. He had no idea what time it was. Martin hadn't had the decency to provide a clock for his guest room. It was light outside but that didn't mean anything, it hardly seemed to get dark at all up here. 'Jockland', that's what he'd begun to call it. Edinburgh, the Athens of the North, that was a fucking joke. He felt as if a slug had crawled into his mouth while he slept and taken over from his tongue. He could feel a trail of snail-drool on his chin.

He hadn't got to bed until four and dawn was already struggling to make an appearance by then. Tweet, tweet, fucking tweet all the way home. Had he got a taxi or had he walked? He had been drinking in the Traverse Bar long after midnight and he had a vivid, bizarre memory of being in a lap-dancing club on the Lothian Road – 'Shania', if he wasn't mistaken, sticking her crotch in his face. A real skank. The show-case had gone OK, those kind of middle-of-the-day BBC things always attracted an older, well-behaved audience, the kind that still believed the BBC was synonymous with quality. But the ten o'clock show . . . wankers, the lot of them. Bastard wankers.

The sun poked its dispassionate finger through the curtains and he noticed Martin's Rolex was on his wrist. Twenty to five. Martin didn't need a watch like this, he wasn't a Rolex man. What chance was there that Martin might give it to him? Or maybe he could 'accidentally' take it home with him.

The alarm in his head went off again and he realized it was actually the doorbell. Why the fuck didn't Martin get it? Again, longer this time. Jesus. He staggered out of bed and down the stairs. The front door was on the latch rather than fastened with the usual endless series of bolts and locks and chains that Martin barricaded himself in with. The guy was such an old woman about some things. Most things. Richard Moat pulled open the door and was hit by the daylight, knew how vampires felt. There was a guy standing there, just a guy, not a postman or a milkman or anyone else who might have claimed the right to be waking him at this hour.

'What? It's not even five o'clock. It's still yesterday, for fuck's sake.'

'Not for you,' the man on the doorstep said, pushing him roughly inside, 'for you it's tomorrow.'

'What the—?' Richard Moat said as the man shoved him into the living room.

The guy was huge, his nose swollen and ugly, as if he'd been in a fight. He was very nasal, English, a bit of something flat, Nottingham, Lancaster, perhaps. Richard Moat imagined himself giving a description afterwards to the police, imagined himself saying, 'I know accents, I'm in the business.' He had tried his hand at acting in the early Nineties, there'd been a bit part in *The Bill* where he'd played a guy (a comic so he wouldn't have to 'stretch' himself) with a crazy female stalker who wanted to kill him and one of the Sun Hill detectives counselled his character that to be a survivor you had to *think* like a survivor, you had to picture yourself in the future, *after* the attack. This advice came back to him now, but then he remembered that his character had actually been killed by the crazy stalker.

The insane stranger was wearing driving gloves and Richard thought this probably wasn't a good sign. The gloves had holes from which the guy's knuckles protruded, little atolls of white flesh, and Richard thought there was a joke in there somewhere, perhaps you could reference those classic yob knuckle-tattoos 'love' and 'hate', but try as he might he couldn't render this thought into anything remotely coherent, let alone funny. From nowhere the guy produced a baseball bat.

What followed ought to be in slow motion, no sound, a music track instead – Talking Heads' 'Psycho Killer' or perhaps something poignant and classical – the cello – Martin would know. Richard Moat's legs buckled suddenly and he fell to his knees. He'd never experienced that before, you heard talk about it but you didn't think it happened.

'That's good,' the man said, 'get down on the floor where you belong.'

'What do you want?' His mouth was so dry he could hardly speak. 'Take anything, everything. Take everything in the house.' Richard Moat flipped desperately through a mental inventory of everything in Martin's house. There was a good stereo, a fantastic widescreen TV over in the corner behind him. He tried to gesture with a nerveless arm in the direction of the television, spotted Martin's Rolex on his wrist, tried to bring it to the man's attention.

'I don't want anything,' the man said (quite calmly, his calmness was the worst thing).

Richard's phone rang, breaking the strange, intense intimacy between them. They both stared at it, sitting on the coffee table, a bizarre intrusion from outside. Richard Moat tried to calculate whether or not he could reach for it, flip it open, shout down the line to whoever was phoning him at this hour, *Help me, I'm with a crazy guy*, prove he wasn't joking, give the address (like someone in a movie, a sudden remembered image of Jodie Foster in *Panic Room*) but he knew it was no good, before he could even touch the phone the crazy guy would have brought his baseball bat down on his arm. He couldn't even bear thinking about the kind of pain the crazy guy could inflict. He started whimpering, he could hear himself, like a dog. Jodie Foster was made of sterner stuff, she wouldn't whimper.

The phone stopped ringing and the crazy guy pocketed it, laughing, singing the Robin Hood theme song. 'Bunch of faggots if you ask me,' he said to Richard, 'don't you think?'

Richard felt a warm trickle of urine working its way down his thigh.

'I didn't like what you did today.'

196

'The show?' Richard said in disbelief. 'You're here because you didn't like the *show*?'

'Is that what you call it?'

'I don't understand. I've never met you before. Have I?' He had gone through his life indifferent to whether or not he offended people, it struck him now that maybe he should have taken more care.

'Stay down on your knees and face me.'

'Do you want me to suck your cock?' Richard offered desperately, trying to make himself sound eager, despite his cotton mouth, despite the warm stain on his boxers. He wondered what he would do to save himself from being hurt by this man. Probably anything.

'You filthy bastard,' the man said. (OK, he'd read that one wrong.) 'I don't want you to *do* anything, Martin. Just shut the fuck up, why don't you?'

Richard Moat opened his mouth to say that he wasn't Martin, that Martin was asleep upstairs in his room and he would very happily show him the way so he could hurt Martin instead of himself, but all he managed was to croak, 'I'm a comedian,' and the man threw back his head and laughed, his mouth open so wide that Richard Moat could see the fillings in his back teeth. He felt a sob break in his throat.

'Oh you fucking are, there's no doubt about that,' the guy said and then quickly, quicker than in Richard Moat's imagination, he brought the bat down and Richard Moat's world exploded into pieces of light – little filaments, like in old-fashioned light bulbs – and he realized he had told his last joke. He could have sworn he heard applause and then all the little filaments burnt out one by one until there was only darkness and Richard Moat floated into it.

His last thoughts were about his obituary. Who would write it? Would it be good?

17

JACKSON WOKE IN THE TAILSPIN OF A NIGHTMARE. SOMEONE, a shadowy figure he didn't recognize, had handed him a package. Jackson knew that the package was very precious and if he dropped it something unspeakably awful would happen. The package was too heavy and awkward though, it had no fixed centre of gravity and seemed to move around in his arms so that no matter how hard he tried he couldn't hold on to it. He woke up with a start of horror at the moment when he knew the package was about to slip out of his arms for ever.

He hauled himself up and sat on the edge of what passed for a bed. He felt dog-rough, as if his body had been fed through a giant mangle during the night, and his eyes seemed to have been poached – or possibly fried – while he slept. His ribs ached and his hand was throbbing, it had swollen up nicely, the imprint of a boot clearly visible on it.

The seawater that had sluiced through his body yesterday had diluted his blood and it was going to require gallons of hot, strong coffee to restore its viscosity, to restore Jackson to some semblance of life. He wondered what kind of toxins and pollutants swam around in the water. And sewage, what about sewage? Best not to think about that probably.

He remembered the dead woman – not that he was about to forget her – and wondered if she had washed up somewhere overnight.

If he was in France he would be going for a swim in his *piscine* round about now. But he wasn't in France, he was in a holding cell in St Leonard's police station in Edinburgh.

He had never been in a jail cell before. He had put people in them, and taken people out of them, but he had never actually been locked in one himself. Nor had he journeyed from a holding cell to a sheriff court in the back of a Black Maria, which was like travelling in a cross between a public convenience and what he imagined a horsebox would be like. Nor had he been up before a court on the wrong side of the rails, and he had certainly never before been pronounced guilty and fined a hundred pounds for assault and gone from being upstanding citizen to convicted felon in the slow blink of the reptilian eye of the sheriff. From moment to moment the novelty just grew. He remembered thinking when Louise Monroe was questioning him that it was interesting to be on the other side. 'Interesting' – there was that word: he had obviously activated the Chinese curse yesterday.

When he came out of the court he phoned Julia on her mobile to tell her he was a free man again. He'd expected to get her voicemail, he thought he remembered her saying that she had a preview at eleven – but she answered, sounding sleepy as if he'd woken her up, 'Oh, gosh, sweetie, are you OK?' This morning there was genuine and touching concern for his welfare in her voice, whereas last night there had been un-Julia-like defeat when he phoned to tell her what had happened.

'Arrested? What a wag you are, Jackson,' she had sighed.

'No, really – arrested and charged,' he said. *Wag?* What kind of a word was that?

'For *brawling*?'

'I believe the technical term is assault. I'm up before the sheriff in the morning, I have to stay in jail overnight.'

'For God's sake, Jackson, do you *have* to go looking for trouble?'

'I didn't go looking for it, it found me all of its own accord. Are you going to ask me if I'm all right?'

'Are you all right?'

'Well, my hand hurts like hell, and I'm wondering if I've got at least one cracked rib.'

'Well, that's what happens when you go in for tom-foolery.'

'Tomfoolery?' His predicament seemed to have brought out the (even more) bizarre elements of her vocabulary. He'd thought she would be sympathetic but she had more or less put the phone down on him, although he supposed he had woken her up in what was the middle of the night by the time he'd been charged and processed. He thought perhaps she might have left him a nice message on his phone while it waited for him with his other belongings, but there was nothing.

He knew that whatever happened he mustn't mention the dog to Julia.

'You killed a *dog*, Jackson?'

'No! The dog just died, I didn't kill it.'

'You killed it with the power of your thoughts?'

'No! It had a heart attack, or a stroke maybe, I'm not sure.' He heard Julia light up a cigarette and drag hard on it. Her accordion lungs going in and out, wheezing their sickly tune.

He had watched in paralysed horror as the snarling dog had lumbered towards him, like an overweight gymnast going for the vaulting horse, and thought, Holy Mother of God, because divine intervention seemed the only thing that could rescue him. He steadied himself, reminded himself of the drill, *grab its legs, pull it apart*, and, lo and behold, the Virgin Mary herself must have interceded on his behalf because just as the furious beast reached him it dropped at his feet like a balloon that had been pricked. Jackson stared at it in dumbfounded astonishment, waiting for it to pull itself together and carry on ripping him apart with its teeth, but there wasn't even a twitch left in its tail. Honda Man roared with some horrible inner dog-loving pain and fell to his knees next to the animal, and even though he was a crazy, enraged psychopath Jackson couldn't help but feel a twinge of sympathy for someone in the throes of so much grief.

He scratched his head, Stan to Honda Man's Ollie, and wondered what to do. Running seemed like a good option, but somehow it didn't feel right just to walk away. Before he could decide on a course of action – kill Honda Man or comfort him – a policeman arrived on the scene. They might have been in a dark by-water of an alley but they were close to the Royal Mile and had been making enough noise to wake poor old Greyfriars Bobby, sleeping the big sleep no more than a stick's throw away. So shouting did work, he must remember to emphasize this fact to Marlee. And Julia.

Jackson supposed that, through a policeman's eye, it didn't look good – Honda Man on the ground, his nose a mashed-up mess, sobbing over his dead dog, Jackson standing over them both, scratching his head in bemusement, his mouth almost dripping with blood that wasn't his own. Perhaps he should just have put his hands up and said, 'It's a fair cop, you've got me bang to rights, officer,' but he didn't, he protested a great deal (*It was self-defence, he attacked me, he's insane*) and ended up being cuffed and forced into the back of a squad car.

His appearance in court this morning had been swift and brutal. The arresting officer read out a statement to the effect that he had come across 'Mr Terence Smith' on the ground in a pool of blood, sobbing over the body of his dog. The victim accused the defendant of killing the dog, but there were no visible marks on the dog. The defendant appeared to have bitten Mr Smith's nose. Mr Smith himself made an almost credible victim – sharp-suited in Hugo Boss, his nose purple and swollen in a way that clearly incriminated Jackson. He had been a man going about his own business, walking his dog. Walking his dog, was there any more innocent pastime that a citizen could indulge in?

Jackson had refused to see the police doctor last night, claiming he was 'fine'. It was stupid male pride that made him reluctant to admit to injury. 'You are a visitor in our city, Mr Brodie,' Sheriff Alistair Crichton admonished him, 'and I am only sorry that this isn't the good old days when you would have been run out of town.' Instead he fined him a hundred pounds for assault and told him to 'watch his step'.

'Why didn't you plead not guilty?' Julia asked. 'You're an idiot, Jackson.' She no longer sounded sleepy, quite the opposite in fact.

'Thanks for the sympathy.'

'And so, what now?' she asked.

'Dunno. Guess I'll try to go straight from now on.'

'It's not funny.'

'Unless you like the idea of being a gangster's moll.'

'It's not funny.'

Jackson could hear a door opening and closing and then voices in the background. A man asked a question that Jackson couldn't catch and Julia turned her mouth away from the phone and said, 'Yes, please.'

'Are you in a shop?'

'No, I'm in rehearsal. I have to go, I'll see you later.' And she was gone. She couldn't be in rehearsal, her venue was so far underground that no phone signal could penetrate the rock. Jackson sighed. Hard times in Babylon.

18

LOUISE HAD TO SPEND TWENTY MINUTES WAKING ARCHIE UP. If she didn't put the effort in he would still be in his bed when she came home from work. He had been in the shower for almost half an hour. She wouldn't be surprised if he'd fallen asleep again in there, he certainly never seemed any cleaner when he came out. She didn't like to think what other things he might be doing in there with his man/boy body. It was hard to remember that he had once been brand-new, as pink and unsullied as Jellybean's paw-pads when he was a kitten. Now he sprouted hair and stubble, erupted in spots, his voice was on a rollercoaster, swooping and plummeting at random. He was undergoing some kind of unnatural transformation, as if he was changing from a boy into an animal, more werewolf than boy.

It was almost impossible to believe now that Archie had come out of her own body, she couldn't see how he had ever fitted in there. Eve was made from Adam's body but in reality men came from *inside* women – no wonder it did their heads in. Man that is born of a woman is of few days, and is full of trouble. Sometimes you wondered why anyone bothered crawling out of the cradle when what lay ahead was so darn difficult. She shouldn't think like that, depressive mothers produced depressive children (she had read a clinical study), she had thought that she could be the one to break the cycle but she hadn't done a very good job.

She drank coffee and glared at the urn, still sitting on the draining board. Woman is born of woman. Perhaps she could just scatter the contents in the garden like fertilizer. There was hardly any topsoil out there – thank you, Graham Hatter – so for the first time in her life her mother could perform a useful function. She realized she had bitten her lip until it bled. She liked the taste of her own blood, salty and ferric. She was sure she had read somewhere that there was salt in the blood because all life began in the sea but she found it hard to believe that – it seemed more poetic than scientific. She thought of an embryonic Archie, more fish than fowl, curled in his watery environment, tumbling like a seahorse inside her.

She sighed. She couldn't deal with her mother yet. 'I'll think about it tomorrow,' she murmured. The ghost of Scarlett passed through her and she acknowledged her with a little salute, *Good to see you, Ms O'Hara*.

It could have been the first murder case on which she was senior officer in charge and instead it was turning out to be a mirage. The divers had gone in at first light and found nothing. She'd sent Sandy Mathieson out there to cover for her. Somehow she had known the divers wouldn't come up with anything. She would probably get hauled over the coals for wasting money and resources. She would like the dead woman to turn up, not because she wanted a woman dead but because she would like to prove that she wasn't a figment of Jackson Brodie's imagination. She wanted to justify Jackson. The justified sinner. Was he a sinner? Wasn't everyone?

Yesterday, Jessica Drummond had checked his credentials with the Cambridge police. Yes, he used to be a detective inspector with them but he had left a few years ago to set up as a private investigator. 'A gumshoe, a private *dick*,' Jessica snorted (she really did snort), '*Boy's Own* fantasy stuff.'

Eager-beaver, Louise had heard Jessica called. She was trying so hard to become one of the boys that she looked as if she might have started shaving. Compared to her, Louise felt like a great big puffy pink marshmallow of womanhood.

Worse, Jessica went on, Brodie had inherited money from a client and buggered off to retire in France.

'How much money?' Louise asked.

'Two million.'

'You're joking.'

'No. Two million pounds from a *very* old lady. You can't help but wonder how much *coercion* that involved. Confused old lady changes her will in favour of some sweet talker. I think there's something wrong with our Mr Brodie,' she tapped her forehead, 'you know, an elaborate hoaxer, misses being a policeman, having a real job, sets about making himself the centre of attention. A fantasist.'

'That all sounds a bit soap opera,' Louise said. 'And I didn't see any evidence of sweet talking.' Quite the opposite if anything. He had two million in the bank and he was travelling on buses? He didn't look like the kind of guy who took a bus. *Not everyone has someone who'll notice they've gone.* Was he talking about himself? He had looked right at her when he said it, did he think she didn't have anyone who would miss her? Archie would miss her. Jellybean would miss her. Jellybean would miss her more than Archie. Archie would hole up in his bedroom, playing Mercenaries – Playground of Destruction, watching *Punk'd* and *Cribs* and *Pimp My Ride* and ordering in pizza on her credit card.

But then what, when the money ran out? He was a boy who could barely open a tin of beans. If she died before her time, then Archie would be an orphan. The idea of Archie as an orphan was a kick to her heart, the next worst thing to his own death (don't think that). But then everyone became an orphan eventually, didn't they? She was an orphan herself now, of course, although the difference between her mother being alive and her mother being dead seemed minimal.

For Archie's sake rather than her own, Louise hoped that she would die a natural death in her own bed when she was a contented old woman and Archie was completely grown-up and independent and was ready to let her go. He would have a wife and children and a profession. He'd probably turn out to be a right-wing investment banker and say things to his kids like 'When I was your age, I was a bit of a rebel too.' She would be dead but everyone would be OK about that, including Louise, and her genes would carry on in her child and then in his child and in this way the world was stitched together.

Louise could imagine being old but she couldn't imagine being contented.

Women aren't noted for drowning. She supposed Jackson Brodie was right. Louise made a mental list of women who had drowned – Maggie Tulliver, Virginia Woolf, Natalie Wood, Rebecca de Winter. True, they weren't all real and, technically speaking, Rebecca didn't drown, did she? She was murdered, and she had cancer. The Rasputin of romantic literature – bad women need killing several times over apparently. You could keep a good woman down but not a bad one. Louise had gone straight into the police after she graduated from St Andrews with a first in English. Never a backward glance to academia. They had wanted her to do an M Phil but what was the point, really? In the police you could be out there, on the street, doing something, making a difference, breaking down doors and finding small helpless children at the mercy of their drunken mothers. And you would have the power to take those small helpless children away from their drunken mothers and save them, give them to foster parents, put them in an orphanage, anything rather than leaving them at home to be a witness to their own ravaged childhood. Jackson Brodie didn't seem like a hoaxer, but then that was the thing about hoaxers and conmen, wasn't it, they were plausible. Perhaps he had fallen in the water and panicked, hallucinated, made something out of nothing. Invented a corpse out of malice or delusion or plain old insanity. He'd wrong-footed her at first by being so professional – his description of the body, the circumstances in which it was found, were all what she would expect from one of her team – but who was to say he wasn't a pathological liar? He had taken photographs but there was no sign of a camera, he had found a card but it had disappeared, he had tried to pull a dead woman from the water but there was no body. It was all very shaky.

He could have gone over earlier, left his jacket and then simply entered the water from Cramond, but as hoaxes go it seemed very elaborate.

Or perhaps there *was* a dead girl and it was Jackson Brodie who had killed her. First person to discover the body – always a prime suspect. He was a witness and yet he felt like a suspect. (Why was that?) He said he'd tried to pull her out of the water to stop her floating off on the tide but he could just as well have put her *in* the water. Deflecting suspicion from himself by being the one who called it in.

She heard Archie stumbling down the stairs, falling into the kitchen, grunting something that was almost certainly not 'Good Morning'. His face was raw with spots, his ham-skin looked as if it had been boiled. What if Archie didn't undergo a transformation? What if this wasn't his pupa stage, what if this was *it*?

She put Weetabix in a bowl, poured milk on it, gave him a spoon. 'Eat,' she said. A dog would be more capable. Being fourteen meant he had slipped back down the evolutionary ladder to some pre-social rung. Some men of Louise's acquaintance had never climbed back up again.

She wanted to talk to him about the shoplifting. She wanted to talk to him about it in a reasonable way, not losing her temper, not yelling at him, telling him what a stupid fucking idiot he was. Lots of kids shoplifted and didn't go on to a career of crime, take herself, for example. Although of course she had gone on to a career of crime, it was just she was on the good side. Hopefully.

Maybe it was regular, maybe it was only the once, she didn't know. Louise had been with him at the time so she had to presume that it was some kind of rebellion against her, some psychological acting out. They were in Dixons in the St James Centre, celebrating her mother's death by buying a big flat-screen TV in anticipation of the insurance money. Louise had taken out life insurance on her mother years ago, deciding she would never profit in any way from her life so she might as well cash in on her death. It was a small policy, she couldn't have kept up big payments on it and once or twice it had struck her that if it had been really serious money (*two million*) she might have been tempted to knock her mother off. A simple accident, drunks fall down stairs all the time, after all. And a detective knows how to cover her tracks.

Archie had taken something stupid – a pack of AA batteries that he could easily have paid for. It wasn't about paying, of course. She was at the other end of the shop when the door alarm went off and then a security guard ran past her, pouncing on Archie as he exited, laying firm hands on a shoulder and an elbow, turning him round and propelling him back inside. The professional part of her brain registered the catch as businesslike and efficient. The unprofessional part of her brain considered leaping on the security guard's back and jamming her thumbs in his eyes. No one ever warned you about how ferocious mother love could be. Let's face it, no one warned you about anything.

She thought about looking helpless and throwing herself on his mercy. Unfortunately, looking helpless was not one of her greatest talents. Instead she marched up to the pair of them, flipping out her warrant and coolly asking if there was anything she could do. The security guard launched into his explanation and she said, 'It's OK, I'll take him in, have a word with him,' frogmarching Archie out of the shop before the security guard could protest, before Archie could say something stupid (like *Mum*). She heard the security guard shout after her, 'We always prosecute!' She knew they'd be on tape and spent some anxious time afterwards waiting to see if anything came of it but nothing did, thank God. She could probably have found a way of making the tape disappear. She would have *eaten* the tape if necessary.

Outside, in the underground gloom of the multi-storey car park they had sat together in the cold car, staring out of the windscreen at the oil-stained floor, the concrete pillars, the mothers hustling toddlers in and out of car seats and pushchairs. Oh God, but she hated shopping centres. There wasn't even any point in asking him why because he'd just shrug his shoulders and stare at his trainers and mutter, 'Dunno.' The artful dodger.

She could see that from his point of view it was unfair – she had so much power while he had absolutely none. A contraction of pain seized up her insides. Another turn of the corkscrew. That was love. As strong as the first time she touched him after he was born, lying on her chest like a barnacle, in the labour suite of the old Simpson Memorial Maternity Pavilion (now, at the new hospital, it was renamed the Simpson Centre for Reproductive Health, it wasn't the same somehow). Louise knew, at that first touch, that, one way or another, they were stuck together for ever.

It seemed to her, sitting there in the car park, that he was as helpless now as he was then and she wanted to turn round and punch him in the head. She had never hit him, never, not once, but she'd come close to it a thousand times, most of them in the last year. Instead she put her hand on the horn and kept it there. People in the car park looked around, thinking it was a car alarm. 'Mum,' he said finally, quietly, 'don't. Please stop,' which was the most articulate thing he'd said to her in weeks. So she stopped. It all seemed a high price to pay for a desperate, drunken bout of sex with a married colleague who never even knew he'd fathered a child.

She had a sudden, unwelcome flashback to the bump and grind of Archie's genesis. PC Louise Monroe in the back of an unmarked squad car with DI Michael Pirie, the night of his leaving do. He had a new promotion and an old wife but that hadn't stopped him. People used to think that the circumstances of a child's conception shaped his character. She hoped not.

'What?' Archie said, glaring at her, a moustache of milk around his mouth.

'Ophelia,' Louise said. 'She drowned. Ophelia drowned.'

Louise went up to the bathroom and opened the window, cleaned the shower, picked up sodden towels, flushed the toilet. She wondered if he would ever be housetrained. It was impossible to modify his behaviour. She wondered what would happen to him under the threat of torture, perhaps she should sell him to science or the army. The CIA would find him a fascinating subject – the boy who couldn't be broken.

She put in her contacts, applied make-up, enough to have made an effort, not enough to be blatantly a woman, a white shirt beneath a trim black suit from Next, court shoes with a slight heel, no jewellery apart from a watch and a pair of modest gold studs in her ears. She would go back out to Cramond as soon as she could, join her team to dot the i's and cross the t's on the case that never was, but this morning she was due to give evidence in Alistair Crichton's court – a car scam, stealing high-end cars in Edinburgh and selling them in Glasgow with new plates. She and a DS, Jim Tucker, had worked doggedly to put a case together for the procurator fiscal, Crichton was an old bastard and a stickler for procedure and she didn't want her appearance to get in the way of her evidence. She had done Jim a big favour last year. He had a teenage daughter, Lily, one of those clean-cut types, thick hair, lots of good orthodontic work, all her grade exams on the piano. Lily had just triumphed in her Highers and was set to go to university on a Royal Navy scholarship to study medicine, and then Louise had helped to

214

net her in a drugs raid in a flat in Sciennes. It turned out to be just a bit of dope, sixth-years from Gillespie's and a couple of first-year university students. Louise had recognized Lily straight away. They were all taken down to the station and a couple of them were charged with possession. It was one of those jobs that looked like overkill afterwards, lots of shouting and breaking down of doors and in the confusion Louise had arm-locked Lily and walked her out of the flat and hissed in her ear, 'Scarper,' and more or less pushed her down the stairs, into the night and into her safe, high-achieving future.

Jim was a good sort, he was so grateful he would have cut off a limb and presented it to her in a glass case if she'd asked. Lily must be honest beyond the call of duty because she told her father about it. Louise couldn't imagine herself owning up at that age. Any age, come to that. Louise wouldn't have said anything to Jim about the bust, didn't think it was nice to tell tales. The way she looked at it, if Jim ever found him-self in a similar situation with Archie, Archie would have a get-out-of-jail-free card and at least one member of the Lothian and Borders Police on his side. Two with his mother, of course.

She emptied half a packet of Tic Tacs into her mouth and she was as ready as she ever would be.

19

RICHARD MOAT DIDN'T WAKE. HE LAY UNTROUBLED IN MARTIN Canning's living room in Merchiston. It was a large neo-Gothic Victorian mansion, with something of the manse about it. The front lawn was dominated by a single, enormous monkey-puzzle tree, planted when the house was still quite new. The house was masked from the road by ranks of mature trees and shrubbery. Nowadays the intricate cabling of the monkey-puzzle tree's roots extended far beyond the front lawn, curling around gas and sewer pipes in the street and poking silently into other people's gardens.

The smashed-up Rolex on Richard Moat's wrist showed he had died at ten to five (a flat line, appropriately), watched over only by the little red demon eye on the television set – the 'fantastic' one that for a second he had hoped to barter for his life – and with nothing for company but the faint noises of the suburban world, growing louder as the morning wore on. The milk van had rattled its way along the street. It was the kind of affluent suburb that still had milk vans delivering glass bottles on the doorstep. The post had slipped through the letterbox in a subdued way. In London, the day never began for Richard Moat until the post arrived. He always felt that days when there was no post (although there was always post) never really began at all. Today there was post, nearly all of it for him, redirected 'c/o Martin Canning' – a cheque from his agent, a postcard from a friend in Greece, two fan letters balanced by two hate letters. Despite the arrival of the post, however, this day was never going to begin for Richard Moat.

It was the maid who found him. The maid was Czech, a physics graduate from Prague. Her name was Sophia and she was spending the summer 'working her arse off' for a pittance. They weren't 'maids', they were cleaners, maids was a stupid old-fashioned name. They were employed by a firm called Favours and they arrived mop-handed in a pink van under the supervision of a gang leader who was called 'the housekeeper' – a woman who came originally from the Isle of Lewis and who was mean to all the maids. With agency fees and hidden bonuses it cost three times as much to hire Favours as it would have done to have a cleaner come in a couple of days a week. So, generally speaking, the houses they went to belonged to people who were too rich or too stupid (or both) to think of a cheaper alternative. They had little pink calling cards on which the strap-line read, 'We have done you a Favour!' Sophia had learned the word 'strap-line' (and the word 'arse' and many other things) from her Scottish boyfriend, who was a marketing graduate. When the maids finished they were supposed to leave one of the little pink cards, after they had written on them, 'Your maids today were Maria and Sharon'. Or whoever. Half the maids were foreign, most of them Eastern European. Economic immigration they called it but really it was just slave labour.

The housekeeper gave them a checklist of tasks. This checklist had been agreed beforehand with the owner of the house and always said obvious things like 'Clean bathroom sink', 'Vacuum stairs', 'Change beds'. It never said 'Clean up cat sick', 'Change spunky sheets', 'Take hair out of bathroom plughole', which would have been more like the truth. Some people were pigs, they left their nice houses in a disgusting state. 'Spunky', obviously, was a word Sophia had learned from her Scottish boyfriend. He was a good source of the vernacular even though he was very shallow, but a great fuck (his words), which was what you wanted in a foreign boyfriend, otherwise why bother?

The housekeeper usually drove them in the pink van and dropped them off and then did God knows what, nothing too strenuous, probably. Sophia imagined her sitting somewhere in a comfortable chair eating chocolate biscuits and watching *Good Morning*.

They had three houses to clean in Merchiston, all close to each other so it was probably word of mouth – because whatever else they were, the Favours maids were good at cleaning. The house with the monkey-puzzle tree (very nice, Sophia fantasized about living there) was somewhere they went every week. The owner was hardly ever there, when they came in the front door he disappeared out of the back door, like a cat. He was a writer, the housekeeper said, so don't ever disturb any papers, any writing. It was the cleanest, tidiest house they went to, nothing ever out of place, beds made, towels folded, all the food in the fridge inside neat plastic containers from Lakeland. You could have sat in the kitchen and drunk coffee and read the newspaper and then left without doing any cleaning and the housekeeper would never have known. But Sophia wouldn't do that. She wasn't lazy. In this house she polished and swept and vacuumed even more because the writer deserved it for being so clean himself. And now also because the writer had a visitor who was a pig, who smoked and drank and left his clothes on the floor and if he caught sight of her said filthy, suggestive things.

He had offered money to one of the other maids, a sad Romanian girl, and she had gone upstairs with him ('to have it off') and then he had only given her half the money and a signed photograph of himself. 'Wanker', all the maids agreed. Sophia had taught them the word, courtesy of her Scottish boyfriend. It was a very useful word, they said. But the girl was stupid to have gone with him. She cried for days afterwards, spilling tears on to nice polished surfaces and using up clean towels. She was a virgin, she said, but she needed the money. Everyone needed money. Lots of the girls were here illegally, some had had their passports confiscated, some disappeared after a while. Sex traffic. It would happen to the Romanian girl, you could see it in her eyes. There were rumours about bad things that had happened to some of the girls who worked for Favours, but there were always rumours and there were always bad things happening to girls. That was life.

Sophia liked to think that the writer wasn't too rich or stupid to hire a regular cleaner but that he maybe liked the impersonal nature of Favours' service. Sophia imagined that writers were people who didn't like to get too close to other people in case it stopped them writing.

Today they were short-staffed because there was flu going round and the housekeeper said, 'Start on your own,' and so Sophia rapped on the door of the writer's house. She had a key but they were supposed to knock first. She rapped again loudly. The writer had a good brass doorknocker in the shape of a lion's head and there was something satisfying about using it, like being the police. When there was no answer she let herself in with the key and announced, 'Favours here,' in a loud singsong voice just in case the writer was in bed having it off with someone. Very unlikely, no sign of a sex life with a woman or a man anywhere in the writer's house. Not even any porn. A few photographs in frames, she recognized Notre Dame in Paris, Dutch houses along a canal – tourist photographs like post-cards, no people in them.

He had a set of Russian dolls, matryoshka, the expensive kind. The tourist shops in Prague were full of Russian dolls these days. The writer's dolls were lined up on the windowsill, she dusted them every week. Sometimes she put them inside each other, playing with them like she had done with her own set when she was a child. She used to think they were eating each other. Her matryoshka had been cheap, crudely painted in primary colours, but the dolls that belonged to the writer were beautiful, painted by a real artist with scenes from Pushkin – so many artists in Russia with no jobs now, painting boxes and dolls and eggs, anything for tourists. The writer had a fifteen-doll set! How she would have loved that when she was a girl. Now, of course, she had put away childish things. She wondered if the writer was gay. A lot of gay men in Edinburgh.

There was a shelf of his books in his study, a lot of them in foreign languages, even in Czech! She had glanced through them, they were about a girl called Nina Riley who was a private detective. *Put the gun down, Lord Hunterston! I know what happened out on the grouse shoot, Davy's death was no accident.* Shite, as her Scottish boyfriend would have said. At Favours they referred to the writer as Mr Canning but that was not the name on his books, on the books he was Alex Blake.

All nice as it was every time. Scented roses from the garden in a bowl on a table in the hall. He always left ten pounds extra, tucked under the bowl, a generous man. Must be very rich. No ten-pound note today, not like him. The dining room unused as usual. She opened the door to the living room. The curtains were closed, which they never were. It felt gloomy as if there was a fog in the room. Even in the half-light she could tell that something bad had happened. She picked her way across the carpet and glass crunched underfoot as if a bomb had gone off. She opened the curtains and sunlight poured in, illuminating the mess

– the mirror above the fireplace, all of the ornaments, even the pretty glass shades in the antique light fitting, all smashed to splinters and shards. A coffee table turned over, a table lamp lying on the floor, its yellow silk shade bent and broken. Everything upside down, as if elephants had passed through the room. Really clumsy elephants. The writer's matryoshka dolls were scattered everywhere, little skittles knocked flying. She picked one up without thinking and put it in the pocket of her jacket, feeling the smooth, round, satisfying shape of it.

Sophia had a funny feeling in her stomach, like when something very exciting was going to happen, something that had never happened before. Like the time she watched a huge block of flats being demolished. Boom! And a great cloud of thick grey dust, like a volcano erupting, like the Twin Towers coming down, only it was before the Twin Towers.

Then she cried out, 'Oh God, oh my God,' in her own language. She made the sign of the cross even though she wasn't religious and said, 'Oh my God,' again. They seemed to be the only words she could remember. The sight of the man on the floor had temporarily eradicated the entire database of Sophia's vocabulary, English and Czech.

She was a scientist really, not a cleaner, she reminded herself, she should be able to observe dispassionately, objectively. She forced herself to move closer. The man, it must be the writer, was lying on the floor as if he had toppled over backwards while at prayer. It looked like an uncomfortable position but he probably didn't care too much any more. His head all caved in, an eye popped out. Brain everywhere like Scottish porridge. Blood. A lot of blood, soaked into the red carpet so she hadn't seen it at first. Blood on the red-painted walls, blood on the red velvet sofas. It was like a room that had been waiting for a murder, waiting to absorb it into its walls like a sponge.

She was getting used to looking at him now. Words were coming back as well – English words. She realized she could shout 'Help!' or 'Murder!' but now she'd got over the shock that seemed a little bit stupid so she walked quietly back through the house and out of the front door and into the street, where she found the housekeeper still unloading plastic buckets and mops from the back of the pink van and informed her that the writer's house wasn't going to be cleaned any time today.

20

'I HEARD YOU KILLED A DOG. YOU LOOK LIKE SHIT. WANT TO grab a coffee?'

Louise Monroe. Louise Monroe grinning at him and pointing across the road to the Royal Museum opposite the Sheriff Court.

'Fraternizing with the enemy?'

'They've got a good café in there,' she said. She scrubbed up nicely – black suit, white shirt, heels. Yesterday she had been in jeans and a T-shirt, a suede jacket. He liked her best in jeans, but the suit was nice. She had good ankles, 'turned on a lathe' his brother would have said. Jackson was a bit of an ankle man. He liked all the other bits that went into the making of a woman, but he particularly appreciated a good pair of ankles. It was the bad Jackson, obviously, that was thinking about Louise Monroe's ankles, the evil doppelgänger who lay in ambush within his brain. Good Jackson, Bad Jackson. The pair of them seemed to be having quite a tussle these days. Jackson didn't like to think what would happen if Bad Jackson won.

Had Dr Jekyll won over Mr Hyde? Which one was good and which one was bad? He had no idea, he'd never read the book, only seen that *Mary Reilly* movie, half of it anyway, on video – Josie's choice – before falling into a post-pizza sleep on the sofa.

'I didn't kill the dog,' Jackson said. 'It just died. Dogs do die of natural causes, despite what everyone thinks. I take it you haven't found her then? The dead girl?'

'No, sorry.'

Not yet would have been a better answer. She said 'sorry' as if looking for the dead girl had been a personal favour to him rather than a police case. Jackson suddenly caught sight of Terence Smith leaving the Sheriff Court, a phone glued to his ear. 'Hey, you,' Jackson shouted, starting after him. Louise Monroe caught his sleeve and held him back, saying, 'Easy, tiger, you don't want to end up straight back in court.' Terence Smith gave him a two-finger salute and stepped into a taxi.

'Lying bastard,' Jackson muttered.

'That's what they all say.'

'So you pleaded guilty even though you were innocent?' Louise Monroe mused over a latte while Jackson downed a triple espresso like medicine. 'You must be a Catholic.'

'My mother was Irish,' Jackson said. 'She was very religious. I was a disappointment to her.'

'I'm a Scottish Catholic, that's a double whammy – all the same crap but a chip welded on the shoulder as well.'

'And were you a disappointment to your mother?' Jackson asked.

'No. She was a disappointment to me.'

'It just seemed easier to plead guilty.'

'And that makes perfect sense where you come from, Mr Brodie, in Topsy-Turvy Land?'

Mr Brodie. That was how Julia used to address him, in the early days, making his surname suggestive and intimate as if he was a character in a Regency romance. Now she said 'Jackson' sharply, like someone who knew him too well.

'I just thought it would be quicker, rather than going to trial and having to come back, get a solicitor, all that rigmarole. I had no witnesses, the guy was injured and I never mentioned my own injuries when I was charged.' He held out his hand for her to see, deciding against lifting his shirt and displaying his other purple trophies in the genteel environment of the museum. 'My sword hand,' he said ruefully.

'He stamped on your hand?' she said. 'When you were on the ground? And you didn't plead self-defence? You're an idiot.'

'So I'm told.'

'You're an ex-policeman, a man of previously good character, it's your first offence.'

'I've crossed over to the dark side.'

'Why?'

'I wanted to know what it was like.'

'And?'

'Dark.' He sighed and winced at the pain in his ribs. He'd had enough of this conversation. 'What about Favours,' he said, 'find anything?'

'I put Jessica on to it yesterday. There's no entry in the phone book for them—'

'Surprise, surprise.'

'Nothing at Companies House, no email address, no website and thousands of internet hits for everything ranging from dog-walking to hardcore porn, although none that's obviously Edinburgh-based. Vice say they've never heard of a sauna called Favours, ditto a lap-dancing club.'

'You should look for the pink cards – phone boxes, toilets, pubs, clubs.' Jackson began to feel something he hadn't felt for a while, for a moment he couldn't identify it and then he realized what it was – he was working a case – all the excitement of trying to put something together, of trying to *get* somewhere. (*Let's face it, Jackson, you feel unmanned.*) 'Have you asked the girls on the street?'

She said, 'I can see your police antennae waving. Put them away.'

She had bitten her lip so that it had bled, he could see a scar or a scab, indicating it was a habit. She looked so in control and yet the whole drawing-your-own-blood thing hinted at all kinds of inner neuroses. He thought of the snake eating its own tail, devouring itself. He wondered what she'd been doing at the Sheriff Court. He didn't ask. Instead he said, 'The man who attacked me last night, Terence Smith, aka Honda Man, was involved in a road-rage incident yesterday. He was a maniac, completely out of control. Viking berserkers come to mind.'

'You saw it? What are you, some kind of professional witness, travelling around looking for crime scenes?'

'No, I'm cursed.'

She laughed and said, 'Who cursed you?' and he said, 'I think I did it to myself.' Because he was an idiot obviously. She looked like a different person when she laughed.

'I saw him take a baseball bat to someone in the street and a few hours later the guy has a go at me, threatening me, telling me to keep my mouth shut about what I saw. He knew my *name*. How could he know that?'

'So you were the only witness to this road rage?'

'No,' Jackson said, 'there were dozens of other witnesses. He didn't see me, and he had much more reason to go after the guy who stopped him – some guy threw a briefcase at him. Maybe he's warned him off as well.'

'Or maybe he was just a run-of-the-mill mugger and you imagined him threatening you.'

'Imagined?' The way she'd been listening to him he'd thought she believed him. He felt suddenly let down.

'Look at the evidence,' she said. 'You say you witnessed a road-rage incident, you claim the alleged perpetrator of the incident then assaulted you – although you yourself pleaded guilty to assaulting *him* – you claimed you found a dead body, but there is no evidence to support that claim. You're a millionaire but you're hanging around finding trouble in all the wrong places. Let's face it, Jackson, on paper you just don't look good.'

The unexpected use of his first name took him more by surprise than the reference to his personal circumstances, but then of *course* she would have run a background check on him. She wasn't the stupid one here, he was the one with the bruises and the criminal conviction. He said, 'You've got blood on your lip.'

21

MARTIN WAS WOKEN BY THE DAWN CHORUS. EVEN WITH HIS brain furred by sleep it struck him as unlikely, he seemed to be in a place where no birds sang and, sure enough, after a while he realized it was actually his mobile rather than an avian choir.

He fumbled for his spectacles, knocking the phone to the floor as he did so. Even with his spectacles on he felt as if his eyes had been smeared with Vaseline. By the time he had recovered it, the phone had ceased chirping. He peered at the screen – *1 missed call*. He went into the phone's call registry. *Richard Moat*. Richard was probably wondering what had happened to him last night, although he wasn't exactly the type who would care. More likely he wanted the loan of something.

He put the phone down on the bedside table and found himself looking at a woman being burnt at the stake. Her mouth was open in a gulping howl of oval as the flames from the piles of wood surrounding her began to catch at her body. It was a print of a woodcut, hanging on the wall, 'Old Edinburgh' a label beneath it declared. When they drained the Nor' Loch to make Princes Street Gardens they discovered it was not just the repository of the town's sewage and refuse but was also the final resting place of the town's witches – their trussed-up skeletons tied thumbs-to-toes like birds ready for roasting. And those were the innocent ones, the ones who sank. Martin had never understood that, you would think that innocence would be an airy substance that would make you float, that evil would be heavy, sinking you to the bottom, to the slimy, stinking mud.

Now, on the site of the witch burnings, there was an expensive restaurant where the cream of the Edinburgh bourgeoisie dined. That was what the world was like, things improved but they didn't get better.

Martin's neck ached and his limbs felt as if they'd been tied up in knots all night, as if he himself had been trussed. He was in the bed, but he had no recollection of lying down next to Paul Bradley. No recollection of removing his spectacles or his shoes. He was relieved that he was still fully dressed. The smell of frying bacon penetrated the room and made him feel sick. He peered at the digital clock on the radio next to the bed – twelve o'clock, he couldn't believe he'd slept so long. Of Paul Bradley there was no sign – no holdall, no jacket, nothing – the man might never have existed. He remembered the gun and his heart gave a little flip. He had spent the night in a hotel room (in the same bed!) with a complete stranger and a gun. An assassin.

He unfolded his body cautiously and lowered his legs to the floor. A spasm in his lower back stopped him and he had to wait for it to pass before he could stand up and wobble on jelly-legs to the bathroom. The inside of his mouth felt like cardboard and his head seemed enormous, too heavy for the stalk of his neck. He felt as if he'd been given an anaesthetic and for one paranoid moment his heartbeat spiked as he wondered if Paul Bradley had been part of some complex scam to harvest organs off innocent bystanders. Or carbon monoxide poisoning? The beginning of the famous summer flu or the end of an Irn-Bru hangover?

He slaked an outrageous thirst with chemical-tasting water from the tap and checked himself in the bathroom mirror but he couldn't find any visible operation scars. Rohypnol? Date rape? (Surely he would know?) Something had happened to him but he had no idea what. Had he been given some mind-altering drug that was making him mad? But why would anyone want to do that? Unless it was the gods who were going to destroy him next. They had bided their time, it was more than a year since Russia, since the *incident*.

The last day, their guide, Mariya, had let them loose in a market somewhere behind Nevsky Prospekt where there was stall after stall displaying tourist wares — nesting Russian dolls, lacquered boxes, painted eggs, communist memorabilia and fur hats decorated with Red Army badges. But mostly there were dolls, thousands of dolls, legion upon legion of matryoshka, not just the ones you could see but also the ones you couldn't — dolls within dolls, endlessly replicating and diminishing, like an infinite series of mirrors. Martin imagined writing a story, a Borges-like construction where each story contained the kernel of the next and so on. Not Nina Riley obviously — linear narratives were as much as she could cope with — but rather something with intellectual cachet (something good).

Martin had never given matryoshka much thought before but here in St Petersburg their ranks seemed omnipresent and unavoidable. His fellow travellers on the tour, overnight connoisseurs of Russian folk art, chatted all the time about which kind they were going to buy to take home. They speculated about how much doll they were going to get for their roubles and the general feeling was that the Russians were out to rip them off but that they would do everything they could to rip the Russians off in return. 'They've embraced capitalism,' one man said, 'so they can take the bloody consequences.' Martin couldn't tell if 'bloody' was being used as an expletive or merely a descriptive. Martin had noticed before that these kinds of trips tended to generate a good deal of xenophobia, so that even when enjoying the Wonders of Prague or the Beauties of Bordeaux the tourists, little Britishers fighting a permanent rearguard action, regarded the inhabitants of those places as hostile miscreants.

The shop in the foyer of their cockroach-infested hotel — hot, brightly lit, its walls mirrored with glass — sold dolls with inflated price tags attached. No one ever bought anything in the shop and Martin spent an evening hour in there browsing beneath the disappointed eye of the woman in charge (*just looking*, he murmured apologetically), studying, evaluating and comparing dolls in readiness for the reality of a raw retail transaction out on the streets of St Petersburg. There were big ones and small ones, tall ones and squat ones, but the features always seemed to be the same, little pouty rosebud mouths and big blue eyes, with eyelids fixed open in a permanent stare of sex-doll horror.

There were also dolls in the shape of cats, dogs, frogs, there were American presidents and Soviet leaders, there were five-doll sets and fifty-doll sets, there were cosmonauts and clowns, there were crudely made dolls and ones that had been exquisitely painted by real artists. By the time he left the hotel shop Martin felt dizzy, his eyes swimming with endless reflections of dolls' faces, and when he went to his narrow, uncomfortable bed he dreamed he was being watched by a giant Masonic eye in the sky which turned into the eye painted at the bottom of his grandmother's chamber pot with its prurient inscription, 'What I see I'll never tell'. He woke up in a sweat, he hadn't thought about his grandmother – let alone her chamber pot – in years. She had been born in a Victorian century and had never really left it, her working-class Fountainbridge tenement a dark and gloomy space draped with chenille and musty velvet. She died a very long time ago and Martin was surprised that he remembered anything about her at all.

'Going to take one of those dolls home for my little grand-niece,' the dying grocer said as they surveyed the rows of stalls. It was beginning to snow again, big wet flakes of early snow that melted on contact with tarmac and skin. It had snowed the day before and now the streets were grim with grey slush. The air was hostile with a damp kind of cold and the grocer decided to buy a fur hat with ear-flaps, haggling with the stallholder over the price. Martin wondered what the point of bargaining was when you were so near to death. He was beginning to wonder if the grocer really was dying or if he had made the claim simply in order to get attention.

Martin managed to give him the slip while he was entrenched in the negotiations over his hat. The man was ruining the Magic of Russia for Martin, that very morning he had trailed on Martin's heels through the Hermitage complaining all the way about the excesses of the décor (but surely that was the point) and imagining what 'god-awful pigswill' they would be served up for supper. Even the Rembrandts didn't shut him up: 'Miserable old bugger, wasn't he?' he said, contemplating a self-portrait of the artist. Martin knew it could only be a temporary respite, no doubt the minute he had his new hat on his head the grocer would ferret him out from amongst the souvenir stalls and spend the rest of the afternoon complaining about being taken to the cleaners by the hat seller, a scrawny man who looked as if he was going to beat the grocer in the race to scramble through the door to the next world.

Martin intended to buy a set of dolls for his mother. He knew they would sit, dusted but neglected, on a shelf amongst her other cheap knick-knacks, the porcelain 'figurines', the dolls in national costume, the little cross-stitched pictures. She took no pleasure in anything he bought her but if he didn't buy her something she would complain that he never thought about her (her logic was indefatigable). If someone had given Martin a piece of rock wrapped in paper he would have been grateful because they had gone to the trouble of finding the rock and wrapping it in the paper, just for him.

He would buy her something ordinary, he decided, because she deserved nothing better than ordinary – a little peasant set, aprons and headscarves, he was holding one in his hand, feeling its smoothness, its fertility symbol shape, thinking about his mother, when the girl on the stall said, 'Is very nice.'

'Yes,' he said. He didn't think it was nice at all. He tried not to look at the girl because she was so pretty. She was wearing fingerless woollen gloves and a scarf wrapped around her blond hair. She came out from behind the stall and started picking up different dolls, opening them up, cracking them like eggs, setting them out. 'This one beautiful, this one also. Here this doll special, very good artist. Scenes from Pushkin, Pushkin famous Russian writer. You know him?' It was a soft sell that it would have seemed discourteous to resist and in the end, after perhaps more contemplation than either the task or the dolls merited, he bought an expensive fifteen-doll set. They were attractive things, their fat-bellied stomachs painted with 'winter scenes' from Pushkin. Works of art really, too good for his mother, and he decided he would keep them for himself. 'Very beautiful,' he said to the girl. 'No dollars?' she queried sadly when he handed over his fistfuls of roubles.

She was wearing ankle boots with a high heel and an old-fashioned, serviceable kind of coat. All the girls in St Petersburg wore high-heeled boots, picking their way dextrously through the icy slush while Martin found himself slipping and sliding like a slapstick comedian.

'You want coffee?' she asked unexpectedly, confounding him with the question. He thought she was going to produce a flask from somewhere, but she shouted something harsh at the man selling old Red Army insignia at the next stall and he shouted something equally harsh back and then she picked up her handbag and set off, swinging her bag and beckoning to Martin as if he was a child.

They didn't have coffee. They had a bowl of bortsch, followed by hot chocolate, thick and sweet, served in tall mugs, alongside some kind of custard pastry. She ordered it and wouldn't let him pay, waving her hand at the thin plastic carrier bag that contained his newspaper-wrapped dolls, snugly inside each other now, so he wondered if this was his reward for having forked out way over the odds for his purchase. Maybe this was how business was transacted in Russia, maybe if you gave someone enough money to live off for a week they took you into warm, steamy cafés and blew their cigarette smoke all over you. On holiday in Crete once (Discover the Ancient Wonders of) he found that every time he bought another item in a shop the shopkeeper insisted on giving him something else for free, as if they wanted to soften the harsh edges of capitalism. These gifts usually took the form of a crocheted doily, so that Martin had quite a pile of them in his suitcase by the time he returned home. He gave them to an Oxfam shop.

'Irina,' she said, sticking out her hand and shaking his. When she unwrapped her scarf her hair fell down her back.

'Martin,' Martin said.

'Marty,' she said, smiling at him. He didn't correct her mistake. No one had ever called him Marty before. He liked the way 'Marty' seemed a more entertaining man than he knew himself to be.

He tried to explain to Irina that he was a writer but he couldn't tell whether she understood him or not. 'Dostoevsky,' he said, 'Pushkin.'

'*Idyot!*' she exclaimed, her pretty doll face suddenly animated. 'Here is *idyot*.' It was only later that he realized the café they were in was called the Idiot.

He wanted to impress her a little with his success. He never talked about his professional good fortune with anyone. Melanie, his agent, thought it was never good enough and he could do better, the few friends he had weren't in the least successful and he didn't want them to think he was boasting in any way, his mother was indifferent and his brother was jealous, so he had found it best to keep his small triumphs to himself. But he would have liked Irina to know that he was a person of a little consequence in his native country (*His sales build with every book*) but she just smiled and licked the crumbs of pastry from her fingers. 'Sure,' she said.

When she had finished eating she stood up

suddenly and, without looking at her watch, said, 'I go.' She drained her cup while shrugging into her coat, there was a kind of greed in the gesture that Martin admired.

'Tonight?' she said, as if they had already made an arrangement. 'Caviar Bar in Grand Hotel, seven o'clock. OK, Marty?'

'Yes, OK,' Martin said hastily because she was already dashing for the door, raising her hand in farewell without looking back.

When he left the café he found it was snowing thickly. It seemed very romantic, the snow, the girl with blond hair wrapped in a scarf, like Julie Christie in *Doctor Zhivago*.

He stared at his reflection in the slightly foxed mirror of the Four Clans' bathroom. Maybe he felt so nauseous because he was starving? He couldn't remember when he last had anything proper to eat. A shiver went through his body and the next moment he was on his knees, holding on to the toilet bowl and being violently sick. He flushed the toilet and as he stared into the vortex of vomit swirling with some nasty blue chemical that must be in the cistern, he was hit by a sudden thought—

Robbed? Of course!

He hurried out of the bathroom and searched for his wallet in his jacket pocket. Gone. He sighed heavily at the thought of all those tedious phone calls he was going to have to make to his bank and credit card companies. His driving licence and a hundred pounds in cash had also been in the wallet, and then – nightmare

– he remembered the little lilac Sony memory stick, the sliver of plastic that contained 'Death on the Black Isle'. Gone. A cold wave of panic passed through his body, followed by a hot one of relief – the novel was backed up on a CD in his 'office'. Martin had saved Paul Bradley's life and in return he had stolen from him. Martin was so hurt by this betrayal that he actually felt tears pricking his eyes.

In the fug of bacon and tartan in reception, there was a sense of *Marie Celeste*-like abandonment. He rang the brass bell and after a long wait a youth dressed in a kitchen-staff uniform appeared. With fantastic sluggishness he ran his finger down the register and confirmed that Paul Bradley had checked out.

'Nothing to pay,' he said, wiping his nose with the back of his hand. 'You're free to go,' he said, as if he was letting Martin out of jail.

Martin didn't mention to the boy that he had been robbed, he didn't seem like someone who would care. And why should he? Martin couldn't help feeling that somehow he had got what he deserved.

22

GLORIA WOKE EARLY AND PADDED QUIETLY DOWNSTAIRS AS IF there was someone else in the house whom she might wake, although she was wonderfully alone. When Graham was here the house crashed and boomed with noise, even when he was still asleep in bed. Without him, the day fell into its own quiet pattern, soft colours and slants of light that Gloria never saw otherwise.

She felt the lamb-like nub of the oatmealy Berber stair carpet between her bare toes and the smooth glide of the red Oregon pine of the banister beneath her palm. She spared a thought for the hundred and fifty years or so of polishing that had gone into creating this satin, some by her own hand, not with Mr Sheen but a hard block of beeswax. Gloria had schooled herself to appreciate small joys, of which there were many to be had in the house, a house that would be standing long after Gloria herself was in the ground.

Every day was a gift, she told herself, that was why it was called the present. They were going to lose this house. It would be dragged into the whole sorry mess Graham had created, it would come under the Proceeds of Crime Act (she had been reading up about it online) and be taken and sold to make some reparation for all Graham had done over the years. A house of cards, that's what he had created, an illusion. His death or the Fraud Unit, whichever came soonest, would reveal everything, throw open the curtains and the shutters and let the light in on every filthy corner.

Gloria opened the French windows in the living room and stood for a few minutes breathing in the early morning air, watching a sparrow hopping delicately along the fence. An ounce of brown feather and black bib. It would be nice to think that God's eye was on it, but failing that, both Gloria and the CCTV cameras would notice its fall. A magpie came swooping and chattering and Gloria chased it off.

The house in the Grange (Providence, named long before Gloria and Graham took ownership of it) had nothing in common with the jerry-built, overpriced rubbish that had made Graham rich. The houses Graham built had badly hung cabinet doors, imitation-stone cement fireplaces and cheap contract carpeting. They were houses that smelt as if they were made from plastics and chemicals. Last year, Graham had talked about moving from their house in the Grange, he said they were 'too rich' for it and he 'had an eye' on an estate up north, acres of land where he could fish for trout and surprise unsuspecting birds by shooting them from the sky. Over the years the Grange house had moulded itself comfortably around Gloria and it seemed cruel suddenly to shuck it off in favour of some cavernous pile in the middle of nowhere.

Gloria said she didn't see how you could be too rich. If you were too rich you could give some of your money away until you were just rich. Or give it all away and be poor. And they weren't really rich anyway, it had all been smoke and mirrors, their lives predicated on dirty money.

She moved into the kitchen and made the first pot of coffee of the day, inhaling the aroma of the beans before putting them in the grinder. The Italian marble tiles on the kitchen floor were cold and inert, like walking on tombstones. They were incredibly expensive but Graham had acquired them incredibly cheaply (naturally). Last year the house had been renovated, using the more qualified members of Graham's workforce. Amongst other things, they had knocked through and installed a vast American kitchen. 'Nothing's too good for my wife,' Graham said expansively to his architect. 'How about it, Gloria – a larder fridge, a Gaggenau hob, one of the ones with an integral deep-fat fryer?' So she said she would like a pink sink because she'd seen one on a home makeover show on television and Graham said, 'Pink sink? Over my dead body.' So there you go.

Gloria liked to visit any new Hatter Homes development. The further afield the estates, the more of an outing these visits were. She might pack a picnic or find out where the local tearooms were. She liked to look round the show home, listen to the selling shtick (*This is a lovely room, a real family room*). Graham never knew about these little excursions.

Occasionally, Gloria posed as a prospective buyer –

a wild-eyed divorcee or a recently bereaved widow who was 'downsizing' into a husband-free apartment. On other occasions, she was looking at 'family homes' on behalf of her daughter or a 'starter home' for a son working abroad. It was harmless and it gave her the opportunity to open and close the cupboards and peer into the tiny en-suites, only big enough for a malnourished person. Everything was built to the tightest specifications, as little garden as possible, the smallest bathroom – it was as if a very *mean* person had decided to build houses.

Before Easter, she had driven over to a development in Fife. The builders had finally moved out and the last of the residents were moving in, although there was still a show home and a sales office Portakabin on site and the flag still flew above their heads emblazoned with 'Hatter Homes – Real Homes for Real People'. A flag of convenience.

She had felt particularly bad for the new householders because the estate was built on a landfill dump and the gardens had been created out of a few inches of topsoil. ('But surely that's not legal?' she said to Graham. '*Caveat emptor*, Gloria,' Graham said, 'it's the only Latin I've ever needed to know.')

Maggie Louden had been in the sales Portakabin and had regarded her with alarm. 'Mrs Hatter? Can I help you?' She looked different out of her cocktail clothes, more frumpish and decidedly less festive.

'Just looking,' Gloria replied, feigning nonchalance. 'I like to keep an eye on things,' but her little day out was spoiled now. She had been intending to pose as the mistress of a rich man who was planning to set her up in a house. The irony of the situation was not lost on her now.

Gloria had gone back secretly, at night, like a terrorist, and left a nice pot plant on every doorstep. It hardly made up for a garden, but it was something.

Gloria sometimes wondered if Graham was building homes for families because he found his own family so unsatisfactory. They had been to see a production of *The Master Builder* at the Lyceum – Hatter Homes was some kind of sponsor – and Gloria couldn't help but make comparisons. She had wondered then if Graham would fall from a spire one day, metaphorically or otherwise. And he had done. So there you go.

The coffee-maker hissed and spat and finally came to its usual furious climax. Gloria poured her coffee and carried it through to the peach-themed living room and settled herself on the couch. She breakfasted on the remains of a packet of chocolate digestives. When Graham was here they always ate at the kitchen table. He liked something cooked – scrambled eggs, an Arbroath smokie, bacon, sausages, even kidneys. While they ate they listened to *Good Morning, Scotland* on the radio, ceaseless disembodied chatter about politics and disasters that Graham considered important and necessary yet it made no difference to their lives whatsoever. There was more to be gained from watching a pair of blue tits pecking away at a bird-feeder full of peanuts than from cursing the Scottish Parliament over your porridge.

She turned the dial on the radio to Terry Wogan. Wogan was a Good Thing. The phone rang. The phone had been ringing at regular intervals since Gloria had woken at five. She had already phoned the hospital to ascertain Graham's unchanged condition and she really wasn't interested in speaking to all the people who wanted to know why Graham had disappeared off the face of the planet in the middle of the working day and wasn't answering his mobile. She let them talk to the answering machine, it was less taxing than lying.

While she stood in the hallway listening to the latest message (*Graham, you old bugger, where are you, I thought we were playing golf today*) the morning newspapers clattered through the letterbox.

What kind of a person bites the head off a kitten? What kind of a person walks into the back garden of a complete stranger, picks up a three-week-old kitten and *bites its head off*? *And doesn't get prosecuted!* Gloria dropped the newspaper to the floor in disgust.

What would be the correct punishment for a person (a man, naturally) who bit the head off a three-week-old kitten? Death, obviously, but surely not a swift and painless one? That would be like an undeserved gift. Gloria believed in the punishment fitting the crime, eyes for eyes, teeth for teeth. Heads for heads. How would you go about biting a person's head off? Unless you could somehow employ a shark or a crocodile to do the job for you, Gloria supposed you would have to settle for simple decapitation.

The man who bit the head off the kitten was, according to the newspaper, high on drugs. That was not an excuse! Gloria had once smoked a joint during her brief period at university (but more from politeness than anything) and had imbibed a considerable quantity of alcohol in her time, but she was sure that she could have consumed any amount of illegal substances and not felt the urge to bite the head off an innocent household pet. A little basket of kittens – Gloria imagined long-haired tabbies with ribbons round their necks, like something you would find on an old-fashioned chocolate box. Tiny, helpless. Innocent. Did chocolate boxes still have those pictures? She had bought a lovely painting on eBay, two kittens, basket, balls of wool, ribbons – the works, but she still hadn't found the right place to hang it. And, of course, Graham said it was 'twee', being more of an about-to-be-murdered-stag connoisseur himself.

There was a barbecue, 'a family barbecue' in progress and the man strode in, uninvited, unannounced, and picked up one of the kittens from the basket and bit its head off as if it was a lollipop. Had the man eaten the kitten's head? Or just bitten it off and spat it out?

You could put the man who bit the head off the kitten into a cage of tigers and say, 'Go on, then, let's see you bite the head off one of those.' But then it would be wrong to put the tigers in a cage. There was that Blake poem about tigers, wasn't there? Or was it robins?

Bill, the gardener, announced himself with the muffled clanking and thudding of tools in the shed as if he wanted Gloria to know he was there but didn't want actually to talk to her. His surname was Tiffany, like the jewellers. Graham had bought her a Tiffany watch for their thirtieth wedding anniversary.

It had a red leather strap and little diamonds all round its face. She dropped it in the fish pond yesterday. All of the fish in the pond, except for one – a big golden orfe – had been gradually picked off by the neighbourhood heron. Gloria wondered if the watch was still keeping time, ticking away quietly in the mud and green slime at the bottom of the pond, marking off the days left to both the big orange fish and to Graham.

Gloria made more coffee, buttered a scone, switched her computer on. Gloria was good with computers. She had learned way back when it was the old Amstrads with their black and green screens and infuriating habits. In those days she used to help keep the accounts for Hatter Homes. He was cooking the books even then but the sums were still relatively small. Hatter Homes had remained a family business, owned by Graham and Gloria. It had never been floated on the stock exchange, never subject to rigorous external scrutiny. The auditing was done by his own accountants. There was a web of complicity stretching as far as the eye couldn't see, accountants, lawyers, secretaries, sales force (sales force-cum-mistresses). Gloria herself had signed anything put in front of her for years, papers, documents, contracts. She hadn't questioned anything and now she seemed to do nothing but question. Innocence was not ignorance.

Gloria had a nice little laptop of her own, hooked up to a broadband connection in the kitchen – which was where she spent most of her time, after all, so why not? Graham never used her computer, he did all his dirty business in the office. She could imagine him going on pornography sites, watching one of those webcams where a woman in a room somewhere (anywhere) in the world performed for him.

The only messages Gloria tended to get – apart from the odd missive from her children – were invitations to enlarge her penis or special offers from Boots.com. She would have liked to check Graham's email but it was password-protected. Gloria had been worrying away at it long before the events of yesterday but she hadn't yet come up with the open sesame – she had tried that too, along with every other word and combination of words she could think of. 'Kinloch', 'Hartford', 'Braecroft', 'Hopetoun', 'Villiers' and 'Waverley'. Nothing. They were the names of the six basic models of Hatter Homes. The 'Kinloch' was the cheapest, the 'Waverley' the most expensive. The 'Hartford' and the 'Braecroft' were semi-detached. Nowadays Graham built a lot more detached houses than he used to. People like detached no matter how small. The 'Kinloch' was so tiny it reminded Gloria of a Monopoly house.

Next month Gloria would be sixty. She had heard on the radio someone say that sixty was the new forty. She had never heard anything so stupid in her life. Sixty was sixty, there was no point in pretending otherwise. Who was going to provide for her in her old age? Whether Graham was dead or alive wasn't going to make any difference to the police and the courts, they were going to destroy Hatter Homes. Quite rightly, in Gloria's opinion, but it would have been nice if she could have salvaged a little pension for herself before they did. She imagined that somewhere there was a big black book that contained all of Graham's secrets, all of his money. The Magus's book. As with capitalism, it was too late to ask him about it now.

She gave up on the password and checked her online bank account. They had a joint account which was mainly for day-to-day bills and housekeeping. Gloria was entirely dependent on Graham for money, a shocking realization that had taken several decades to sink in. One minute you're sitting on a bar stool drinking a gin-and-orange, worrying about whether or not you look pretty, the next minute you're a year away from a bus pass, staring bankruptcy and public humiliation in the face. And sixty was the same old sixty as it ever was.

The housekeeping account was drip-fed automatically from a Hatter Homes account, whenever money was debited from it, more was credited, whatever went out one day was topped up overnight. It was almost like magic. No one seemed to have noticed the five hundred a day that Gloria had been siphoning off. Her nest egg. It was entirely legal, it was a joint account, her name was on it. Five hundred a day, every day except Sunday, Gloria's day of rest, monitored by her Baptist conscience. The new money-laundering regulations made it difficult to move large sums of money around but five hundred a day seemed to keep her below the radar of both the Hatter Homes accountants and the bank. Sooner or later, she supposed, an alarm bell would ring, a flag would go up, but by then the accounts would probably all be frozen and, if there was any justice in the world, Gloria would be gone with her black plastic bag of swag. Seventy-two thousand pounds wasn't a lot to start a new life on but it was better than nothing, better than what most people in the world had.

Gloria emptied Graham's belongings out of the bag and laid them on the maple-wood draining board of the laundry room. His shoes, polished to a liquorice-like shine, the jacket and trousers of his suit, the Austin Reed shirt, his expensive silk socks that someone, a nurse presumably, had rolled into a ball, the cotton vest and boxer shorts from Marks and Spencer – his underwear seemed particularly depressing to Gloria – and, lastly, his blandly corporate tie, curled limply at the bottom of the plastic bag like a dispirited snake.

It was strange to see his clothes laid out like that, flat and two-dimensional, as if Graham had suddenly become invisible while wearing them. Now they had all been swapped for a cotton gown that showed his Roquefort legs and his not-so-firm buttocks. The cotton gown would in turn soon be swapped for a shroud. With any luck.

Gloria had a sudden image of her brother's mutilated body when it had been shown to his family in the hospital mortuary, wrapped up in white sheets, like a mummy or a present. Gloria wondered which of her parents had thought it was a good idea to let their fourteen-year-old daughter view the dead body of her brother, nicely wrapped or not.

Jonathan had a place at college to do an HND and was only working in the mill for the summer between school and college. There had been several mills in

251

Gloria's home town when she was a child, now there was none. Some had been demolished but most had been converted into flats or hotels, one into an art gallery and another into a museum where ex-mill workers demonstrated to the public the jobs they used to do in a past which was now officially history.

The week before her brother died he had taken Gloria inside the mill. He was proud of where he was working, doing a 'man's job'. It wasn't dark and satanic, as she had imagined from singing 'Jerusalem' in school assemblies, rather it was full of light and as big as a cathedral, a hymn to industry. Tiny strands and puffs of wool floated in the air like feathers. And the noise! The 'clattering, shattering, shuttling noise' – she had written a poem later for her grammar school magazine 'in the style of Gerard Manley Hopkins', thinking it might heal some part of the grief, but the poem was poor ('wool-dappled white air') and came from the head, not the heart.

There had been talk of prosecution after Jonathan's death – all kinds of health and safety laws had been flouted in the mill – but it never progressed beyond talk and Gloria's parents lacked the passion to pursue it. Her sister (so recently dead) was twenty at the time and upstaged their brother by turning up in a pair of jeans and a black polo-necked sweater for his Baptist funeral. Gloria had fully admired her sister's gesture.

The only other time Gloria had been inside a real cathedral of industry was long ago on a school visit to Rowntree's factory in York, when her class had marvelled at every step of the way, from the Smarties being tumbled around in what looked like copper cement mixers, to the packing room where women were tying ribbons around boxes of chocolates with (yes) pictures of kittens on them. At the end of the tour they had been given bags of mis-shapes of all kinds and Gloria had returned home triumphantly bearing dozens of two-fingered Kit Kats that had, like Jonathan, been mangled by the machinery.

She took the phone from Graham's jacket pocket. What had Maggie Louden said last night? *Is it done yet, is it over? Have you got rid of Gloria? Have you got rid of the old bag?* Was that what she was – an old bag? Maggie Louden was well over forty, she'd be an old bag herself soon enough.

The phone had run out of battery (rather like its owner). Graham's suit could do with going to the dry cleaners, but really why bother? If he died all of his suits were going to the Oxfam shop on Morningside Road, apart from the one he would wear for his funeral. This one might do, a bit of a brush and a press, no point in getting something cleaned when it was going into the ground to rot.

She plugged Graham's phone into the charger in the kitchen and carefully typed out a text to Maggie Louden. She tapped out *Am in thurso speak to you tomorrow g* – she was pretty sure Graham wouldn't bother with any punctuation or grammar – but then changed it to *Sorry darling am in thurso speak to you tomorrow g* and then redrafted it a third time to *Sorry darling am in thurso not much of a signal here don't bother phoning speak to you tomorrow g.*

What Gloria remembered most was that York was a town that smelt of chocolate whereas she came from a town that smelt of soot. Of course, you could no longer go on tours of Rowntree's, now it was owned by some multinational conglomerate that didn't want anyone inside their gates, watching what they were doing. Now that her sister was dead, Gloria was the only person who remembered her brother. It was extraordinary how quickly a person could be erased. Death triumphant.

She took a bag of bird seed from underneath the sink in the laundry room and filled a bowl with it. Outside she broadcast the seed around the lawn and for a moment felt quite saintly as all the birds of Edinburgh descended on her garden.

23

LOUISE SURVEYED THE CORPSE ON THE SLAB DISPASSIONATELY. She considered it best to leave her emotions at the door when it came to post mortems. There were a lot of programmes on television these days where the police and the forensics all banged on about how a dead body wasn't just a dead body, it was a *person*. The pathologists were always addressing the deceased as if they were alive (*Who did this to you, sweetheart?*) as if the victim was suddenly going to sit up and give them the name and address of their killer. The dead were just dead, they weren't people any more, they were only what was left over when the person was gone for ever. The remains. She thought of her own mother and reached for the Tic Tacs.

The mortuary was crowded with the usual suspects, a photographer, technicians, forensics, two pathologists – a Noah's Ark of post-mortem specialists. Jim Tucker was standing off to one side, Louise knew he had a poor stomach for this kind of thing. He saw her and frowned, surprised to see her there. She gave him a thumbs-down signal and saw him mouth, 'Oh, shit.'

Ackroyd, the pathologist, caught sight of her and said, 'You've missed a lot of the good stuff, stomach, lungs, liver.' Ackroyd was a bit of a pillock.

The second pathologist, on the sidelines, acknowledged her with a little nod and a smile. She'd never seen him before. Only the most routine post mortems were done with one pathologist, two were considered necessary 'for verification'. One and a spare. 'Neil Snedden,' he said with another smile, as if they were at a social event. Was he flirting with her? Over a corpse? Nice.

'You here for her?' he asked, nodding at the woman on the slab.

'No, I need a word with Jim – DS Tucker.'

The dead girl looked unhealthy, more unhealthy than just straightforward dead. Ackroyd hefted her heart in his hand. An assistant, a girl named Heather, if Louise remembered correctly, hovered nearby, holding a metal pan like a baseball mitt, as if the pathologist might be about to toss the organ in her direction. When it was placed, rather than thrown, in the dish, Heather took the heart away and weighed it as if she was intending to bake a cake with it.

Louise reached out and touched the back of her hand against the nerveless one of the girl. Warm flesh against cold clay. The quick and the dead. She had a sudden memory of her mother in the undertaker's, her face like cold, melted candlewax – the Wicked Witch of the West. Jim Tucker raised an enquiring eyebrow in her direction and she gestured him to one side.

The dead woman's clothing was on a nearby bench waiting to be bagged and taken to forensics at Howdenhall. The bra and pants weren't a matching set but they both displayed Matalan labels. This was why you should wear matching underwear, Louise reminded herself, not for the off-chance of a sexual encounter but for eventualities like this. The dead-on-a-fishmonger's-slab scenario where the whole world could see that you bought your oddly matched underwear in cheap shops.

'Working girl, found in a doorway in Coburg Street. Drug overdose. Vice knew her,' Jim Tucker said. He dropped his voice. 'What happened?'

'Crichton threw the case out on a technicality. Non-appearance of a witness.'

'You're joking? He could have held off, asked us to find the witness.'

'We'll go to appeal,' Louise said. 'It'll be fine.'

'Shit.'

'I know.' Something caught her eye, on the bench with the clothing – a little pile of business cards sitting on a Petri dish. 'What are these?'

'Found in her pocket,' Jim Tucker said. 'The lady's calling cards.'

Pale pink, black lettering. *Favours*. A mobile number. Just like Jackson Brodie had said.

'We thought maybe a call-girl agency,' Jim Tucker said. 'We've not been able to get anything from the phone number.'

'She's got a call-girl's calling card but you think she's a street girl?' Louise puzzled.

'She was a druggie, I'm guessing it didn't really

matter to her whether she was in a hotel room or a doorway.'

Louise didn't think that was true for a minute. If she was selling herself she'd rather be doing it in a nice, warm hotel room knowing someone knew where she was. 'I've been looking for Favours myself, we've come up with nothing so far.'

'Something I should know about?' Jim Tucker asked.

'Not really. A missing girl, but I'm not convinced she existed in the first place.'

'Ah, your so-called dead body yesterday. I heard you called out all the troops for nothing. She hasn't turned up?'

'Not yet.'

'What was that I heard about a body in Merchiston?' Ackroyd shouted across to her.

'No idea,' she said. 'That's Edinburgh South, nothing to do with me.'

'I live in Merchiston,' Ackroyd grumbled.

'There goes the neighbourhood, Tom.' Neil Snedden laughed. He winked at Louise. Louise wondered if she could have sex with someone who was so twinkly in the face of death. She supposed it would depend how good-looking he was. Snedden wasn't remotely good-looking.

Ackroyd took out a small electric saw and began to slice the top of the girl's head off as if it was a boiled egg. 'Look closely,' he said to a green Jim Tucker, 'this is the only time you ever really get to see what's inside a woman's head.'

The sight of Jackson Brodie walking out of the Sheriff

Court this morning had given her a start. That little flip-flap to the tell-tale heart.

Louise wondered what Jackson Brodie had been like when he was fourteen. Did he have all his virtues (and drawbacks) in place by then, could you have looked at the boy and seen the man in him? Could you look at the man and see the boy?

The pink cards existed. Louise had the proof in her pocket, the top one swiped from the pile while everyone was looking at Ackroyd performing his party piece. OK, so it was tampering with evidence but it wasn't as if it was the only card. At the end of the day what did it matter if there was one less? Really?

She phoned Jeff Lennon, he was the guy at the station who knew everything. A DS a few weeks away from retirement, the face of a tortoise, the memory of an elephant. Handicapped by a bad knee, he was seeing out his last days doing a reluctant catch-up on paperwork and she knew he would be glad of an excuse to do something else.

'Do me a favour?' she asked him.

'If you ask nicely.'

'Nicely. Can you find out about a road-rage incident in the Old Town yesterday? The attacker drove off. Can you check that someone caught the registration?' Jackson said there were 'dozens of other witnesses' but when Jeff phoned back a few minutes later it was to report that no one had remembered, although 'someone thought the car was blue'.

'Well, I'm the bearer of good news,' she said. 'Blue is correct and what's more it was a Honda Civic and I can give you a registration. I've got a witness.' She had called him 'Jackson' to his face. It had felt un-professional, even though it wasn't.

'Jeff? One more wee favour? Get me an address for a Terence Smith, in court this morning.'

Jim Tucker had a dead girl carrying a card for Favours with her. Jackson Brodie had a dead girl carrying a card for Favours with her. Jim's girl was definitely a prostitute of some ilk, therefore there was a good chance that Jackson's girl was too. She realized that she was thinking about Jim Tucker and Jackson Brodie as if they were equals. Write out ten times, *Jackson Brodie is not a detective*. He was a witness. A possible suspect as well, even if the charge was only wasting police time. And he was certified guilty of assault, even if he claimed he was innocent. Let's just say it again, Louise – he was a witness, a suspect, *and* a convicted felon.

24

THERE WAS NOTHING LIKE A NIGHT IN THE CELLS TO GIVE YOU an appetite. Jackson was starving, but raking round the cupboards of the tiny kitchen he could find only dried-up instant gravy granules and some perforated teabags that smelt herbal and repellent. That was something useful he could do today, find a supermarket or, preferably, a good deli, stock up on decent stuff and cook something for them to eat tonight, something wholesome. Jackson's culinary repertoire consisted of five dishes that he could cook well, which was five more than Julia could cook.

He imagined how his local market in France would look this morning, overflowing with tomatoes, basil, cheeses, figs and big, fat French peaches, ripe enough to burst. No wonder northerners were miserable buggers, evolving for thousands of years on harvests of wet grains and thin gruels.

Julia hadn't looked as though she'd eaten at all yesterday, she'd had 'a drink' with Richard Moat at lunchtime. Still, having seen him, Jackson now felt relatively safe from any rivalry with him, no way would Julia be attracted to anyone that untalented. The guy had *died* on stage.

Propped up against the kettle was a note from Julia. Her bold hand announced simply, 'See you later, love J.' Her initial was accompanied by only one kiss and no exclamation marks. She was a person who used exclamation marks liberally, she said they made everything seem more friendly. Jackson thought they made everything seem startling but found that he missed them when they weren't there. He was being over-analytical, there wasn't much you could read into *See you later, love J.* Was there? The absence of exclamation marks, the paucity of x's, the initial rather than a name, the vagaries of time and place of *See you later* – see him later where?

She'd had a preview (but had she?) and then he remembered her saying that Tobias was giving them 'notes'. He was sure she had nothing this evening. He could cook her penne pasta with pesto, a good salad, strawberries, no, she preferred raspberries. Some gorgonzola, she liked that; he couldn't abide it. A bottle of champagne. Or would champagne feel too celebratory? Would it highlight the fact that they had very little to celebrate? When had he started thinking so much?

He had a shower, a shave, changed his clothes. He didn't quite feel like a new man but he looked a lot better than the shabby criminal who had stood up in court. His boots were still damp from yesterday but there was not much he could do about that, he'd experienced worse. His face was unmarked, which was something to be grateful for. He would have liked to strap his hand up – more for aesthetic reasons than anything else – but it wasn't a good idea to compress bruises. He'd done enough first aid in field courses to know a bit about fixing people up. He flexed his hand a few times, agonizing but it still worked. He would have known by now if there'd been any broken bones.

At least the bruises were hard evidence of the fight with Honda Man. The girl in the water, on the other hand, hadn't left a trace in his life. He was beginning to doubt his own experience. Maybe he *had* hallucinated the whole incident out at Cramond. Maybe he had wanted something to happen, something interesting, and so he had fabricated it. Who knew what weird things the brain was capable of? But no, he had touched her pale skin, he had looked into her sightless sea-green eyes. He had to believe the evidence of his senses. She was real and she was dead, and she was out there somewhere.

After fuelling up on coffee and a proper breakfast at Toast round the corner from the flat he set off to walk into town across the Meadows.

There were a lot of people on the Meadows, none of them doing anything that could be called useful. Didn't any of these people have jobs to go to? There were Japanese drummers, a group of people (Scots by their pallor), mostly middle-aged, doing t'ai chi – Jackson didn't get t'ai chi, it looked OK on the television when you saw people doing it in China, but in Scotland it looked, let's face it, arsy. There were some people dressed like extras from *Braveheart*, lolling around on the grass in a way that would have made William Wallace shudder. Re-enacters, that's what they were called. Julia had done re-enactment for a couple of weeks last summer, playing Nell Gwyn for some National Trust place ('for a pittance and the oranges'). Julia 'rented herself out by the hour' (her words) on any number of mundane jobs from banqueting wench to bingo caller. All jobs were acting, she claimed, whether you were a prostitute or a shop girl you were in a role. 'And what about when you're being Julia?' he asked. 'Oh,' she said, 'that's the greatest show on earth, sweetie.'

He had another cup of coffee as he walked, dispensed from a kiosk that used to be a blue police box, a Tardis. It was a strange world, Jackson thought. Yes, sirree.

Edinburgh was like a city where no one worked, where everyone spent their time *playing*. And so many young people, not one of them over twenty-five, looking carefree and careless in a way that irritated him. He wanted to tell them that no matter how golden they were feeling now, life was going to disappoint them on a daily basis. It was going to wipe the smiles off their faces. Jackson was alarmed by this surge of something bitter, the black bile of envy if he wasn't mistaken. It wasn't his, it belonged to his father. He could hardly claim it as his when his own life consisted of nothing more taxing than lapping his turquoise swimming pool.

A young guy in one of those idiotic jester's hats was blocking the path in front of Jackson. He was practising juggling with three oranges, almost as if

Jackson had conjured him up by thinking of Nell Gwyn. Julia was perfect for Nell Gwyn, of course, her curvy, busty figure, her compulsion to flirt. She sent him a photograph of her in costume, her tightly corseted breasts, as round as oranges, although considerably bigger, being offered up to the camera in a way that was extraordinarily provocative. Jackson wondered who took the photograph. 'What do you do when you're Nell Gwyn?' he'd asked and she'd put on a kind of yokel accent, Devon or Somerset, and said, '*Oranges, who'll buy my lovely oranges?*'

Nell Gwyn wasn't really an orange seller, Julia said, 'she was actually a bona fide actress.' 'Just like you,' Jackson said. It had possibly sounded more sarcastic than he'd intended. Or perhaps it had sounded exactly as sarcastic as he'd intended. Julia would have made a perfect mistress for a king, a perfect mistress for any man. And a terrible wife. He knew that in his heart, that was what made it worse.

Stifling a desire to shoulder Juggling Boy off the path, Jackson scowled at him and said, 'Excuse me,' in a pointed, sarcastic tone. It would have been no trouble for Jackson to have simply walked round the boy on the grass like everyone else but it was the *principle* of the thing. Paths were for people to walk on, not for idiots in hats to juggle on.

Juggling Boy said nothing but moved slowly to the side, his eyes never leaving the oranges. Jackson bumped into him as he walked past, catching his elbow, and the oranges went rolling in three different directions across the grass. 'Sorry about that,' Jackson said, unable to keep the pleasure off his face.

'Wanker,' the boy muttered after him. Jackson turned on his heel and marched back, planting himself on the path. 'What did you say?' he asked, sticking his face menacingly near to the boy's. Adrenalin chased the bile in his bloodstream, a little voice in his head accompanied it, saying, *Bring it on*. He had an uncomfortable flashback to last night, to Terence Smith's jeering, ugly features.

The boy took a step back in alarm and whined, 'Nothing, man. I didn't say anything.' He looked cowed and sullen and Jackson realized that he couldn't be more than sixteen or seventeen, almost a child (although Jackson had joined the army at that age, a boy soldier who thought he was a real man). He remembered Terence Smith yesterday, stepping out of the car with his baseball bat swinging in anger. This is what road rage felt like. Path rage. Jackson laughed, a sudden unexpected harshness that made the boy flinch. Sheepishly, Jackson chased after the oranges, picked them up and handed them back. The boy took them gingerly as if they might be hand grenades. 'Sorry,' Jackson said and walked away quickly to spare the boy any more humiliation. You bastard, Jackson said to himself, you total fucking bastard. He was turning into his enemy, his own worst version of himself.

25

MARTIN FILLED UP ON PETROL AT A GARAGE ON LEITH WALK. He had been relieved to find his car still waiting for him in the St James Centre car park, like a patient pony in the corral – his brain was in some kind of nervy overdrive, jumping terrible metaphorical somersaults. It took him half an hour to find the car as Richard Moat's instructions weren't exactly helpful – *Your car's parked outside Macbet on Leith Walk, cheers, R*, scrawled on the envelope that his ticket had been in yesterday. When he found the car it was plastered in parking tickets.

At the petrol pump next to his, a small boy in the back seat of a Toyota was making faces at him, horrible, imbecilic faces that made Martin speculate the child was handicapped in some way. The mother was in the shop, paying for her petrol, and Martin wondered if he would dare to leave a child alone in a car. If the car was locked it might catch fire (all that petrol) and the child would burn to death. If it wasn't locked someone might steal the child or it might slip out of the car and run on to the road and be crushed under the wheels of a lorry. One of the compensations for not having a child of his own was that he wasn't responsible for making life and death decisions on its behalf.

If you were a woman and you couldn't find a partner you could always go to a sperm bank, but what could a man do? Apart from buying a wife, he supposed you could pay a woman to bear your baby, but it was still a commercial transaction and how would you ever explain that to a child when it asked who its mother was? He supposed you could lie but you always got caught out in lies, even if it was only by yourself.

Perhaps he *should* have become a monk, at least then he would have had a social life. Brother Martin. He would perhaps run the infirmary, wandering in the walled herb garden, tending the medicinal plants, the bees humming gently, the tolling of a bell somewhere, the scent of lavender and rosemary in the warm air. From the chapel wafted the soothing sounds of plain-song or Gregorian chant – were they the same thing and if not, what was the difference between them? The simple meals in the refectory, bread and soup, sweet apples and plums from the monastery's own orchards. On Fridays, a fat carp from the fish ponds. Hurrying through the cold cloisters in winter, his breath like white clouds in the icy air of the chapter house. Of course he was thinking of a pre-Reformation monastic life, wasn't he? Another time, another place, a hybrid of the Cadfael novels and 'The Eve of St Agnes' rather than an historic reality. And anyway, there was no such thing as 'historic reality', reality was this nanosecond, right now, not even a breath but an atom of a breath, the littlest, littlest thing. Before and after didn't exist. Everyone was clinging on by their finger-nails to the thread they were hanging by.

His nameless, imaginary wife, a woman who had come with no price attached (although it was above that of rubies) lived with him in a cottage that was in a perfect village from which you could get up to London in an hour if you so wished. The cottage they lived in was chintzy and had beams and a lovely garden and was very like Mrs Miniver's. Martin had recently watched the sequel to *Mrs Miniver – The Miniver Story* – on early morning TCM and was still nursing an outrage that they had killed off poor Greer Garson *for no reason whatsoever*, as if there was no further use for her in the post-war world. Which there wasn't, of course, but that wasn't the point. And she hadn't even fought back against her unnamed illness (obviously cancer); her only concern was to make her death no bother to anyone else. No sickness, vomiting, blood and pus, no brain matter spattered round her living room, no raging against the dying of the light – she just kissed her husband goodbye, went up the stairs and closed her bedroom door. Death wasn't like that. Death happened when you least expected it. It was an argument in the street, it was a crazy Russian girl opening her mouth to scream. The littlest thing.

His noble post-war wife knew, Miniver-like, how to mend and make do, she knew how to soothe troubled brows and lift drooping spirits, she had known tragedy but she was stoic in the face of it. She smelt of lilies-of-the-valley.

It was usually early spring, the sky pale and austere, the wind sharp, new daffodil shoots spearing their way out of their earth silos. It was also nearly always Sunday morning for some reason (probably to do with spending weekends in a boarding school). A leg of lamb (no animal was harmed in the making of this fantasy) was sizzling in the old cream Aga in the kitchen. Martin had already chopped mint, grown in their own garden. They sat in the living room, in armchairs covered in William Morris's 'Strawberry Thief' fabric, and drank a small sherry each while listening to a recording of the *Goldberg Variations*. This woman with no name harmoniously shared his taste in all music, poetry, drama. After they had eaten their lamb (with gravy and peas and roast potatoes) they had a home-made custard tart – a trembling pale yellow with a freckling of nutmeg. Then they did the washing-up together at the old-fashioned porcelain sink. She washed, he dried, Peter/David put away (*The serving spoons go in this drawer, darling*). And then they shook the crumbs from the tablecloth and went for a walk, naming the birds and the early spring flowers, climbing over stiles, splashing through puddles. Laughing. They should have a dog, a friendly terrier full of vim. A boy's best friend. When they came home, flushed and fit, they would drink tea and eat something home-made and delicious from the cake tin.

In the evening they made sandwiches from the leftover lamb and did a jigsaw together or listened to the radio, and after Peter/David was in bed they each read their books, or they played a duet together, her on the piano, him on the oboe. To his everlasting sorrow he had never learned a musical instrument but in his imagination he was proficient, occasionally inspired. She did a lot of knitting – Peter/David's Fair Isle sweaters and rather effeminate cardigans for Martin. In winter they sat by a roaring coal fire, and sometimes Martin would toast pikelets or teacakes on a brass toasting fork. He liked to read poetry to her occasionally, nothing too modern.

Then, of course, it was their own bedtime. Martin wound the clock, checked the locks, waited while the woman had done whatever she did in the cold, slightly damp bathroom. One day, inevitably, this cottage would be modernized, bathroom suites and kitchen units, electric cookers and central heating installed, but now there was a certain sense of privation about it necessary to its time and place in British social history. Then he too would climb the stairs (narrow pine, a runner and brass rods) and enter their bedroom beneath the sloping eaves of the roof where she would be waiting for him, in a flower-sprigged nightdress, sitting up in their mahogany bed from a previous century, reading her book in a homely pool of light from the parchment-shaded lamp above the bed. *Marty, come to bed.*

No, that was wrong, she never called him Marty. That was wrong. Wrong, wrong, wrong. *Martin*, she called him Martin, the ordinary name of an ordinary man whom no one ever remembered.

The mother of the boy in the Toyota came hurrying out of the garage shop, clutching crisps and cola and chocolate bars. She glared at Martin (for no reason at all as far as he could see) and passed the results of her foraging to the boy in the back seat before driving off in a haze of exhaust. The boy turned to face Martin and held one finger against the glass of the window in an unmistakable gesture.

It was only when he went inside the shop to pay that he remembered he didn't have his wallet.

When Martin pulled up in the street outside his house he discovered his driveway had been cordoned off with crime scene tape and was being guarded by a uniformed constable. Martin wondered if there had been a fire or a burglary at his house, wondered if he had inadvertently committed a crime – perhaps during those hours of oblivion in the Four Clans. Or had they finally come for him? Had he been traced through Interpol and now they were coming to arrest him and extradite him to Russia?

'Officer,' he said, 'has something happened here?' (Was that what people said – *Officer* – or was that what people said on American TV? Martin still felt horribly befuddled.)

'There's been an incident, sir,' the policeman said. 'I'm afraid you can't go up to the house.'

Martin suddenly remembered it was Wednesday. 'It's Wednesday.' He hadn't intended to say that out loud, he must sound like an idiot.

'Yes, sir,' the policeman said, 'it is.'

'The cleaners come on a Wednesday,' Martin said. 'Favours – it's an agency – has one of them had an accident?' Martin had only briefly met one or two of the pink-clad women who cleaned his house. He didn't like the idea of being there while they scrubbed

272

and polished, servants doing his dirty business, and he always tried to escape from the house before they saw him.

Had one of the 'maids' electrocuted herself because he had faulty wiring, slipped on an over-polished floor, tripped on a badly fitted stair carpet and broken her neck? 'Is one of the cleaners dead?'

The constable muttered something into the radio on his shoulder and said to Martin, 'Can I have your name, sir?'

'Martin, Martin Canning,' Martin said. 'I live here,' he added and thought perhaps he should have mentioned that earlier in the conversation.

'Do you have any identification on you, sir?'

'No,' Martin said, 'my wallet was stolen last night.' It didn't sound convincing even to his own ears.

'Have you reported the theft, sir?'

'Not yet.' In the garage on Leith Walk he had turned his pockets out and found four pounds and seventy-one pence. He offered to write an IOU for the rest, a proposition that was greeted with hilarity. Martin, who believed everyone should be treated as honest until they proved themselves otherwise (a policy that frequently left him fleeced), felt surprisingly pained that no one would afford him the same grace. In the end the only thing he could think of was to phone his agent, Melanie, and ask her to pay with her credit card.

The policeman on guard outside his house gave him a long, level look and muttered something else into his radio.

An old woman walked by slowly with an equally

old-looking Labrador. Martin recognized the dog rather than the woman as a neighbour. Dog and woman lingered by the gateway. Martin realized there were several people on the other side of the road – neighbours, he supposed, passers-by, a couple of workmen on their lunch break – who were all loitering in the same way. He was reminded for a moment of the spectators yesterday at Paul Bradley's bloody street theatre.

The old woman with the Labrador touched Martin on the arm as if they were old acquaintances. 'Isn't it terrible?' she said. 'Who would have thought, it's so quiet around here.' Martin rubbed the moth-eaten dog's head behind its ears. It stood four-square, immobile, only a faint quiver in the tail indicating enjoyment. The dog reminded him of the push-along dogs on wheels that children played with. He and his brother Christopher had one when they were little, some sort of generic terrier. Their father tripped over it one day and was so enraged that he picked it up by the handle and flung it as hard as he could, through the living-room window. That was regarded as acceptable behaviour in their home. Not home – 'home front' was what their father called it. That had been a dress rehearsal for his throwing their real dog, a mongrel, through the window of the living room in married quarters in Germany. The toy dog survived, the real dog didn't. Martin remembered throwing his laptop yesterday – was there something in him that had enjoyed that aggressive moment? Something, God forbid, of his father in him?

'And to think, no one heard a thing,' the old woman with the Labrador said.

'Heard what? What happened?' Martin asked her, glancing at the policeman, wondering if he was allowed to ask, if there wasn't some great secret here that he wasn't allowed access to. Perhaps they'd discovered Richard was a terrorist – unlikely given his complete lack of interest in anything that wasn't Richard Moat. Richard! Had something happened to Richard? 'Richard Moat,' he said to the policeman, 'the comedian, he was staying with me, has something happened to him?' The constable frowned at him and spoke into his radio again, more urgently this time, then he said to the woman with the Labrador, 'I'm afraid I'll have to ask you to move away, madam.'

Instead of moving away, the old woman shuffled closer to Martin and said in a conspiratorial whisper, 'Alex Blake, the crime writer – he's been murdered.'

'I'm Alex Blake,' Martin said.

'I thought you were Martin Canning, sir?' the policeman objected.

'I am,' Martin said, but he could hear the lack of conviction in his voice.

An earnest man introduced himself to Martin as 'Superintendent Robert Campbell' and walked through the house with him as if he was an estate agent trying to sell a particularly troublesome property. Someone gave Martin what looked like paper shower caps to put over his shoes (*Still an active crime scene, sir*) and Superintendent Campbell murmured softly, 'Tread carefully, sir,' as if he were about to quote Yeats.

In the shambles of the living room, Martin glimpsed

a couple of crime-scene technicians still at work – studious and unremarkable people, not glamorous and good-looking like the characters on *CSI*. There were no technicians of any kind in Martin's novels, crimes were solved by intuition and coincidence and sudden hunches. Nina Riley occasionally resorted to asking advice from an old friend of her uncle's, a self-styled 'retired criminologist'. *Oh, dear old Samuel, what would a poor girl do without a brilliant mind like yours to call on?* Martin had no real idea what 'criminologist' meant, but it covered a lot of gaps in Nina Riley's education.

The criminologist lived, in fact, in Edinburgh and Nina had just been to visit him in his house near the Botanics. She was currently on page one hundred and fifty, on her way back to the Black Isle, hanging from the Forth Bridge while the Edinburgh-to-Dundee train 'thundered like a dragon' above her. Did dragons thunder? *Well, Bertie, this is quite a scrape we've got ourselves into here, isn't it? Thank goodness that wasn't the King's Cross-to-Inverness express train, that's all I can say!* From his living room there drifted the scent of offal. Was Richard still in there? Martin twitched, he found his left hand was shaking. No, no, Superintendent Campbell reassured him, the body had already been removed to the police mortuary. The house had been polluted by the living Richard Moat and now it was being polluted by the dead one. There was no reality, he reminded himself, only the nano-second, the atom of a breath. A breath that was scented like a butcher's shop. He was glad now that he had eaten neither breakfast nor lunch.

'How did he die?' Did he really want to know?

'We're still waiting for the results of the autopsy, Mr Canning.'

Martin was waiting for the right moment to say, 'I've just spent a drugged night in a hotel with a man who had a gun,' but Campbell kept asking him if he could tell if there was 'anything missing' from the house. The only thing Martin could think of was his watch but that had disappeared the day *before* yesterday.

'A Rolex,' he said, and the detective raised an eyebrow and said, 'An eighteen-carat oyster Yacht-Master? Like the one that Mr Moat was wearing?'

'Was he? Do you think Richard was killed in the course of a burglary that went wrong? Did someone break in thinking the house was empty (*because I was spending a drugged night in a hotel with a man who had a gun*) and Richard came downstairs and took him by surprise?' Martin could hear himself talking like a *Crimewatch* presenter. He tried to stop but it seemed he couldn't. 'Did he disturb an intruder?'

'It has all the hallmarks of an opportunistic crime,' Campbell said cautiously, 'a burglar surprised in the act, as you say, but we're keeping an open mind. And there was no break-in, Mr Moat either opened the door to his killer or he brought him home with him. We estimate his time of death to have been somewhere between four and seven o'clock this morning.'

A uniformed policewoman passed them on the stairs. There were strangers everywhere in his house. He felt like a stranger himself. The policewoman was carrying a large plastic box that reminded Martin of a bread-bin. She was holding it carefully away from her body as if it contained something dangerous or delicate. 'Crossing on the stairs,' she said cheerfully to her superintendent, 'that's bad luck. And all those broken mirrors downstairs,' she added, shaking her head and laughing. Campbell frowned at her levity.

'We haven't found the murder weapon,' he said to Martin. 'We need to know if there's anything missing from the house that might have been used to kill Mr Moat.'

It seemed ridiculous to be using words like 'weapon' and 'kill' in his lovely Merchiston house. They were words that belonged in Nina Riley's lexicon. *So you see, Bertie, the murder weapon that killed the Laird was actually an icicle taken from the overhang on the doo'cot. The murderer simply threw it in the kitchen stove once he had used it – that's why the police have been unable to find it.* He suspected he had stolen this plot device from Agatha Christie. But didn't they say there was nothing new under the sun?

'We can't discount the fact that this might have been personal, Martin.' Martin wondered at what point had he segued from 'sir' into 'Martin'.

'You mean that someone came here *intending* to kill Richard?' Martin said. Martin could understand that, Richard could provoke you into murderous thoughts.

'Well, that certainly,' Campbell said, 'but I was thinking about you. Do you have any enemies, Martin? Is there anyone who might want to kill *you*?'

A miasma of Usher-like doom seemed suddenly to rise up and fold itself around the house like a wet shroud. Death had stalked its rooms. He had a terrible headache. Death had found him. It might not have taken him, but it had found him. And it was coming to exact retribution.

Robert Campbell escorted Martin to 'his friend's room'. Martin wanted to say 'he's not my friend' but that seemed cruel and heartless considering what had happened.

Martin hadn't been in the room since he had first shown Richard into it, saying, 'If there's anything you want, just say.' Then it had been 'the guest room' with a pretty blue-and-white toile de Jouy on the walls, a cream carpet on the floor and a neat pyramid of white guest towels on the French sleigh bed, with a cope-stone of Crabtree and Evelyn's lily-of-the-valley soap. (*Are you always this anal, Martin?* Richard Moat laughed when he walked in the room. *Yes*, Martin said.)

Now the guest room was like a dosshouse. It smelt ripe, as if Richard had been eating takeaways – and indeed, beneath the bed there was a pizza box that still held a slice of old, cold, pepperoni pizza and a foil container of something possibly Chinese, along with plates and saucers full of cigarette butts. The floor was littered with balled-up dirty socks, underpants, used tissues (God knows what was on them), all kinds of bits of paper that were scribbled on, a couple of porn mags. 'He wasn't the tidy sort,' Martin said.

'Is there anything missing from this room, do you think, Martin?'

'I'm sorry, I can't really tell.' Richard Moat was missing, but that seemed like stating the obvious.

279

A police constable was rifling through a plastic carrier bag full of correspondence. 'Sir?' he said to Robert Campbell, handing him a letter which he held gingerly by one corner in his gloved hand. Robert Campbell read it with a frown and asked Martin, 'Did anyone have a grudge against Mr Moat?'

'Well, he got a lot of fan mail,' Martin said.

'Fan mail? What kind of fan mail?'

'*Richard Moat you're a wanking wanker.* That kind.'

'And was he?' Robert Campbell asked.

'Yes.'

'Can I ask you where you were last night, Martin?' Campbell asked, his broad, friendly features betraying no indication that he held Martin responsible in any way for what had happened in his house, to his 'friend'. He sighed, a great deep sigh, the kind a very sad horse might give, while he waited for Martin's reply.

Martin felt a burning pain, like indigestion, beneath his ribcage. He recognized it as guilt even though he was innocent. Of this at least. But did it matter? Guilt was guilt. It had to be assigned somewhere. Paid for somehow. If there was cosmic justice at work, and Martin was inclined to think there was, then at the end of the day the weights had to balance. An eye for an eye.

'Last night?' Campbell prompted.

'Well,' Martin said, 'there was a man with a baseball bat.' It sounded like the beginning of a story that could go anywhere – *and he was a champion player in the major league.* Or sad – *and when he found out that he*

was dying he willed the bat to his favourite grandson.
The shape that the real tale had taken seemed unbelievable in comparison to its fictional alternatives.
In the end Martin didn't mention the gun, he could see
it might be considered a detail too far.

26

BILL, THE GARDENER, APPEARED LIKE AN APPARITION AT THE French windows, giving Gloria a start. It had begun to spit with rain outside but Bill never seemed to notice the weather. Whenever Gloria commented on it, *Isn't it a lovely morning?* or *Goodness, it's cold today*, and so on, he would glance around with a perplexed expression on his face as if he was trying to see something invisible. It seemed an odd trait in a gardener, surely the weather should be part of his nature? She offered him coffee, as usual, although he had never in five years accepted. Bill always brought a khaki canvas satchel in which he carried an old-fashioned Thermos flask and various greaseproof-paper packets of food – sandwiches, Gloria supposed, and cake, perhaps a hard-boiled egg, all prepared by his wife.

Gloria used to prepare a packed lunch for Graham. That was a long time ago when the world was much younger and Gloria took pride in making 'traybake' cakes and sausage rolls and filling little Tupperware containers with lettuce and tomato and carrot batons, all for Graham to consume mindlessly in a lay-by somewhere. Or perhaps he just threw the contents of the little Tupperware containers in the nearest bin and went and ate scampi and chips in a pub with an eager-breasted woman. Sometimes Gloria wondered where she had been when feminism occurred – in the kitchen making interesting packed lunches, presumably. Of course, Graham hadn't eaten a packed lunch in decades, wasn't eating at all now, instead had mysterious substances added and subtracted from his body by tubes, like an astronaut.

Gloria wondered why Bill wasn't unwrapping his little paper parcels of food in the privacy of the shed. He cleared his throat in a self-conscious way. He was very small, like a jockey, and he made Gloria feel like an elephant.

'Can I help you with something?' she asked him. He was always 'Bill', while she was always 'Mrs Hatter' and she had long ago given up saying, 'Call me Gloria.' He used to work for some kind of aristocrat in the Borders and was more comfortable in a mistress/servant relationship. Gloria almost expected him to tug his forelock.

She was distracted by the sight of a smear of chocolate on her white blouse. She supposed it was from the chocolate digestives she had breakfasted on. She imagined the little factory of cells that was her body taking in the chocolate and fat and flour (and probably carcinogenic additives) and sending them off on conveyor belts to different processing rooms. This industry, dedicated to the greater good that was Gloria, was run on co-operative, profit-sharing lines. In this model Gloria factory, the cells were a cheerful, happy workforce who sang along to *Workers' Playtime* from a tannoy radio. They were unionized and benefited from subsidized housing and healthcare and never became entangled in the factory machinery and mangled to death like her brother Jonathan.

Bill's wife, it transpired, had a brain that was 'turning into a sponge', according to Bill, and therefore he was going to have to give up coming on Wednesdays ('if you don't mind, Mrs Hatter,') and tend his sponge-brain wife instead of Gloria's garden. Gloria thought about mentioning Graham's present condition to him – having a damaged spouse was the first thing they had found in common – but they had already had the longest conversation ever and she decided he probably couldn't bear any more.

The phone rang for the hundredth time. Bill didn't question Gloria's standing patiently waiting for it to stop. Gloria wondered what it would have been like to have been married to such a passive man. Infuriating, probably. Say what you like about Graham, he had given her a good run for her money.

After he'd delivered his news Bill disappeared into his shed and, presumably, ate his lunch as usual, because thirty minutes later he emerged, brushing crumbs from his moustache, and began to aerate the lawn with a device that looked like an instrument of torture. Gloria made herself a cheese and chutney sandwich (gooseberry chutney, her own recipe, the gooseberries picked a few weeks ago out at Stenton Farm) and ate it standing at the kitchen counter and then went into the hall and listened to the messages on the answering machine. There were so many now that the later ones had erased the earlier ones. Gloria thought this was how her own memory worked, except the opposite way round.

Everyone wanted Graham for one reason or another. His absence was causing a rising tide of panic in the Hatter Homes offices, already under mental siege from the Fraud Unit. *You've not done a Robert Maxwell, have you?* said the fraught voice of his second-in-command, Gareth Lawson.

Pam fluttering, *Oh, Gloria, can I have your recipe for Turkish cheesecake, I know I've written it down somewhere but I can't put my hands on it.* It was a very good recipe – a packet of Philadelphia, a tin of Fussell's sterilized cream and half a dozen eggs beaten together and poured into a caramel-coated mould and cooked gently in a bain-marie. It was the kind of recipe a person treasured once they had been given it. Careless Pam would not be getting it off Gloria a second time.

A short, barking *Graham, still in fucking Thurso?* from Murdo Miller, endless *Mother? Mother-where-are-you?* from Emily. An abrasive West Coast voice that Gloria recognized as their accountant, saying, *What's going on, Graham, you're not answering your mobile, you didn't turn up at our meeting yesterday.* The stentorian tones of Alistair Crichton blared, *Where the fuck are you, Graham? You seem to have disappeared off the face of the fucking planet.* Gloria thought that she wouldn't like to be a criminal appearing in his court. A judge who, if he were judged himself, would be found seriously wanting. 'Justice has nothing to do with the law,' he once remarked airily to her, over a tray of canapés at some do or other. *Graham, why aren't you answering your mobile? We have to talk, do you understand? I hope you're not bailing out on me.*

The phone rang before this message was finished and the answering machine summarily ditched Sheriff Crichton and began recording the unhappy tones of Christine Tennant, Graham's long-suffering secretary of ten years. ('PA, actually, Gloria,' she continually, apologetically, corrected but Gloria knew that if you typed and took notes and answered a phone you were a secretary. Call a spade a spade.) Her usual rather whiny tones now had a near-hysterical edge to them. *Gloria, everyone's looking for Graham, he's really needed here. Do you know how I can contact him in Thurso?* Over the years, Gloria had occasionally wondered if Graham had ever had sex with Christine Tennant. She had been with him for ten years, after all, and yet still seemed unnaturally enamoured of him. Surely only a woman suffering from unrequited passion could remain that fond of Graham? On the other hand, Graham was a man of clichés and therefore sleeping with his secretary would be the kind of thing he would do. That would be a rather good epitaph for his headstone. *Graham Hatter – A Man of Clichés.* You didn't have headstones if you were cremated, did you? You had nothing, an epitaph written on the wind and water.

Of course, the first thing you did when someone was missing was phone the hospitals, everyone knew that, yet it never seemed to have crossed the mind of any of these people who were so desperate to get their hands on Graham, when all this time he was simply lying there on his catafalque in the ICU, hidden in plain sight, waiting to be discovered.

Gloria's eye was caught by something, a flicker in the rhododendrons, a flash of something reflective catching the light. She reached for the binoculars that she kept handy for birdwatching. It took her a while to adjust the focus on the binoculars but then the glossy green leaves came suddenly into focus, revealing a face, Ovidian amongst the greenery. The face melted back into the foliage. At any rate she was sure now that it wasn't a bear or a horse. Nor was it a woman meta-morphosed into a tree, or vice versa. Gloria strode out into the garden, scattering sparrows in her wake, but when she reached the rhododendrons there was no intruder, only Bill urinating discreetly in the shrubbery.

The electronic gates swung open to let Gloria's Red Golf out. She always felt as if she was making a get-away from a crime when she drove through them. She headed for George Street, where the parking gods found her a space right outside Gray's, where she bought a radiator key and a Stain Devil (for chewing gum, glue and nail varnish) before schlepping along to the Royal Bank on the corner of Castle Street, where she withdrew her five hundred pounds cash for the day.

When she returned Bill was packing up, putting his tools in the boot of his car. Although they had every kind of tool possible in the shed, Bill preferred to bring his own with him, some of them so old they could have been displayed in an agricultural museum.

'Well,' he said, laconically, 'I'll be going then.' Gloria supposed that if she hadn't returned when she had, he would have left without even saying goodbye. Five years and all she got was 'I'll be going then'. Graham's last words to her had been something similar. She tried to remember what he had said to her yesterday morning. *I'll probably be late* – nothing new there, something about *the fucking fraud cops*, and then *I'm off now*. How prescient of him.

She should give Bill a farewell gift of some kind; she should have bought something in town but she never thought. She could give him money but money always seemed an impersonal gift. From an early age, both Ewan and Emily had asked for money for their birthdays and Christmases. Gloria liked to give gifts, not money. Money was good but it wasn't *personal*. It was business.

Bill slammed the boot of his car shut and she said, 'No, wait a minute,' and hurried inside the house to look for something suitable. It was hard to know what a man of so few words might like. She considered a pair of dainty Staffordshire Dalmatians sitting pertly on royal blue cushions – he looked like a man who might like dogs – or a nice limited-edition Moorcroft vase? Then she remembered him standing at the French windows one day – he had never once crossed the threshold in five years – admiring the stag at bay on the wall. She unhooked the painting, which was much heavier than it looked, and carried it outside to Bill.

He was reluctant to take it. 'Worth a lot, Mrs Hatter,' he mumbled shyly.

'Not *that* much,' Gloria said. 'Come on, take it, God doesn't give with two hands.' She thought of Bill's wife with her spongy brain. Sometimes God seemed to give a little with one hand and take away a lot with the other.

Eventually he was persuaded into giving a home to the doomed stag, sliding it into his boot on top of his tools before driving away for the last time. Gloria had neither liked nor disliked him but now she felt a surprising pang of sorrow that she would never see him again. Even though they barely interacted with each other she thought of Wednesday as 'Bill's day'. Monday was 'Hospice day' when Gloria put on a ludicrously cheerful smile and trundled a tea trolley round the local hospice – good china, home-made biscuits – everything nice because they were dying and they knew it.

Friday was 'Beryl's day'. It seemed now that Beryl would outlast her son. She lived in a nursing home just a few streets away and Gloria visited her there every Friday afternoon, although Beryl had no idea who Gloria was as her brain had also softened into a sponge. Gloria felt her own brain turning into something harder, less friendly; coral perhaps. They had seen 'brain coral' on holiday in the Maldives when Gloria had made a timid foray into the underwater world of snorkelling. She had worn an old navy blue one-piece that she wore for swimming in Warriston Baths and was acutely aware of how, from shoulder to hip, her body had taken on the prowed shape of a lizard's. Every other woman on the hot white beach seemed to be slim and brown and wearing a tiny expensive bikini.

They always took a tropical holiday in January – the Seychelles, Mauritius, Thailand – staying at the most expensive hotels, waited on hand and foot. Graham liked being a rich man, liked people to see that he was a rich man. If he recovered, if he lived, perish the thought, could he bear to be a poor man? Probably not. So Death might be a Good Thing for him.

There had been a lot of Russians staying in their hotel in the Maldives. The women were thin and blond and taken up with children, while the men were big and hairy and reminded Gloria of walruses, basking all day long in their gold jewellery, oily skins and swimwear that was too tight. 'Gangsters,' Graham said to Gloria matter-of-factly. Gloria was puzzled as to who the Russian men reminded her of until she realized it was Graham. They out-Grahamed Graham, which was quite an achievement.

That was the last time Gloria had sex with Graham, in the Maldives, on the tight white coverlet of the bed under a tropical hardwood ceiling spiralled into the shape of a snail. It had been an awkward and slightly confrontational act.

Gloria wondered if anyone would visit *her* if she was in a nursing home. She couldn't imagine Emily turning up regularly, with new underwear, hand cream, a potted hyacinth. She couldn't imagine Emily sitting opposite her week in, week out, brushing her hair, massaging her hands, keeping up a one-sided meaningless conversation. She couldn't imagine Ewan visiting her at all.

The phone was ringing. Gloria went into the hall and looked at it. It was developing a personality of its own – irritating and unforgiving, not unlike the voice now shouting 'Mother!' into the answering machine. The *Evening News* was poking like a tongue through the letterbox and Gloria tugged it out and glanced through it while Emily continued with her one-note, two-syllable chant – she had done this as a child, a repetitive mantra, *Mummy-mummy-mummy-mummy*, but when Gloria asked her what she wanted she would shrug and look blank and say 'nothing'.

'Mother! Mother! Mother! I know you're there, pick up the phone. Pick up the phone or I'll call the police. Mother, mother, mother, mother.'

The last time they had all been together as a family was Christmas. Ewan worked for an environmental agency and had flown home from Patagonia. Working for the environment didn't mean Ewan was a particularly nice person. He was very self-righteous about the fact that he didn't want any share in Graham's business empire, which apparently was playing its own small part in 'the global capitalist conspiracy'. That didn't stop him taking money from Graham whenever he was home. Ewan had always been a disappointment to Graham, never interested in the tenets of Scottish religion – alcohol, football, feeling badly done by – that formed the backbone of Graham's faith. Graham was about to fulfil his lifetime ambition of owning a Premier League football team when fate tagged him yesterday – he had the unsigned contracts with him in his briefcase when he collapsed beneath Tatiana.

When Ewan had declared himself a member of the Green Party his father's only comment was 'Silly little fucker.' Emily had no principles at all when it came to Graham's money. Of course, Graham should have been grooming her to take over, she would have made an excellent capitalist profiteer.

Emily had been a lovely child, sweetness and light, a child who worshipped Gloria and everything she did. And then one day Emily woke up and she was thirteen and she'd been thirteen ever since as far as Gloria could make out. She was thirty-seven now and married with a child of her own but motherhood had, if anything, only served to sour her disposition even further. She lived in Basingstoke, with her husband Nick ('project development manager in IT' – what did that *mean*?), and devoted a lot of time to harbouring grudges.

The main topic of conversation for both Ewan and Emily at Christmas had been how much their lives had changed, evolved, grown, but from one year to the next they expected Gloria to stay exactly the same. If she mentioned anything new in her life – 'I've joined a gym' (she had tried, and failed, at a class called Nifty Fifties. After that there was Sensational Sixties. After sixty there didn't seem to be anything.) or 'I was think-ing of doing French conversation at the French Institute' – their response was always the same: 'Oh *Mother*,' said in an exasperated tone as if she was a particularly stupid child.

Last Christmas Eve, when Graham was still a fully functioning member of the family and not yet an astro-naut floating through space, she had been in the kitchen making the chocolate log. They always had a chocolate log on Christmas Day along with the pudding. Gloria made a roulade mix, no flour, only eggs and sugar but heavy with expensive chocolate, and when it was cooked she rolled it up with whipped cream and chestnut purée and decorated it with chocolate butter cream, scored and marked to look like wood, and then sprinkled it with icing-sugar snow. Finally, she cut ivy from the garden, frosted it with egg white and sugar and then twined it round the log before perching a red plastic robin on top. She thought it looked lovely, like something from a fairy tale, and if she had been still bothering with Weight Watchers it would have used up all her points for a whole year.

When it came to the time to eat it, Ewan would say (because they were like actors with an immutable script), 'None of that stuff for me, I'll just have Christmas pudding,' and Emily would say, 'God, Mother, that kind of thing is toxic to the system,' and now that she had Xanthia she would add threateningly, 'And don't give any to Xanthia either,' because, of course, one-year-old Xanthia had been weaned on *millet* as far as Gloria could tell, and then, inevitably, Graham would say, 'I don't know why you make that shite, no one eats it,' and Gloria would say, '*I* eat it,' and she would cut herself a big slice. And eat it. And every day after that she took it out of the fridge and cut another big slice until only the piece with the robin was left and she would put that one out for the squirrels and the birds, but minus the robin, of course, in case the squirrels accidentally ate it. Or another robin attacked it, thinking it was a miniaturized, paralysed trespasser into its territory.

Their parts were fixed – Graham was the villain, Ewan took the role of worthy leading man, Nick was his long-suffering sidekick and Emily was forever the adolescent ingénue, the moody daughter whose life had been blighted by everyone else (apparently). Gloria herself was offstage, playing the woman in the kitchen. They wheeled out Graham's mother, Beryl, for Christmas Day and she sat on the sofa dribbling. An extra with a non-speaking part.

'You have such a classic passive-aggressive personality,' Emily had hissed at Gloria while she was basting the Christmas turkey. Gloria wasn't sure she knew what a passive-aggressive personality was, classic or otherwise, but clearly it wasn't to Emily's liking.

'You're always so *nice* to everyone,' Emily said.

'Is that a bad thing?' Gloria asked.

Emily carried on as if Gloria hadn't spoken, slamming down the tureen of roast potatoes on to the countertop, 'But underneath you're so *angry*. And do you know something I've come to understand recently?' Emily had been having some kind of counselling, every Wednesday afternoon in Basingstoke, from a man called Bryce who was 're-programming' her brain 'into more positive patterns'.

'No, what have you come to realize?' Gloria asked, wondering whether, if she were to hit her daughter about the head with the basting spoon, that wouldn't reprogramme her brain a lot faster and more cheaply than someone called Bryce.

'I've realized that I have spent my entire life not being *me.*'

'Who have you been then?' Gloria knew that she should try to be more sympathetic but she just couldn't somehow.

'Oh very clever, Mother. I haven't put my energy into being *me*, because my whole life has been defined by my terror of becoming *you*.' Gloria didn't think of herself as a nice person at all, quite the opposite in fact, but she supposed these things were relative; compared to Emily most people were in line for canonization.

The only item on the Christmas menu that Emily had prepared was a starter of fig and Parma ham. All Emily had done was buy the figs and ham from Harvey Nichols' food department and put the ruddy things on a plate but nonetheless her starter was given a rousing introduction, *Now this is going to be something really lovely for a change*, before being applauded to the rafters (by herself) afterwards, *Wasn't that gorgeous? Isn't it nice to have something different?* The starter had also come with a warning as Emily placed the plates on the table, this warning directed specifically at Nick and uttered with a manic kind of cheerfulness, 'Now, darling, don't you dare *critique* this.' Emily had done an MA in literature at Goldsmiths' and it had made her into the kind of person who used critique as a verb. And applied it to food. She was 'not getting on very well with Nick', she confided to Gloria in the kitchen, she had even been thinking of 'a trial separation'. Horror clutched at Gloria's chest at the idea that Emily might move back home.

'For better for worse,' Gloria said and Emily replied, 'What – like you and Dad, staying together when neither of you can stand the sight of each other?' Children were not necessarily a Good Thing.

If they had known that it might be their corrupt, adulterous fraudster of a paterfamilias's last Christmas would they have done things differently? Gloria might have roasted a goose instead of a turkey, he liked goose, but that was probably as far as she would have been prepared to go.

Gloria sat on the peach-damask sofa in the peach-themed living room and drank tea and ate a sandwich she had bought in town. The sandwich contained mozzarella, avocado and rocket. None of the ingredients existed in the museum that was Gloria's past. Gloria could remember a time when all you could buy was lettuce. Soft, limp lettuces that tasted of nothing. English lettuces. She could remember a time before mozzarella and avocado, before aubergines and courgettes. She could remember seeing her first yoghurt in the corner shop in the northern town that had been her home and still was even though she hadn't visited it for over twenty years.

She could remember a time when there was no take-out food, no Thai restaurants, when Vesta packets were the nearest you came to anything exotic. A time when food was herrings and mince and luncheon meat. She had mentioned to Emily once that she could remember a time before aubergines and her daughter had snapped, 'Don't be ridiculous,' at her. She finished her lunch with a slice of Genoese sponge (the secret was in the addition of a spoonful of hot milk). She had already hung her Victorian kittens-in-a-basket painting in place of the gloomy stag at bay, although its ghostly impression was still visible, thanks to a faint outline of grime. It was only last year that the room had been redecorated, after the new security system was installed, but it never ceased to surprise Gloria how quickly dirt gathered. The kittens looked completely at home on the wall.

She was so far lost in the contemplation of innocent kittenhood that she wasn't aware of the lumbering shape that appeared at the French windows until it raised a meaty paw and knocked on the glass. Gloria nearly fell off the sofa.

'For God's sake,' she said crossly, heaving herself off the peach damask and opening the window. 'You nearly gave me a heart attack, Terry.'

'Sorry.'

Terence Smith. Graham's golem, formed from the slime at the bottom of a pond of low-lifes somewhere in the Midlands. Sometimes Murdo borrowed him to work on the doors or do bodyguard duties (Murdo's security firm looked after fragile celebrities when they made appearances in the capital), but most of the time he was simply Graham's pet thug, driving him around if he was too drunk to find the steering wheel – Graham refused to crush his ego into Gloria's Red Golf – or hanging about in the background with the same air of doltish fidelity as his dog. Gloria fed cake to both man and dog and kept them away from cats and small children. There was no sign of the dog today. 'Where's your dog today, Terry? Where's Spike?'

He made an odd, choking noise and shook his head but when he spoke it was to ask the whereabouts of Graham, his puppet-master.

'He's in Thurso,' she said. It was funny but the more she said that the more it seemed true, in a meta-physical sense at any rate, as if Thurso was a kind of purgatory to which people were banished. Gloria had been to Thurso once and found that to be pretty much the case.

'Thurso?' he repeated doubtfully.

'Yes,' Gloria said. 'It's up north.' She doubted that Scottish geography was high on Terry's list of specialist subjects. She frowned at him. His face, always ugly, had acquired a new and disturbing florescence. 'Terry – what happened to your nose?' He put his hand over his face as if he'd grown suddenly bashful.

The phone rang again and they both listened in silence to Emily's bleating. *Mother-Mother-Mother*.

'That's your daughter,' Terry said eventually, as if Gloria had failed to recognize Emily.

Gloria sighed and said, 'Tell me about it,' and, against her better judgement, went and picked up the receiver.

'I've been ringing for ever,' Emily said, 'but all I get is the answering machine.'

'I've been out a lot,' Gloria said. 'You should have left a message.'

'I didn't want to leave a message,' Emily said crossly. Gloria watched as Terry lumbered down the path. He reminded her a little of King Kong, but less friendly.

'Mother?'

'Mm?'

'Is something going on?' Emily asked sharply.

'Going on?' Gloria echoed.

'Yes, going on. Is Dad OK? Can I speak to him?'

'He can't come to the phone just now.'

'I have some news for you,' Emily's less than dulcet tones announced. 'Good news.'

'Good news?' Gloria queried. She wondered if Emily was pregnant again (was that good news?), so she was taken aback when Emily said, 'I've found Jesus.'

'Oh,' Gloria said. 'Where was he?'

27

LOUISE STARED THROUGH THE WINDSCREEN AT THE RAIN. THIS could be a God-forsaken country when it rained. God-forsaken when it didn't.

The car was parked down by the harbour at Cramond, looking out towards the island. There were three of them in the car, herself, DS Sandy Mathieson and eager-beaver Jessica Drummond. They had steamed up the inside of the car like lovers or conspirators although they were doing nothing more exciting than talking about house prices. 'Where two or more people are gathered together in Edinburgh,' Louise said.

'Supply and demand, boss,' Sandy Mathieson said. 'It's a town with more demand than supply.' Louise would have preferred 'ma'am' to 'boss', 'ma'am' made her sound like a woman (somewhere between an aristocrat and a headmistress, both ideas quite appealing), whereas 'boss' made her one of the boys. But then didn't you have to be one of the boys to cut it? 'I read something in the *Evening News*,' Sandy Mathieson continued, 'that there aren't enough expensive houses in Edinburgh. There are millionaires fighting over the high-end stuff.'

'The Russians are moving in,' Jessica said.

'The Russians?' Louise said. 'What Russians?'

'Rich ones.'

'The Russians are the new Americans apparently,' Sandy Mathieson said.

'Someone paid a hundred thousand for a garage last week,' Jessica complained, 'how insane is that? I can't even afford a starter home in Gorgie.'

'It was a double garage,' Sandy Mathieson said. Louise laughed and cracked a window to let out some of the hot air. The tide was dropping and she caught a faint smell of sewage in the damp atmosphere. She never knew whether or not Sandy Mathieson was being funny. Not seemed more likely, he never seemed sharp enough to be witty. He was true to his name, from his gingery hair to his little beard to his giraffe-coloured freckles. He made Louise think of a biscuit, shortbread or gingerbread, perhaps a digestive. He was a straight-down-the-middle type, married, two children, docile dog, season ticket to Hearts, barbecues with the in-laws at the weekends. He had told her once that he had everything he had ever wanted and would die protecting any of it, even the season ticket to Hearts.

'That must be nice,' Louise had said, not really meaning it. She wasn't the sacrificing kind. Archie was the only thing she would die for.

'Where do *you* live, boss?' Jessica asked.

'Glencrest,' Louise said reluctantly, having no desire

to start chatting about her private life with Jessica. She knew the type from her schooldays, winkling out intimacies and then using them against her. *Louise Monroe's mother's an alkie, Louise Monroe gets free school meals, Louise Monroe is a liar.*

'That Hatter Homes development out by the Braids?' Sandy Mathieson said. 'We looked at that. Too pricey, we decided.' The 'We' sounded emphasized, Louise noticed, underlining his little world, *Me and my wife and my two children and my docile dog*. Not a woman on her own with a kid whose paternity had always been a matter for speculation. Sandy was a plodder, too unimaginative to be unfaithful to his wife, too stolid to rise above the rank he was at now. But he would always do the right thing by his kids and he didn't dodge and weave with the truth, didn't seed favours – a blind eye here, a deaf ear there. Wouldn't screw a DI in the back of a police car, too drunk to remember that sex was a biological imperative with only one goal. (*I'm pulling rank on you, Louise*. Hilarious, how they'd laughed. Jesus.)

'It's a very small house,' Louise said defensively.

'Still . . .' Sandy said, as if he'd proved a point.

'Didn't there turn out to be some problems with Glencrest?' Jessica asked.

'Problems?' Louise said.

'Subsidence or something.'

'What?'

'*Real Homes for Real People*,' Jessica said. 'Word on the pavement is that Graham Hatter's going down.'

' "Going down"? You sound like an extra off *The Bill*.' Yes, that would be Jessica, Louise could just see her going home at night, putting her clumpy feet up, eating a takeaway in front of *The Bill*. ' "Going down" for what?'

'Well, a little bird says they're after him for money laundering, amongst other things. But apparently it's huge, corruption in high places and all that.'

'A little bird?' Louise said.

'I have a friend in fraud.'

'Really? You have a friend?'

'Name me a famous woman who drowned,' Louise said. Jessica gave her a worried look as if she suspected this was part of some kind of intellectual hazing, some arcane knowledge that you needed in order to be in plain-clothes. Her pudgy brow puckered with the effort of remembering something she didn't know in the first place.

'You see,' Louise said, when no answer was forthcoming, 'women aren't known for drowning.'

'I think I prefer I-Spy,' Sandy Mathieson said.

All morning while Louise had been in court, her small flu-diminished team had been busy, mostly on door-to-door inquiries. Had anyone seen anything unusual, had anyone seen a woman go into the water, had anyone seen a woman on shore, had anyone seen a woman, had anyone seen anything? A negative on all counts. The divers had come up with nothing. Louise had watched them emerging from the water. Frogmen, they used to be called, you didn't hear that much any more. They reminded her of *The Man from Atlantis*.

They were chasing a wild goose, a trick of light on water.

'I see dead people,' Jessica intoned.

The only excitement in Cramond over the last few days had been an unattended car alarm and a dog that had been run over. The dog was making a good recovery, apparently. Fantastically low crime rate – that's what you got for paying a small fortune to live in one of the nicest parts of Edinburgh.

She had showed her team the pink card that she'd taken from the mortuary, didn't mention how she'd come by it, told them to ask around to see if anyone had heard of Favours, but it seemed the good burghers of Cramond didn't move in the kind of society where girls handed out little pink cards with phone numbers on.

Louise had sent a couple of uniforms on a trawl of the cheap jewellery shops in town for gold earrings in the shape of a cross. 'I can't believe how much nine-carat crap there is out there,' one of them had reported back. More crucifix earrings than you might have thought, it turned out, but no one remembered a five-foot-six, hundred-and-twenty-pound blonde buying a pair.

'The Girl with the Crucifix Earring', like a lost painting of Vermeer. Louise had seen *Girl with a Pearl Earring* at the Filmhouse, in the company of friends, two other single women. It was a film meant for single women of a certain age – muted, poignant, full of art, ultimately depressing. It had (briefly) made her want to live in seventeenth-century Holland. When she was young she had often fantasized about living in the past, mainly because the present had been so awful.

'Who's on the Merchiston murder?' she asked.

'Robert Campbell, Colin Sutherland,' Jessica said promptly. 'High-profile celebrity murder gets the big fish high up the food chain.'

'Celebrity?'

'Richard Moat,' Sandy Mathieson said dismissively, 'Eighties comedian. Did you hear what happened?'

'No, what?' Louise said. The name sounded vaguely familiar.

'They ID'd the wrong person,' Jessica said.

'You're kidding.'

Sandy laughed. 'He lived with this other guy, a writer, wasn't it?' he checked with Jessica (Christ, they were like a double act), who nodded and took up the story. 'And he was wearing his boyfriend's watch,' she said.

'Who was?' Louise was totally confused.

'Richard Moat,' Jessica said with theatrical patience, 'was wearing the other guy's watch. His boyfriend. And, the boyfriend, get this, is a crime writer.'

'Life imitating art,' Sandy said, as if he'd just invented the phrase. 'Alex Blake. Ever heard of him?'

'No,' Louise said. 'They ID'd him by his *watch*?'

'Well, his face was gone apparently,' Jessica said, in the offhand way you might say, 'Do you want vinegar on your chips?'

Louise could have eaten a horse, she'd had nothing since breakfast. 'Have you got anything to eat?' she said to Jessica.

'Sorry, boss.' Cheeky cow. Louise didn't believe her, you didn't get that fat without having constant access to food. Louise supposed she should have warm and fuzzy feelings towards the sisterhood, they were only

305

25 per cent of the force, they should support each other, yada yada, but quite honestly she'd like to corner Jessica and give her a few vicious playground pinches.

There was a constant undertow of communication on the police radio. A lot of shoplifting. What would happen if Archie's foray into thieving hadn't been a one-off? What would she do if he was caught next time? Louise checked her watch, he should be home from school by now.

Sandy turned to her and asked unexpectedly, parent to parent, 'How's that lad of yours doing?'

'Fine,' Louise said, 'Archie's doing fine. Great,' she added, trying to introduce a more upbeat note, 'he's doing great.' Sandy had a boy, but he was only six or seven years old, still harmless.

She climbed out of the car, waving her mobile at Sandy and Jessica in a shorthand that said only too plainly, *I'm going to make a call I don't want you to hear.* She wondered what they said about her when she wasn't there. She didn't really care as long as they thought she was good at her job.

She walked out on to the causeway, only one bar of signal on her phone. Jackson Brodie said he couldn't get a signal at all, that was why he hadn't phoned the police from the island.

She walked back and caught a signal. Her answering machine clicked in after a couple of rings and she listened to an assertive male voice informing her that no one was available to answer the phone just now so 'leave a message'. Nice and neutral, no 'please' or 'thank you' (I'm a polite woman asking to be

306

offended), no 'sorry, there's no one at home' (open invitation to burglars), no promise that anyone would actually return the call. The male voice belonged to a friend's husband drafted in to record the message after Louise had been plagued by nuisance calls, even though she was unlisted. Some guys just dialled every number until a woman answered. There were thousands of them out there, seeing out the wee small hours by dialling the Samaritans and Childline and unsuspecting women. Wankers, in every sense of the word. She had an uncomfortable feeling that the perpetrator of the nuisance calls was Archie's friend Hamish.

'If you're there, Archie, can you pick up?' When hell froze over. Louise didn't know why she was bothering, he never answered the phone unless he thought it was one of his friends. She tried his mobile, but it went straight to his answering machine. If she could she would have a tracking device implanted in his scruff.

Finally she gave in and, using the only lingua franca understood by fourteen-year-old boys, texted him, *Are u home? Eat something from the freezer. I may be late. Love mum x.* It was odd to give herself that appellation, to commit it to writing; she never thought of herself as 'mum'. Maybe that was where she'd gone wrong. Had she gone wrong? Probably.

Archie could just about manage to take a pizza or a burger from the freezer and put it in the microwave. There was no point in trying to get him to do anything more challenging (*An omelette, surely you can manage an omelette?*).

Her phone rang, not Archie but Jim Tucker. 'My girl

died of a heroin overdose,' he said without preamble, 'no identity yet. The forensic dentist said her mouth was, and I quote, "Full of crap," by which he meant foreign fillings. East European, by the look of it.'

'No dental records then,' Louise said.

'No, and I don't know if it's likely but someone said that they thought Favours were cleaners.'

'Cleaners?'

As soon as she'd said goodbye to Jim Tucker her phone rang again. 'I've been trying to phone you,' Archie complained.

'I try to phone you all the time and you *never* answer.'

'Can Hamish stay over tonight?'

'It's a school night.'

'We've got a geography project we have to do together.'

'What project?' A short, muffled conversation ensued, Hamish tutoring Archie, no doubt, before he came back on the line and said smugly, '*Discuss the transport factors influencing the location of industry.*'

It was plausible, Hamish was good. 'Does his mother say he can?'

'Of *course.*'

'OK.'

'And can we get a takeaway?'

'OK. Do you have money?'

'Yes.'

'Will you remember to feed the cat?'

'Whatever.'

'That's not the answer I'm looking for.'

'*Yessss.* OK? Jesus.'

Louise sighed. She really, really wanted a drink. A lime daiquiri. Cold enough to freeze her brain. And then she'd like to have a lot of sex. Casual, mindless, faceless, emotion-free sex. You would think casual sex would be easy, but no. She'd hardly had any since Archie hit adolescence. You couldn't just bring a guy home and shag him while your teenage son was playing Grand Theft Auto on the other side of a wafer-thin plasterboard wall. Every year there was a fresh surprise, something you didn't know about having a kid. Maybe it went on like that for ever, maybe when Archie was sixty and she was in her eighties she'd be thinking, 'Well, I didn't realize sixty-year-old men did *that*.'

She watched a uniformed PC tap on Jessica's window and hand her something.

'What did the UB want?' she asked, climbing back in the car.

'Brought this,' Jessica said, handing her a copy of the *Evening News*, helpfully turned to an inside page where she pointed out the small headline, 'Police ask public for help with their inquiries'.

'It's not very obvious, is it?' Sandy said. '*Police are asking if anyone saw a woman go into the water* – "Go into the water"? That's very vague.'

'Well, it *is* very vague,' Louise said. 'She was found in the water and somehow or other she got into it.'

'If she exists,' Jessica said. She sneezed and Sandy said, 'Hope you're not getting the flu.' Louise didn't care if Jessica got the flu.

Louise felt suddenly incredibly tired. 'Bugger this

for a game of soldiers. They're putting out something on Radio Forth tomorrow but in reality that's it for now. If there's a body out there then it'll probably wash up eventually. I don't see what more we can do.'

'I don't think there ever was a body,' Jessica said. 'I think Brodie made the whole thing up. I know where the nut is and it's not on the tree.'

'I didn't like the guy,' Sandy said, with the certainty of one who thinks his own moral judgement is un-impeachable. 'I'm all for calling it a day.' He turned to Jessica and said, 'Home, James.'

28

JACKSON HAD A HELLISH VISION OF BEING STUCK ON ONE BUS or another for ever. This time it was one of the open-top tourist ones that lumber around British cities, holding up the traffic. Jackson had taken Marlee on the Cambridge one last year, thinking it would be an easy way of absorbing some (probably revisionist) history but now he couldn't remember a thing they had been told. It was cold on the upper deck and a miserable wind seemed to have whipped itself across the North Sea with the sole intention of hitting Jackson on the back of the neck. This, Jackson reminded himself, was why he had moved to another country.

The Royal Mile was beginning to feel almost familiar to Jackson now. He felt like turning to the nearest person and pointing out to them St Giles Church and the new parliament building (ten times over budget – how could anything be ten times over budget?). The real tour guide was a melodramatically inclined middle-aged woman working for tips. It was the kind of job that a hard-up Julia would take.

The bus trundled along Princes Street – no dark Gothicism here, only ugly high-street chain shops. It began to spit with rain and less hardy foreign souls sought out the shelter of the lower deck, leaving only a scattering of Brits huddled under umbrellas and cagoules. He was half listening to the tour guide telling them about witches (otherwise known as women, of course) being thrown alive into the Nor' Loch, 'which is now unrecognizable as our "world-famous" Princes Street Gardens' (everything in Edinburgh was 'world-famous' apparently. He wondered if that was true – famous in Somalia? In Bhutan?), when he noticed a pink van, a Citroën Combo, in the lane next to them. They were at a red traffic light and when it changed to amber the van moved off. Jackson wasn't thinking anything much at the time except for 'you don't see many pink vans', but a semi-conscious part of his brain read the words emblazoned on the side panel of the van in black lettering – 'Favours – We Do What You Want Us To Do!' and another semi-conscious part of his brain dredged up the little pink card that had been in the dead girl's bra yesterday.

The two semi-conscious parts of Jackson's brain finally communicated with each other. This was a slower process than it used to be – Jackson imagined signal flags rather than high-speed broadband. One day, he supposed, the different parts of his brain would find they were unable to interpret the messages. Flags waving helplessly in the wind. And that would be it. Senility.

Jackson sprinted down the stairs, past the huddled masses in steerage, and asked the driver to open the

312

doors. The pink van was further up Princes Street now. Jackson could have kept up with it at a jog but sooner or later it was going to untangle itself from the traffic and then he would lose it. He dashed across the street, in front of a hooting bus bearing down on him (buses had somehow become the bane of his life), and at the taxi rank on Hanover Street threw himself into the back of a black cab. 'Where to?' the driver asked and Jackson felt absurdly pleased with himself that he was able to say, 'See that pink van? Follow it.'

They weaved their way through the leafy pleasantness of suburban Edinburgh. ('Morningside,' the cab driver said.) No mean streets these, Jackson thought. The black cab felt lumbering and obvious, hardly the ideal vehicle for covert activity. Still, the driver of the pink van didn't seem to notice, perhaps the black cab was so obvious that you couldn't see it. He supposed he should phone it in. He had Louise Monroe's card with her station number on it. The phone was answered by some kind of minion who said 'Inspector Monroe' was 'out of the office' and did he want to leave a message? He didn't, thank you. He redialled the number (in his experience, a phone was hardly ever answered twice in a row by the same person) and had Louise Monroe's out-of-the-office status reiterated. He asked for her mobile number and was refused. If she had really wanted him to keep in touch she should have given it to him, shouldn't she? No one could say he hadn't tried. It wasn't his fault if he had gone rogue, the renegade old lone wolf. Solving crimes.

The Combo drew to a halt and Jackson said to the

cab driver, 'Keep on going, round the corner,' where he paid and got out of the cab and then walked nonchalantly back round the corner.

'We Do What You Want Us To Do!' A Julia-like exclamation mark. Jackson wondered if that was strictly true. Could they, for example, turn *Looking for the Equator in Greenland* into a good play? Heal the sick and make the lame to walk? Find his dead woman in the Forth?

'It's a slogan,' the mean-faced woman unloading buckets and mops from the van on to the pavement said. She had an embroidered badge on the pocket of her pink uniform that said 'Housekeeper', an appellation that Jackson found vaguely menacing. The Mafia were supposed to call contract killers 'cleaners', weren't they? (But probably only in the fiction he occasionally read.) What would that make a 'housekeeper'? A kind of *über*-killer?

'Favours,' Jackson said pleasantly, 'that's a nice name.'

'It's a cleaning agency,' the mean-faced woman said, without looking at him.

'I wondered,' Jackson said, 'if you had the address for your office, I haven't been able to find it anywhere.'

She looked at him suspiciously. 'Why would you want it?'

'Oh, you know,' Jackson said, 'just to go in and have a chat, about getting the cleaners in.' It sounded even more like Mob-speak when you put it like that.

'Everything is done on the phone,' the housekeeper said. She looked as if she breakfasted on lemons,

314

'thrawn-faced' his father would have called her, but she had an accent as soft as Scotch mist.

'Everything on the phone?' Jackson said. 'How do you get new business?'

'Word of mouth. Personal recommendations.'

A sallow young woman, built like a peasant and radiating hostility, came out of the nearest house and without a word picked up the buckets and mops and carried them inside.

'I'll be back to pick you up in two hours,' the house-keeper shouted after her and then she got into the van and drove off without giving Jackson a second look.

Jackson loped off in the opposite direction, trying to appear insouciant in case the housekeeper was watching him in her rear-view mirror. When the pink van was out of sight he doubled back and entered the house through the front door. He could hear the sound of running water in the kitchen and someone clattering about upstairs. The noise of an aggressively wielded vacuum cleaner came from the back of the house so Jackson reckoned there were at least three women in there. They might not all be women, of course. Don't make sexist assumptions, they always got you into trouble. With women, anyway.

He decided to target the one in the kitchen. Slow down, Jackson, he said to himself, you're not in a potential threat situation here. Army-speak. The army felt so long ago now and yet it remained like a pattern in him. Sometimes he wondered what would have happened to him if his father had let him go down the pit instead of joining up. Every aspect of his life would have been different, he himself would have been a different man. He would be on the scrap heap now, of course, redundant, unwanted. But wasn't that what he was now anyway?

In 1995, he remembered the year, remembered the moment, he had been at home in Cambridge, when his wife was still his wife, not an ex, and he was a policeman and she was hugely pregnant with Marlee (Jackson imagined their baby tightly packed like the heart of a cabbage inside his wife) and Jackson was washing up after dinner (when he still called it 'tea', before his language was buffed into something more middle class and southern by his wife). They ate early at the end of her pregnancy, any later and she said she was too full to sleep, so while he washed the pots he listened to the *Six O'Clock News* on Radio 4 and somewhere in the middle of that night's bulletin they announced the closure of the pit his father had worked in all his life. Jackson couldn't remember why that pit had made the news when so many had closed by then with so little fuss – perhaps because it had been one of the largest coalfields in the area, perhaps because it was the last working mine in the region, but whatever, he had stood with a soapy plate in his hand and listened to the newsreader and without any warning the tears had started. He wasn't even sure why – for everything that had gone, he supposed. For the path he hadn't taken, for a world he'd never lived in. 'Why are you crying?' Josie asked, lumbering into the kitchen – she could hardly get through the door by that stage. That was when she cared about every emotion he experienced. 'Fucking Thatcher,' he said, shrugging it off in a masculine way, making it political not personal, although in this case there was no difference.

And then they got a baby and a dishwasher and Jackson continued on and didn't think again for a long time about the path he hadn't chosen, a way of life that had never been and yet that didn't stop him aching for it in some confused place in his soul.

His target maid was at the sink too, wringing out a cloth and vigorously wiping the draining board back and forth, back and forth. No crucifixion ears as far as he could see, although she had her back to him and was singing along to the radio in a foreign accent. There was so much background noise in the house that Jackson was unsure how to proceed without startling her. He was struck by three things, one – she wasn't the peasanty one that the housekeeper had barked at, and two – she had a great behind, made greater by the tight skirt of the pink uniform. *Two hard-boiled eggs in a handkerchief*, his brother used to say. His brother had been a connoisseur of women. One day, one day too soon, men would look at his daughter in the same way. And if he saw them looking at her like that he would beat ten kinds of crap out of them.

Jackson had spent half his life in uniform without thinking much about it beyond that it made getting up in the morning easier when you didn't have to make a choice about what to wear, so the effect a woman in uniform could have always struck him as curious. Not all uniforms obviously, not Nazis, dinner ladies, traffic wardens. He tried to recall if he had ever seen Julia in a uniform. Offhand he couldn't really think of one that would suit her, she wasn't really a uniform kind of girl. Louise Monroe's black-suit, white-shirt combo was a kind of uniform. She had a little pulse that beat in her throat. It made her look more vulnerable than she probably was.

He never really got the third thought to the front of his brain because the woman in this particular uniform caught sight of him at that moment and reached into the dishwasher, plucked a big dinner plate from the rack and in one smooth action sliced it through the air as if it was a frisbee, aiming straight for his head. Jackson ducked and the plate crashed through the open kitchen doorway into the hall. He put his hands in the air before she reached for another plate. 'You don't take any prisoners, do you?' he said.

'University discus champion,' she said, without any apparent remorse for having nearly decapitated him. 'Why are you creeping?'

'I'm not creeping, I was looking for someone to clean my flat,' Jackson said, trying to sound like a helpless male ('Shouldn't be too hard,' he heard Josie's voice say in his head). 'I saw the van and . . .'

'We're not called cleaners. We're called maids.' She relented a little. 'I'm sorry, I'm nervous.' She sat down at the table and pushed her hands through her hair, hands that were red and raw with some kind of dermatitis. She said, 'This morning, Sophia, a maid, a friend, found a man who was murdered in a house we go to. Was terrible,' the foreign girl said mournfully.

'I'm sure it was,' Jackson said.

'We're not paid enough for that.'

Money. Always a good starting point, in Jackson's

experience. He removed five twenty-pound notes from his wallet and placed them on the table. 'What's your name?' he said to the girl.

'Marijut.'

'OK, Marijut,' Jackson said, flicking the switch on the electric kettle. 'How about a nice cup of tea?'

'A young woman,' Jackson repeated patiently, 'I want to know if she's on your books.' There was a listless air in the offices of Favours. The girl in charge, who appeared to be the only person in the building, spoke a poor kind of English and seemed to want wilfully to misunderstand everything Jackson said to her. He automatically converted to a kind of simplistic pidgin because deep in his atavistic native soul he believed that foreigners couldn't be fluent in English, whereas, of course, it was the English who were incapable of speaking foreign languages. 'Ears? Crosses?' he said loudly.

The office was in a neglected cobbled close off the High Street. The soot had long since been blasted off the face of Edinburgh but the stonework in this place was still encrusted with the black reminder of the capital's reeking past. It was a cold, unloved place, strangely untouched by the hand of either the Enlightenment or the property developer.

Favours was squeezed in between a restaurant (a self-styled 'bistro') and Fringe Venue 87. Jackson peered into the dim and meaty interior of the bistro where the last few lunch customers still lingered. He made a mental note never to eat there. From the outside, the Fringe venue looked like a sauna but it proved to be housing a disgruntled group of American high-school children playing *The Caucasian Chalk Circle* to an audience of two men who looked as if they might also have mistaken the venue for a sauna. Julia had warned him about Edinburgh 'saunas'. *Don't for one minute imagine that they are actually saunas, Jackson.*

The office had an unremarkable black-painted street door on whose jamb was fixed a cheap plastic name-plate that read 'Favours – Import and Export'. No exclamatory promise to fulfil his desires, he noticed. 'Import and export', if ever there was a phrase that covered a multitude of sins it was that. There was a security camera above the buzzer so that it was im-possible to stand at the door without being scrutinized. He put on his most trustworthy face and got in by posing as a courier. No one ever seemed to ask couriers for their ID.

He had to go up a stair and along a corridor that was stacked with industrial-sized containers of cleaning fluids. 'Hazardous materials', one of them said. Another sported a black skull-and-crossbones but the writing on the container was in a language that Jackson didn't recognize. He thought about Marijut, wringing the cloth out, cleaning the draining board with her washerwoman hands. If nothing else, he could report Favours to Environmental Health. Another wall of boxes, all stencilled with one mysterious word, 'Matryoshka'.

Perhaps Favours were some kind of crime cartel that was running everything in the city. And what was it with the crucifixes? A Vatican-run crime cartel?

'This woman had crucifixes in her ears,' Jackson said to the receptionist. 'Crosses.' He took a pen from her desk and drew a crucifix on a pad of paper and pointed at his ears. 'Earrings,' he said, 'like yours,' he pointed towards the silver hoops in the receptionist's ears. She looked at him as if he was mad. Marijut had told him that she didn't recall seeing any girl with crucifix earrings. His description, 'Five-six, hundred and twenty pounds, blond hair,' could easily have fitted half the girls she knew. 'Me, for example,' she said. Or the receptionist.

Jackson tapped the computer monitor and said, 'Let's look in here.' The girl gave him a surly glare and then scrolled idly down the screen.

'What do you want her for?' she asked.

'I don't want her *for* anything. I want to know if she's on your books.' Jackson craned his neck to catch a glimpse of the screen. The girl opened a file that looked like a CV; there was a thumbnail photograph in the top left-hand corner, but she closed it down immediately. 'Stop,' he said. 'Go back, go back to that last one.' It was her, he could swear it was her. His dead girl.

'She doesn't work for us any more,' the receptionist said. She gave a little hiccup of laughter as if she was making a joke, 'Her contract is terminated.' She clicked the files shut with an air of finality and turned off the screen.

'This woman I'm looking for,' he enunciated each word slowly and clearly, 'this woman is dead.' Jackson made a slashing movement across his throat. The girl shrank away from him. He wasn't very good at miming. He could have done with Julia, no one played Charades with as much enthusiasm as Julia, except perhaps for Marlee. How *did* you portray dead? He crossed his arms over his chest and closed his eyes. When he opened them, 'the Housekeeper' was standing in front of him, regarding him quizzically.

'He says he's courier,' the girl at the computer said sarcastically.

'Does he?' the Housekeeper said.

'I'm looking for someone,' Jackson said stoutly, 'a girl who's gone missing.'

'What's her name?' the Housekeeper asked.

'I don't know.'

'You're looking for someone and you don't know who she is?'

'I can give you someone else,' the girl at the computer screen offered.

'I don't want someone else,' Jackson said. 'What kind of agency *are* you?'

The girl leaned closer to him over the desk and, giving Jackson a predatory kind of smile, said, 'What kind of agency would you like us to be?'

29

'NO ROOM AT THE INN,' THE POLICEWOMAN ASSIGNED TO look after Martin said. They were sitting in a car outside the police mortuary, waiting while a civilian on the radio back at headquarters tried to find him somewhere to stay for the night. He couldn't sleep amongst the aftermath of the carnage in his 'active crime-scene' house, wouldn't have wanted to if he could. 'You don't have any friends you could stay the night with?' the policewoman said. No, he didn't. She gave him a sympathetic look. There was his brother in the Borders, of course, but little in the way of sanctuary was to be had in his household and he doubted he would be welcome anyway.

'Clare' ('PC Clare Deponio') looked like one of the policewomen who had come to Paul Bradley's aid yesterday, but they all looked alike in their uniforms. The police car was parked almost exactly where the Honda and the Peugeot had faced off against each other yesterday. Who would have thought that event would have faded into such insignificance?

'The Festival,' Clare said, coming off the radio, 'no hotel rooms anywhere apparently.'

Superintendent Campbell had handed Martin over to someone only slightly more menial ('Detective Chief Inspector Colin Sutherland'). He took ('accompanied') Martin from his own house to a police station where Martin had his fingerprints taken – it was exactly like the Society of Authors' tour. The inspector said it was 'for comparison', but after that it stopped being like the Society of Authors' tour because they gave him a white paper boiler suit to wear and took all his clothes away while they put him in an interview room and questioned him for a long time about his relationship with Richard Moat and his whereabouts at the time of Richard's death. Martin felt like a convict. He was given tea and biscuits – Rich Tea, to denote his change in status. Pink wafers and chocolate bourbons for the innocent members of the Society of Authors, plain Rich Tea for people who spent drugged nights in dodgy hotel rooms with men. (*So you and Mr Bradley slept together? In the same bed?*) He still hadn't mentioned the gun. Inspector Sutherland enjoyed pretending to be baffled. 'I'm having trouble getting my head round this, Mr Canning – you saved a stranger's life, you spent the night with him but he disappeared before dawn. Meanwhile, in your own house, your friend was being bludgeoned to death.'

Paul Bradley had an address in London, Martin remembered the nurse in A and E copying it down, the same address that he had watched him write in the hotel register.

'The Met are looking into it for us,' Sutherland said.

324

Sutherland reminded Martin of someone but he couldn't think who. He had this unsettling way of smiling at inappropriate moments, so that Martin, who tended to smile when he was smiled at, found himself responding with an inane grin to statements like *Mr Moat's skull was shattered by a blunt instrument.*

A female detective sergeant sat next to Sutherland. She was silent throughout, like a mute. There was a mirror on the wall and Martin wondered if it was two-way. He couldn't think why else you would have a mirror in an interview room. Was someone in the looking-glass world watching him dunk his convict-grade biscuit into his tea?

'He did exist,' Martin said.

'No one's doubting his *existence*, Mr Canning,' Sutherland said, like a pedantic philosopher. Martin missed Superintendent Campbell's amiable 'Martin', as if they were old acquaintances. 'He was involved in a road-rage incident,' Sutherland continued. He smiled and paused rather pointedly before saying, 'the same one you claim you yourself were involved in.'

'I was,' Martin said. 'I made a statement.'

'The incident was logged just after midday yesterday, the victim – your Paul Bradley – was treated at the Royal Infirmary for a minor head injury, he signed the register of the Four Clans. Hundreds of people saw him during the course of yesterday, his existence is not in doubt. The problem is . . .' Another well-timed pause for a smile. It stretched the edges of his face, the Cheshire Cat would have struggled in a contest with Chief Inspector Sutherland. 'The problem, Mr Canning, is that no one remembers *you*.'

'The police took a statement from me in the hospital.'

'But after that?'

'I was with Paul Bradley.'

There was a knock on the door and a constable came in and put a piece of paper on the desk in front of the silent sergeant. She read what was on the paper, her sphinx-like features revealing nothing, and then passed the paper over to Sutherland.

'The mysterious Mr Bradley,' Sutherland murmured.

'He's real,' Martin protested. 'His name's in the hotel register.'

'Yours isn't, though, is it?' He waved the piece of paper at Martin. 'We asked the Met to check the address that Paul Bradley gave and it turns out it's a row of lock-ups. The mysterious Mr Bradley doesn't seem to exist after all.'

The previously silent female detective leaned forward suddenly and said to Martin, earnestly, as if she wanted to help him, as if she was a therapist or a counsellor, 'Were you and Richard Moat lovers, Martin? Did you have a tiff?'

'A tiff?'

'An argument that got out of hand, escalated into violence? Was he jealous that you had gone to a hotel with another man?'

'It wasn't like that. It was *nothing* like that!' He removed his spectacles and rubbed his eyes. He wished people would stop asking him questions.

'Or, let me run this by you,' Inspector Sutherland

suggested amiably, 'you were involved in a gay lovers' threesome that went horribly wrong.'

Richard Moat's parents had travelled up from Milton Keynes to identify their son. Richard had a whole repertoire of jokes in his routine about his parents, about their politics, their religion, their bad taste. None of the things he said about them on stage seemed pertinent to the heartbroken, bewildered couple grieving in the police mortuary. The identity of the corpse had become a vexed issue for the police. Reluctant to expose the Moats to the full horror of what had happened to their son, they had muddled matters more by showing them the flatlined Rolex that Richard had taken from Martin. They had cried with relief because it 'definitely wasn't Richard's'.

They showed the watch to Martin and he said yes, it belonged to him (there was a crack across the glass, he tried to imagine how that might have happened), and Mr Moat shouted, 'There you are, you see!' pointing at Martin as if this was proof that he was the dead man, rather than their son. Richard Moat seemed to have appropriated everything that belonged to Martin, including his identity.

'We could wait for dental records,' the relentlessly polite Sutherland murmured to Martin, 'but that would take some time and the whole thing has become so . . . *confused*.' Martin knew he was being asked to step up and didn't really see how he could not. *Be a man.* Do as you would unto others. The meek shall inherit the earth. He wanted Sutherland to think well of him, so after a considerable briefing – *You have to prepare yourself for a shock* and *the injuries are very unpleasant* – he was taken into the small room that smelt not only of antiseptic but also of something sweet and unpleasant and there, beneath a white sheet, were the battered remains of Richard Moat. Neither better nor worse than he had imagined. Simply different, and in some way artificial, as if Richard Moat had been made up for a film – Martin thought of Michael Jackson's *Thriller* video – but it was definitely Richard. There was no doubt at all about that. Martin waited to be overcome by the horror of it, wondered if he would faint or vomit, but none of these things happened; he just found himself feeling grateful that it was Richard Moat lying there and not him. Worse things had, after all, happened to him than viewing Richard Moat's corpse.

'There but for fortune,' Sutherland said.

'I don't understand,' Martin puzzled, 'who identified me as Richard Moat? Who identified Richard Moat as me?' It depended on which way you looked at it, he supposed.

'I believe it was your brother, Mr Canning,' Sutherland said.

'My *brother*?' His own brother had mistakenly identified him? Somehow that said everything about what was wrong with their relationship.

Sutherland tapped his wrist. Martin wondered if it was a Masonic gesture of some kind but he said, 'The watch, we showed him your watch, Martin. It was an informal ID, we would have got to the truth eventually.'

'I'd better phone him,' Martin said.

'Probably.'

*　*　*

It had proved to be an odd kind of conversation ('I'm
not dead, Chris, the police made a mistake') and
hadn't gone well. Christopher was still driving home.
'I'm just passing Haddington,' he said as if his
geographical location was relevant. 'Wait a minute,
I'm not on the hands-free.' This was followed by the
noise of fumbling, a curse that seemed to indicate the
phone had been dropped, scrabbling, and finally,
'Wouldn't want to get pulled up by a fucking policeman.' Martin wondered if Sutherland, sitting across a
desk from him, heard this slur.

Christopher proceeded to run through a range of
emotions – disbelief, shock, disappointment and
finally an irritable 'For fuck's sake, Martin,' as if
Martin had committed some kind of deranged
prank. Martin supposed his brother had spent the previous couple of hours of bereavement getting used to
the idea of being in possession of Martin's copyright
for the next seventy years, to say nothing of the
Merchiston house.

Thank goodness they hadn't phoned his mother
down in Eastbourne. He tried to imagine how his
mother would have responded to the news of
his death. He expected she would have been
underwhelmed.

The anonymous civilian came back on the phone and
Clare rolled her eyes at the news that they were still
having trouble finding him a room for the night.

'You would think,' she said, a sentence that
apparently didn't need completing.

Martin sighed and said, 'I think I know a place that will have vacancies.'

'It's all been a bit of a cock-up, hasn't it?' Clare said cheerfully to Martin. 'It made the papers, you know. Your death.'

'My death,' Martin echoed. His death had been pronounced. A murder is announced. It was like a witch doctor laying a curse on him, dooming him to invisibility or death. Isn't that what happened? The witch doctor told you that you were going to die and so you did, by the power of suggestion rather than any actual ability on his part to hex, but the means were moot when the result was certain.

Martin asked Clare to stop at a newsagent's on George Street. One good thing about being in a police car, perhaps the only good thing, was the fact that they could stop anywhere they wanted. '*Local Writer Murdered*,' he read out to her from the *Evening News* as he climbed back into the car. 'The reports of my death have been greatly exaggerated,' he added.

'Well, yes,' she said, puzzled, 'because you're not actually dead, are you?'

'No, I'm not,' he agreed. There was a photograph beneath the headline. It looked like some kind of poor-quality holiday snap that Martin couldn't recollect ever seeing before and he wondered where on earth they had got it from.

The traffic forced them to a halt outside the Assembly Rooms, where a poster announcing a gala benefit for Amnesty still displayed Richard Moat's name, in smallish print near the bottom of the bill.

Clare took the opportunity to scan the newspaper, 'You're quite famous,' she said, sounding surprised. '*Alex Blake, whose real name was Martin Canning, trained for the priesthood before becoming a religious studies teacher*,' Clare continued, '*. . . turned his hand to writing late in life.*'

'I was never a priest,' Martin said, 'that's misinformation. And forty-two,' Martin said, 'I hardly think that's late in life, do you?'

She said nothing, merely smiled in that sympathetic way again. He wondered how old she was; she looked about twelve.

He opened a packet of Minstrels he'd bought in the newsagent's and tipped some into her palm. 'What kind of books do you write then?' she asked.

'Novels.'

'What kind of novels?'

'Crime novels,' Martin said.

'Really? That's ironic, isn't it? Fiction stranger than truth and all that.' They set off again, ploughing through the clotted traffic as far as the next zebra crossing, where a seemingly endless line of people trailed in front of them. 'They go slow on purpose,' Clare said, 'gives them a false sense of power, but at the end of the day, they're on foot and I'm in a car.

'*The author of seven novels based on private detective Nina Riley*,' she continued to read relentlessly. 'It's good you have a woman heroine,' she said. 'Is she a real kick-ass?'

Martin pondered the question. He liked the idea of Nina Riley being kick-ass, it elevated her out of the tweed and pearls post-war world into something more dynamic. She knew how to fly a plane and climb mountains, she had driven a racing car, she could fence, although the opportunities for swordplay were few and far between, even in the Forties. *The blighter's getting away, Bertie. I need a weapon – throw me that hockey stick!* 'Well, in her own way, yes, I suppose she is.'

'So do you make a living from it?' Clare asked.

'Yes, better than most people. I'm lucky. Do you read much?' he added, in an attempt to steer the conversation away from himself.

'No time.' She laughed. Martin couldn't imagine a world where there was no time to read.

'His agent, Melanie Lenehan – wow, there's a tongue-twister – *was quoted as saying, "This is a tragedy in every sense of the word. Martin was just beginning to enjoy the fruits of his phenomenal success. He was writing at the top of his game."'* Martin felt a pang of disappointment that Melanie had not bothered to come up with anything better than platitudes. Or perhaps that's what she believed he merited.

Clare accompanied him into the Four Clans and rang the brass bell on the counter. The thing about the police, Martin was beginning to notice, was that they behaved like people who didn't need to ask permission, because, of course, they didn't. Paul Bradley had possessed the same authority. It was something natural and unstrained; these people didn't spend their lives being apologetic.

A woman appeared reluctantly from the room at the

back of the reception. She wiped a crumb from the corner of her mouth and gave them both an unfriendly stare. She had a bulky figure and her ill-fitting grey suit and severe hairstyle, not to mention her demeanour, reminded Martin of a prison governor (or rather his *idea* of a prison governor, never having met one in real life. Not yet anyway.). She was wearing a badge that said 'Maureen' but she looked too formidable to be addressed with such intimacy. Through in the back room he caught a glimpse of a table on which was a well-thumbed copy of the *Evening News* and a plate containing a half-eaten toasted sandwich. Even from where he was standing Martin could see the blaring headline, 'Local Writer Murdered', and make out his own grainy features in the photograph.

'Maureen' checked him in, unfazed by the fact that he was accompanied by a police officer. No mention was made of how he was going to pay the bill. He was handed the key to his room as if he was a prisoner who was allowed to lock himself in his own cell.

'Right, I'll be off now then,' Clare said. 'Good luck, with the writing and . . . everything.'

On his weary way up the stairs Martin caught the eye of the stag. It regarded him mutely, an expression of moody indifference on its mouldy features.

30

'MURDERED, JACKSON!' JULIA SAID, HER FACE A PANTOMIME of round-eyed horror but she couldn't keep the excitement out of her voice.

'Murdered?' Jackson echoed.

'I was eating lunch with Richard Moat yesterday and today he's dead. Caught the umpire's eye and Bob's your uncle – gone.' She pronounced 'gone' as 'gawn' in a Dick Van Dyke kind of cockney. She seemed positively euphoric compared with this morning. 'The police have been round interviewing everyone. *Murdered*, Jackson,' she said again, relishing the word. They were standing at the door of the sweat-box that passed for a female dressing room in Julia's venue and into which actresses from another play were also crammed, most of them in their underwear. Jackson tried not to look. He felt as if he was backstage at a strip show, albeit a rather highbrow one where people said, 'I can't believe it, he was in my light *the whole show* yesterday.' Julia herself had changed out of her sackcloth and ashes costume but was still dithering, unwilling to leave the world of performance behind. Of course, for Julia every day was a performance.

'You said you had a drink with him,' Jackson said, 'you didn't say you *ate*.'

'Does it matter?' Julia frowned.

'Well, not *now*,' Jackson said.

'What do you mean, "not *now*"? Would it have mattered if he was still alive?' Julia's husky voice rose to a more theatrical pitch. She could have played to the whole of the Albert Hall without amplification if she'd wanted to. 'I had a cheese roll, he had pasta, it was hardly *cunnilingus*.'

The underwear-clad actresses all turned to stare at them. '*Please*,' Jackson hissed. When had everything between them become so jagged? Had Richard Moat paid for lunch? No such thing as a free lunch, except for the biggest fish.

'And how are you feeling, Julia?' Julia said. 'How did your preview go?'

'Sorry,' Jackson said. 'How did your preview go?'

'I don't want to talk about it.'

'Another preview? Tonight?' Jackson said.

'Well, God knows we need one,' Julia said, drawing hard on a cigarette and then breaking out into a fit of filthy coughing. They were standing in the street outside the venue. Just over twenty-four hours ago Jackson had witnessed Honda Man trying to kill Peugeot Guy on this very spot.

'I told you this morning,' Julia said vaguely when her scarred lungs had recovered from the coughing bout.

'I didn't see you this morning,' Jackson said.

'You don't listen,' Julia said. What a strangely wifely thing for her to say.

'I didn't not *listen*,' Jackson said, 'I didn't *see* you. I was in jail.'

'But you're coming to the preview? You don't have other plans?'

He sighed. 'No, I don't have other plans. What about now? We could have a drink. Afternoon tea?' Surely she would respond to those two words.

'It's much too late for afternoon tea,' Julia said crossly. Her left eyelid twitched and she took another long, desperate drag on her cigarette. 'And Tobias is about to give us notes.'

'You always have notes,' Jackson grumbled.

'Well, thank goodness for that,' Julia snapped, 'because we certainly need as much help as we can get.' She ground out the cigarette beneath the sole of her boot. She was wearing black lace-up boots with a high heel that made Jackson have unchaste thoughts about Victorian governesses.

'I'm sorry,' she said, suddenly contrite, pressing herself against him. He felt her body slacken, as if her strings had just been cut, and he rested his chin on the top of her head. She was taller than usual because of the boots. They both kept their arms by their sides, just leaning against each other like two unbalanced people trying to hold each other up. He smelt her perfume, something spicy like cinnamon that she hadn't worn before. He noticed for the first time that her earrings were tiny porcelain pansies. He didn't think he'd seen them before either. Her hair was mad as usual, you really could imagine birds nesting in it. He wouldn't have been surprised if one evening a flock of rooks returned to roost there. ('Wouldn't that be wonderful?' Julia said.) A chopstick that, in a victory of creativity over physics, seemed to be holding the whole edifice in place nearly poked Jackson's eye out.

There was a poster on the wall behind them for *Looking for the Equator in Greenland*. It showed Julia reaching out to the audience in a manner that Julia said was supposed to be beseeching but to Jackson looked whimsical. The faces of the other cast members were stacked in a kind of pyramid around her, in a way that was, unfortunately, reminiscent of Queen in the video for 'Bohemian Rhapsody'. It was pasted next to one for Richard Moat's *Comic Viagra for the Mind*. Someone had taken a felt-tipped pen and scrawled 'Cancelled' across his face.

She stepped away from him and said, 'The preview should be finished about nine, although we ran over this afternoon. We'll probably go for something to eat, then for a drink. Come and join us, help us lick our wounds.' He wished she was in a good play, one the critics would rave about, one that might end up transferring to the West End.

He had a sudden, horrible thought. 'Your sister's not coming up for your first night, is she?'

'Amelia?'

It was odd the way she said that, as if there was a choice of sisters, as if Olivia and Sylvia were still alive. Maybe they *were* still alive for Julia.

'Yes, Amelia.'

'No. I told her to come later, when the play's run in

a bit. She won't like it anyway, it's not her kind of thing. She likes Shakespeare, Ibsen, Chekhov. I thought she could come up and stay for a few days. That would be nice, wouldn't it?'

'Hold me back.'

'Don't be like that, Jackson. Amelia's all I've got.'

Jackson refrained from saying the obvious, *You've got me*, in case it provoked more arguments.

'Oh, I nearly forgot,' Julia said, suddenly animated (when had her moods started changing so quickly?). She reached into her big carpet bag, pulling out an assortment of God knows what before finding what she was looking for. 'Free tickets!' she said with an enforced gaiety. When Jackson made no attempt to take them she pushed them into his hand.

'Who did you have lunch with to get those?' he said. Why couldn't he keep his mouth shut? He'd meant it to come out as a joke (not a good one, admittedly) but it ended up sounding offensive. Julia just laughed though and said, 'Oh, sweetie, I had to fuck two clowns and an elephant to get those tickets. The *circus*, Jackson, they're tickets for the circus, they were handing them out for free, drumming up trade, the circus wallah chappie gave them to me. It'll be good sport. Go. Relive the childhood you never had.'

'A lime daiquiri and a Glenfiddich, please,' Jackson said to the barman. It was a nice old-fashioned pub, no music or games machines, lots of polished wood and stained glass. He wasn't a whisky drinker by nature yet he seemed to have drunk a lot of the stuff since arriving. It must have been in his Scottish blood all this time, calling to him.

'And yet you've never visited Scotland before?' Louise Monroe said. 'That's odd, don't you think? Do you think you're avoiding something? Psychologically speaking?' No small talk then, Jackson thought, none of that getting to know you stuff, pussyfooting around each other's past, *I was in France on holiday/ Oh, what part?* or *You like country music? What a coincidence, so do I.* Cutting straight to the chase instead – *Are you psychologically damaged? Are you in avoidance about something?*

'I don't know,' Jackson said. 'Are you? Avoiding something?'

'Question with a question,' she said, as if he'd just failed a test. 'The psychopathology of it is interesting though, isn't it?'

'That's a big word,' Jackson said. 'Pretty *and* smart, huh?'

'You may behave like an idiot, but you're not stupid.'

Jackson wondered if that was supposed to be a compliment.

'Anyway, cheers,' she said, taking a healthy swig of her lime daiquiri.

'Confusion to kings and tyrants,' Jackson responded, raising his glass. He was under the impression that a daiquiri was the kind of drink you were supposed to sip. He avoided cocktails in case they arrived encumbered with parasols and sickly-sweet cherries on sticks but the daiquiri looked clean and inviting.

'Try it,' she said, holding the glass out to him, and he

felt shocked by the sudden intimacy of the offer. He had been brought up in a parsimonious household where they tended to steal food off each other's plates, not offer it up willingly. He could still see his brother, Francis, winking at him while he filched a sausage off his sister – and getting a box on the ear from Niamh for his efforts. Julia, on the other hand, would share with a dog, she was forever pushing forks and spoons into his mouth, *try this, eat this*, licking her lips, sucking her fingers, he'd never met anyone for whom the line between food and sex was so thin. The things she could do with a strawberry were enough to make a grown man blush. He had a sudden image of her in the Nell Gwyn costume, volunteering her breasts to the photographer, oranges are the only fruit. He had seen that on television, Julia had read the book, that was the difference between them. She had a little gap between her front teeth that gave her the slightest of lisps. It was funny – he'd always been aware of that and yet he'd never really thought about it before.

'No, you're all right,' he said to Louise Monroe, lifting his glass to prove that he was happy with his own choice of alcohol, and she said, 'I wasn't offering to share DNA with you.'

'I didn't think you were.'

The pub was in a street off the Royal Mile, close to the offices of Favours.

'I see you found the soot-blackened, whisky-soaked, blood-sodden metaphysical core of the wen that was Edinburgh,' she said when she met him in the cobbled close.

'Right,' he said. She could be quite wordy once she got going. Like Julia. He had finally managed to get a call through to Louise Monroe and all she could say was, 'You should have phoned me before you came here. Oh no, wait a minute, you're not a policeman, are you? *You shouldn't have been here in the first place.*'

'I couldn't get hold of you, you didn't give me your mobile number.'

'Well, I'm here now and what exactly am I looking for? I see what appears to be a dodgy sauna housing a doomed production of *The Caucasian Chalk Circle*.'

'Shit,' Jackson said, staring at the entrance. There was no longer any sign saying 'Favours – Import and Export', no sign saying anything at all. No buzzer, no camera. The door was still there, Jackson was relieved to see, so he hadn't entered some parallel universe, and when Louise Monroe gave it a push it opened with the theatrical kind of creak that a sound effects man would have been proud of. They made their way up the stairs. If they had been Americans they would have had their guns out by now, Jackson thought, but as it was, being Scottish and half-Scottish, they had nothing to defend themselves with but their wits.

'First floor,' Jackson whispered.

'Why are you whispering?' Louise asked in a loud voice that echoed in the stairwell. 'I thought you said they were a cleaning agency.'

'They are,' he said. 'Sort of.'

'Sort of?'

'No, they are, definitely,' Jackson said. 'I mean I've seen them cleaning – scrubbing, hoovering, that sort of thing. They wear pink uniforms.' He had an image of Marijut's buttocks moving rhythmically and immediately dismissed it. 'It's just there's something . . . odd about them. I don't know. A lot of industrial cleaning firms take on ex-cons, you know, maybe there's a link. The girls I saw in Morningside were definitely legit cleaners. I thought I saw the dead girl's photograph on their database.'

The place was abandoned, no computer, no filing cabinet or desk. The Housekeeper and the receptionist had packed up and gone. The place felt as if it had never been occupied in the first place. The cheap contract carpeting, slightly tacky underfoot, the chipped paintwork and the unwashed windows, all bore no hint that a couple of hours previously there had been a business here. There was a smell of something stale and slightly rank.

'What database would that be then?' Louise Monroe murmured, looking around the empty space. 'The one on that invisible computer over there?'

'I don't understand,' Jackson muttered. He spotted something on the carpet, a tiny painted wooden doll, no bigger than a peanut. He picked it up and peered at it and Louise Monroe said, 'You need spectacles, you shouldn't be so vain.'

Jackson ignored the comment. 'What is that?' he asked, holding the little doll up for her inspection.

'It's from one of those Russian doll sets,' she said, 'the ones that nest inside each other. Matri-something.'

'Matryoshka?'

'Yes.'

'This one doesn't open,' Jackson said.

'That's because it's the last one. The baby.'

Jackson pocketed the doll. It was less than two hours since he was here: how could they have just packed up their tents and slipped away without leaving a trace behind? No, they had left something – he spotted something on a windowsill. A pink card. *Favours – We Do What You Want Us To Do!* He pounced on it and held it up for Louise Monroe's inspection. 'See,' he said triumphantly. 'I didn't make it up.'

'I know,' she said, producing an identical card from her pocket. 'Snap.'

'Where did you get that?'

'From the body of a dead prostitute.'

'Dead? As in murdered dead?'

'No, she OD'd. No foul play, apart from drug trafficking, prostitution, economic exploitation, illegal immigration, of course. It's not my case,' she said with a shrug as if she didn't care. Jackson was pretty sure that wasn't so.

'Two dead girls turning up within twenty-four hours of each other,' Jackson said, 'both with these cards on their bodies? What does that say to you?'

'The cards are the only thing that links them.'

'But that's enough,' Jackson persisted. 'I'll bet you the cleaning agency's a front, maybe it's a way of getting girls into the country, maybe they pick out the more vulnerable ones, take their passports, threaten people they've left behind. You *know* the kind of stuff that goes on, for Christ's sake. There's a connection between the two girls, there has to be. It leads back to this place.'

'Could just be a coincidence.'

'You're playing devil's advocate. And I don't believe in coincidence,' Jackson said. 'A coincidence is just an explanation waiting to happen.'

'So much wisdom from one so foolish and I would just like to remind you once again that you are not a policeman and this is not your case.'

'No, it's *your* case.' Frustration was beginning to get the better of him. He wished he'd slapped a pair of handcuffs on the 'Housekeeper' and secured her to the nearest heavy object. Or if he could only have anchored his dead girl to a buoy or clamped the pink van this afternoon, taken Marijut into custody, anything that would have provided immovable evidence rather than this shifting mirage. He felt as if he was trying to hold on to water. 'If you believed me it would help,' he said, sounding more pathetic than he'd intended.

He thought she might get stroppy with him (yet again) but she walked over to one of the filthy windows and gazed out at the view – a stone wall opposite. Then she sighed and said, 'Well, the sun's over the yardarm and I'm off the clock. And I want a drink.'

'You like *country* music?' Louise Monroe said doubtfully. 'Good-hearted women and bad-living men and all that stuff?'

'Well, it's not all like that.'

'And you live in France?' This was more like an interrogation than a conversation. He thought he preferred it when she was casting doubts on his 'psychopathology' and calling him an idiot.

'I've never been to France,' Louise said.

'Not even Paris?'

'No, not even Paris.'

'Not even Disneyland?'

'Christ, I haven't been to France. OK?'

'OK. Do you want another one?' he asked.

'No thanks, I'm driving. I shouldn't be drinking at all.'

'And yet you are.' Their conversation had been restricted to an almost masculine neutrality, although Jackson admitted to a divorce and she shrugged and said, 'Never married, never saw the point.' He had learned that she liked Saabs, she had fast-tracked to inspector, 'climbing over the bodies on the way up', she wore contacts ('You should try them'). But then she suddenly said, 'Do you have someone?' and he said, 'Julia. She's an actress.' He could hear himself sounding apologetic, as if an actress was something to be embarrassed by (which it frequently was). If Louise hadn't asked, would Jackson have owned up to Julia? The sad, male answer was no. 'She's in a play at the Festival.'

'What's Julia like?'

'She's an actress.'

'You said that already.'

'I know, but it does kind of *explain* her. I don't know, she's short, she's an optimist. Usually,' he added.

'You described a dead body to me better than that,' Louise said.

'Julia's hard to explain,' he said, gazing at the dregs of his whisky as if they held the key. Julia was impossible to describe, you had to know her to understand her. 'She's like . . . herself.'

'Well, that's a good thing, isn't it?' Louise said.

'Yes, I suppose it is,' he said. And yet it didn't feel like that. That was the trouble, of course. You started off liking someone because of who they were and you ended up wanting them to be different.

He liked Louise because she was bolshy and cynical and sure of herself, but give them a few months and those would be the things that would drive him crazy. *Give them a few months*, what was he thinking?

'Well, thanks for the drink,' Louise Monroe said abruptly, standing up and putting on her jacket. 'I should go.'

He would have offered to help her with the jacket but he didn't know if she would like that. He did hold the door open for her though. His mother had instilled manners into him, mostly by cuffing him about the head. *Always hold open a door, always offer your seat. No gentleman would let a lady walk on the outside of the pavement.* She had been brought up in a backward part of Ireland where they didn't even have pavements but she didn't want her sons to grow up like their father. He'd never really understood about the outside of the pavement. (*So you can die first if a horse and carriage swerves out of control, of course*, Julia explained.)

He walked up the High Street with Louise. The further up the street they got the more revellers they encountered, plus all the usual suspects – fire-eaters, jugglers, unicyclists, or any combination of the three. A guy on a unicycle juggling with flaming torches, really pushing the envelope. There was a woman pretending to be some kind of living statue of

Marie-Antoinette. Was that really a suitable job for a woman? For anyone, come to that? How would he feel if Marlee grew up and announced she wanted to do that for a living?

'Oh, I don't know,' Louise Monroe said, 'doing absolutely nothing all day, I could do with some of that.'

'It's not all it's cracked up to be, trust me.'

They hesitated awkwardly on the pavement at a crossroads for a few seconds as if they were both unsure of the correct form of farewell address. For a delusional moment Jackson thought she was going to kiss him on the cheek; one half of him hoped she would, the other half was terrified she would, good and bad Jacksons having a little tussle. But she just said, 'Right. I'll let you know if anything turns up.'

'Anything?'

'Your girl.'

'His' dead girl, he ruminated. She *was* his girl, for better or worse, no one else wanted to own her or claim her or even acknowledge her existence.

'Well, good night,' she said.

'I don't suppose you want to go to the circus, do you?'

31

MARTIN WAS IN A DIFFERENT ROOM IN THE FOUR CLANS. HE was lying on the bed, trying to have a nap. His body was exhausted but his brain had apparently discovered a secret amphetamine factory and was popping pills at will. The picture on the wall opposite his bed was a print of Burke and Hare caught in the act of gleefully digging up a dead body, almost, but not quite, trumping the flaming witch of the previous room. He sat up and twisted round in order to see what was hanging above the bed. The Battle of Flodden Field, the slaughter of the Scots in full swing. Twenty-four hours ago he didn't even know the Four Clans existed, now his entire life seemed contained within its tartan walls. He was being brainwashed by plaid.

He turned the television on and caught an evening bulletin of Scottish news. *The comic Richard Moat . . . battered to death . . . home of crime writer Alex Blake . . . earlier in an extraordinary mix-up . . . reclusive writer Alex Blake whose real name was . . . a spokesman for Lothian and Borders Police said that they are appealing for witnesses to the murder . . . the Merchiston area of Edinburgh.* He turned the television off.

He didn't have any books with him, or his laptop, of course, so he could neither read nor write. Martin hadn't realized how much of his life was taken up by these two activities. How would he manage if he became blind? At least if he was blind he could get a guide dog – there was an upside to everything, a silver lining of helpful Labs and noble German Shepherds eager to be his eyes. What if he became deaf? They had dogs for the deaf too, but Martin wasn't sure what they did. Tugged at your sleeve a lot probably while looking meaningfully at things.

His phone chirruped and he listened to the rich Dublin tones of his agent. 'Are you dead, Martin?' she asked. 'Or not dead? Only I wish you'd make up your mind, because I'm fielding a lot of questions here.'

'Not dead,' Martin said. 'It said on the television news that I'm a recluse. Why would they say that? I'm not reclusive, I'm not a *recluse*.'

'Well, you don't have a lot of friends, Martin.' Melanie dropped her voice as if there were other people in the room with her and said, 'Did you kill him, Martin? Did you kill Richard Moat? I know we always say that no publicity is bad publicity but murder's a line you can't really cross. You know what I'm saying?'

'Why on earth would I kill Richard Moat? What would make you think that?'

'Where were you when he died?' Melanie asked.

'In a hotel,' Martin said.

'With a woman?' she said, sounding surprised.

'No, with a man.' Whichever way he said it, it wasn't going to sound right. He couldn't imagine what she would say if he told her about the gun. The gun had become a guilty secret he was carrying around with him. He should just have told the police, brazened out their incredulity, but spending the night with an armed assassin didn't seem like a very good alibi.

'Jesus,' Melanie said, 'do you have a lawyer, Martin?' She let pass what she obviously thought was a decent interval and then said, 'How's the book going anyway?'

Did she honestly think he was writing while all this was going on? Someone, someone he knew, had been murdered in his house. There were lumps of *brain matter* on his coffee table.

'An antidote,' she said, 'art can be an antidote to life.'

Nina Riley was hardly art. *This is pretty spiffing, Bertie, we should think about taking a cruise more often. Now all we have to do is prove that our cat burglar is Maud Elphinstone and that the name on her birth certificate is Malcolm Elphinstone.* It was, let's face it, crap. 'Are you still there, Martin? You know you've got the Book Festival tomorrow, so you have. Do you want me to come up and give you moral support?'

'No, I don't. I'm going to cancel.'

'There'll be a lot of interest.'

'That's why I'm cancelling.' He put the phone down and returned to staring at the ceiling.

*   *   *

Martin was running on empty, he had eaten nothing since yesterday apart from the packet of Minstrels he had shared with Clare in the police car. He had spent a large part of the day feeling nauseous for one reason or another – the lurid hangover of earlier this morning, the blood and gore besmirching his lovely house, the sight of Richard Moat's zombie face – but now he felt suddenly ravenous. He would have liked a proper high tea – poached orange-yolked eggs on hot, buttery toast. And on the table a big china pot of tea and a cake shaped like a drum – a cherry Genoa or a frosted walnut. And his wife, quietly knitting in a corner somewhere.

He was in a different room in the Four Clans but the mini-bar was still devoid of anything edible. The sight of a can of Irn-Bru lurking in its innards made his stomach turn. He wanted to go home. He wanted to go to his house and crawl into his own bed and pull the covers over his head and make it all go away, but it would never go away because this was his punishment. And his punishment wouldn't be finished until his entire life had been dismantled and all the little pieces of it had been fed through a mangle until they were flat and no one would ever be able to put him back together again. One minute he was a fully fledged member of society and with a tick of the clock, a turn of the screw, he had become an outcast. It took only the littlest thing. The arc inscribed by the baseball bat, a bowl of bortsch and a girl unwrapping her hair.

*   *   *

A beautiful girl with blond hair wanted to meet him (*Marty*) in the Caviar Bar of the Grand Hotel Europe. He wondered if, being a foreigner, she found something attractive in his hesitant, stuttering Britishness, if instead of dullness she saw reticent charm.

He had taken the grocer to the Grand Hotel Europe for afternoon tea, but the man had made a great performance of examining the little sandwiches and cakes and saying, 'You don't get much for your money, do you?' as if he was paying, not Martin. There were a lot of girls around, very well-dressed Russian girls, and the dying grocer raised his eyebrows at Martin and nodded his head in the direction of one of them and said, 'We know what they are, don't we?' and Martin said, 'Do we?' The grocer snorted at what he saw as Martin's ignorance and made a face. 'St Petersburg brides,' he said and laughed. A flake of smoked salmon had adhered to one of his fleshy lips. Martin wondered what was the point of anything. Being with the grocer was like being with a walking, talking memento mori. 'No, really,' he said earnestly to him, 'I think they're just attractive young women, I don't think they're . . . you know.'

'Yes, but what would *you* know, Martin?' the grocer said patronizingly.

They had taken tea in the light, airy space of the café but the Caviar Bar was a darker, more sophisticated place with its stained glass and copper, Russian *style moderne*. 'We call it Art Nouveau,' he said to Irina. '*Da?*' she replied as if it was the most fascinating thing anyone had ever said to her.

Even now, a year later, he could see the red and

black pearls of caviar glistening on their little glass dishes of crushed ice. He didn't eat any; the idea of fish was bad enough, but the thought of fish eggs was repellent. Irina didn't seem to notice, she ate all of it. They drank champagne, Russian and cheap, but surprisingly good. She had ordered it without asking him and then clinked his glass and said, 'We have good time, Marty.' She had changed for the evening, her hair was pinned up and her boots had been exchanged for shoes but her dress was high-necked and modest. He wanted to ask her why she was selling souvenirs from an outdoor stall – had she fallen on hard times or was it a vocation? – but he couldn't communicate something so complex.

He had spent the intervening hours between the Idiot and the Grand Hotel thinking about this up-coming encounter. He had imagined them chatting happily, her English magically improved and his few words of uneasy Russian transformed into fluency. He should have been with everyone else on an outing to the ballet at the Mariinskiy Theatre but had claimed a 'bit of a tummy bug' when the grocer had come calling for him. The man went away disgruntled, an upset stomach not a valid excuse apparently to a man dancing with death.

Martin had worried that Irina might have mis-interpreted this whole scenario, that she would want payment, but the fact that she had footed the bill in the café seemed to imply that she wasn't selling herself. Perhaps she wanted to find a husband. He wouldn't mind, not really. No one would look at her in the St James Centre the way they would a Thai bride. You wouldn't be able to tell just by looking at her that she'd been purchased. (Or would you?) *Yes, Irina Canning, my wife. Oh, she's Russian, you know. We met in St Petersburg and fell in love. A very romantic city.* She would learn English, he would learn Russian. They would have small half-Russian children, *Sasha and Anastasia.* He would provide her with what she wanted – financial security, a lovely home, children brought up in the affluent West, healthcare for an age-ing mother, an education for a younger sibling, and in return she would give him the illusion of love. Profit and loss, goods and services, that was what it was all about, after all. Business. At some point they had stopped drinking champagne and started drinking vodka. The vodka was so cold it gave him neuralgia across his scalp.

Martin realized he was quite drunk. He wasn't a drinker, one glass of good wine in the evening was his limit, and he didn't have either the head or the stomach for cheap champagne combined with 80 per cent proof Russian vodka. Time began to lurch forward in a series of snapshots: one minute he was rifling through his wallet looking for enough roubles to pay the bill and the next he was in the front seat of a taxi being driven at a reckless and frightening speed. He wondered if he had been kidnapped. He heard Irina murmur something in Russian to the taxi driver. Martin tried to fasten his seat belt but the taxi driver growled '*Nyet*' at him and then said something to Irina that made her laugh. 'Not necessary,' he said, as if Martin had insulted his driving skills. Martin laughed as well, he had given over control of his life to a crazy

Russian taxi driver and a Russian would-be bride. He experienced an unexpected feeling of buoyancy. Something was going to happen, something was going to change.

In a drawer in his bedside table in the Four Clans he found a glossy plastic card with the menus and phone numbers for local takeaways. His stomach rumbled and a jet of acid caught him in the throat. He could phone for a pizza but he knew that when it arrived it would look as unappetizing as it did in the photograph on the menu, and anyway he didn't have enough money to cover it. 'Just nipping out for a bite to eat,' he said to the receptionist. He knew there was no reason for him to account to her for his movements but Martin couldn't shake off the oppressive sense of being in custody in the Four Clans. He had hardly any money to his name but he supposed he could get chips or maybe a bowl of soup somewhere cheap.

'Good for you,' the receptionist said indifferently. She had a smear of what looked like blood on her chin but Martin thought it was more likely to be tomato ketchup.

He ended up in an internet café where the prices were cheap. It looked like an old-fashioned corner shop, except that it was painted black and written in some kind of Day-Glo purple on the outside was the name 'e-coffee'. Inside it smelt of old coffee grounds and artificial vanilla. Martin ordered a tomato soup that tasted of stale dried oregano but came within his meagre budget.

Surrounded by the computers of the internet café, he realized again how acutely he missed the constant companionship of his laptop. He had mentioned its disappearance to Inspector Sutherland, who hadn't shown much interest beyond taking a note of the details. Martin could see that it must be quite low down on his list of priorities. 'An awful lot of things seem to have happened to you in the last twenty-four hours, Mr Canning,' he said. 'Still,' he added cheerfully, 'just think, one day, when this is all over, you'll be able to write about it.'

For a brief moment Martin thought about logging on to the internet. He vaguely wondered if his death had made any difference to his position on Amazon (it could go either way, he supposed). He decided, however, against looking at Amazon or googling his own name (or Richard's). He really didn't want to find evidence of his own death disseminated all over the web.

When he had paid for the soup with the change from his pockets he was left with sixty-one pence to his name. He was only a ten-minute walk from his office – he made a determined effort to get rid of the inverted commas – and thought he might take a stroll along there and check it out. Perhaps tomorrow he could escape the Four Clans, buy a blow-up airbed and bivouac on the laminate flooring of the office. Martin couldn't imagine ever moving back into his own house. Even when the police were finished with it, how would he ever get rid of the memory of Richard Moat's murder from his (ironically named) living room? And how would he ever get the room cleaned up? He couldn't imagine the women of Favours in their nice pink overalls scrubbing bits of Richard Moat's brain matter off the carpets and walls.

The office had a toilet and a tiny kitchen with kettle and microwave. Everything he needed really. In the office he could live his life simply and without ornament, like the monk he had never been.

They had gone camping quite a lot when he was young – with the Scouts (Christopher fitting in with jovial fakery, Martin getting by) and several times with their parents when their mother took on the role of Harry's obedient corporal, endlessly boiling kettles on the rickety Primus stove while Harry himself instructed his pint-size troops in the blacker survival arts (breaking a rabbit's neck, tickling a trout, wrestling an eel). Survival, it seemed, wasn't possible without killing something else.

Nina Riley was a great one for camping, of course. She had learned to love the outdoor life in Switzerland during the war and frequently loaded up provisions in the boot of her Bristol and took to the hills of her Highland home. She had a pair of stout walking boots, an army-style tent and an old-fashioned canvas rucksack with leather straps in which she carried her Thermos and thick sandwiches of beef and mustard. She boiled up water from peat-brown burns to make tea. She caught fish – trout in the rivers or mackerel from a sea loch – then she fried it for breakfast before setting off on a day-long hike, during the course of which she might well come across someone suspicious and have to spy on them. *Looks jolly dubious to me, Bertie. I think our friend's a bit of a blackguard.* Bertie himself never got to speak much. The television producer had suggested to Martin that Nina and Bertie should 'have some sexual tension going on. They're both a bit *bland*, you know?' Martin wondered if he was going mad, if this was what it felt like.

He passed the circus on the Meadows on his way from the café to the office. He had always found circuses unsettling, the performers fragile and quite superfluous to the needs of the planet and yet they seemed to Martin to behave as if they knew things he didn't. The Mysteries. A Russian circus. Of course. What else? The whole of Mother Russia come to town to bring him to justice over their lost daughter. *Here this doll special, very good artist. Scenes from Pushkin, Pushkin famous Russian writer. You know him?* Kafka had taken over the authorship of his life. He was being deleted, wiped out of memory and history, and quite rightly because that was what he had done to Irina. He had thrown her away like rubbish. He had erased her from the earth and he in turn was being erased.

Someone had been in the office. The place hadn't been trashed or turned over, it was little things – the microwave door was open, and in the bin in the kitchen there was a polystyrene box, a half-eaten burger and an empty Coke can. There was a sweet wrapper on the floor, a chair was on the other side of the room to where it usually was. The different-coloured pads of Post-it notes he kept squared up against each other on the desk had all been moved around. It wasn't so much as if a thief had been in, it was more as if an untidy secretary without enough work to do had spent the afternoon in here being bored.

He opened the drawers of the desk. Everything was still in order, the pens and pencils neatly aligned, the paper clips and the highlighters in the right place. Only one thing was missing. Martin knew what it would be, of course, before he even opened the drawer. The CD that was the backup of 'Death on the Black Isle', the last refuge of his novel. He slumped into the high-end office chair that came with the rental. That was when he noticed that a pink Post-it note had been torn off the pad and stuck in the middle of the unadorned white wall opposite the desk. Someone had written a message for him on it. *Fuck you, Martin*. He felt a tattoo of pulses and thuds in his chest. Something *viral* was happening to him. From his wake-up call this morning to his incarceration in the Four Clans this evening, everything had been unrelentingly awful.

His wake-up call this morning! It had been from Richard. *1 missed call*. He'd been in too much of a stupor to answer and then he had forgotten all about it. He must tell the police. It was an important piece of evidence. He took out his phone and discovered that it was down to its last bar of battery.

He wished now that he had answered the phone this morning, he might have been the last person Richard spoke to. 'Oh my God,' Martin said out loud, his mouth making the same oval of horror as the flaming witch on the engraving in his room at the Four Clans. What if Richard had phoned him during ... his ordeal? What if he'd been looking desperately for help? If Martin had answered the call – could he in some way have prevented Richard's death? (*Stop, you blackguard!*) Martin put his head on the desk and moaned. But then he had a thought. He lifted his head and gazed at the pink Post-it note stuck to the wall. Richard had phoned at ten o'clock, Martin remembered looking at the time on the clock radio by his bed in the Four Clans, but Superintendent Campbell said that Richard died between four and seven o'clock in the morning, so he couldn't have phoned at ten. *Unless he had phoned him from beyond the grave.* On cue, in a way that even Nina Riley couldn't have arranged, the phone in his hand chirped. The tom-tom thuds of his heart grew wilder, more erratic. *Richard Moat*, the screen said.

He was on the Pirate Boat again, feeling it lift on its terrible unstoppable ascension, taking his body with it but leaving his mind behind, moving towards its zenith, the nanosecond of a pause at the top of its curve. It wasn't the rise that was the terror, it was the fall.

His imaginary wife bravely took up her knitting. She had recently begun a fisherman's guernsey for him. 'To keep you warm this winter, darling.' Martin was toasting pikelets on a brass toasting fork. The fire was roaring, the pikelets were piping hot, everything was safe and cosy. Richard Moat had gone beyond the grave *and knew everything.* Martin's heart was beating so hard it actually hurt. Was he having a heart attack? His wife said something to him but he couldn't hear her because the fire was roaring so loudly. Irina's doll-blue eyes suddenly flew open. No, she wasn't here. She couldn't be in his lovely cottage. It wasn't allowed. He was fading, falling, a curtain was coming down. Something black and monstrous was inside him, its wings beating in his chest. His wife's needles clacked furiously, she was trying to save him with her knitting.

Martin spoke tentatively into his phone. 'Hello?' he said. No one spoke. His phone gave a last feeble cheep and died. Crime and punishment. An eye for an eye. Cosmic justice had come to town. He started to cry.

32

THERE WERE NO ELEPHANTS, OF COURSE. YOU DIDN'T SEE animals in circuses any more. Jackson remembered only one circus from his childhood; contrary to what Julia thought, he had been through a childhood (of sorts). The circus he remembered from forty years ago (could he really be that old?) had been pitched on a field owned by the colliery at the edge of town, in the shadow of a slag heap. It had been full of animals — elephants, tigers, dogs, horses, even — Jackson seemed to remember — an act that featured penguins, although he might have got that wrong. He could still remember the intoxicating smell of the big top — sawdust and animal urine, candyfloss and sweat — and the lure of exotic people whose lives were so different from Jackson's that it had hurt him like a physical pain.

Louise Monroe had refused his invitation. Julia had only given him one ticket anyway, although he would have bought another one if Louise had said yes.

The circus on the Meadows didn't hold out the same promises and terrors as the circus of long ago. It was a

Russian circus, although there was nothing particularly Russian about spinning plates, trapezes and high-wire work. Only the clowns acknowledged their national origins in an act based on Russian dolls – 'Matryoshka', it declared in the programme. The word of the day. He thought of the boxes that had been stacked in the hall of the Favours office, stencilled with 'Matryoshka'. He felt the peanut-baby doll in his jacket pocket. The layers of the onion. Chinese boxes, Chinese whispers. Russian whispers. Secrets within secrets. Dolls within dolls.

The ringmaster (what Julia had meant by 'circus wallah chappie' presumably) looked like ringmasters the world over, the black top hat, the red tailcoat, the whip – he looked more like he was about to orchestrate a foxhunt than MC a load of spangled kitsch. He was way too tall to hold any attraction for Julia. The circus, the programme also said, shared space with 'The LadyBoys of Bangkok'. Jackson was relieved some passing LadyBoy hadn't given Julia tickets for his/her show.

'*Murdered*,' Julia said. Last night he had watched Richard Moat on stage, now the poor guy was in a refrigerator somewhere. Jackson would have applauded him more generously if he'd known it was his final appearance. Was he murdered because he wasn't funny? People killed for less. The reasons people killed other people had often seemed trivial to Jackson when he was in the police, but he supposed it was different from the inside. He had once been in charge of a case where an eighty-year-old man had hit his wife on the head with a mash hammer because she'd burnt his morning porridge and when Jackson said to the old bloke that it didn't seem like a reason that was going to stand up in court he said, 'But she burnt it every morning for fifty-eight years.' ('You could have had a word with her about it earlier,' a DS said dryly to him but that wasn't how it worked in a marriage, Jackson knew that.) When you retold it, it seemed almost funny, but there had been nothing comical in seeing the old woman's brains all over the worn linoleum or watching the old guy, all rheumy eyes and shaking hands, being put in the back of a police car.

To be honest, Jackson was surprised that more people didn't kill each other. Julia was definitely lying to him about something.

One face in the sea of faces across the other side of the ring caught his attention. It wasn't just a cliché, it really was a sea of faces, he was finding it almost impossible to focus on one. He'd been under the impression that long sight was supposed to improve with age and short sight deteriorate (or was it the other way round?) but he seemed to be losing out on both of them. But if he concentrated, no, it was actually better if he didn't concentrate, he could make out the girl. Her face was tilted upwards watching the trapeze artists, her expression serene, beatific. Her eyes only half open as if she was watching but thinking of something else. She was so like the dead girl it was impossible. His girl, curled up on the rocks, a mermaid dreaming and he had disturbed her sleep. He squinted, trying to make out the features of the girl in the audience, but his focus slipped and she was gone, swimming off into the sea of faces.

He fell asleep while a human pyramid was being constructed out of acrobats and when he woke he felt disorientated. The roof of the big top was dark blue, spangled with silver stars, and it reminded him of something but he couldn't think what and then he realized it was the roof – the vault of heaven – in a side chapel in the Catholic church where his mother dragged them three times a day on a Sunday when they were very small, until she ran out of energy and let the devil have them.

Maybe Julia wasn't lying exactly, just not telling the truth.

When Jackson exited the big top on the Meadows along with the rest of the audience he was greeted by a pearly dusk. The gloaming. It was so much lighter up here, a transient Nordic light that spoke to his soul. He took a seat on a bench and turned his phone on. There was a text from Julia, *In the trav bar come and find us* (not even a '*J*' or a single '*x*' this time, he noticed. Let alone '*love*' or punctuation). It sounded more like a challenge or a treasure hunt than an invitation to a drink. He guessed 'the trav' was the Traverse, which was both good and bad, good because it was nearby and he was sure he knew how to get there, bad because he'd been there the first night with Julia and the cast and it was a smoky underground place full of posers up from London. Maybe he could persuade her out of there, take her to one of the many Italian restaurants around this part of town. He seemed to remember a plan to cook for her tonight. The best-laid plans of mice and men. They had studied that book at school, that is to say his fellow pupils had studied it at school, Jackson had looked out of the window or played truant. He remembered the little plaque in the Scottish War Memorial. *The Tunnellers' Friends.* He felt strangely bereft.

Although there were still plenty of people milling about, light was fading fast on the Meadows and away from the street lamps that bordered the paths there were now murky pools of darkness presenting opportunities for all kinds of transgression. Everything suddenly seemed darker and Jackson realized that the lights on the big top had been switched off. Something seemed to drop inside him, a leaden weight, a memory of walking home from that circus forty-odd years ago, holding his mother's hand – his mother was no more than a shadow of a memory now – walking away up a hill, it was a town built on hills, and looking back and seeing the big top, ablaze with lights, being abruptly plunged into darkness. It had disturbed him in a way that, as a small boy, he couldn't put words to. Now he knew it was melancholy. Melancholic, choleric, phlegmatic – that was what Louise Monroe had called him yesterday, *you seem remarkably phlegmatic, Mr Brodie.* What was the fourth? Sanguine. But melancholy, that was his own true humour. A miserable bastard, in other words.

The lamps are going out all over Europe, he thought. God, that was a wretched quotation. He had been reading a lot of military history lately, courtesy of Amazon. He thought of the Binyon poem again. *At the going down of the sun.* The rest of the verses were crap. Viscount Grey was actually watching the street lamps being *lit*, not put out, although, of course, some people thought it was an apocryphal quotation. God, would you look at him, a sad middle-aged loser sitting on a park bench at twilight thinking about an old war he never took part in. Jackson rarely thought about the wars he *had* taken part in. All he needed was a can of lager. When had he started thinking of himself as a loser? *We shall not see them lit again in our lifetime.* He wouldn't blame Julia if she had grown bored with him.

And then, instantly, his self-pity was forgotten because there she was. It was her, it was his dead girl. He hadn't imagined her in the big top, she had been there and now she was *here*, walking across the Meadows, in and out of the shadows cast by the trees, coming towards him.

She was wearing heels and a short summer skirt so that you couldn't help but admire her perfect legs. He stood up abruptly and set off towards her, wondering what he should say – *Hey, you look just like a dead girl I know*? As opening conversational gambits went, it left something to be desired. He knew she wasn't really his dead girl, unless the dead had begun to walk, which he was pretty sure they hadn't. He couldn't imagine the kind of chaos that would ensue if they did.

And then – and in Jackson's opinion this was becoming just a wee bit tiresome – who should slip out of the shadows but his old enemy, Honda Man. Terence Smith creeping up on tiptoe behind the not-dead girl in a way that reminded Jackson of a cartoon character. The man was a juggernaut, juggernauts shouldn't try and tiptoe. The girl might not be dead but it looked as if Terence Smith was intending to make her that way, not with his trusty bat in his hand but a length of what looked like nylon rope. Dog, bat, rope, he was a one-man arsenal. 'Hey!' Jackson yelled to get the girl's attention, 'Behind you!' Did he really say that? But it was no pantomime joke and no pantomime thuggee – Terence Smith already had the rope round her neck. Jackson's warning cry had alerted her, however, and she had managed to get her hands on the rope, tugging on it for all she was worth to prevent Terence Smith tightening it.

Jackson sprinted along the path towards the two of them. There were other people closer but they seemed benignly unaware of a girl being strangled in front of their eyes. Before Jackson reached them the girl managed to do something swift and admirably effective that seemed to involve the heel of her shoe and Honda Man's groin and poor old Terry collapsed on to the ground with an ugly noise. *Unmanned*, Jackson thought. The girl didn't hang around, instead she kicked off her shoes and started running back the way she had come, in the direction of the circus, and by the time Jackson reached Terence Smith, now retching with shock, the girl was out of sight.

Honda Man's moans attracted a couple of passers-by, who seemed to be of the opinion that he was the victim of an assault and that the perpetrator of the assault must be the man standing over him. Been here, done this, Jackson thought. His brain was lagging vital seconds behind, still trying to compute the convergence of himself, his old pal Terry and a girl who looked like the dead girl in the Forth. He had seen the crucifixes in her ears as she struggled with her assailant. You say coincidence, he thought, I say connection. A baffling, impenetrably complex connection, but nonetheless a connection. Jackson was torn between wanting to interrogate Terence Smith, with the added bonus of then beating him to a pulp, or running after the dead girl lookalike.

The decision was made for him by the arrival of a police car containing two uniformed constables, one male, one female, a breeding pair, who were soon out of the car and walking along the path in that determined way that Jackson remembered well, slow enough to assess a situation but ready to accelerate at the drop of a hat. One of the passers-by pointed at Jackson and shouted, 'This is the man who did it!' Oh thanks, Jackson thought, thanks very much. He'd been convicted of assaulting Terence Smith once already today, a second time would probably send him straight to jail. He took a deep breath, which hurt, and ran.

One of the police, the female of the pair, stayed with Terence Smith, who was still making a fuss over his manhood. Jackson would have quite liked to know what exactly the girl did back there and hand on the arcane knowledge to the women in his life the next time they found themselves being lifted off their feet with a rope round their neck. God forbid.

The other constable lumbered along the path after Jackson. He was on the hefty side and normally Jackson could have outrun him easily, but he was handicapped by his bruised ribs and so he darted off the main drag into the tangle of caravans and lorries that surrounded the big top. He stumbled and tripped, knocked something flying. Someone shouted abuse at him but he carried on running, weaving in and out of the assortment of vehicles that made up the circus laager.

He paused to catch a breath inside an avenue of trucks. He could hear the policeman talking to someone. He rather hoped that some vagabond instinct amongst the members of the circus troupe would lead them to help him and misdirect the law (*He went that way*). No such luck. The police constable, unfit but dogged, passed across the top of the avenue of trucks. Jackson flattened himself against the side of a huge generator, but too late, the guy had spotted him, yelling something inarticulate in surprise at suddenly coming upon his quarry. The policeman in Jackson wanted to reassure him that he wasn't dangerous. The guy didn't have his partner with him, no one covering his back and had no idea what Jackson was capable of, so he was probably more scared than Jackson was. What *was* he capable of? he wondered.

He didn't hang around to find out, instead he was off again, helter-skeltering around the parked convoy. The chase was telling on him, his ribs aching so much he could barely keep upright. Just when he thought he was going to have to give up this game of hide-and-seek, someone or something (he hoped it was someone) grabbed him by the arm and pulled him into the dark.

Not entirely dark, just enough light to make him realize he was somewhere in the hinterlands of the big top, the space where the performers waited to make their entrance. Ahead of him a tunnel led to the ring itself, reminding him for a moment of the Colosseum. He had taken Marlee to Rome last year. They had eaten a lot of ice cream and pizza. All his recent memories were of holidays.

There was enough light, too, to catch a glimpse of the knife glinting near his throat. His first thought was that it was Terence Smith with his Cluedo armoury but there was surely no way he could have got here so fast. He twisted his neck round, felt the knife scratching dangerously near an artery. The dead girl lookalike. She smiled. She had a feral look about her that didn't invite smiling back. All that was needed were a few clowns and the nightmare would be complete.

'Shut up, OK?' she said. She sounded foreign. He didn't know why that should be a surprise, everyone he encountered seemed to be foreign.

'OK,' he agreed. She moved the knife an inch away from his neck. He was so close to her that he could smell the cigarette smoke on her mingled with perfume, it made him want a cigarette. It made him want sex. An idea that surprised him, considering the circumstances. He wondered if the earrings were the sign of a cult, some born-again Christian thing. She didn't look like any Christian he'd met before, but you never could tell. Had she saved him from the police in order to kill him? That made no sense, but then nothing made any sense.

'You look like someone who's dead,' he whispered. Yes, he had decided this was a conversation-killer but here he was using it anyway.

'I know,' she said. This was an unexpected answer. She lowered the knife a little more.

'Your sister?' he hazarded.

'No, friend,' she said, and with a shrug, 'we look alike, that's all.'

'Honda Man – Terence Smith – why did he attack you?' Her green eyes narrowed and she laughed. 'The gimp?' she said contemptuously. 'He's idiot.'

'Yeah, I know he's idiot, but he still tried to kill you.'

She made some kind of gesture that he suspected was obscene where she came from. Russia, by the sound of her. '*Da*,' she agreed. She seemed impressively unflustered by the fact that someone had just tried to kill her. He wondered if it happened to her a lot.

'I saw you at the circus,' he said.

'Circus is illegal now?' she said. She wasn't good at small talk.

'What's your name?' he ventured. 'My name's Jackson Brodie.' *I used to be a policeman.*

'I don't have a name, I don't exist,' she hissed, 'and you won't if you don't shut up.' Really bad at small talk.

'We're on the same side,' Jackson said. It seemed unlikely, but wasn't his enemy's enemy his friend?

'I'm not on *side*. Listen—' A little jab of the knife in his ribs to get his attention.

'That hurts.'

'So?'

He couldn't imagine why he had worried about her being attacked. Another little poke with the knife in his ribs.

'OK, OK, I'm listening,' he said.

'Stop putting your nose in places, I'm taking care of it.'

'Taking care of what?'

She dug the point of the knife further into his ribs, the bruised, aching ribs, and said, 'We can go now,' in a decisive way that brooked no argument. She walked him across the circus ring, eerily dark and robbed of illusion, and made him crawl under the flap on the other side, behind the tiers of empty seats. Out on the grass, in the cool night air, there was no sign of Terence Smith or the police.

'I save your bacon,' she said, and laughed, apparently pleased with her mastery of English metaphor. 'Now get lost.' She started walking away. She was barefoot but she didn't seem to notice. He followed her, limping along, a lame dog. 'Fuck off,' she said without looking back at him.

'Tell me about your friend, the dead girl in the water,' he persisted. 'Who was she?' She carried on walking but raised the knife so he could see it. It was smaller than he had thought but it looked sharp and she definitely had the air of someone who would use it without any qualms. He had respect for knives, he'd seen a lot of stabbing victims in his time and most of them weren't around to talk about the experience.

'Did Terence Smith kill your friend?' They passed a knot of people who didn't even give them a second glance – the barefoot girl, the knife, the limping man, the dubious dialogue. Jackson supposed they were taken for Fringe performers.

'You're big nuisance, Jackson Brodie,' the girl shouted. They reached a main thoroughfare and suddenly there was traffic and people everywhere. Jackson vaguely recognized the street, it was near the museum on Chambers Street, near the Sheriff Court, scene of his disgrace this morning. Hard to believe it was still the same day.

He was desperately trying to make sense of things before she escaped him. Terence Smith had tried to kill the crazy Russian girl. The crazy Russian girl was a friend of his dead girl. Terence Smith had attacked him and told him to forget what he had seen. Jackson thought he meant the road-rage incident but what if he meant what had happened on Cramond Island? Because he was the only witness who knew the girl was dead, apart from the crazy Russian girl? And Terence Smith had just tried to kill *her*. For the first time since he'd taken his unwelcome dip in the river he could see something that made sense. A tangible connection, not just a coincidence.

The Russian girl was waiting to cross the road, hovering on the edge of the pavement looking for a gap in the cars, like a greyhound impatient for the trap to open. The traffic slowed to a halt at the red light just as he caught up with her and he made a grab for her arm to hold her back. He half expected to be stabbed or bitten but she just glared at him. The green man on the pedestrian crossing flashed and beeped behind them. It turned back to red and she was still glaring at him. He wondered if he was going to turn to stone.

A sudden loud bang made Jackson jump. He had once watched his own house explode and tended to be wary of loud noises.

'It's firework,' the girl said, 'for Tattoo.' Sure enough, in the distance, a huge flower of glittering sparks bloomed above the Castle and fell slowly to earth. Then, without warning, she leaned towards him and put her lips close to his ear as if she was going to kiss him but instead she said, 'Real homes for real people,' then she laughed as if she had made an incredibly funny joke.

'What?' She turned to go, pulling her arm away, and he said, 'Stop, don't go, wait. How can I get in touch with you again?'

She laughed and said, 'Ask for Jojo.' And then she crossed on the red man, holding up the cars with an imperious salute. She really did have perfect legs.

By the time he ducked into the Traverse, Julia and the rest of the company were long gone. He presumed Julia would be at home but when he finally made it back to the flat there was no sign of her, even though it was after midnight. He tried phoning but her phone was turned off. He was so tired that he hardly noticed when she slipped into bed next to him.

'Where were you?' she said.

'Where were *you*?' he said. *Question with a question*. It felt like an old war, one he'd fought several times. His phone rang before hostilities escalated. Louise Monroe asking him what he was like when he was fourteen. She had a son, it turned out. He wouldn't have figured her for a mother.

'Why are women phoning you in the middle of the night asking you about your teenage years?' Julia asked sleepily.

'Maybe they find me interesting.'

Julia chuckled, deep and throaty. It set off a cough and by the time she'd recovered it was too late to ask her why she found that so funny.

33

LOUISE DIALLED HIS NUMBER FROM HER CAR AND BEFORE HE even had time to say anything asked, 'What were you like when you were fourteen?'

'Fourteen?'

'Yes, fourteen,' she repeated. The sound of his voice was a kick. He was just the right side of wrong.

'I don't know,' he said finally. 'I was no altar boy certainly. A bit of a tearaway, I suppose, like a lot of lads at that age.'

'I know absolutely nothing about fourteen-year-old boys.'

'Well, why should you?'

'My son's fourteen.'

'Your son?' He sounded astonished. 'I didn't realize you were . . .'

'A mother?' she supplied. 'I know it's hard to believe, but there you go, it's the old story – sperm meets egg and bam. It can happen to the best of us.' She sighed. 'Fourteen-year-olds are a nightmare.' She realized that she was clutching the steering wheel of the car as if she was in rigor mortis.

'What's his name?'

'Archie.' *What's his name?* That was a question a parent would ask, Louise thought. When Archie was born the people who asked, 'How much does he weigh?' all had babies themselves. Guys who weren't fathers hadn't been interested in Archie's weight or what she was going to call him. So, she deduced, Jackson Brodie had kids. She didn't want to know about that, wasn't interested in second-hand guys with baggage. Kids were baggage, stuff you lugged around. Luggage.

'You have kids?' she asked. Just couldn't help herself.

'Just one, a girl,' Jackson said. 'Marlee. She's ten. I know nothing about ten-year-old girls if it's any consolation.'

'Archie's not a criminal,' Louise said, as if Jackson had accused him of something. 'He's basically harmless.'

'I nearly landed in court for stealing when I was fifteen.'

'What happened?'

'I joined the army.'

Jeez. Archie in the army, there's a thought.

'This is why you're calling?' he asked. 'For advice about parenting?'

'No. I'm calling to tell you that I'm on a housing estate in Burdiehouse.'

'Great name for a housing estate.' He sounded weary.

'I'm outside a shop that's been boarded up. I think it

used to be a post office. There's a fish-and-chip shop on one side, a Scotmid on the other side. Single-storey, commercial properties, no flats above, nothing remotely residential.'

'Why are you telling me this and should you be there in the dark on your own?'

'That's very gallant of you but I'm a big girl. I'm telling you because I thought you'd like to know that this is the address that Terence Smith gave to the court this morning.'

'Honda Man gave a false address?'

'Which is an offence. As you know. I told you that you were an idiot to plead guilty. And by the way, no one else caught the registration of the car involved in the road-rage incident, so you held up the investigation by withholding vital information.'

'So sue me,' Jackson said. 'I've just seen him actually, he was trying to kill someone else.'

'Terence Smith?' she said sharply. 'Please tell me you didn't have another go at him?'

'No, although the police were keen to question me.'

'Jesus, what is it with you?'

'Trouble is my friend.'

'He was trying to kill someone? Is that one of your fantasies?'

'I don't have fantasies. Not about people killing each other anyway. If I tell you what happened you'll think I'm even more paranoid and delusional than you do already.'

'Try me,' she said.

'I saw a girl who looked like my dead girl, she even had the earrings.'

'You're even more paranoid and delusional than I thought.'

'Told you.'

'You see dead girls everywhere.'

'No, I see the same dead girl everywhere.'

He was, officially, a lunatic, she decided. Strangely, that didn't make him less attractive. She sighed and said, 'Anyway, cheers. I'm off home. Sleep well.'

There were rules. The rules said, you don't fool around with witnesses, you don't fool around with suspects, you don't fool around with convicted felons. And Jackson Brodie managed to be all three at once. Yes, Louise, you surely know how to pick them. And, of course, you didn't fool around with a man who already had a woman.

At least that explained why he was in Edinburgh. 'For the Festival,' he had said when she first interviewed him but he hadn't seemed like the Festival type. Still didn't. But *Julia* was in a play.

'What's Julia like?' The naming of her had provoked an unexpected, visceral spasm of jealousy in Louise. Hold your tongue, bite your lip.

'She's an actress.' That had surprised her. He frowned when he said her name.

Be honest. Honest was hard sometimes, even with herself. She was a natural dissembler. Even the word 'dissembling' was a way of dissembling, of not just saying *liar*. Be honest, Louise, you fancy Jackson. Such an inane, adolescent word, 'fancy'. *Louise Monroe fancies Grant Niven* written in the school toilets in Fourth Year. PC Louise Monroe and DI Michael Pirie

379

in the back of an unmarked squad car in the wee small hours of his leaving do. *Christ, I've always fancied you rotten, Louise*, the dull gleam of his wedding ring in the dark, the push and shove of unbridled lechery that kick-started Archie. How odd that babies, the absolute innocents at the top of the moral heap, were created out of such vulgarity. The beast with two backs. Maybe it wasn't that she fancied Jackson exactly, maybe she just saw in him someone who had weathered the world and still had something left to give. 'You can't have it both ways,' one of her girlfriends said, 'Tough *and* tender. Men are like steaks, it's one or the other.' Tough and tender, a contradiction in terms, Hegelian synthesis. Dualism, the Edinburgh disease. It was possible, Louise was sure, but perhaps only in a far-flung corner of the galaxy. Or with Jackson Brodie. Maybe.

She had noticed a chickenpox scar beneath his eyebrow. Archie had one in almost the same place, a tiny shield-shaped depression in the skin that she supposed would last for ever.

His dark hair was flecked with slate. At least he hadn't done the middle-aged male thing of growing a beard to hide a double chin, not that he had a double chin. He probably wouldn't look too bad with a beard. When she was younger she could never have imagined that she would find middle-aged men with greying hair or beards even remotely attractive. It just went to show. But let's not forget *Julia*. Still, she was an actress *and* he frowned when he mentioned her name. Two strikes against Julia.

It was odd how you could feel so attracted to

someone by the simplest things, the way they handed you a drink and said, *There you go.* The dent of a chickenpox scar, the cast of despair on their features when they said *Julia*.

Louise slipped her car into the garage. She remembered Sandy Mathieson saying that a garage had just sold for a hundred thousand. The thing about Edinburgh was that even some of the best addresses in town didn't have garages, leaving the rich nobs stuck with the horrors of on-street parking, whereas Louise in her modern, characterless (but still mind-blowingly expensive) estate house had a double garage. Thank you, Graham Hatter. The urn that contained her mother was now sitting on a shelf in the garage, between a half-empty two-litre can of paint and a jar of nails. She gave the urn a mock salute as she got out of the car, 'Hey, Mom.'

Jellybean was waiting behind the front door to greet her. A deep thumping bass pulsated out of Archie's bedroom. Jellybean followed her up the stairs. He had to put all four paws on a step before he could move on up to the next. It wasn't long since he'd been like quicksilver on the stairs. The corkscrew in her heart moved a quarter turn.

I was a bit of a tearaway, I suppose. 'Tearaway' was a good word, she could use that next time Archie got into trouble. *Archie's a bit of a tearaway, but he's OK.* More and more she had this troubling vision of sitting in a courtroom, watching Archie in the dock, seeing his whole life go down the pan, and her life with it. *You placed him in a nursery when he was three*

*months old and went back to work, Ms Monroe? You
have always put your career first, haven't you?
You don't know who his father is?* Of course she knew,
she just wasn't going to say. Harmless, my ass, she
thought. He was a little shit, that's what he was.

She knocked on the door of Archie's room and went
in quickly, without waiting for an answer. Always try
and catch suspects off guard. Archie and Hamish
(damn, she'd forgotten about Hamish) were huddled
around Archie's computer. She heard Hamish's sotto
voce warning, 'Incoming, Arch.' Archie turned off the
computer screen as she came in the room. Porn probably. She turned the music off. She shouldn't do that
really, he had rights after all. No, he didn't.

'OK, boys?' she said. She could hear herself sounding like an officer of the law, not a mother.

'We're fine, Louise,' said Hamish, giving her a big,
cheesy grin. Fucking little Harry Potter. Archie said
nothing, just glared at her, waiting for her to leave. If
she'd had a girl they would be having little chats now,
about clothes, boys, school. A girl would lie on her
bed and look through her make-up. A girl would share
her secrets, hopes, dreams, all the things Louise had
never done with her own mother.

'You've got school tomorrow, you should be asleep.'

'You're so right, Louise,' Hamish said. 'Come on,
Archie, time to go bye-byes.'

Little fucker, she thought as she left the room. She
walked away and then tiptoed back to listen at the
door. The music remained off and they seemed to be
reading from a book, first one voice, then the other.
Not porn anyway, although they were both sniggering

as if it was. Hamish's confident tones, more masculine when incorporeal, declared, ' *"You know, I think there's more to this than meets the eye, Bertie,"* Nina said. *"Maud Elphinstone seems whiter than the proverbial driven snow but methinks the lady doth protest too much."* ' And Archie's swooping, cracked voice said, ' *"Why, Bertie, I do believe you're blushing."* '

Were they gay? How would she feel if her son was gay? Actually it would be quite a relief, she wouldn't have to deal with any of that macho bullshit in the future. Someone to go shopping with, that's what they always said, mothers of gay sons, didn't they? She didn't like shopping, so that might be a bit of a problem.

' *"I do believe you have a pash on the lovely Maud, Bertie."* '

For a moment, when they were saying goodbye, she thought Jackson was going to kiss her. What would she have done? Kissed him back, right there in the middle of the street, like a teenager. *Louise Monroe has a pash on Jackson Brodie.* Because Louise Monroe was an idiot, obviously.

34

GLORIA SPENT THE EVENING AT THE HOSPITAL. SHE WATCHED Graham closely and wondered if he was faking it, if he had decided that being dead to the world was a way of dodging all the problems that were piling up around him. 'Can you hear me, Graham?' she whispered in his ear. If he could he was keeping schtum about it.

The colossal wreck now as weak as a kitten, as quiet as a mouse. Ozymandias toppled. *Half sunk, a shattered visage lies.* Gloria had been very fond of Shelley when she was younger. She had given Graham a beautifully illustrated Folio Society copy of the collected poems for his sixtieth birthday, on the basis that you should give a present you would like to receive yourself.

Naturally, being Graham, he had misread the poem, seeing only the triumphal hubris of *My name is Ozymandias, King of Kings:/Look on my works, ye Mighty, and despair!* Gloria couldn't think, offhand, of a present she had ever received from any member of her family that she had actually wanted. Last

Christmas, Emily ('and Nick') bought her a food mixer, an inferior brand to the one she already owned, and Graham gave her a Jenners' gift token, which hardly required much thought and had probably been bought by his sales-woman-cum-mistress-cum-would-be-wife, Maggie Louden. Gloria had had no intuition that the woman standing in front of her Christmas tree, waving away a mince pie, was planning to be the next Mrs Graham Hatter. *The hand that mocked them, and the heart that fed.*

She drank a cup of tea that a nice nurse brought her and flicked through a copy of the *Evening News* that she had bought from the shop downstairs. *Police are asking if anyone saw a young woman go into the water.* Her eye was caught by the words *earrings in the shape of crucifixes.* She put her tea down and read the short piece from the beginning again. *Going into the water –* what did that mean?

When she got home, Gloria went down to the basement to set the security system for the night. Something moved on one of the CCTV screens, a pair of eyes glowing monstrously in the night – a fox, a big dog-fox, carrying off the remains of Gloria's supper from last night. Then, unexpectedly, the screen went blank.

Then all the other screens went blank, one by one. No little robots moving this way and that, keeping their electronic eyes on things. The lights on the alarm system flickered and went out and then all the electricity in the house failed. This was what it would be like for Graham when he died.

A fuse must have blown, Gloria told herself. Nothing to worry about. She felt her way in the absolute dark of the basement towards the wall where the fuse box was. Then she heard a noise. A footfall, a door opening, a floorboard creaking.

Her heart started thudding so loudly that she thought it must be like a beacon pinpointing her position in the dark. A man had been beaten to death in Merchiston this morning, who was to say the murderer hadn't moved on to another suburb on the south side? She wished she had a weapon. She made a mental inventory of what was available. The garden shed provided the biggest arsenal – weedkiller sprays, an axe, the electric hedge-trimmer, the strimmer – she imagined you could probably do quite a bit of damage to someone's ankles with a strimmer. Unfortunately there was no way she could get to the garden shed without passing whoever was in the house. Did they have eyes of diamond and jet, were they as tall as a bear?

She suddenly remembered Maggie Louden's words. *Is it done yet, is it over? Have you got rid of Gloria?* What if she wasn't talking about divorce, what if she was talking about murder?

Of course, that was exactly what Graham would do! If he divorced Gloria he would lose half of everything he had and no way in the world would Graham be prepared to do that, but if Gloria died he could keep everything. It was as melodramatic a concept as anything in *Emmerdale* and yet somehow perfectly credible. He would hire someone – Graham had a way of never getting his own hands dirty. He would pay someone to get rid of her. Or he would use Terry. Yes, that was what he would do, he would use Terry.

Gloria held her hand over her heart in an attempt to muffle its tell-tale thumping. Another floorboard creaked, much closer this time, and Gloria realized that there was someone standing at the top of the basement stairs, a figure outlined faintly with an aura of moonlight from the atrium skylight in the hall.

The figure started to descend the stairs. Gloria took a deep breath and said stoutly, 'I think you should know before you come any further that I am armed.' A lie, of course, but in these circumstances truth was hardly a weapon. The figure hesitated, bent down to get a better view of the basement and then a familiar voice said, 'Hello, Gloria.'

Gloria gave a little scream of horror and said, 'I thought you were dead.'

35

WHEN MARTIN RETURNED TO THE FOUR CLANS HE FOUND THE prison-governor receptionist had been replaced by the night porter from last night. Hadn't Sutherland said he was on holiday? He handed Martin his key, barely looking up from the *Evening News* that was spread out on the cheap veneer of the reception counter. A cigarette teetered precariously from the edge of his lip.

'Do you remember me?' Martin asked. 'Do you know who I am?'

The night porter tore himself away from the newspaper, an inch of ash dropping from his cigarette. He glanced up at Martin and then, as if seeing nothing of interest, returned to his paper. 'Yeah,' he said, turning over a page, 'you're that dead guy, aren't you?'

'Yes,' Martin agreed. 'I'm that dead guy.'

Thursday

36

A ROOSTER CROWED. THERE WAS NO BETTER ALARM CLOCK. He remembered it was Sunday, his favourite day of the week, and he stretched all four limbs luxuriously in the bed. No need to get up and go to work. He was no longer writing, thank God, he had found an odd kind of liberation in donning a suit and tie every weekday morning and commuting up to London to toil in a conservative office with high ceilings and big, old-fashioned desks, a place where the juniors and the secretaries called him 'Mr Canning' and the chairman clapped him on the back and said, 'How's that wonderful woman you married, old chap?' He didn't know what he did in the office all day, but at lunchtime he went out to a restaurant where the waitresses wore white broderie anglaise aprons and little caps on their heads and brought him oxtail soup and steamed puddings with custard. And in the afternoon, at three on the dot, his secretary (June, or perhaps Angela), a cheerful young woman with crisp shorthand and soft twinsets, brought him a cup of tea and a plate of biscuits.

The rooster didn't know it was a day of rest. He was soon joined by the other birds. Martin could pick out the thread of the joyful warble of a blackbird from the tapestry of birdsong but the identity of the others in the pattern was a mystery. His (wonderful) wife would know, she was a country girl, born and bred. A farm girl. A wholesome, milk-fed farm girl. He propped himself up on an elbow and studied her wholesome farm-girl face. In repose, she was even more lovely, although it was the kind of loveliness that inspired respectful admiration in other men rather than lust. Even the idea of lust would have sullied her. She was beyond reproach. A strand of her soft brown hair lay across her face. He moved it gently away and kissed the priceless ruby bow of her lips.

He would make her breakfast in bed. A proper breakfast, eggs and bacon, fried bread. For lunch today they would roast a piece of good English beef, although meat was still on the ration but the village butcher was a friend. Everyone was their friend. (He wondered why he was so frequently a carnivore in this other life.)

The morning would follow its usual happy Sunday pattern. When lunch was nearly ready – the gravy thickening, the beef resting – he would laugh (because it was their little joke) and say to her, 'A little pre-prandial, darling?' and bring out the Waterford sherry decanter that had belonged to her parents. Then they would sip their amontillado and sit on the armchairs covered in 'Strawberry Thief' and listen to Schubert's 'Trout Quintet'.

He could hear a tap running in the bathroom and the tread of feet along the hallway and down the stairs. Peter/David was making aeroplane noises, fighting the Luftwaffe single-handed. Martin heard him say, 'Take that, you filthy Nazi!' before making the *ack-ack* sounds of a machine gun. He was a good boy, he would grow up like his father the fighter pilot, not like Martin. Yesterday evening when they had been sitting in their cosy living room (roaring fire, etc.), Martin toasting crumpets, his wife knitting yet another Fair Isle pullover, after Peter/David had kissed them both goodnight and gone up to bed, his wife paused over her needles and with a smile said, 'I think he deserves to have a little brother or sister, don't you?' A moment to treasure in a life of treasures.

He stretched again and put his arms round his wife and smelt her lily-of-the-valley hair. She wriggled a little, a sign that she was awake and willing. He put a hand inside the folds of her nightgown and found the apple roundness of a breast and pressed his body against hers. He should say something loving at this point, something tender. He always had trouble with the intimacies of conversation with her for some reason, perhaps if he gave her a name it would help. She rolled over and returned his embrace. 'Marty,' she said.

He woke with a start. The cheap digital clock-radio on the bedside table informed him that it was six o'clock in the morning. He wondered if he should check under the covers to make sure he hadn't turned into a giant insect.

Daylight had already overtaken the street lamp

outside and filtered through the thin orange curtains, bathing the room in the glow of a post-nuclear sunrise. The lurid Lucozade light washed over Martin's face. He couldn't imagine how he would get back to sleep again. The walls of the room were tissue-thin. Every toilet flushed, every hawking phlegmy cough, every sexual act attempted or achieved, all seemed to be finding a direct conduit to Martin's room.

What if somehow he was stuck here, if he had entered some surreal loop where he must wake up every morning in a different room in the Four Clans? How many rooms were there in the hotel? What if it was an infinite number, what if it was one of those *Twilight Zone* places with a non-existent thirteenth floor and a staff who were really the ghosts of previous guests? A hotel you could never check out of?

He knew, in the sober light of day, that it was not Richard Moat who had phoned him last night. Which was most likely after all – that Richard Moat was phoning him from the afterlife or that the person who killed Richard Moat had stolen his phone? A murderer phoning him was preferable to a corpse phoning him. Of course this was something he should tell the police about, but the idea of having to encounter Sutherland again was too depressing. He wondered what Richard Moat's killer would have said to him if his phone hadn't run out of battery. *You next*, perhaps. An eye for an eye.

He had said to Melanie last night that he was going to cancel his appearance at the Book Festival but now it struck him that it would be a badge of courage to turn up. *Pull yourself together, boy! Face the thing you're frightened of.* He might have been reduced to a plaything of the gods but he was still Alex Blake. This was his life, this was his arena: it might not be a very noble one but it was all that was left to him.

He had lost his laptop, his wallet, his novel, his home, his identity over the course of the previous forty-eight hours. All he had left was Alex Blake.

Reception was now being manned by a boy in a striped satin waistcoat and a bow tie who looked as if he belonged in a barbershop quartet.

'Can I use the phone?' Martin asked and the boy said, 'Certainly, Mr Canning. My mother's read all the Alex Blake books, she's your number one fan.'

'Thank you, thank *her*. That's very kind.'

From his pocket he fished out the flyer that had been given to him a lifetime ago. *If you need any help*, the man had said. Well, he did need help. He needed just one person to be on his side. *Face the thing you're frightened of. Pull yourself together, you fucking fairy. You're an old woman, Martin.*

He was not going to be cowed by unfounded suspicion, or by dead men phoning him. He was going to hold his head high and carry on. Cosmic justice could come and get him but it would be on his own terms.

He dialled the number and when it was answered said, 'Mr Brodie? I don't know if you remember me?'

37

JACKSON ROLLED OVER IN THE BED AND SPOONED JULIA'S HOT body. She usually slept naked but was now wearing a pair of horrendous pyjamas that were much too big for her and might at some point have belonged to her sister. Jackson knew the pyjamas were significant but he didn't particularly want to think what that significance might be. He missed the feeling of skin on skin, the peachy roundness of Julia. He fitted himself into the familiar curves and cambers of her body but instead of pushing back and settling into his shape she shifted away from him, murmuring something incomprehensible. Julia talked a lot in her sleep, all of it gibberish, but nonetheless Jackson had taken to listening intently in case she divulged something secret and hidden that he would feel better (or, more likely, worse) for knowing.

He moved closer to her again and kissed her neck but she remained steadfastly asleep. It was difficult to wake Julia up, short of shaking her. Once, he had made love to her while she slept and she'd hardly even twitched when he came inside her, but he didn't tell her about it afterwards because he wasn't sure how she would react. He couldn't imagine her being particularly put out (this was Julia, after all). She would probably just have said, 'Without me? How could you?' Technically it was rape, of course. He had arrested enough guys in his time for taking advantage of drunk or drugged girls. Plus, if he was honest, Julia was such a sound sleeper that there had been a touch of necrophilia about the whole thing. He'd put a necrophiliac away once: the guy worked in a mortuary and didn't 'see where the harm was' because 'the objects of my affection have moved beyond earthly matters'.

Between Amelia's pyjamas and necrophilia, Jackson had pretty much managed to kill off any desire he might have woken up with. Julia was probably still annoyed with him anyway. Jackson placed his ear to her back like a stethoscope and listened to her rattling breath. He had done the same for a three-year-old Marlee when she'd had bronchitis. Julia's lungs would kill her in the end. There was something about her that suggested she would never make old bones. Long before she was drawing her pension she'd have emphysema and be lugging around an oxygen tank as tall as herself. She wriggled further away from him.

Everything was subject to entropy, even sex, even love. A slow erasure of passion. Not his love for his daughter, obviously, that was the one unbreakable bond. Or his sister. He had loved his sister with a true heart but Niamh was too far 'beyond earthly matters' now for him to feel the tug and urgency of love. The sadness was all that was left.

He propped himself up on an elbow and studied Julia's face. He had a feeling that she wasn't really asleep, that she might be acting.

'Don't,' she said and rolled over, pressing her face into the pillow.

When he woke again, Julia was kneeling on the bed next to him wearing only a towel and holding a tray on which he could see coffee, scrambled eggs, toast. 'Breakfast!' she announced gaily. Jackson's watch said seven o'clock. 'For a minute I thought you were Julia,' he said.

'Ha, funny. I couldn't sleep.' Her damp hair was bundled into a demented ponytail on one side of her head and she smelt soapy clean. She was naturally spotlit by the sun, caught in a lozenge of light, and he could see the dark rings around her eyes, the shadow of something mortal on her brow. Maybe it was just disappointment. She settled cross-legged on to the bed and read out his horoscope to him. '*Sagittarians are having a tough time at the moment. You feel as if you're getting nowhere but never fear, there is light at the end of the tunnel.* Are you? Having a tough time?' she asked.

'No more than usual.'

He didn't ask her what her stars said, that would have been to give a kind of credence to something he considered to be nonsense. He suspected Julia thought it was nonsense as well, and it was all part of some affectation.

'Are you having a tough time? Oh, yes, you are, aren't you? Fighting in the street, *brawling*, killing dogs . . .'

'I didn't kill the dog.'

'Thrown in jail, convicted of an offence. They'll never take you back in the police now, sweetie.'

'I don't want to go back to the police.'

'Yes you do.'

It was surprising what a burnt offering for breakfast could do to a man's spirits. The eggs were rubbery and the toast was charred but Jackson managed to get it all down. He had been expecting to breakfast on the cold leftovers of last night's argument so the eggs and Julia's general air of benevolence were a pleasant surprise.

Julia sipped a cup of weak tea and when he asked her why she wasn't eating – Julia loved food the way a dog does – she said, 'Funny tummy. First-night nerves. The press is going to be in, how ghastly is that? The idea of the show being reviewed is terrifying, almost as terrifying as it *not* being reviewed. And you know it's the Festival, so we won't get a proper theatre critic, they're too busy on The Next Best Thing, we'll get some nerd who usually subs the sports section. If only we had another preview.'

'How did it go last night?'

'Oh, you know.' She shrugged. 'Awful.'

Jackson's heart went out to her.

'I'm sorry I was grumpy with you,' Julia said.

'I was grumpy too,' Jackson said magnanimously. He didn't think he had been really but it didn't hurt to be a little chivalrous, especially as he presumed the logical outcome of Julia in a towel making him breakfast in bed was going to be sex, but when he made a playful grab at her she jumped off the bed as neatly as a cat and said, 'I have to get on, I've got so much to do.' At the door to the bedroom she turned back and said, 'I love you, you know.' At the beginning of a relationship, Jackson had noticed on more than one occasion, people looked happy when they said, 'I love you,' but at the end they said the same words and looked sad. Julia looked positively tragic. But then that was Julia, always overacting.

Jackson's phone rang and he considered not answering it. Good news always sleeps till noon, isn't that what they said – or were they the lyrics to a Cowboy Junkies song? He answered it and had to riff on his memory for a while before the name meant something. Martin. Martin Canning, the guy who threw the briefcase at Terence Smith. An odd little guy.

'Hey, Martin,' Jackson said, adopting a false kind of camaraderie because the man sounded slightly unhinged. 'How can I help you?'

'I wonder if you could do me a favour, Mr Brodie?'

Jackson could no longer hear the word 'favour' without thinking it had dark implications. 'Sure, Martin, I haven't got anything else to do today. And it's Jackson, call me Jackson.'

'What are you going to do today?' Julia asked, fully dressed now and too distracted by her own day to be truly curious about his. She was applying her make-up in a little mirror propped up on the kitchen table. A light dusting of face powder had fallen on a pyramid of oranges balanced in a glass oven dish. Jackson didn't remember buying any fruit.

'I've got a job,' he said.

'A job?'

'Yes, a job. Some guy wants babysitting today.'

'Babysitting?'

Jackson wondered if she would just keep echoing back to him what he said to her. Wasn't this what the Queen was supposed to do? It gave the impression of polite conversation, it gave the impression that you were genuinely interested in what the other person was saying without you having actually to engage with them on any meaningful level, or even listen to them. Testing the theory, he said to Julia, 'And then I thought I might go and drown myself in the Forth,' but instead of parroting, 'The Forth?' Julia turned and gazed at him thoughtfully, seeing him rather than looking at him, and said, 'Drowned?'

Jackson sensed the mistake immediately. Julia's eldest sister, Sylvia, had drowned herself in the bath, a formidable act of will that Jackson almost admired. She was a nun so Jackson supposed all those years of discipline had put the iron in her soul. His own sister hadn't drowned, she had been raped and strangled and then dumped in a canal. Water, water, everywhere. They were linked, he and Julia, by these things. 'Like some kind of karmic concatenation,' she had ruminated once. He had to look up the word 'concatenation'; it had sounded Catholic, but it wasn't. From the Latin 'catena', a chain. The chain of evidence. Chain of fools. He wished now he'd had a classical education rather than an army education. A good school, a degree, the world his own daughter was growing up in. The world Julia had grown up in, but then look how fucked up that had been. He wanted to tell Julia about the woman in the Forth, about his own near-drowning experience, but she had returned to herself, applying lipstick, peering at her lips in the mirror with professional detachment, smacking them together and making a face as if she was kissing her reflection.

Jackson wondered what it said about a relationship when you were unable to tell the 'object of your affection' that you had been pulled out of the water like a half-drowned dog. 'Lucky' – inevitably – had been the name of the dog that had scooted with joy off the pier at Whitby. The owner of the dog, the first man to drown that day, had a wife and an eight-year-old daughter and Jackson had wondered what had happened to the dog. Had they taken Lucky home with them?

'But you'll be finished in time for the show?' Julia said.

'The show?'

As she was going out of the door Julia said, 'Oh, while I remember, can you do me a favour? I dropped the memory card off in the chemist next to the flat. I thought if you didn't have anything better to do you could pick up the photographs.'

'And what if I do have something better to do?'

'Do you?' Julia said, curiosity rather than sarcasm in her voice.

'Hang on,' Jackson said, 'back up – what photographs? What memory card?'

'The one from our camera.'

'But I lost the camera,' he said. 'I told you I lost it at Cramond.'

'I know and I told *you* that I phoned up the police lost property at Fettes and someone had handed it in.'

'What? You didn't tell me that.'

'Yes, I did,' Julia said, 'unless there was someone else lying next to me in bed *pretending* to be Jackson.'

When had Julia had time to drop things off at the chemist, to fill up the fruit bowl, to make phone calls, have lunch with Richard Moat? And yet she hadn't had a second to give *him*.

'Scott Marshall,' she continued blithely, 'that nice boy who plays my lover, drove out to Fettes and picked it up for me.'

'They just handed it over to him?' Jackson said, astonished (*my lover*, the way she said it, so casual). 'Without any proof?' He thought of the image of the dead girl trapped in the camera. Had someone looked at it, developed it?

'I described the first three photographs on the memory card over the phone,' Julia said, 'and that seemed to satisfy them. And I told them that someone called Scott Marshall would be picking up the camera. He showed them his driving licence. Crikey, Jackson, do we have to dissect every aspect of police procedure regarding lost property?'

'What *are* the first three photographs on the memory card?' Jackson asked.

'Are you testing me?'

'No, no, I'm intrigued. *I* have no idea what they are.'

'They're of you,' Julia said, 'they're of you, Jackson.'

'But—'

'I have to dash. Sorry, sweetie.'

No wonder identity fraud was such a fast-growing crime. The chemist was as lax as the police. Jackson had no receipt, no proof that the photographs were his, yet they were handed over promptly to him when he said that 'Julia Land' had dropped them off this morning. The chemist (a man) smiled at him in a knowing way and said, 'Yes, of course,' so Jackson presumed that Julia had used the full force of her orange-selling charms on him. If you were a man you could be eighty with a Zimmer and Julia would flirt with you while she helped you across the road — because, and this was one of the reasons he loved her, she was the kind of person who walked old people across the road, helped blind people in supermarkets, scooped up lost cats and injured birds.

She couldn't help the flirting, it came automatically to her as if it was embedded in her personality. Julia flirted with *dogs*, for heaven's sake. He had even seen her flirt with inanimate objects, cajoling a kettle into boiling faster, a car to start, a fire to catch. *Oh, come on, sweetie, if you just try a little bit harder you can do it.*

Perhaps he should look on it as a social service rather than a threat, send her out to old people's homes to give old guys the illusion of virility, make them feel good about themselves again. *Viagra for the mind*. There was something pathetic about old men. Guys who had fought in wars, witnessed empires topple, strode around boardrooms and factory floors like kings, won the bread, paid the dues, walked the walk, talked the talk and now they couldn't even piss without help. Whereas old women, no matter how frail, never seemed as pitiful. Of course there weren't as many old men around as there were old women. Dry and brittle as old kindling maybe, but they were built to last.

He took the photos into Toast and settled into a booth. He felt an emotion similar to that of un-wrapping a gift, the same anticipation, the same surge of excitement, only on the dark side – the obverse, that was the fancy word for it, the word Julia would have used. The photograph would be welcome proof that he hadn't hallucinated his experience in the Forth; un-fortunately it would also be unwelcome proof that someone, somewhere was dead.

A waitress brought over his coffee and when she was safely back behind the counter he opened the packet of glossy six-by-fours. They were printed in the order they had been on the memory card – the first three were indeed of Jackson, taken in the snow in France on Christmas Day, Julia trying out her new camera. He looked much the same in all three, striking awkward poses, managing a half-smile in the last one after much coaxing on Julia's part. *Oh, come on, sweetie, if you just try a little bit harder you can do it.* He hated having his photograph taken.

Then there were a couple more of France and then nothing until Venice because Julia had accidentally left the camera behind when she returned to London after New Year. She had packed in haste, typical Julia, and they had made love, a last minute farewell thing, when she should already have been on the road to the airport.

He dialled Louise's mobile number. The phone rang for a long time.

Venice still looked beautiful but now, rather than simply being holiday photographs, the little Canalettos looked like poignant images of halcyon days, a record of their golden age together as a couple. Just before the cracks appeared. *A couple? Is that how you think of us?*

When Louise Monroe called him 'Jackson' yesterday (*Let's face it, Jackson, on paper you just don't look good*) it felt like a switch had been thrown, just that little buzz of an electrical current kicking in. Bad dog, Jackson. He had thought better of himself than that.

She was, let's face it, his type. Julia was so much not his type that she was off the radar. *Louise.* This was what happened when you went over to the dark side. When you became bad Jackson, you started to lust after other women. *Watch out for Pisceans*, Julia had said. Was Louise Monroe a Piscean? She would be a new path. Not necessarily a good path or a better one, just a new one.

After several rings a male voice (posh Edinburgh) answered, 'The Monroe residence, can I help you?' Jackson was caught off guard, he hadn't expected a man to answer, much less a pretentious-sounding wanker. Before he could say anything she came on the phone with a snappish 'Yes?'

'It's Jackson, Jackson Brodie,' he said.

He had reached the last photograph of Venice. It was

the view from their hotel window, over the lagoon, taken at the last moment by Julia (*Wait – we'll forget this view*) before they boarded the Cipriani's launch to St Mark's Square for the last time. She was right, he would have forgotten the view if there had been no record of it. But at the end of the day, no matter how beautiful, it *was* just a view. He could see what she meant about having people in photographs – if she had been standing at the window with the lagoon behind her it would have been a completely different photograph.

Then there was the photograph of him next to the One O'Clock Gun, with the Japanese, then the photograph of the National War Memorial building. There was only one more photograph after that. It was black, entirely black. Puzzled, Jackson rifled through the pictures again. Same result – nothing. No sign of the dead girl at all. Only the black photograph. He was reminded of the black square that Julia gazed into every night, the raging Arctic storm. He was wondering if the photograph of the dead girl had been erased, perhaps accidentally. He knew that you could never erase anything completely, it wasn't deleting a file that destroyed it, it was writing new data over it. There were programmes designed for retrieving images. It would be easy enough for a camera shop to do. Or police forensics.

'Did you want something?' Louise asked. 'Or did you just ring to annoy me?'

'You're not really a morning person, are you?' he said. He suddenly realized what had happened. In his hurry to take the photograph – dead body, rising tide and so on – he had left the lens cap on. Oh *shit*. He banged his head on the table. The other patrons of Toast looked at him in alarm.

'Hello? Calling Jackson.'

'Nothing, I don't want anything. You're right, I was just ringing to annoy you.' He remembered something, something the crazy Russian girl said to him last night, and he asked Louise what she knew about real homes for real people.

'Squirrels are eating my house,' Louise Monroe said unexpectedly.

'OK,' Jackson said slowly, unable to think of any kind of response to that statement. He wondered if they were particularly big squirrels.

38

LOUISE WAS STRUCK BY AN ODD KIND OF TERROR, SOME vague memory of a documentary or a film – fact or fiction, she didn't know – a man waking up in a stupor and discovering that his entire family had been butchered while he slept, stumbling from room to room and finding their bodies.

She woke up suddenly, too suddenly, tachycardiac and sweating, and it took several seconds before she was convinced it was a dream. That was when she heard the scrabbling. In the walls? Or above her head? Above her head. Claws or nails on wood, scratching, something running. It stopped. Started again, stopped again. She tried to imagine what was making the noise. Rodent Olympics in the attic. A couple of years ago and she would have been able to put Jellybean up there, the feline terminator. Asleep on the bed, he shifted against her foot. She would have liked his professional opinion on the scratching, scrabbling things but she didn't want to disturb him. He slept nearly the whole day and night now. She had begun to think in terms of last days, that this might be his last breakfast, his last wash, his last walk outside. She no longer bought him cat food, instead she went to Marks and Spencer's food hall and chose organic smoked salmon, slices of cooked chicken breast and cartons of fresh custard, none of which he was able to take more than a few half-hearted mouthfuls of, more to please her, Louise suspected, than from any real hunger. The last supper. Archie complained that he didn't get fed as well as the cat and he was right.

She hauled herself out of bed and padded along the hall, where she opened the door to Archie's bedroom – she just needed to be completely sure that the nightmare had been a nightmare. Both boys were sprawled in sleep, Archie in his bed, Hamish in a sleeping bag on the floor. The room stank of boys. Louise imagined a girl's room would smell of nail varnish, pencils, cheap candy sweets. Archie's room was essence of testosterone and feet. In the gloom, she could just make out the rise and fall of Archie's breathing. She didn't bother examining Hamish for signs of life, boys like him should be culled as far as she was concerned.

Retrieving her heavy police-issue Maglite from under her pillow, she pulled down the Ramsay ladder from the trapdoor in the landing ceiling. She climbed up and lifted the trapdoor cautiously, imagining things jumping on her head and getting tangled in her hair, nibbling on her ears and lips.

The tiny attic skylight let in more of the morning than she'd expected and extra illumination was provided through gaps in the slates. Louise was pretty sure there shouldn't *be* gaps between the slates. It wasn't really an attic, just a loft space that contained the water tank and had no flooring or power. An electric cable snaked across the floor instead of being snugged away in trunking, and she could see that part of the plastic outer covering had been eaten through, exposing bare wires. The rafters and joists were rough and splintery and there was no insulation. Louise wondered if it was illegal to build new houses without insulation. The loft seemed to underline the fact that the house had a permanently unfinished feel to it.

Something moved in the far corner, something small and nimble, a grey whisk of tail and then it was gone, through a tiny hole where the roan-pipe met the small overhang above the downstairs living room. A squirrel.

Louise swept her Maglite over the wall. She could see quite clearly now where the squirrel had made his getaway – a chink in the fabric of the house where a lump of cement must have fallen out, or (more likely, knowing Hatter Homes) had never been there in the first place. She ran the torch over the gable wall, an archaeologist opening up a pharaoh's tomb, and frowned as she traced a crack that ziggurated down the mortar between the bricks. It didn't look like something you could blame on squirrels.

She made the awkward journey back through the trapdoor and down the ladder. As she reached the bottom rung she nearly jumped out of her skin when a hand touched her bare arm. Hamish held out a mug of coffee to her, the image of a helpful butler, except that he was wearing nothing but a pair of boxers. Advanced for his age. She was suddenly acutely aware of the shortness of the old T-shirt she had slept in. The little fucker had been looking up it the whole time she'd been climbing down the ladder.

'I put in milk but no sugar, Louise,' he said. 'I thought you looked like someone who watched their figure.' She considered punching him but she didn't want coffee all over the hall, or a lawsuit from his banker daddy, an arsehole whom Louise had met at a parents' evening. No coincidence that banker rhymed with wanker.

'Thank you,' she said and took the coffee from him. 'You'd better get a move on, Hamish, you're going to be late for school.' She emphasized the word 'school', just to remind him that he was actually, technically, a *child*. She wanted to see a little scowl of humiliation on his smooth, bourgeois features but instead he said, 'Goodness, Louise, you really need to chill.'

Louise pulled on shapeless sweats and went outside. She was still fuming at Hamish – now making breakfast in her kitchen, as comfortable as if he was in his own home. He made a surprisingly good cup of coffee though. Archie had no idea how to make coffee unless it was instant. Louise wondered if Hamish made coffee for his own mother. It must be nice to have someone who did things for you. Perhaps in his own house he was as asocial and uncomfortable as Archie was at home, and perhaps, conversely, when he went to Hamish's house, Archie went around like Little Lord Fauntleroy, saying, 'Can I get you more tea, Mrs Sanders?' to Hamish's mother. No, that was a fantasy too far.

She stood on the pavement on the opposite side of the road sipping her coffee while scrutinizing her house for flaws in the brickwork.

From somewhere inside the house she could hear her mobile start to ring.

'That's quite a crack,' a voice said. She turned and saw her next-door neighbour unlocking his car. He nodded his head in the direction of her front door and climbed into the driving seat, his family piling in after him. Louise moved smartly away from where she'd been standing and, looking up, saw a fissure crow-stepping its way down between the brickwork above the porch. *I'll huff and I'll puff and I'll blow your house down.* In the story, the Big Bad Wolf hadn't been able to blow down the house made of bricks, built by the sensible pig. Unfortunately, a sensible pig hadn't built Louise's house. Louise's house had been built by the Big Bad Wolf himself, Graham Hatter. What had Jessica said? *Subsidence or something.*

'Fuck,' she said.

The neighbour winced. He was some kind of Christian, he had one of those fish stickers on his car, and he obviously expected better of the police force. Weekday mornings he drove his children to school, Saturday morning to the swimming, Sunday morning to church. Mr Straight Guy. The Vanilla Family. She hated them. 'Fuck,' she said to see him wince again. 'Fuck, fuck, fuck.' He drove off in a cloud of disapproval.

Hamish appeared at the front door, holding her phone aloft. 'You have a gentleman caller,' he said. He was very camp sometimes, so maybe he wasn't the salacious hetero he pretended to be. Would she be able to say to her colleagues at Corstorphine, *My son is gay*? Say it loud and say it proud. It was a conversation she just couldn't imagine somehow. Fourteen, she reminded herself: they were still children, they had no idea what or who they were. She crossed back over the road and snatched her mobile off Hamish.

'Yes,' Louise said sharply into the phone and then was sorry because it was Jackson Brodie, and then she was even more rude to him, punishing him for the fact that she had experienced a twitch of pleasure at the sound of his voice.

'I just wondered,' he said, 'if the words "real homes for real people" meant anything to you?'

'What?'

'Real homes for—'

'I heard you. You're not still sleuthing around, are you? "Real Homes for Real People" is the slogan of Hatter Homes. Their headquarters are in Edinburgh, still a family business. Graham Hatter's a Scottish bigwig, millionaire businessman, etc. I live in a Hatter Home. It's a pile of shite. Squirrels are eating my house.'

She had waited until Archie and Hamish were sprawled in the living room watching MTV with their breakfast, oblivious to anything that wasn't their own stupid little world, and then she had snuck into Archie's bedroom. She struck the space bar on the hibernating screen of his computer and a page of text came up. She scrolled down and read, *'You know, Bertie, you've got to remember the rich aren't like us.'*

'I know, miss. They've got more money.' It was a story or a novel. Archie was writing a novel? When pigs flew. And if Archie wrote a novel it wouldn't be this kind of novel, it would involve the destruction of the world by robotic cyber machines, with compliant sex-doll women thrown in for good measure. She went into My Documents. The novel was on a CD. Definitely not Archie's. There was correspondence from an 'Alex Blake', apparently replying to fan letters. Other correspondence with the same address from a Martin Canning. There was a part of a manuscript, a novel – several chapters of something called 'Death on the Black Isle'. This was what Archie and Hamish had been reading out loud last night. *'I think there's more to this than meets the eye, Bertie.'*

Then it had hit her – 'Alex Blake' was the name of the guy whose house Richard Moat had been murdered in. Martin Canning was his real name – or was it the other way round? Her son, her *harmless* son, was in illegal possession of something that must have come from a murder scene. What else had they done? She felt something scooped out and hollow where her stomach used to be.

39

GLORIA HAD INTENDED THE EARLY-MORNING BLAZE IN THE garden brazier to be symbolic, a pyre for the past Gloria (Graham's wife) and a signal for the future Gloria (Graham's widow). She had imagined herself emerging from the flames like a phoenix so it was rather disappointing that her wardrobe hadn't made more of a show, even if it was only a couple of evening dresses – expensive, designer things that she had worn for company dinner-dances. Gloria had an uncomfortable vision of herself teetering into a succession of hotel ballrooms over the past thirty-nine years, mutton dressed as mutton, her body stuffed into the glittering carapace of a spangled dress and her small feet ('pig's trotters', Graham called them) bound in unsuitable shoes.

Because he *would* soon be dead, she felt sure of it. Dead as a dodo. Dead as mutton. Dead as a doornail. Why a doornail? Why was a doornail deader than anything else? (The door itself, for example – equally dead, surely?) Did dead exist in the comparative?

Could something be deader than something else? Dead, deader, deadest. Graham would be deader than Gloria. He would be superlatively dead. It had taken a lifetime for Gloria to realize how much she disliked Graham.

There was more smoke than fire so she threw a firelighter into the brazier and watched the little tongues of green and blue flame as they began to lick at a rhinestone-encrusted bolero jacket by Jacques Vert. Mineral to mineral, dust to dust. The clothes hadn't reduced to the soft, powdery ash she had imagined.

The electronic gates opened and closed several times. If Gloria hadn't known that the man from the security company was down in the basement checking the system she would have thought that a crowd of invisible people were being slowly filtered on to the property.

She watched a thrush pulling an elasticated worm from the lawn. Birds (apart from magpies) were Good Things. Even when they were killing other things. The birds ate the worms, the worms might soon be eating Graham. Graham had eaten birds (chicken, turkey, duck, pheasant, grouse, partridge) and so the cycle of life would be complete. Since Graham's authoritarian regime was suspended unexpectedly, Gloria hadn't eaten anything that breathed. Graham always said he wanted to be burnt, not buried, at the end, but Gloria thought it would be a shame to deprive all those small industrious creatures of a good meal.

Let the punishment fit the crime. She had attended a particularly rousing amateur production of *The Mikado* at the King's last year. She was very fond of Gilbert and Sullivan opera, at least the better-known ones. Some things were obvious – a man who kicked a dog to death, for example, should himself be kicked to death, preferably by dogs but that wasn't really possible, the anatomy of a dog didn't lend itself to kicking. Which said a lot about dogs, if you thought about it. Gloria would be happy to undertake the kicking herself if necessary. But as for Graham – what would be a suitable punishment for him?

Perhaps he should be forced to sit (or, better still, stand like a Victorian clerk) in an airless, windowless office all day, shuffling his way through endless sheaves of papers – insurance claims, VAT returns, tax returns, double accounting ledgers – all of which he would have to fill in accurately and truthfully by hand. Or, better still, he would have to stand all day and all night for the rest of time counting other people's money without ever being allowed to pocket so much as a farthing for himself. Gloria missed farthings, the littlest coin with the littlest bird on it.

She gave the brazier one last poke. Perhaps she should cremate Graham after all, just to make absolutely sure he couldn't come back.

In the paper (she must cancel the newspapers, they weren't healthy) there was an article about a court case – a teenager had broken into an old people's home and stolen wallets and purses and watches from the rooms and then he had taken an old woman's pet budgerigar from its cage, wrapped Sellotape round and round its body and thrown it out of the window – five floors up. And this was civilization! How satisfying it would be to wind that teenager in Sellotape and throw *him* out of a fifth-floor window. Was there no one meting out justice in this world? Were the yobs and the magpies and the Grahams and the kitten-eating men and the budgie-taping teenagers *just going to get away with it*?

Upstairs in her bedroom, Gloria pushed aside the black plastic bag of twenty-pound notes in her wardrobe and retrieved a little-worn red velour 'leisure suit' that had been stuffed in the back of the wardrobe after only one outing because Graham had despised it at first sight, saying it made her look like a giant tomato. She regarded the image reflected back to her by the vast mirrors of the built-in wardrobes. A touch of the tomato it was true and it made her arse look enormous, but it covered her matronly bosom and iguana belly and it was comfortable and rather jaunty, the sort of thing a sporty Mother Christmas might have worn. Graham had never liked her using words like 'arse', he said a woman should be 'ladylike', like his own mother, Beryl, who, before she acquired her sponge-brain syndrome, had always referred to her rear end as her 'derrière', possibly the only French word she knew.

'Arse, arse, arse,' Gloria said to her mirrored behind. The red velour suit felt soft and snug, she imagined this was how babies felt in their clothes. She put on the trainers she had bought for her Nifty Fifties class, still more or less box-white and unsullied. As she made her way downstairs she felt lighter on her feet, as if she was ready for something. Ready to run.

Gloria sighed. She could hear Graham's whiny secretary, Christine Tennant, speaking to the answering machine again, *Graham, you're really needed here!*

Gloria picked up the phone and said, 'Christine, what can I do for you?' adopting the efficient tones of a woman who had worn heels and little business suits instead of slipping off a bar stool and following her prospective husband like a dog.

'The Fraud Unit have been here again,' Christine said. 'They want to question Graham. He's not really in Thurso, is he?' she added, sounding sad rather than bitter. 'He's betrayed us all, hasn't he? He's run off and left everyone else to face the music.'

'I don't know, Christine.' She replaced the receiver. She almost felt sorry for Christine, all those years of faithful service and nothing to show for it. Perhaps she could send her flowers or a fruit basket. A fruit basket was a nice thing to receive.

The man from the security company emerged unexpectedly and mole-like from the basement. 'There's something wrong with the sensors on your gates,' he announced, with more histrionics than seemed strictly necessary to Gloria. 'I've got your screens back up, and your panic buttons, but I'll have to come back later with new parts. I don't know what's been going on down there.'

He was a short man with many of the character problems of short men, Gloria noticed. He drew himself up to his full pompous height and said, 'You haven't let anyone suspicious in, have you?'

'Why would I let anyone suspicious in?' Gloria puzzled.

This didn't appear to be a satisfactory answer to him and with a promise that he would be back later he strutted his way down the garden path like a cock of the walk. A robin hopped along the path in the opposite direction, man and bird ignoring each other. The path was edged with borders of summer bedding plants – antirrhinums and salvias, neither of which were to Gloria's taste, but Bill had been an old-fashioned kind of gardener and she hadn't liked to request of him anything more avant-garde in the way of horticulture. If she were to stay in this house she would plant archways of roses and honeysuckle. Row after row of sweet peas. But she wasn't staying.

The strong aroma of coffee hit Gloria's nostrils and she followed its vapour trail, like an addicted Bisto Kid, back inside the house. It led her to the kitchen where Tatiana was sitting at the table, smoking and reading the newspaper. She tapped the headline ('Massive manhunt sparked by murder of Fringe comic') with a painted fingernail and said, 'Lot of bad people about.'

Tatiana had slept and breakfasted in a serviceable pair of Gloria's pyjamas but had now changed into something more sophisticated. She wore a pair of dainty shoes, 'Marc Jacobs,' she said, displaying her foot and admiring it, and was dressed in simple black trousers and a silk print top, 'Prada,' she said, stroking it. 'Prada is truth,' she added, blowing smoke up towards the ceiling. 'I know many truths, Gloria.'

'Really?' Gloria said. 'You'd better be careful then.'

Gloria's heart had nearly stopped when Tatiana walked into the basement last night. 'I thought you were dead,' Gloria said to her, and Tatiana laughed and said, 'Why would you think that? Front door isn't locked,' she added. 'Someone can kill *you* in your bed, Gloria.'

'I'm not *in* my bed,' Gloria said, following her up the stairs and into the kitchen, where she fumbled in a drawer for candles and matches. Before she could find either, the power came back on.

'It said in the newspaper that the police thought a girl who was wearing crucifix earrings might have drowned.'

'Ah, yes,' Tatiana said. 'Wasn't me.'

'Who was it?'

'You didn't call me, Gloria,' Tatiana said, ignoring the question, her mouth making a little moue of disappointment.

'I didn't know I was supposed to.'

'I gave you phone number.'

Gloria had given her phone number to a lot of people in her time and never expected any of them to call her back. Tatiana started raking through cupboards looking for something to eat and Gloria had sat her down and fixed them both toasted sandwiches. When she finished her sandwich Tatiana lit a cigarette and tore into a satsuma. Gloria had never seen anyone eat fruit and smoke at the same time. She made smoking look so enjoyable that Gloria wondered now why she had ever given it up. Something to do with pregnancy, but really had that been a good enough reason?

'Graham has a mistress,' Gloria said.

'Ah yes, Maggot,' Tatiana said. 'Voddabitch. He's going to leave you.'

Is it done yet, is it over? Have you got rid of Gloria? Have you got rid of the old bag? Not planning to kill her but to leave her, which was a relief. 'He should live so long,' Gloria said.

Tatiana had lost interest in the conversation. She stretched and yawned and said, 'I have to go to bed now,' so Gloria had put her in Emily's old room, where she snored like a trooper most of the night before waking up and asking for bacon sandwiches, 'With pickles. You have pickles?'

'Just Branston,' Gloria said.

It wasn't every day that a strange Russian dominatrix appeared out of nowhere and prowled around your house. Gloria followed Tatiana into the living room and watched her pick up and inspect several ornaments. The Moorcroft seemed to meet with her approval but not the Staffordshire figures, particularly the pair of 1850 creamers in the shape of cows which she judged 'vile'. She inspected the fabric of the curtains, sniffed the flowers, tested the chairs for comfort. Gloria wondered if she howled at the full moon.

Tatiana proceeded to play with the Bang & Olufsen remote control, particularly taken with the button that turned the lights on and off, before stopping her pacing to scrutinize herself in the mirror. Then she picked an apple from the fruit bowl and while she ate it (very loudly) she went through every station on the radio, pausing only to turn the volume up for Celine Dion's 'My Heart Will Go On'. And on and on and on. 'This is great song,' she said.

Gloria was fascinated. It was like being stuck in a cage with a restless and opinionated animal. Tatiana seemed utterly foreign in all ways. If you had sliced into her with a knife (although it was more likely to be the other way round) Gloria suspected she would have tasted of raw reindeer meat and smoky black tea and the iron tang of blood. Someone else's.

Finally, Tatiana threw herself on the sofa and blew air out of her mouth as if she were about to die of boredom. She scrutinized each of her fingernails in turn before fixing Gloria with a level gaze and saying, 'OK, Gloria. Shall we make a deal?'

Gloria had never made a deal in her life. She stood at the French windows and watched a huge wood pigeon, built like a cargo plane, waddling across the lawn. She turned back to look at Tatiana, another kind of wildlife, lying on the sofa and working her way through the channels on the television.

'A deal?' Gloria said. 'What kind of a deal?'

40

'CRIME WRITERS FOR LUNCH' — AS IF THEY WERE GOING TO BE eaten by their audience. 'Lunch' was coffee and filled white rolls, which were free and served from a bar at the back of the Spiegeltent. And the writers were the entertainment. Dancing bears. They used to teach bears to dance by putting the cubs on hot coals. That was humanity for you. Martin had seen a bear — not a dancing one — in St Petersburg. It had been with its owner, out for a walk on a lead, a brown bear as big as a big dog, on a small area of grass near the Neva. A couple of people were photographing it and then giving money to the man. Martin supposed that was why the man had the bear, to make money. Everyone was trying to make money in St Petersburg: teachers with no pensions selling books, gnarled old babushkas selling bits of knitting, girls selling their bodies.

The book event was being chaired by a gaunt woman whose credentials seemed vague, but in her introduction she claimed to be a 'huge fan' of 'genre writing', and 'What a wonderful privilege it was to have a group of such diverse writers with us this lunchtime.' Clap, clap, clap, hands raised high towards the three of them, a little geisha bow of obeisance.

Martin was sharing a platform with two other writers. One was an American woman by the name of E. M. Watson who was on a book tour, 'trying to break into the British market', and who wrote violent, edgy books about serial killers. In person, Martin had expected her to be precise and severe, dressed in black with a hint of Harvard about her, but she turned out to be a slightly frowzy blonde from Alabama with yellow teeth and a general air of sloppiness. When she spoke she put her hand in front of her mouth. Martin thought it was because of her yellow teeth but she turned to him and said, 'I don't want to open my mouth, they'll all hate my accent,' which came out more like '*Ahdantwanopnmamarth, theyolol hayet ma-acksent.*' No they won't, Martin reassured her. But they did.

Their little trio was completed by Dougal Tarvit, who lived up north, on Nina Riley's patch, and who wrote 'psychological thrillers' that were loosely based on real-life crimes. Martin had tried reading a couple but was put off by the fact that nothing really happened in them.

The Spiegeltent was full. Martin supposed the large audience was due to economics – free food, and three writers for the price of one – but in the lull before they began, it slowly dawned on him that *he* was the subject of the attention. People were talking to each other about him, quite loudly in some cases, as if he wasn't actually present. He distinctly heard a tightly querulous Morningside voice say, 'But I thought he was dead,' in a way that implied that the female owner of the voice had been cheated by his live appearance.

E. M. Watson leaned across and said, 'Hey, Alex, are you OK, honey?'

Martin reassured her he was. 'My real name's Martin,' he added. What did E. M. Watson call herself, he wondered, not Em, surely?

'No.' She laughed. 'It stands for Elizabeth Mary — two queens for the price of one, my momma used to say, but people call me Betty-May.'

'Christ,' they both clearly heard Dougal Tarvit mutter, 'it's like being trapped inside fucking *Steel Magnolias*.

Tarvit, slumped in his chair as if languor and bad posture were a mark of masculinity, seemed to hold his two fellow writers in contempt — E. M. Watson for being a woman and Martin for writing 'populist shite', words that were actually thrown in Martin's direction in the course of what turned out to be a dismayingly quarrelsome sixty minutes. ('Well, the scalpels seem to be out today,' the gaunt woman said, glancing nervously around as if marking possible exits from the Spiegeltent.)

'I thought this was just a reading,' E. M. Watson whispered to Martin. 'I didn't realize it was a debate.'

'It's not supposed to be,' he whispered back. Dougal Tarvit glared at them both. Martin regretted now that he had refused Melanie's offer to fly up; if nothing else, his agent was good for a scrap. Dougal Tarvit was all polemical bluster and would have been no match for Melanie. If slicing him with her tongue didn't

427

work, she would have beaten him to death with her bare fists.

'He's just jealous,' Betty-May whispered to Martin. 'You being involved in a real-life murder and all.'

'If you could each just read for ten minutes,' the gaunt woman said to them before they began, 'then there'll be time for lots of questions at the end.'

The audience was predominantly middle-aged and female, as usual at these events, although Dougal Tarvit's scathing presence had attracted a younger, mostly male element. Martin's typical audience was almost exclusively women older than he was. He looked for Jackson and saw him standing near the bar, straight-backed with his hands in front as if he was going to stop a penalty shot. All he was missing was the black suit and the earpiece to make him look like a presidential Secret Service agent. Jackson was standing very still, alert like an intelligent sheepdog, but his eyes roamed restlessly round the room. He had the reassuring demeanour of someone who knew what they were doing. Martin felt an absurd twinge of pride in Jackson's professionalism. He was the right stuff.

'Nothing's going to happen to you on my watch, Martin,' Jackson said laconically. Martin thought people only said that in films.

Betty-May read first, too fast and too breathless. The poor woman was stopped three times, twice by members of the audience asking her to 'speak up' or 'speak more clearly' and once by a mobile phone suddenly playing the opening bars of Beethoven's Fifth.

Tarvit, on the other hand, hammed it up like an old pro. His reading introduced the element of dramatic tension to his books that Martin hadn't found on the flat page. He read for a long time, much longer than his allotted ten minutes. Martin glanced surreptitiously at his watch and found only naked wrist – he still wasn't accustomed to it not being there. What had Richard Moat felt in the last minutes and seconds left to him? It didn't bear thinking about. Why had the person who killed Richard Moat phoned him? Was he going to come back and kill him as well? Had he intended to kill him all along and only just realized that he got the wrong person?

Martin's stomach growled so loudly that he was sure everyone must have heard it. It was a bit much to have to sit there and watch other people eat, especially when he'd had nothing so far today. Betty-May pressed a mint into his hand and gave him an encouraging yellow-toothed smile.

Tarvit had the audience in thrall, so that when he finished there was a collective sigh of deflation as if they wanted him to carry on. Please, no, Martin thought. The gaunt woman came on to the platform again and said, 'That was wonderful, Dougal, a pretty hard act to follow but I'm sure Alex Blake will try to live up to the challenge.' Thanks, Martin thought. 'If you could cut it a bit short, Alex,' she murmured to him.

When it came to question time, hands shot up everywhere. Young people, student types, ran around with microphones and Martin braced himself for the usual questions (*Do you write with a pen or a computer? Do you have a daily routine?*) Of course, he had once been on the other side of the platform, asking just those questions of the writers he admired. *Mr Faulks, who have been your literary influences?* I was that reader, Martin thought glumly. He was beginning to wish he had never crossed over.

But to his horror there were a barrage of questions aimed at Martin's new-found notoriety – *What did it feel like to be at the centre of a real-life murder investigation? Had it put his own work in perspective? Was it true that Richard Moat had been decapitated?* The gaunt woman stepped in anxiously, 'Perhaps these aren't appropriate questions, and I really don't think we should be talking about what is, after all, an on-going police investigation. Let's have some questions about the *work*, shall we? That's what we're here for, after all.' All the questions about the *work* were for Betty-May and Tarvit, not for Martin, except for a stout and insistent woman who wanted to know whether his faith helped his 'creativity' or was it the other way round? ('Hard to say,' Martin said.)

The gaunt woman – Martin had no idea what her name was and now never would probably – clapped her hands and said, 'Well, I'm sorry that's all we have time for, it's been such a treat, but if you all want to make your way over to the signing tent you will be able to buy copies of the books by our authors here and have them signed. So if you would just put your hands together, please . . .'

In the signing tent they sat at three identical tables. Every time an eager reader approached him Martin felt a little knock of panic to his heart, imagining each newcomer reaching across the table as he signed his name and stabbing him with a knife, shooting him with a gun. Or indeed, suddenly producing whatever weapon had been used to smash Richard Moat's skull and bringing it down on top of his own. Of course, most of them were ladies of a certain age, half of them wearing tweed, for heaven's sake. 'Death Wore Tweed', Martin thought gloomily. It would be a good title for a Nina Riley book.

Jackson was standing behind him, in the same bodyguard pose as before, and after a while Martin began to relax into the rhythm of things. '*And who shall I sign this to? To you? Or is it for someone else?*' '*Is that a Clare with an "i" or without an "i"?*' '*To Pam, with all best wishes, Alex Blake.*' '*And one for your friend, Gloria? Certainly.*'

When the last of the queue had dribbled away and they were returning to the 'authors' yurt', Betty-May Watson caught his sleeve and said, 'How about a crime writer for lunch?' Martin couldn't help but notice the faint six o'clock shadow on her lip.

'I'm afraid he has to go,' Jackson said, taking hold of Martin's elbow and steering him firmly away.

'Gosh,' Martin heard Betty-May Watson murmur, 'your publicist is so *strict*.'

41

NOW THIS WAS WHAT YOU CALL A MURDER INQUIRY. PEOPLE who were busy, busy, busy. People with a real body and crime scene photographs pinned up to prove it. A room humming with life because of a death. Louise studied the colour photographs of Richard Moat's corpse pinned up in the Major Incident Room at St Leonard's. The police station at Howdenhall was too small to accommodate something this big. Louise had worked out of St Leonard's when she was still in uniform. It was like going back to your old school. It felt familiar and alien at the same time.

'Nasty whack to the head that,' someone said behind her, making her jump. She turned and found Colin Sutherland standing behind her, smiling for Scotland. If he was in *The Bill* he'd be known as something like 'Smiler Sutherland' but, this being real life, he was usually referred to as 'that tosser, Sutherland'.

'Were you looking for me?' he asked, a hopeful expression on his face.

Louise smiled back at him and said conversationally,

'What's this guy Canning like? Is he a suspect?'

'Nah,' Campbell said. 'He's a funny little guy, bit of an old woman if you ask me, but I doubt he's the killing kind.'

'So,' Louise said casually, 'are you thinking burglary? Is anything missing from the house?'

'His phone, we think.'

'Nothing else?'

'Not that we know of.'

She could hardly be blatant and say, *No computer disks or anything like that?* Would they notice if a CD was missing? Probably not but Martin Canning would know, wouldn't he?

'Where is he? Canning?'

'In a hotel, the Four Clans, I believe.'

She wanted to say, *So you're not thinking two fourteen-year-old boys might have broken in and beaten the victim to death?* She gazed at a photograph of Richard Moat, he'd made a very messy corpse. Could her son be responsible for that? No, definitely not. Hamish maybe, but not her baby.

'You're very interested in this case, Louise. Do you want me to find room for you on the team? We've lost a couple of people to the flu. We could bring you over from Corstorphine if you're not busy over there.' He moved a step closer to her and she moved a step back. Perfect rhythm, they'd be doing the foxtrot next.

'No, no, just idle curiosity, boss.' Lies came easier than the truth. She pulled out a name from the past. 'Actually I was looking for Bob Carstairs.'

'Went upstairs a few months ago, Louise, didn't you hear?'

'Upstairs?'

'To meet the big boss.' The man was like a walking riddle. 'Dead. Heart attack,' Sutherland said with a huge grin. 'One minute here, the next minute gone.' He snapped his fingers like a magician. 'Just like that.'

Back at Corstorphine she went looking for Jeff Lennon and found him hiding away in a corner of the open-plan office, sitting at his desk, eating a bar of chocolate. Louise imagined him in retirement, lardy and bored. Or, more likely, on his way upstairs to meet the 'big boss'.

'Did you check the owner of that Honda, Jeff?'

Jeff took in a deep nose-breath as if he was in a yoga class. Louise had tried yoga but she found herself wanting to yell at the teacher to get a move on. Now she wanted to yell at Jeff Lennon. 'Certainly did,' he said eventually. 'I was just coming to find you.'

He didn't seem like a man who was planning on looking for anything in a hurry.

'It's a business called Providence Holdings.'

'Not Terence Smith then?' What did that mean, that Jackson Brodie had been wrong (or lying) when he said that Honda Man had been involved in the road rage? Or was Honda Man driving someone else's car, someone he worked for? Providence Holdings. 'Never heard of it,' she said. 'Does it mean anything to you?'

'No, but I did you a favour and looked it up in Companies House.'

'And?'

'The director is one Graham Hatter.'

'*The* Graham Hatter?'

'One and the same,' Jeff said.

'So Honda Man – I mean Terence Smith – works for Graham Hatter?' And Jackson had been asking about 'Real Homes for Real People' this morning. Making his bloody 'connections' everywhere. What did he know that he wasn't telling her? Withholding evidence, that was an *offence*, for God's sake. What was wrong with the man?

'I handed the info on to the team investigating the road rage,' Jeff Lennon said.

'It's a *team*?'

'Well, no, a couple of wee lassies.' Ah, sexism, thy name is Jeff Lennon.

'You're a star, Jeff. I owe you one.'

'Aye, you do,' he said cheerfully. 'How's that son of yours? Andy?'

'Archie. He's fine, thanks.'

42

JACKSON WORKED HARD AT SUPPRESSING A YAWN. THE AIR IN the Spiegeltent was thick and overheated. *Deconstructed romantic irony*, said the cadaverous woman who had introduced the writers on the platform, her words seemingly addressed to no one in particular. Jackson had no idea what she meant. She was wearing a low-cut top that revealed a bony sternum and breasts that hung like flaps. Someone give that woman a good meal, Jackson thought. Retaining an impassive expression on his face, he conjured up a picture of Julia's breasts, breasts he hadn't seen enough of recently. Louise Monroe had much smaller breasts, you didn't have to see her naked to know that. But she *had* them, there was no doubt about that. He mustn't think about Louise Monroe naked. He felt a stab of cuckolder's guilt. Very, very bad dog.

And, he noticed, here were *yet more* people who didn't seem to have jobs to go to, how did the economy of the country not collapse? Who was actually working? The foreign and the dispossessed – girls called Marijut and Sophia. And computer geeks, thousands of spotty boys who never saw daylight, the suits in the financial district, a few orange-sellers, and that was it. And the emergency services, of course, they never rested. He wondered how Julia's day was going. He checked his watch discreetly, perhaps she was having *lunch* with someone. Acting wasn't real work, not by anyone's definition of the word.

Martin, who clearly should be lying down in a darkened room listening to soothing music, was hysterically insistent that he appear at the Book Festival today even though it seemed an unnecessary kind of engagement to Jackson. He had already had to have a quiet word with a journalist who wanted to interview Martin. '*Sub judice*,' Jackson said to the man, rather more menacingly than he'd intended. He really wasn't in the mood today to be messed around with.

A lot seemed to have happened to Martin since Tuesday. A lot had happened to Jackson as well, of course, but Martin was winning hands down in the having-a-bad-day stakes.

'My laptop disappeared after I threw it at the Honda driver,' he said breathlessly when Jackson caught up with him at the Book Festival in Charlotte Square. He seemed slightly deranged. Of course, there was deranged and then there was deranged. Jackson wasn't sure he was up to the second kind but Martin seemed lucid and articulate. Perhaps a little too articulate for Jackson's liking.

'I spent the night in a hotel with the Peugeot driver

because the hospital was worried that he might be concussed. His name was Paul Bradley, only it turns out that it wasn't, because there's *no such person*. He doesn't *exist*. But of *course* he exists, you saw him, didn't you? He had a gun. It was a Welrod. But then I passed out because I think he drugged me and then he stole my wallet. I wouldn't mind but I saved his *life*.'

'A Welrod?' Jackson queried. How did Martin know about guns? About *Welrods*, for heaven's sake.

'And someone broke into my office, well, not broke in, there was no sign of a break-in, but there was a *sweet wrapper* on the floor—'

'A sweet wrapper?'

'*I don't eat sweets!* And now it turns out that Paul Bradley doesn't even exist! And he was my alibi.'

'Alibi?'

'For murder.'

'Murder?' Jackson revised his opinion: maybe this was the second kind of deranged.

'A man was murdered in my house! Richard Moat, the comedian, and then he phoned me.'

'Whoa! Richard Moat was murdered in *your* house?'

'Yes. And then he phoned me.'

'Yes, you said that.' Could Martin tell the difference between fact and fiction? He was a writer after all.

'Not him, I know it wasn't him. The murderer must have taken his phone – his phone was missing – and then he phoned me on it.'

'Why?'

'I don't know!'

'OK, OK, stay calm.' Jackson sighed. You said five little words to someone – *How can I help you?* –

and it was as if you'd mortgaged your soul to them.

Despite the fact that everything Martin said sounded outlandish there were little anchors of truth in his story. And who was Jackson to criticize? He had tried to save a dead girl from drowning, he had killed a dog with the power of his thoughts. Jackson wondered if Martin still lived with his mother. Not that there was anything wrong with that, Jackson would quite like to be living with his own mother, his time with her having been cut so short. No, Martin didn't live with his mother, he lived with Richard Moat, didn't he?

'Not *lived*,' Martin corrected. 'He was staying with me while he was up for the Festival. I hardly knew him actually. I didn't even like him. What if his killer is coming after me next?'

'I think you need to talk to the police, Martin.'

'No!'

'Give them your phone so they can try and trace the call.'

'No!'

They were a contentious bunch. He had never heard of Dougal Tarvit, or E. M. Watson. He'd never heard of Alex Blake, come to that, until yesterday evening. On his way over to the Book Festival, he had popped into a bookshop and leafed through one of Alex Blake's books in the coffee shop. It was innocuous stuff, depicting a kind of retro-utopian Britain that was rife with aristocrats and gamekeepers – although no one seemed to have sex (which would fit with Martin's neutered air). It was a nonsensical kind of setting where murders were tidy affairs that resulted in inoffensive corpses, the stuff of Sunday evening television, the equivalent of a hot bath and a warm mug of cocoa. The serfs weren't revolting, they were positively happy in their chains, and the rank smell of death didn't corrupt the genteel, heather-scented air around Nina Riley's head. *'Don't go in there, Miss Riley,' the gillie said, 'it's no' a sight for a bonny young lassie's eyes.'*

Nina Riley had a sidekick, didn't they all? Robin to her Batman. *I've discovered something important, Bertie. I must see you.* There was a guy named Burt who used to be his brother Francis's best friend. Both welders, both rugby players. Burt had broken down at Francis's funeral – it was the only thing Jackson could remember about his brother's funeral – Burt crying at the graveside, ugly masculine sobs, coughed up by a macho guy who probably hadn't cried since he was a baby. Francis had killed himself, in a brutal, casual way that Jackson now recognized as being typical of his brother. 'You stupid fucking bastard, Francis,' Burt had shouted angrily to the coffin as it was lowered, before a couple of guys wrestled him away from the open maw of the grave. Francis had never been 'Frank' or 'Fran', he had always been called by his full name. It had lent him a certain dignity that he had possibly never really earned.

Jackson didn't remember his sister's funeral because he hadn't attended it, staying with a neighbour instead. Mrs Judd. It was a long time since he'd thought about Mrs Judd, the sooty smell of her back parlour with its overstuffed cut moquette, the gold eye-tooth that gave her a slightly rakish, gypsy air although there had been nothing unconventional in a life defined by the pit – daughter of a miner, wife of a miner, mother of a miner.

Jackson was all dressed ready to go to Niamh's funeral – he could recall the black suit he was wearing, made from a cheap, felty material, he'd never seen it before and never saw it again – but when it came to the time to go he simply couldn't, shaking his head mutely when his father said, 'Best get going, son.' Francis said gruffly, 'Come on, Jackson, you'll be sorry if you don't come and say goodbye to her proper like,' but Jackson had never regretted not going to that terrible funeral. Francis was right though, he had never said goodbye properly to Niamh.

He was twelve years old and had never worn a suit before and it would be years before he wore one again – Francis's funeral hadn't merited one apparently – and all he remembered about that day was wearing someone else's ill-fitting suit and sitting at Mrs Judd's little kitchen table with its worn Formica, dotted with cigarette burns, and drinking sweet tea and eating a Bird's Eye chicken pie. Funny the things you remembered. *Bertie, this was no accident, this was murder!*

He had expected someone to come up to him in the coffee shop and ask him with a sarcastic sneer if he was intending to buy the book or just sit there all day and read it for free, but then he realized that no one cared and he could indeed have sat there all day, with a sickly latte and an even more sickly blueberry muffin, and read Alex Blake's entire oeuvre without paying if he so wished. Nobody worked and the books were free.

Jackson didn't read much fiction, never had, just the occasional spy or thriller thing on holiday. He preferred factual books, they gave him the feeling that he was learning something, even if he forgot it almost immediately. He wasn't really sure he saw the point of novels, though he didn't go around saying that because then people thought you were a philistine. Maybe he was a philistine. Julia was a great reader, she always had a novel on the go, but then her whole professional life was based on fictions of one kind or another, whereas his whole professional life had been based on fact.

He wasn't much better with art. All that fuzzy Impressionism didn't do it for him, he'd looked at endless water lilies and thought, what's the point? And religious painting made him feel like he was in a Catholic church. He liked representational art, pictures that told a story. He liked Vermeer, all those cool interiors spoke of an ordinariness he could relate to, a moment in time captured for ever, because life wasn't about legions of Madonnas and water lilies, it was about the commonplace of details – the woman pouring milk from a jug, the boy sitting at the kitchen table eating a chicken pie.

You could tell Tarvit was an arrogant prick and E. M. Watson (what kind of a name was that?) was just plain odd: either a badly put together woman or a man in drag. Transvestism was a mystery to Jackson. He had never in his life worn a single item of female clothing, apart from once borrowing a cashmere scarf from Julia when they were going for a walk and being troubled all afternoon by its perfumed softness around his neck.

Martin seemed blithely unaware of the signals that E. M. Watson was sending his way. The guy definitely had a look of celibacy about him, he reminded Jackson of a vicar or a monk. E. M. – Eustacia Marguerite or Edward Malcolm? Whichever, E. M. was going to have her work cut out with Martin.

Jackson felt faintly ludicrous, standing like a Secret Service agent behind Martin in the 'Signing Tent' (he had originally misread it as the 'Singing Tent' – an idea that had both alarmed and confused him). The Book Festival was a jamboree of tents and reminded him vaguely of an army field camp. He had a sudden flashback to the smell of the big top last night, the familiar scent of grass under canvas. The crazy Russian girl, like a bandit queen, with her knife at his throat.

Martin glanced up nervously as each new person approached him, as if he was waiting for an unknown assassin. Jackson didn't understand why he was doing the event if he was so worried. 'I'm not going to hide away,' Martin said. 'You have to face the thing you're afraid of.' In Jackson's experience it was often best to avoid the thing you were most afraid of. Discretion really was sometimes the better part of valour.

'But at the same time you're worried that someone's after you? The person who stole Richard Moat's phone, the person who broke into your office?'

'No, that's not who's after me,' Martin said. 'Cosmic justice is after me.'

'Cosmic justice?' Martin made it sound like a person, an outrider for the Four Horsemen of the Apocalypse.

'I committed a crime,' Martin said. 'And now I must be punished. An eye for an eye.'

Jackson tried to be encouraging. 'Come on now, Martin, wasn't it Gandhi that said, "An eye for an eye and the whole world will be blind"?' Something like that anyway. He had seen it on a T-shirt once, at a CND demonstration he'd policed in the Eighties. Last year Julia had made him go on an anti-war march. That was how far his world had turned around.

'I'm sorry,' Martin said. 'It's very good of you to do this.'

Jackson didn't mind, it had all the trappings of a job and he was doing something rather than just hanging around (although it felt very like hanging around). Close up and personal wasn't really his thing but he had done bodyguard detail in his time, knew the drill.

'Nothing's going to happen to you on my watch, Martin,' he reassured him. Moviespeak that seemed to make Martin happy.

Jackson wondered what 'crime' Martin had committed. Parking in a bus bay? Writing crap novels?

Martin was doing well, politely signing and smiling. Jackson gave him a thumbs-up sign of encouragement. Then he turned round and there she was, standing next to him.

'Jesus Christ,' he muttered. 'Would you not do that?'

He looked for the knife – just because he couldn't see it didn't mean that she didn't have it. In a previous life, under a previous regime, he expected she would have been a spy (or, indeed, an assassin). Maybe she still was.

'So, crazy Russian girl,' he said, 'how's it going?'

She ignored him and without any preamble handed him a photograph.

It showed a girl standing against a sea wall somewhere. 'Day trip to St Andrews,' the crazy Russian girl said. He couldn't keep on calling her that. She had said – what had she said? *Ask for Jojo*. That sounded pretty unlikely. A working girl's name. 'What's your real name?' he said to her. Real names had always seemed important to Jackson. *My name's Jackson Brodie*.

She shrugged and said, 'Tatiana. Is not secret.'

'Tatiana?' Jackson wondered if that was like 'Titania'. He had seen photographs of Julia playing the queen of the fairies in a drama-school production of *A Midsummer Night's Dream*, barefoot, almost naked, her astonishing hair let loose and garlanded with flowers. A wild girl. He wished he had known her then.

'Yes, Tatiana.'

'And the girl in the photograph?'

'Lena. She is twenty-five.' It was sunny in the photograph and the wind was blowing the girl's hair around, tiny crucifixes just visible in her ears. His mermaid. She looked remarkably like Tatiana, except that her eyes were kinder. 'Everyone says we look like sisters,' Tatiana said.

Tatiana had no grasp of the past tense, Jackson realized. It kept the dead girl in a present she no longer had a place in. He thought of all the other photographs of dead girls he had looked at in his time and felt the leaden weight of melancholy drop again. Josie had album after album of photographs documenting Marlee's existence from the moment of her birth. One day they would all be dust, or perhaps someone would find one in a flea market or a car-boot sale or whatever they would have in the future and feel the same sadness for an unknown, forgotten life. Tatiana nudged him in his bruised ribs with a sharp elbow and hissed, 'Pay attention.'

'What's with the crucifixes?' he asked.

'She buys them in jewellers, in St James Centre. Pair for her, pair for me – gift. She's religious. Good person. Meets bad people.' She lit a cigarette and stared into the distance as if she was looking at something that wasn't quite visible. 'Very good person.'

At the sight of the cigarette, a boy in a Book Festival T-shirt came running towards her. She stopped him at twenty paces with a look.

'I found her,' Jackson said. 'I found your friend Lena and then I lost her.'

'I know.' She took the photograph back off him.

'You told me last night to mind my own business,' Jackson pointed out. 'But now here you are.'

'A girl can't change mind?'

'I take it that Terence Smith is trying to kill you because you know what happened to your friend Lena? Did he kill her?'

Tatiana threw the cigarette on the ground. The boy in the Book Festival T-shirt, still hovering just beyond the range of her petrifying gaze, darted forward and picked up the burning stub. He looked like the kind of boy who would throw himself on a grenade to stop it killing other people.

'How did Terence Smith know my name?' Jackson asked.

'He works for bad people, bad people have ways. They have *connections*.'

That sounded pretty vague to Jackson's ears. 'How do I find him?'

'I tell you already,' she said crossly. 'Real homes for real people.' She leaned closer to him in that rather alarming way she had and fixed him with her green eyes. 'You're very stupid, Mr Brodie.'

'Tell me about it. Did Terence Smith kill Lena?'

'Bye-bye,' she said and waved her hand at him. He hadn't realized until then that it was possible to wave *sarcastically*. And then she was gone, slipping away into the eager, book-loving crowd.

Jackson managed to wrestle Martin away from E. M. Watson's ambiguous clutches. 'She prefers Betty-May,' Martin confided in a whisper.

'Does she?' Jackson said. He was struck by a thought. 'You don't have a car, do you, Martin?'

Martin's car was parked in the street outside his house where he had abandoned it the previous morning. Crime scene tape was strung across the end of his driveway and an assortment of police, uniform and plain-clothes, could be glimpsed coming in and out of the house. Jackson wondered if he had been identified last night on the Meadows. It was unlikely but it still might be best to avoid the long arm of the law. Martin certainly seemed to feel the same, shielding his face with the property newspaper that Jackson had just picked up. If Martin really had been phoned by Richard Moat's killer then he was withholding evidence, and by extension Jackson was now party to that. He sighed at the thought of how many charges he was stacking up.

He thought of Marijut in her pink uniform, *a maid, a friend, found a man who was murdered in a house we go to.* And this was the house. Favours again. They seemed to spread their tentacles everywhere that Jackson went. You say connection, I say connection. What did Martin know about them?

'Nice women,' Martin said, 'good cleaners. Wear pink.'

'How did you pay them?'

'Cash in hand to the Housekeeper. I always leave them a tip.'

'None of them ... How shall I put this, Martin? None of them ever offered extras?'

'Not really. But there was a nice girl called Anna who offered to defrost the fridge.'

'Right. Shall I drive?' Jackson said, feeling suddenly perky at the idea. Martin's car was an uninspiring Vectra but nonetheless it was four wheels and an engine.

'No, no, it's OK,' Martin said politely, as if he was doing Jackson a favour, for God's sake, sliding into the driving seat and turning on the engine. They set off in a series of kangaroo hops.

'Easy on the clutch there, Martin,' Jackson murmured. He hadn't actually meant to say that out loud, nobody liked a back-seat (or in this case, front-seat) driver, or so his ex-wife had constantly informed him. Men had no purpose on earth whereas women were gods walking unrecognized among them.

'Sorry,' Martin said, nearly skinning a bicycle courier. Jackson considered wresting the helm off Martin but it was probably good for the guy to feel he was in control of something, however badly.

'Where are we going, by the way?' Martin asked.

'We're going to buy a house.'

43

'WE'RE GOING TO BUY A HOUSE?'

'Well, we're going to *look* at houses,' Jackson said, rifling through the property newspaper. 'We're going to look at new developments. Hatter Homes, you know them?'

'Real Homes for Real People. I looked at one but it was a bit shoddy. I don't really like new housing estates.' He worried that Jackson might live in a new house on an estate and would be offended but Jackson said, 'Me neither. We're not *really* looking to buy,' he added. Martin wondered if Jackson thought he was simple. 'We're just going to pretend. I'm looking for someone. Watch out for that bus, Martin, I think it's going to sideswipe you.'

'Sorry.'

'This is a lovely room, a real family room.' The woman showing them round the Braecroft show home hesitated. Martin supposed that he and Jackson didn't look like a real family. The woman had a name badge that said 'Maggie' and was dressed like a holiday rep in sky-blue suit and multicoloured cravat. Martin wondered if he could get a name badge made – 'William' or 'Simon' or anything that wasn't Martin. It could be a very easy way to change your identity.

'Lovely,' Jackson said in a deadpan kind of way. It was a north-facing room, all the light seemed to be funnelled away from it. Martin felt an ache for his own home. Was he going to move back in when the police finished with it and spend the rest of his life living with the ghost of Richard Moat? Would he be able to sell it? Perhaps he could employ 'Maggie'. He imagined her showing prospective buyers around, saying brightly, *This is the living room, a lovely room, a real family room, and this is the spot where Richard Moat had his brains splattered.*

'Of course, all sorts of people enjoy living in Hatter Homes,' Maggie said, 'not just families. And what is a family anyway?' She frowned as if she was giving serious thought to this question. She seemed tense and overwound.

They traipsed after her up the stairs. 'Are you on a tight budget?' she enquired over her shoulder. 'Because the Waverley is more roomy and has a bigger garden – not that there's anything wrong with the Braecroft of course, it's an ingenious use of space.'

'Deceptively small,' Jackson muttered.

'And this is the master bedroom,' Maggie announced proudly, 'en-suite, of course.'

Martin sat down on the bed. He wanted to lie down and go to sleep but he supposed that wasn't allowed.

'Well, thank you, Maggie,' Jackson said, making his way back down the stairs, 'you've certainly given us a lot to think about.' She seemed to droop with disappointment, sensing a sale lost.

'Come into the Portakabin and I'll just take a note of your name,' she said.

Outside the light seemed harsher. The estate was in a dip between two hills and had strange acoustics so that you could hear the constant rumble of a motorway even though you could see no cars. A pot of dusty red geraniums sat next to the door of the Portakabin, the only sign of organic life. A JCB trundled past. The estate was still a building site even though half the houses were already occupied. There were some hard chairs in the Portakabin and Martin took a seat on one of them. He was so tired.

'And you are?' Maggie said to Jackson. 'David Lastingham,' Jackson said promptly.

'And your partner?' she asked, looking at Martin.

'Alex Blake,' Martin said wearily. It was his name, it belonged to him in a way that he suspected David Lastingham didn't belong to Jackson.

'And a contact phone number?' Jackson reeled off a number. Martin wondered if it was genuine.

'Oh, by the way,' Jackson said casually to Maggie, 'I'm an old acquaintance of Terry Smith's from way back – you don't know where I can get hold of him, do you? It would be great to catch up.'

A look of distaste passed across Maggie's face. 'I've no idea where Terry is today.' A mobile started to ring, and she dug into her handbag and said, 'Excuse me a minute,' and went outside. To Martin's surprise

Jackson leaped like a cat burglar over to the filing cabinet and started raking through it.

'I think that's illegal,' Martin said.

'I think you're right.'

'I thought you used to be a policeman.'

'I did.'

These were the kind of circumstances that made Martin feel nervous and he stood anxiously in the doorway and watched Maggie pacing around as she talked into her phone. She seemed to be having to raise her voice because of a poor signal and stopped every few seconds to say, 'Are you still there?' He heard her say, 'He's in Thurso, apparently. I know, I don't believe it either. I think he's abandoned me, after all his promises.' Her face seemed to collapse as she talked. She finished the call and dabbed at her eyes.

'She's coming back!' Martin hissed at Jackson.

By the time she returned to the Portakabin, her mask firmly in place, Jackson was engrossed in a brochure containing photographs of the various Hatter Homes on offer. 'They're all so lovely,' he said, 'I don't see how I could possibly choose.' He sighed and shook his head. He wasn't the least bit convincing. 'Anyway,' he said, turning to Martin, 'back to the batmobile, Robin.'

'Here, I think,' Martin said, drawing to a halt in front of a pair of electronic gates that stood wide open. They were in the Grange, at an address that Jackson had apparently stolen from Maggie's filing cabinet. 'Providence', a sign said on the gate.

'Who lives here?' Martin asked.

'Graham Hatter. Owner of Hatter Homes. He

employs Terence Smith so I'm thinking that he might know his whereabouts.'

'And who's Terence Smith?'

'It's a long story, Martin.'

I've got time, Martin thought, but he didn't say it. Time was the only thing he did have, nanosecond after nanosecond ticking down. 'I'll just stay here while you go in.' He yawned. He wondered if the Irn-Bru cocktail that the so-called Paul Bradley had given him had permanently affected his metabolism in some way. One minute he was so edgy he was twitching, the next he was so tired he couldn't keep his eyes open.

'Won't be long,' Jackson said.

Martin looked through his glove compartment for something to read. All he could find was a wad of flyers for Richard's show, miniature versions of his 'Comic Viagra for the Mind' poster that he must have left in there on Tuesday.

He closed his eyes and was just falling into a sickly doze when he suddenly heard an unmistakable tune. The hairs on the back of his neck stood up like bristles as the familiar opening bars of the *Robin Hood* theme tune wafted in through the car window. His heart bumped against his chest wall. Richard Moat's phone was ringing. In the street. Close by. Martin spun round, looking for the source of the fugitive theme. A blue Honda had driven up and parked behind his own car. A blue Honda. A blue Honda? No, there were thousands of blue Hondas around, it wasn't necessarily the one that belonged to the insane base-ball-bat-wielding driver. The theme to *Robin Hood* started up again. Martin opened the door and stumbled out of his car. There was no sign of anyone. Then he spotted him, walking up the driveway of the Hatters' house, the phone to his ear. It really was the Honda driver from Tuesday. The Honda driver had Richard Moat's phone. How could that be, unless he had killed Richard Moat? And why would he kill Richard Moat – unless it was the Honda driver who had picked up his laptop, found his address and come to Merchiston to kill Martin? Something grasped his heart and squeezed it. Fear.

Martin was expecting him to ring the doorbell and announce himself in the usual way but instead the Honda driver crossed the lawn and stood in front of the French windows. He finished his call and produced the baseball bat, again out of nowhere. He raised it high as if he was preparing to hit for the outfield, but instead he smashed it into the glass of the windows.

44

THIS WAS THE DEAL. WHEN CELINE DION HAD SUNG HER LUNGS out, when Tatiana had eaten her way through the fruit bowl, she reached into her bra, conjured out a memory stick, and said, 'Do you know what this is, Gloria?'

'A memory stick, I believe,' Gloria said.

'Whose memory stick, Gloria? Whose?'

'Yours?' Gloria hazarded, wondering if she was being subjected to some form of Slavic Socratic irony. 'I know it's not mine,' she added.

Tatiana handed her the memory stick and said, 'No, it's *ours*, Gloria. You share with me, fifty–fifty.'

'Share what?'

'Everything.'

The Magus' Book. Graham's secret accounts, all contained on one tiny tablet of plastic that Tatiana had taken from the pocket of Graham's summer-weight wool, as he lay flapping like a fish on his Apex bed.

'I thought you tried to resuscitate him,' Gloria said thoughtfully. Tatiana made a sad clown face. 'Don't,' Gloria said with a shudder.

There had been something on the radio this morning about horses. Someone had left dozens of horses locked up in a stable and gone away and all the horses had starved to death. Gloria thought about the big brown eyes of horses, she thought about *Black Beauty*, the saddest book ever written. She thought about all the horses with sad brown eyes that you could help if you had a lot of money. The headless kittens, the Sellotaped budgies, the mangled boys.

'Hm,' she said.

Gloria gazed thoughtfully at her screensaver of Border collie puppies for a while and then tapped the space bar and brought her computer back to life. She typed in 'Ozymandias' and, just like that, she entered into Graham's occult books.

'How did you know the password?' she asked Tatiana.

'I know everything.' Gloria could think of a lot of things that Tatiana probably didn't know (how to make scones, the whereabouts of the Scilly Isles, the terror of ageing) but didn't bother challenging her. She was oddly touched that Graham had used the title of the Shelley poem for his password. Perhaps he had, after all, appreciated the gift she had given him. Or perhaps he was just looking for the most obscure word he could find.

Graham's memory stick contained a lot of the humdrum of commerce – *feasibility studies, projected figures, tight margins*. The world seemed full of so many vague concepts but you had to wonder – were these actually important? (Were they even real?)

457

Shouldn't a person's life be based on simple, more tangible things – a bed of sweet peas staked in a garden border, a child on a swing, a certain slant of winter light. A basket of kittens.

There was a dismayingly large cache of emails that Graham had saved from Maggie Louden, little electronic billets-doux of the *my darling, what we have is so wonderful* type. Tatiana read out, in a drawling vampiric accent that rendered the sentiments ludicrous, '*Have you talked about the divorce with Gloria yet? You promised you would talk to her this weekend.*'

Attached to one of the emails was a folder of photographs, some of Graham and Maggie, although mostly of Maggie alone, taken by Graham presumably. Gloria couldn't remember the last time that Graham had taken her photograph.

'Voddabitch,' Gloria said.

He had taken her to York Races for Ladies' Day, something Gloria herself had suggested to Graham that they might do together, *a day out*. Maggie and Graham had stayed at Middlethorpe Hall (*Really lovely, darling, you are a god*). He had bought her a pink diamond – *Gorgeous, gorgeous, gorgeous. It's huge! (like you!). Someone's going to get a treat tonight!*

His emails to her tended to be more prosaic. *The new Ivanhoe is going to be a four-bedroom terrace, integral garage. We're trying to nail down sales before construction begins. Make a point of the laundry room. It's a big selling point.* Everything was business, even love.

Gloria couldn't have a pink sink but his mistress

could have a pink diamond as big as the Balmoral. It seemed a shame now that Graham's imminent demise might rob Gloria of the satisfaction of watching him squirm in the divorce courts. Half his income, half his business.

'Half of nothing, Gloria,' Tatiana said to her. 'Remember, Proceeds of Crime Act, 2002.'

Somehow Gloria wasn't surprised that Tatiana was up to date with the criminal justice system.

'It's all there, Gloria,' Tatiana said, and she was right, it was – the false accounting, the illegal bank transfers, the shell companies, the tax evasion. The money that Graham had passed through Hatter Homes' accounts, not just for himself but for other people – the man was a money launderer for hire, scrubbing away at the filthy lucre as if it was a vocation. There were codes and passwords for bank accounts in Scotland and in Jersey, in the Caymans, in Switzerland. The breadth and sprawl of it all was astounding. He owned the whole world.

'He owns Favours?' Gloria asked, squinting at the screen. 'With Murdo?'

'Everything is business, Gloria. Business and lies. You're old woman, you should know that by now. Move,' she commanded. Gloria shifted out of her seat and Tatiana took over at the computer, her hands poised above the keyboard like a virtuoso pianist about to commit to the performance of her career.

Gloria was intrigued. 'What exactly are you doing? Are you transferring money? Into the housekeeping account?' she added hopefully.

'If I tell you I have to kill you,' Tatiana said. She was like a comedy Russian. Gloria wondered if she really *was* Russian. There was no reason why she should be who she said she was. No reason why anyone should be who they said they were. People believed whatever they were told. They believed Graham was in Thurso. In the future, the future that was just beyond the path edged with antirrhinums and salvias, Gloria could be whoever she wanted to be.

Tatiana burst out laughing and slapped Gloria on the arm (quite hard) and said, 'Just joking, Gloria. I'm moving it into one of the Swiss accounts. Take fraud cops for ever to find it, long after other accounts are frozen and by then you and me—' She snapped her fingers in the air, 'Pouf! We are gone.'

'But how will we get the money out?' Gloria puzzled.

'Gloria, you are such *idyot*! It's Hatter Homes' account, you're director of company, you can take what you want out. You're important *businesswoman*. You better phone them and tell them we're coming because this is *lot* of money. Don't worry, Gloria. Remember, I work in *bank*.'

The doorbell rang. It was Pam.

'This isn't really a good time,' Gloria said.

'Your security gates are wide open,' Pam said, walking into the hallway. 'Anyone could walk in. I'm just on my way back from the Book Festival.' She marched, without being invited, into the living room and sat on the peach-damask sofa. Gloria followed, wondering how to get rid of her. Perhaps she could just snap her fingers and *Pouf!* she would be gone.

'I have to say, you didn't miss much,' Pam said. 'As

events go it was very unsatisfactory. It managed to be both argumentative and lacklustre at the same time. And I wasn't convinced by the filled rolls. Dougal Tarvit was all right but as for Alex Blake, what a disappointment.'

'Oh?'

'So short. Definitely something suspicious about him. I'm surprised the police don't have him in custody yet for Richard Moat's murder.'

'Oh?'

'I bought you a signed copy.'

'Oh?'

'Stop saying "oh", Gloria, you sound like a walking zero. Are you going to put the kettle on? I hear poor old Graham got stuck in Thurso.'

The doorbell rang again. 'Oh, for heaven's sake,' Gloria said.

'Inspector Brodie,' the man said, stepping forward and shaking her hand.

'An inspector calls,' Gloria said. She presumed he was a fraud officer but didn't they hunt in packs? He followed her into the living room. She wished she had kept him on the doorstep, like a Jehovah's witness. All these unwanted visitors were an unwelcome distraction from the international banking fraud that Tatiana was committing in the kitchen, overseen by Gloria's red KitchenAid and Delia Smith's *Complete Cookery Course.*

'Tea?' Gloria offered politely, trying to remember if he had shown her any ID. Where was his warrant card? He was saying something about road rage when

Tatiana glided in from the kitchen and said, 'Hello, everybody,' like a poor actress in a farce.

'Oh,' Pam said.

'We have to stop meeting like this,' the policeman said to Tatiana. 'People will begin to talk.'

Whatever else might have been said after that was never spoken because Graham's golem chose that moment to put in the French windows with a baseball bat and Pam started screaming as if she was trying to summon all the demons out of hell and she didn't stop screaming until the stranger appeared in the garden and shot the golem in the heart.

45

JACKSON HADN'T INTENDED TO IMPERSONATE A POLICEMAN, yet when the door was opened and he said, 'Mrs Hatter?' and she said, 'Yes,' it came out automatically. It had seemed the most natural thing in the world to say, 'Inspector Brodie.'

Gloria Hatter was dressed in a red tracksuit that reminded him, in a distant pocket of his memory, of Jimmy Savile on *Jim'll Fix It*. Luckily she wasn't wearing a medallion or smoking a cigar. She seemed to think he was with the fraud squad and he didn't go out of his way to disabuse her of this notion.

When he mentioned the Honda and the road-rage incident she said, 'I didn't see anything,' and he said, 'You were there as well?' in disbelief. A vaguely familiar woman with orange hair was sitting on the sofa holding a copy of Martin's latest book, *The Monkey-Puzzle Tree*. That detail alone sent Jackson's brain spinning. Boxes within boxes, dolls within dolls, worlds within worlds. Everything was connected. Everything in the whole world.

The phone rang and an answering machine some-where kicked in. A woman's hysterical voice that could have been announcing an alien invasion shouted, *Gloria! It's Christine! They're here. They're taking the computers!*

Jackson was distracted from this message by Tatiana's entrance. He thought, this is too much, it really is. When Honda Man, complete with baseball bat, appeared at the French windows like a character in a horror movie and created air where previously there had been glass, Jackson began to wonder if he was on some new kind of reality television show, a cross between *Candid Camera* and a murder mystery weekend. He half expected a presenter to leap out from behind the sofa in Gloria Hatter's living room and shout, 'Surprise! Jackson Brodie, you *thought* you found a corpse in the River Forth, you *thought* you witnessed a man being assaulted with a baseball bat, you *thought* this little Russian lady here whispered clues in your ear (yes, she doubled as that mysterious corpse) but no, it was all a fiction. Jackson Brodie, you are live in front of an audience of millions. Welcome to the future.'

They were all here, Tatiana, Honda Man, the only person missing was Martin. But, lo, he had thought too soon because here came Martin, striding with more purpose than hitherto across Gloria Hatter's admirably well-kept lawns, *and also starring Martin Canning as the deceptively bumbling writer!*

Tatiana shouted something in Russian that sounded like a curse, while Gloria Hatter, less dramatically, said, 'Terry, what on earth do you think you're doing?'

'He's gone,' he shouted at her. Spittle flew out of his mouth, reminding Jackson of his dog. 'Mr Hatter, he's done a runner. He's left me to carry the fucking can, hasn't he?' And then with one easy motion he swung body and bat and smashed a glass display cabinet that contained a host of animal ornaments. The man really liked the sound of breaking glass. He turned back to the room and hesitated for a moment as if unsure what to choose next, time enough for Jackson to herd Gloria Hatter and her orange-haired friend behind the sofa (where there was no TV presenter, thank goodness).

Terence Smith seemed to notice Jackson for the first time and a frown settled on his dumpy features. 'You?' he puzzled. '*Here?* Why?' Then he spotted Tatiana. 'And you as well?' He lifted the bat again and swung it in Tatiana's direction. Jackson made a dive for her, a rather inept rugby tackle, trying to bring her down and shield her with his body. Terence Smith caught him mid-air with a fierce smash at the waist so that Jackson folded in half as if he was hinged and dropped to the carpet. A nice carpet, he noted, one of those thick Chinese ones with a pattern that looked as if it had been sculpted. He had a very close-up view of it. If he turned his head slightly, with great difficulty and much pain, he could also see Martin – still walking purposefully towards the house, his arm stretched straight in front of him as if he was leading a cavalry charge. At the end of the arm was his hand (as you would hope) and in his hand a gun. The Welrod. The Welrod that had puzzled Jackson when Martin mentioned it this morning.

Jackson thought, well, OK, designed for covert

close-up work but still capable of being lethal at a distance, but only in the hands of someone who knew how to shoot because the sight on a Welrod was primitive. And you only got one shot because by the time you'd managed to reload you'd be either dead or arrested. And Martin was, let's face it, a bungler, he was bound to be a crap shot.

The sight of Martin was too much for Honda Man. The wheels in his brain seemed to grind to a halt, apparently from the effort of trying to work out why all the people he wanted to kill were in the same room together. Then he gave up on the whole thinking thing and turned his attention to Jackson. If he had to make a start somewhere, his expression seemed to imply, then it might as well be on the one already on the ground, groaning in agony. He raised the bat. Jackson rolled over into a foetal position and tried to protect his head with his hands. He wondered vaguely what the other people in the room were doing while he was waiting to have his skull broken open. Surely Tatiana could do something useful with her knife? And failing that she could rip open Terence Smith's throat with her teeth. She was doing neither, he could hear her on the phone, speaking in Russian, very fast. He wondered what she was saying. Send lawyers, guns and money? The woman with orange hair was screaming. She was doing the right thing. A lot of noise would bring the police. That would be good.

He was in a cocoon, isolated from the normal rules of time. His own personal end of days, counting every last lamb. He was back at home, the dimly lit kitchen of a small terraced house – the past was always dimly lit in his memory, he wondered if it was because the poor used low-wattage light bulbs – he was sitting at a table, his brother and sister either side of him, his father newly scrubbed from the pit, his mother dishing up some kind of stew. His sister's lovely hair was in plaits (*pleats*, his father called them), his brother's face was pale and open, he was wearing the same secondary school uniform that Jackson would wear in a few years. Not *Candid Camera* but *This is Your Life*. It was just a moment, quite ordinary, the woman pouring milk from a jug. They ate their tea, their mother sat down when they'd finished and ate scraps. His brother hit him on the back of the head and he recognized it was Francis's way of being affectionate even though it hurt. His mother said something but he couldn't catch what it was because an object the size of a house fell on him at that moment. Jackson smelt blood and gunfire, the unmistakable scents of the battlefield. All he'd heard was a tiny *thuck* kind of sound. You had to hand it to the Welrod, when they said silenced they meant silenced. It wasn't a house that had fallen on top of him, it was Terence Smith, felled like big game, and now crushing him to death. Jackson wondered if he could get a new ribcage when all this was over.

Grunting with the effort of it, he rolled the rhinoceros weight off and pulled himself up to a sitting position (great difficulty and much pain, etc.) and looked at his watch. It was an automatic reaction, an echo of other times, other places – *time of death . . . the suspect entered the premises at . . . the incident was logged at . . .* A quarter to eight but High Noon for Jackson. Julia's show was due to start in fifteen minutes. His whole day had pivoted on that one appointment. *But you'll be finished in time for the show?* His watch, he noticed groggily, was spattered with blood.

Tatiana lit a casual cigarette and took Terence Smith's pulse.

'Is dead,' she said, somewhat unnecessarily. He wasn't just dead, he was outstandingly dead, his heart ripped open by a bullet.

'Bull's-eye, Martin,' Jackson murmured. Who would have thought Martin had it in him to be a crack shot? Tatiana came over to Jackson and knelt down next to him. She peered at him and said, 'OK?'

'In some ways.'

'You save my life,' she said.

'I think it was that guy over there that saved you,' Jackson said. Martin was still standing on the lawn with the gun, slack in his hand, aimed at the grass now. He seemed very calm, like someone who'd made peace with themselves. Jackson heard a siren and thought, that was quick, but Gloria Hatter said, 'Panic button,' in a matter-of-fact way to no one in particular.

Tatiana leaned closer to Jackson. Her eyes had that dreamy look he remembered from the circus. She kissed him on the cheek and said, 'Thank you.' He felt strangely privileged, as if a wild animal had allowed him to stroke it.

Jackson didn't really care one way or another that Terence Smith was dead. Maybe he'd seen too many dead people to get upset about another one, or maybe it was just that Honda Man was a bad piece of work and there wasn't enough room on the planet for the good people, let alone all the bad ones. There were starving people, tortured people, just plain poor people who could do with his oxygen. He wasn't the only one in the room to be unperturbed by Terence Smith's passing. 'Eye for an eye,' Gloria Hatter said with magnificent indifference. The only person who seemed upset by what had happened was the woman with orange hair, who was whimpering quietly on the sofa.

Jackson heaved himself on to his feet and approached Martin cautiously. Close up, he had a panicky, wild look in his eye. From past experience Jackson had found it best to treat panicky, wild-eyed guys like scared animals – they might be essentially harmless but they could still kick and bite.

'Stand easy, Martin,' he said gently. 'Come on now, give me the gun.' Martin handed the gun over without any hesitation. 'Sorry,' he said. 'Sorry about that.' Then his knees gave way and he collapsed in a sad little heap on the lawn so there was only Jackson, Welrod in hand, standing over Terence Smith's dead body when the first officer on the scene arrived.

'This looks bad, doesn't it?' Jackson said.

46

LOUISE TURNED INTO THE HATTER HOMES' CAR PARK AT THEIR headquarters on Queensferry Road. Some kind of flunky in a uniform came towards her to question her right to be there and she slapped her warrant card against the windscreen and nearly mowed him down. Real Homes for Real People. How had Jackson found out there was a connection between Hatter Homes and Terence Smith? She would bet her bottom dollar that he was on the hunt. Was there ever such a troublesome man?

She was single-handed. Both Jessica and Sandy Mathieson had succumbed to flu. Before she came here she had swung by the Four Clans but there had been no sign of Martin Canning. The CD was hidden now, safely slipped inside an old Laura Nyro CD. She figured that was the last place anyone would look.

When she got inside, she found the Hatter Homes' offices were in chaos. She recognized a couple of guys from fraud. One of them said to her, 'No sign of Hatter anywhere.'

'Have you tried his house?' she asked and the guy from fraud said, 'Next on our list. The wife's the other director, she's in deep shit as well.'

She went looking for the woman behind the man, Hatter's secretary ('Christine Tennant'), who immediately started whining, 'I haven't done anything. I know nothing. I'm innocent.' The lady was protesting a little too much in Louise's opinion. She remembered the crack down the middle of her house. If nothing else, Hatter was a rotten builder. There was a fruit basket on Christine Tennant's desk. Louise could read the card tied to it with a ribbon: 'Just a little token of appreciation, best wishes, Gloria Hatter'.

'Terence Smith?' she asked Christine Tennant.

'What about him?'

'What does he do exactly?'

'He's horrible.'

'Maybe, but what does he *do*?'

The secretary shrugged and said, 'I don't really know. Sometimes he drives Mr Hatter or runs errands for him, does favours. Mr Hatter's in Thurso at the moment though. *So they say,*' she added darkly.

'Can you give me Mr Hatter's home address? I'd like to talk to his wife.'

Christine Tennant reeled off the address. In the Grange, nice, Louise thought. She'd bet Gloria Hatter's house didn't have a crack in it.

On the way over to the Hatter house, Louise wondered if Archie had come straight home from school or was he roaming around town, creating mayhem and mischief? Archie and Hamish ought to be tethered somewhere, some dark, quiet place where they could do no harm. Instead they'd be in shops, on buses, in the streets, laughing like imbeciles, howling like monkeys, getting into trouble. If he had a father, if he had a father like Jackson – or even a father like Sandy Mathieson – would he be different?

Her radio crackled into sudden life, *ZH to ZHC – personal attack alarm at Providence House, Mortonhall Road. To any set that can attend, your call sign and location please.* Louise didn't bother responding. She was already there. Somehow it seemed unlikely it was a coincidence. What had Jackson said? *A coincidence is just an explanation waiting to happen.*

'This looks bad, doesn't it?' Jackson said.

'Yes,' she agreed. 'But no doubt you've got an outlandish explanation.'

'Not really. You got here fast.'

'Coincidence. Looks like I missed the good stuff again.' He was standing over Terence Smith's dead body with a gun in his hand, covered in blood. Her heart contracted uncomfortably. Was he injured?

'Are you hurt?'

'Yes, a lot, but I'm OK. I don't *think* it's my blood.' There was a man sitting on the lawn mumbling something about taking vows, the next time she looked at him he seemed to have fallen asleep. There was a woman with peachy-coloured hair that complemented the sofa she was sitting on, who was having a mild fit of hysterics. 'Mrs Hatter?' Louise asked her but she didn't respond.

'I don't know who she is,' Jackson said. Very helpful. 'And the guy asleep on the grass is Martin Canning.'

'*The* Martin Canning? The writer? The guy who lives with Richard Moat?' Oh, this was too weird. Weird piled on weird.

'You need to secure the crime scene,' he said. 'No, you know that, don't you? Of course, you're a detective inspector.'

'You're *so* not in a position to be making jokes.'

He wiped the prints off the gun and put it on the ground. Jesus, she didn't believe he'd just done that! She should cuff him and arrest him right there on the spot. He said, 'The gun belongs to someone called Paul Bradley, but he doesn't exist.' He looked around and asked, 'Where are the other two?'

'What other two?'

'Mrs Hatter and Tatiana.'

'*Tatiana?*'

'Crazy Russian girl. They were here a minute ago. Look, I'd really like to stay and chat but I have to go.'

Now he was really having a laugh. 'This is a *murder* scene. My career will be over if I let you go. At worst you're a suspect, at best you're a witness.' She seemed to have been here before. One more time, Louise, *a witness, a suspect, and a convicted felon.*

'I know but I've got something important to do, really important.' They both listened to the sound of a siren coming closer. He looked like a dog hearing a whistle. 'I don't exist,' he said. 'You never saw me. Please. Do me just this one favour, Louise.'

* * *

He was a justified sinner. Like Louise. *Louise*. Just the way he said her name . . . She gave her head a shake, tried to dislodge him from her brain.

He went out the back door at the same time as Jim Tucker strode up the front drive. She was going over in her mind how she would present this to Jim. Was she really going to erase Jackson from the picture? Neither of the other two 'witnesses' looked as if they had the foggiest what was going on. Through the now non-existent French windows she motioned Jim Tucker to go to the front door.

'Louise,' he said. 'I didn't know you were already at the locus.'

She could see a DC and two uniformed police-women at the gate, advancing up the path. And then her phone rang and her world tilted. *Archie*. 'I'll be right there,' she said to him.

'Archie,' she said to Jim. 'I have to go.' He winced, sensing the mess he was about to inherit from her. She tried to make it sound better, which was pretty difficult in the circumstances. 'Look, Jim, I just walked in on this a second ago, I know no more than you do, to all intents and purposes you're the first officer on the scene, but *I have to go*.' The DC and the two constables were approaching the French windows but changed direction towards the front door when they realized they might be about to contaminate a crime scene. One of the policewomen peeled away and approached Martin Canning. Louise heard her say, 'Mr Canning, Martin? Are you all right? It's PC Clare Deponio, do you remember me?'

She could hear more sirens, one an ambulance.

Louise could taste blood from where she had been biting her lip. She didn't say, *Remember the favour you owe me, Jim*, she didn't say, *How's your lovely daughter doing at university, bet she's glad she didn't get a drug rap*. She didn't need to, he knew it was payback time, as you sow so shall you reap. He nodded his head towards the back of the house without saying anything. 'Thanks,' she mouthed at him and disappeared. She wondered how many disciplinary, possibly criminal, acts she'd committed within the last five minutes. She didn't bother to count.

Archie had sounded odd on the phone – strained and slightly desperate – and she thought he must have been arrested or killed someone. But it was worse than that.

47

THEN HE AND IRINA WERE WALKING INTO HIS COCKROACH hotel, past the rather frightening men who hung around at the entrance. A cross between doormen and security staff, they were always dressed in black leather jackets, always smoking cigarettes. They opened doors (sometimes) and called taxis but they seemed more like gangsters. One of them said something to Irina and she waved him away with a dismissive gesture.

And then somehow they were in his room and, without knowing how, he was standing in front of her in his underpants saying, 'Well-upholstered. Built for comfort, not for speed.'

Then time jumped forward again and she was astride him on the narrow bed, wearing only a bra and shoes, making short yipping noises that might have suggested sexual frenzy if her face hadn't remained a blank. Martin contributed hardly anything to the encounter, it had taken him by surprise in its unexpectedness and its haste. He climaxed quickly and quietly in a way that ashamed him. 'Sorry,' he said and she shrugged and leaned over him, her beautiful hair sweeping his chest, a teasing gesture that seemed entirely perfunctory. He saw the dark roots where the bleach had grown out.

She climbed off him. The fog of alcohol in his brain cleared a little and in its place a nauseous, dull depression fell on him as he watched her lighting a cigarette. A woman in a foreign country, a woman you hardly knew, did not strip down to her bra and shoes and ride you like a horse for free. She might not be a prostitute as such, but she expected money.

She picked up her clothes and put them on, the cigarette dangling from her mouth. She caught him looking at her and smiled. 'OK?' she said. 'You have good time? You want to give me little gift for good time?'

He got up and hopped around, trying to get his trousers back on. The evening had taken him to depths of indignity he had previously steered clear of, even in his imagination. He searched through his pockets for money. He had cleared out most of his cash in the Grand Hotel and could find only a twenty-rouble note and small coins. Irina looked in disgust at the money as he tried to explain to her that he could go down to the reception desk and draw money on his Visa. She frowned and said, '*Nyet*, no Visa.'

'No, no,' he said, 'I'm not offering you Visa. I will *change*. I will get dollars for you from downstairs.' She shook her head vigorously. Then she pointed at his Rolex and asked, 'Is good?' She was wrapping the scarf around her head again, buttoning up her coat.

'Yes,' he said, 'it's genuine, but—'

'You give to me.' She was beginning to sound shrill and uncompromising. It was four in the morning (he had no idea how that had happened, when he last noticed the time it was eleven o'clock). There was a retired couple from Gravesend in the room next door. What would they think if they were woken up by a Russian woman demanding payment for sex? What if she started to scream and throw things around? It was ridiculous, the watch was worth more than ten thousand pounds, hardly a fair exchange. 'No, I'll get money,' he insisted. 'And then the hotel will call a taxi for you.' He imagined one of the menacing men in black leather putting her in a taxi, looking at Martin, knowing he'd just paid for sex with her.

She said something in Russian and made a move towards him, trying to grab his wrist. 'No,' he said, dancing out of the way. She made another lunge and he stepped away again but this time she tripped and lost her balance and although she put out her hands to save herself she couldn't stop her head hitting the corner of the cheap veneer desk unit that occupied almost the whole of one wall in the small room. She gave a little cry, a wounded bird, and then was quiet.

She should have got up. She should have got up clutching her forehead. There would be a cut or a bruise and it would be sore. He would probably take the Rolex off his wrist and give it to her to make up for the pain, to stop her making a fuss. But she didn't get up. He crouched down and touched her on the shoulder and said, 'Irina?' tentatively. 'Did you hurt yourself, are you OK?' The scarf had slipped from her hair. She was lying face down on the nasty carpet and didn't respond. The back of her neck was pale and vulnerable.

He tried to roll her over, not sure if that was the right thing to do to someone who had knocked themselves out. She was heavy, much heavier than he'd expected, and awkwardly resistant as if she was determined to give him no help in his manoeuvres. He managed to turn her and she flopped on to her back. Her eyes were wide open, staring at nothing. The shock made his heart stop for a second. He sprang away from her, falling over the end of the bed, banging his shin, hurting his foot. Something rose in his chest, a sob, a howl, he wasn't sure how it was going to emerge and was surprised it was nothing more than a stupid little squawk.

There was no obvious reason for it. A red mark on her temple, that was all. One of those chances in a million, he supposed – a fracture to one of her cervical vertebrae or an intracranial bleed. He read up on head injuries for months afterwards.

The littlest thing. If she hadn't been wearing heels, if the carpet hadn't been fraying, if he had had the sense to realize that no way in the world would a girl like that be interested in him for himself. For a second he saw this scene through the eyes of others – the hotel management, the men in black leather, the police, the British consul, the couple from Gravesend, the dying grocer. There was no way that any of them would interpret it in a way that favoured him.

Panic kicked in. Panic throbbing in his chest,

spinning through his brain like a cyclone, a wave of adrenalin that passed through his body and washed away every thought except one – *get rid of her*. He glanced around the room to see what of herself she had left behind. The only thing he could see was her handbag. He rifled through it to make sure there was nothing to incriminate him, that she hadn't written down his name and hotel address. Nothing, just a cheap purse, some keys, a tissue and lipstick. A photograph in a plastic wallet. The photograph was of a baby, its sex indeterminate. Martin refused to think about the significance of a photograph of a baby.

He yanked the window open. He was on the seventh floor but the windows opened all the way – no health and safety in the cockroach hotel. He dragged her over to the window and then, holding her round the waist in a clumsy embrace like a poor dancer, he hauled her across the sill. He hated her for the way she was like an unwieldy puppet, a sandbag mannequin for bayonet practice. He hated her for the way she hung half in, half out of the room as if she didn't care about anything any more. A Russian doll. The street was deathly silent. If she fell from the seventh floor, if she was found on the pavement, no one would know whether she had jumped or been pushed, or simply fallen in drunken confusion. Her blood must be almost 100 per cent alcohol the amount she had drunk. No one would be able to point up to his window and say, *There, Martin Canning, British tourist, that was whose window she came out of.* There was an enormous builders' skip down below, nearly full of rubble. He didn't want her to fall into that because then it might seem as if someone was trying to dispose of her body rather than her having simply fallen.

He put the strap of her bag around her neck and then pushed her arm through it, like a child's satchel, then he grabbed her round the knees and heaved and shoved until she slipped away.

If he had aimed for the construction skip he would have missed it but because he wanted her to hit the pavement she went straight into the skip, twisting round in the air before crashing face up on to the wood and stone and broken plaster inside it with a kind of crunching noise. A stray dog swerved from its path in alarm but apart from that the street remained unmoved. He closed the window.

He sat on the floor in the corner of the room and hugged his knees. He stayed in that position for a long time, too drained to do anything else. He watched dawn entering the room and thought about Irina's sightless eyes never seeing the light come. A cockroach ran across his foot. He heard the first tram taking to the street. He waited for the builders, imagined them climbing up the scaffold, looking down and seeing the woman lying like a discarded doll. He wondered if he would hear their cries of discovery from his room.

He heard a massive engine, gears grinding, and crawled over to the window. The skip was swinging in mid-air, like a child's toy from this distance. Somehow he had hoped that in the intervening hours she might have disappeared but she was still there, broken and limp. The skip was swung on to the back of the enormous pickup lorry and settled with a great metallic clunk that echoed through the cold air. The lorry drove away. Martin followed its progress, watching it move slowly along the road, turning on to a bridge over the Neva. At the end of the bridge it disappeared from sight.

He had thrown a human being away like rubbish.

At the airport, going through passport control, he waited for one of the terrifying officials to put a hand on his chest and feel his racing heart, to stare in his eyes and see his guilt. But he was waved through with a sullen gesture. He had thought retribution would be swift, but it turned out that justice was going to be measured out slowly, rolling him flat until he simply didn't exist.

In a small duty-free shop he bought a fridge magnet for his mother, a little varnished wooden matryoshka. On the flight home the grocer sat with the couple from Gravesend, squeezed into a seat that was too small for him, and told them that he had ticked off another item from his to-do-before-I-die list. The in-flight meal was served, a sorry concoction of congealed pasta. Martin wondered if Irina's stall remained boarded up or if someone had already taken it over. The grocer took ill as they came in to land. An ambulance collected him on the tarmac. Martin didn't even look.

There was a woman he recognized from the book signing earlier in the day. He had no idea why she was here. She was clutching a copy of *The Monkey-Puzzle Tree* and screaming. He thought about making a joke, saying to her, 'It's not that bad, is it?' but he didn't.

There was a blond girl who shouted something in Russian at the crazy Honda driver. The Honda driver was going to kill the blond Russian girl and then Jackson stepped in to save her, to sacrifice himself. The Honda driver was engorged with rage. There was something wrong with the minds of people like that, people who threw dogs through windows and stuck guns to their wives' heads. Bad brain chemistry. If Nina Riley had been here she would have said, *Lay down your weapon, you dastardly scoundrel*. But she wasn't here. It was just Martin.

Time slowed down. The Honda driver raised the bat in the familiar arc of annihilation. The Russian girl turned to face him. Her features changed. Her blue-doll eyes stared at him unblinking, her little rosebud lips said, 'Shoot him, Marty.' So he did.

48

A PREGNANCY-TESTING KIT.

Jackson had run (literally) back to the flat, dropped his bloodstained clothes on the bathroom floor, jumped in the shower and washed away Terence Smith from his life. For a mad second he had contemplated running all the way from the Hatter house to Julia's venue but he could see that it might look a little *too* dramatic to arrive covered in blood. Save it for *Macbeth*.

He had been multi-tasking (as they said), pulling on clothes, phoning for a taxi, regarding his harrowed face in the steamy mirror, when he happened to glance down and see it.

He plucked the pregnancy test out of the wastebasket and stared at it as if it was an object from the moon. It was the last thing he was expecting to find, and yet why not? It had never happened in the two years they were together, but here it was. Blue. It was blue. Everyone knew what that meant. It explained everything, her mood swings, her loss of appetite (for sex and food), her odd diffidence. Julia was pregnant! What an extraordinary idea — Julia was having a baby. His baby. *We're having a baby*. A baby for Julia. There were a lot of different ways of saying it but it all came down to the same thing: there was a microscopic new life inside Julia, a small creature nestling in a burrow inside the woman he loved. He wondered if it was a boy. Wouldn't that be something, to have a son, to be the father his own father never was? He still had the little peanut-baby doll in his pocket. He shrugged his jacket on and felt for it, like a talisman, a rosary bead, turning it over and over in his hand.

A baby would heal Julia. The lost Olivia would somehow be reborn in Julia's own baby. A baby would make everything right, for Julia, and for the two of them. A couple. If they were going to be parents then, one way or another, she was going to have to come to terms with that word. A baby would heal Jackson too, close up some of his wounds. What had Louise said? *Sperm meets egg and bam. It can happen to the best of us.* And it had happened to Julia.

Not a new path, but a new world to walk in.

49

LOUISE COULD HEAR CLASSICAL MUSIC PLAYING IN THE LIVING room. The house lights were off and instead a scented candle was burning in the hearth. He had put Classic FM on the radio. Her heart broke for the way he had tried to deal with everything. She could see the back of Archie's head above the sofa. *Thou knowest, Lord, the secrets of our hearts, shut not thy merciful ears unto our prayers.* She must have made a noise because he turned his head slightly and said, 'Mum?' She could hear the tearful tremor in his voice.

'Archie?' She approached the sofa slowly. She bit down hard on her lip to try and stop the howl that was trying to escape from some deep, deep place inside. Archie looked up at her and said quietly, 'I'm sorry, Mum.' His eyes were rimmed with red, he looked ghastly. In his arms he was cradling Jellybean as if he were a newborn baby, but he was deflated and shrunk, the life all gone from him. He was wrapped in an old sweater of Louise's. 'I thought he'd like to smell you,' Archie said. Another turn of the corkscrew. Her heart in shreds. 'It's OK to cry, Mum,' he said and the pain finally forced its way out – a terrible wail of lamentation, a high-pitched keening that sounded as if it belonged to someone else.

She hadn't been present at her cat's birth and now she had missed his death. 'But you had everything in between,' Archie said. It was disturbing how like an adult he sounded. 'Here,' he said, carefully passing his sad, swaddled bundle over to her, 'I'll make a cup of tea.'

She unwrapped the cat and kissed him on the head, the ears, the paws. *Even this shall pass.*

When Archie came back with the tea, it was sweet. He must have heard it somewhere on television – hot, sweet tea in times of crisis. She had never taken sugar in tea in her life but there was something unexpectedly comforting about it.

'He had a good life,' Archie said. He wasn't old enough for it to be a cliché to him.

'I know.' Love was the hardest thing. Don't let anyone ever tell you different.

50

'WE HAVE TO LEAVE, GLORIA,' TATIANA SAID.

The machines continued to hiss and pump, Graham continued to float in space. Gloria bent down and kissed Graham on the forehead. A benediction or a curse, or both, because everything could be encompassed in the synthesis that was reality. Black and white, good and bad. His flesh already felt like clay.

What were the true crimes? Capitalism, religion, sex? Murder – usually but not necessarily. Theft – ditto. But cruelty and indifference were also crimes. As were bad manners and callousness. Worst of all was indifference.

Not long after Gloria married Graham they went to his parents', Beryl and Jock's, for Sunday lunch. A skinny roast duck, as Gloria remembered, counterbalanced by a hefty plum cobbler. It never ceased to amaze Gloria that she could barely remember what happened last Friday but could recall in detail meals that she had eaten forty and more years ago.

For some reason their car was in the garage that day

(Graham had brought a Triumph Herald to the marriage), so Graham's father had given them a lift to the modest Hatter Home (the old Pencaitland model, long abandoned) that had been a wedding gift from Jock and Beryl. It had been known as a 'starter home'. No one sold 'finisher homes', did they?

On the way, they made a detour via 'the yard' on some business or other that father and son had to attend to, long forgotten now. At the time Hatter Homes was just a builders' yard with a ramshackle office in one corner. Gloria got out of the car. She'd never been to the yard or the office before and supposed she should take an interest now that she herself was a Hatter. She should never have given up her maiden name of Lewis, of course. Now might be a good time to revert to it, now that she was an outlaw widow. People changed their identities all the time, her own grandfather had changed his name to Lewis after he arrived in Leeds from Poland with nothing more than a cardboard suitcase and a surname that no one could pronounce.

The two Hatter men went into the office and Gloria wandered around the yard with its mysterious pallets and sacks. She couldn't imagine how you even began to build a house. She wondered what would have happened to the human race if it had all been up to her at the point when man first struck flint on flint and made a tool. She would never have managed anything as sophisticated as a shelf, everything would now be kept in hammocks and bags probably. She was a gatherer, Graham was a screwdriver-wielding hunter. He would go out and build things and she would stay inside and rear things. This was only a month after their wedding when the sparkle was still on their union and Gloria was deliriously busy buying matching tea plates and squeegee mops.

At that moment Gloria heard a little mewling noise which proved, when investigated, to be – joy of joys – a nest of kittens, still blind and mole-like, curled up with their mother in a corner of the yard behind a pile of old wood.

Hatters, senior and junior, emerged from the office, her new father-in-law hailing her with 'You found those damn kittens then, Gloria?' Gloria, who was already planning the sheepskin-lined basket she would provide for at least two, possibly all, of the kittens, a Hatter home within a Hatter Home, said, 'Oh, they're so *gorgeous*, Mr Hatter.' Gloria's toes wriggled with the cuteness of the kittens. She still couldn't manage the familiarity of 'Jock' and in fact never did for the three years she was his daughter-in-law, before he had a massive heart attack, dropping dead on site, into the mud in the breeze-block shell of one of his houses, while his men gathered round and stared down at his lifeless body in astonishment. The Titan had left the building. The Olympian, meanwhile, was in the unfinished kitchen, wondering if he could get away with putting in a smaller window.

'Graham,' Jock Hatter said, 'get the bloody things will you?'

'Sure,' Graham said, scooping up all five soft, warm kitten bodies and in one easy movement plunging them into a water butt that stood next to the office. Gloria was so surprised that for a terrible second she merely watched, mute and motionless as if she was under a spell. Then she screamed and made to run to Graham to rescue the kittens, but Jock held her back. He was a small man but astonishingly strong and no matter how much she twisted and turned to get away from him she couldn't escape his grip. 'Has to be done, lass,' he said softly when she finally gave up. 'It's just the way of the world.' Graham removed the five limp little bodies from the water butt and threw them into an old oil-drum that was used for waste.

'Fucking cats,' he said when she became hysterical with him later in the galley kitchen of their starter home. 'You need to stop being so fucking soft, Gloria. They're just fucking animals.'

Murdered. The word had sounded strange falling from Tatiana's lips. It rolled around like thunder, it cracked the sky. Gloria wondered if the cracked sky was going to break into pieces and fall at her feet. Her stomach felt hot and liquid and her heart was beating faster than was healthy in a woman on the verge of a bus pass. Tatiana's friend had been murdered. Lena. A good person.

Gloria knew what Tatiana was going to say. And the worst thing was that she had believed it even before the name was said, so she said it first.

'Graham,' she said flatly.

'Yes,' Tatiana agreed. 'Graham. He is very bad man. He told Terry to kill her. Same thing as killing her himself. No difference.'

'No,' Gloria agreed. 'No difference. No difference at all.'

'Lena was going to cops, tell everything she knew.'

'What *did* she know? About the fraud?'

Tatiana laughed. 'Fraud is nothing, Gloria. Many worse things than fraud. Graham's in business with very, very bad men. You don't want to know, they come after you. We really have to go now.'

Gloria leaned closer to her husband and whispered in his ear, '*Look upon my works, ye Mighty, and despair!*'

They had left the scene of a murder. They were making a real getaway. Gloria was breaking rules, although not her own. She had rescued the black plastic bag of cash and the memory stick but other than that they were fleeing in the clothes they stood up in. Tatiana had made a phone call and a big black car had driven up to the back door and they had stepped into it. It was, if Gloria wasn't mistaken, the same car that had picked Tatiana up from the hospital after Graham's heart attack. The driver remained mute throughout their journey and Gloria didn't ask who the black car belonged to. Big black cars with blacked-out windows tended to belong to bad people. Bad people like Graham.

They were driving south, towards the airport, but Gloria had requested 'a little detour'.

'Why?' Tatiana asked.

'Business,' Gloria said as the mute driver followed her instructions and turned off the main road and into a housing estate. 'A little unfinished business.'

'Glencrest Way,' Tatiana announced, reading the street sign. Glencrest Way was followed by Glencrest

Close, Glencrest Avenue, Glencrest Road, Glencrest Gardens and Glencrest Wynd, the titles of all of which Tatiana insisted on reciting, like an exotic replacement for the black car's satellite navigation system, which refused to work amongst the baffling complexity of the housing estate's streets, shielded by the lingering fog of Graham's presence, the cloud of knowing.

'The Glencrest estate,' Gloria said, rather redundantly as the black car drew to a halt at the kerbside. 'Real homes for real people. Built on old mine workings.' She hauled out the black plastic binbag that contained seventy-three thousand five hundred pounds in twenty-pound notes.

Tatiana leaned against the side of the car and smoked while Gloria dragged the black plastic bag from house to house, distributing bundles of notes on the doorsteps. Not enough for everyone but then life was a lottery.

'Is tragedy,' Tatiana said, shaking her head. 'You're one crazy person, Gloria.'

They climbed back in the black car and drove away. The bundles of notes weren't tied together and the evening breeze began to lift them and toss them around like giant flakes of ash. In the rear-view mirror Gloria caught a glimpse of someone coming out of one of Graham's mean houses – a Braecroft – and looking astonished at the sight of money flying around in the air.

Feared by the bad, loved by the good. They were bandit queens, they were robber girls. They were outlaws.

51

BLACK SPACE. WHITE LIGHT. APPLAUSE. THE APPLAUSE sounded quite vigorous to Jackson's ears, but then, apart from a couple of critics, the audience was weighted with friends and family and hangers-on. He was tonight's representative of all of those things for Julia and he had managed to miss the entire performance, slipping in at the back of the theatre just in time to see the cast taking their bow. Jackson knew that murder and mayhem weren't good enough excuses for missing Julia's show. Perhaps he should have turned up covered in blood after all.

In the bar afterwards the entire cast was giddy with relief, like an over-excited nursery-school class. Tobias made a performance out of making sure everyone had champagne and then giving an extravagant, congratulatory toast that Jackson stopped listening to halfway through. 'To us!' they all concluded, clinking their glasses high.

Julia put her arm through his and rested her head against his shoulder.

'How was it for you?' he asked and he felt her wilt slightly against him. 'Bloody awful,' she said. 'Whole chunks of that scene on the iceberg went AWOL and that idiot boy didn't give me any of the right lines.'

'Scott Marshall? Your *lover*?'

Julia removed her arm from his.

'Still, you were great,' he said, wishing he himself was a better actor. 'You were really great.'

Julia downed her glass of champagne in one. 'And,' she said, 'when that usher came down the aisles and actually asked if there was a doctor in the house – I mean not that I wasn't sorry for the man who had the heart attack, but trying to continue as if nothing was going on . . .'

'These things happen,' Jackson said soothingly.

'Yes, they do, but *not in tonight's show*, Jackson,' she snapped. 'You weren't there, were you? You managed to miss my opening night! What happened that was so important? Did someone die? Or did someone just say, *Help me, Jackson*?'

'Well, as it happens—'

'You are so fucking predictable.'

'Calm down.'

'*Calm down?*' Never say that to a woman, it was on the first page of the handbook that didn't come with them. 'I will not fucking calm down.' She lit a cigarette, sucking deeply on it as if it contained Ventolin.

'You shouldn't,' he said (words also advised against in the handbook). 'You know you're going to have to stop smoking. And drinking.'

'Why?'

'Why do you think?'

495

'I don't know.' There was a new fury in her eyes, a challenge that he knew he shouldn't pick up. And it was ridiculous. It wasn't how he had envisaged this moment at all. He had imagined candles, flowers, a loving kindness enveloping them both like a shawl. 'Because you're pregnant,' Jackson said.

'So?' She tilted her chin up defiantly and blew cigarette smoke towards the ceiling, where it joined the polluted cloud above their heads.

'So?' he echoed irritably. 'What does that mean? *So?*' This conversation shouldn't be taking place in a dingy bar crowded with noisy people but he couldn't think how to manoeuvre her out of the building. He wondered how she had planned to give him the news. The annunciation. The preciousness of it all was being horribly stained. Then a terrible thought struck him. 'You weren't planning to get rid of it, were you?'

She gave him a cold, level look. 'Get rid of it?'

'A termination. Jesus, Julia, you can't be thinking of doing that.' He almost said, *This might be your only chance*, but somehow or other he managed to block that one.

'Just because I've got big tits doesn't necessarily make me maternal, Jackson.'

'Julia, you would make a *wonderful* mother.' She would. He couldn't believe that she didn't want to experience motherhood. They had never talked about children, they had talked about marriage but never about children. Why was that? How could a man and a woman have a relationship and not discuss that?

'We've never talked about having children, Jackson. And it's my body and my life.'

'My baby,' he said.

She raised an eyebrow. '*Your* baby?'

'Our baby,' he amended. Something passed across her face, an immense sadness and regret. She shook her head and stubbed the cigarette out in an ashtray on the bar. Then she looked at him and said, 'I'm sorry, Jackson. It's not. It's not yours.'

Friday

52

'JESUS. ARE YOU SURE? YOU'RE SURE HE'S DEAD? HAVE YOU called the vet?'

The shop assistant was watching him, like there was a magnet between his face and hers. Her features mirrored his horror, as if she'd entered into the drama of his life. Give the girl an Academy Award.

'Everything all right?' she said when he came off his mobile.

'That was my mum,' Archie said. 'Our cat's dead.'

'Oh no,' she said, her face all crumpled. Her lip actually trembled.

'Ooh, that was a good one,' Hamish whispered as they left the shop. 'We should have thought about dead cats before, girls really go for that kind of thing.'

Archie felt bad, using the cat like that, although it had helped him draw on some genuine emotion in his performance. He was sorry about the cat. He hadn't realized he cared until it started yowling. It had been an awful noise, gave him the creeps. Its back legs had gone and it just lay there panting. Sometimes when his mother was out working, especially when she was working at night, he would get this horrid pain clutching at his chest because he thought, what would he do if she died? If she was in a high-speed chase and she crashed? Or if someone shot her or stabbed her? His heart went fluttery and he felt faint if he imagined it.

The way she loved that cat was weird. Her own mother died last week and she'd drunk a toast, 'Here's to the old bitch, may she burn in hell for all eternity.' But the cat died and she'd bawled her eyes out. And his mother, whatever else she was, was tough. He'd hated it when she cried.

He had tried to make it better for her, tried to think what she would have done if she'd been there. Candles and music, almost religious. He wrapped the cat in a sweater that belonged to her and then cradled it. It died in his arms. He'd watched it happen. There was a moment when it was alive and then there was a moment when it was dead and nothing in between. One day that would happen to his mother. His family was too small, just himself, his mother and an old cat, that was it, and now the cat had gone. Hamish had two sisters, a father, grandfathers, grandmothers, aunts, uncles, cousins, he had more relatives than anyone could possibly need. Archie only had his mother. If something happened to her he'd be on his own.

He had cried when the cat died, everything inside him had suddenly felt too big, like it was all going to burst out. His mother came in and hugged him and he'd wanted to be a baby again and they'd cried together. She was crying for the cat and he was crying for the fact that he could never be a baby again. Then he'd made her a cup of tea and gone out and bought chips and they'd watched television and it had been nice despite the cat being dead and his mother being so unhappy about it. She said, 'We'll get him cremated, the vet gave me a leaflet. You can get this little wooden box and have his photograph put on it, a little brass plaque with his name, and we'll keep it on the mantelpiece.' Her own mother was sitting neglected on a shelf in the garage. There was *irony* for you. It had all been so *close* between them at that point that he'd almost admitted everything. About all the thieving, about finding Martin Canning's wallet in the Cowgate (not *stealing*, the guy must have lost it), getting the address for his office from the wallet, breaking into his office (for fun. Which it had been). Hamish could pick locks like a master thief. His goal in life was to rob his father's bank. Hamish hated his father in a way that Archie found scary. But then Archie changed his mind about *sharing* because it seemed mean to do his mother's head in while she was so upset. Some other time.

His mother put her arm round him and said, 'It's OK.' And it was, briefly. He finished her chips for her and let her stroke his hair but then her phone rang and she sighed, 'Sorry, that was the Force Command Centre. I have to go, there's been an incident,' and she'd left him alone. With the dead cat. Other mothers didn't do that.

He heard her car pulling out of the garage and he looked out of the window to watch her drive away. A twenty-pound note floated past slowly, like a small magic carpet.

* * *

'Fuck's sake, Archie, police!' Hamish yelled at him, giving him a shove from behind so his arms wind-milled around as he tried to keep his balance and not fall on his face. Hamish was off, running down George Street, abandoning Archie to his fate. He turned and saw two stocky policemen approaching. He didn't even bother trying to run. He walked towards his fate. It was a moment he'd been walking towards for months. Mostly what he felt was relief.

53

NINA RILEY CLIMBED, HAND OVER HAND, LIKE AN AGILE SPIDER on the rust-red web of girders of the Forth Bridge until finally, slick with sweat from the effort, she made it up to the railway tracks. She had no idea where Bertie was. Perhaps he had fallen to his death in the grey waters down below. She felt remarkably unperturbed by his fate. He had been such an annoying boy, so obsequious (*Miss Nina, you're topping, you really are*). He needed a hefty dose of socialism or a good kick up the backside.

She looked up and down the tracks, no sign of a train. No sign of the Earl of Morybory, or whatever he was called. Her so-called 'arch enemy'. No sign of the circus troupe of clowns that had been dogging her steps for days. A faint cry interrupted her thoughts. It sounded like Bertie. Was he calling for help? She listened intently. A feeble *Help me, Miss Riley* drifted towards her on a stiff estuary breeze. She ignored it. Then a far-off rumbling noise. A train. It was time. She lay down on the tracks, carefully – she didn't want to dirty her new cream-leather trench coat, although, of course, it was probably going to get ruined anyway.

She stretched herself as nice and straight as a railway sleeper across the tracks. If you were going to do something, do it properly. It was a shame there was no one about to tie her to the tracks with rope. It would be good to finish on a Hollywood note. Or perhaps not, that wasn't quite her style and she wasn't a damsel in distress, she was a modern woman doing the sensible thing. The noble thing.

The train was louder now. Closer.

Sacrifice. Self-sacrifice, to be more exact. She was doing this for Martin. She was going to free him of her for ever. She was going to take Alex Blake with her into oblivion and Martin would be liberated. He could have a fresh start, write something good, for heaven's sake, instead of this nonsense. Regrets, she had a few, of course. She had never had sex – Martin wouldn't let her. And she had never been to Wales, she had always wondered what it was like, now she would never know.

A little flicker of something she'd never felt before crossed her features. She thought it might be fear. No going back now. This was it. The nanosecond that would change everything. It was coming. It was here.

She entered the blackness where there were no words. Let there be dark.

'And he just sits there and says nothing?'

'Mm. More or less. The police said that when they arrived he was gibbering about wanting to go into holy orders.'

'Gibbering? Is that a clinical term?'

'Very funny. I haven't made an official diagnosis yet but I would say that he's in some kind of post-traumatic catatonia, a fugue state. He shot someone, killed someone. None of us really know how we would react in those circumstances.'

'Do you think he's faking it? He's a writer, isn't he?'

'Mm.'

'What kind of things does he write?'

54

JACKSON PHONED LOUISE FROM THE CAR. HE HAD HIRED A Mondeo from Hertz and was driving down to London. It seemed he wasn't ready to go back to France yet. Maybe he would never be ready. He was running, gunning for the county line at ninety miles an hour with his tail lights out. He was heading for the Canadian border. He was on the dusty back roads of Texas looking for a little trouble. He was every song he had ever listened to.

He tried the word 'home' in his head and it didn't sound right somehow. *Home is where the heart is*, Julia said. Not usually a cliché kind of girl but then she had never lived down to his expectations of her. He would have said his heart was with Julia but maybe he had just thought that to make himself feel better, to make himself feel less alone. *I'm sorry, Jackson, it's not yours*. He had said he didn't care, that it didn't make any difference who the father was and he shocked himself because it was true, but Julia said, 'Well, it makes a difference to me, Jackson.' And that was that, it was over between them. From nought to sixty in one conversation. *It's better this way, sweetie.* Was she right? He honestly didn't know. What he did know was that he felt as if something had been ripped out of him without anaesthetic. And yet he was such an old dog now that he was just carrying on because that's what you did, you picked yourself up off the ground and, against all the odds, you kept on slugging. *Bring it on.*

But really he wondered if his heart hadn't been buried with his sister all those years ago while he sat at Mrs Judd's worn Formica-topped table eating a chicken pie.

New frontier, new future. London, the home of the dispossessed of the world, seemed like a good place to get lost and found in for a few days. In a service station in the Borders he bought a three-disc set of Tamla Motown greatest hits. He hadn't suddenly changed his musical allegiance but he thought it might be a good idea to have something upbeat for the road, and you had to hand it to those guys (although, as ever, he preferred the girls), they certainly knew how to spin a tune. He couldn't believe what a relief it was to be in a car, in the driving seat, behind the wheel. Even in a Mondeo. He felt like himself again.

'Hello, you,' he said when she answered with a rather tart 'Detective Inspector Louise Monroe.' There was a beat of silence on her end of the phone. The Velvelettes finished looking for a needle in a haystack without finding one, then she said, softer than usual, 'Hello you, back.'

'I'm on the road,' he said. (Four wonderful words.) 'I'm sorry I didn't get to say goodbye.'

'So your work here is done and all that?' she said. 'The mysterious stranger leaves town, looking back long enough to light a chewed-up cigar and wonder what might have been, before digging in his spurs and galloping off.'

'Well, actually I hate to disappoint you but I'm just passing the Angel of the North in a rented Mondeo.'

'And Smokey's singing the blues.'

'Yeah. Something like that.'

'You have to come back.'

'No.'

'You impersonated a police officer. You left a crime scene.'

'I was never there,' Jackson said.

'I have witnesses who say you were.'

'Who?'

Louise sighed. 'Well, one witness is dead obviously.'

'Our friend Terry.'

'Another one is asking to be taken to a monastery.'

'That would be Martin then.'

'But the third one is pretty coherent now apparently,' Louise said.

'The third one?'

'Pam Miller.'

'The woman with orange hair?'

'Well, I would say it was more peach, but yes. Wife of Murdo Miller, her husband runs a huge security out-fit. He's a crook but semi-respectable.'

'What about the other two women? Gloria Hatter and Tatiana.'

'Gone. Did a bunk. Like you. Mrs Hatter's wanted by the fraud boys. And Graham Hatter seems to have disappeared off the face of the planet. Everyone's very agitated by this case.'

'You're running it then?' he asked. 'Your first murder?' It sounded odd, like a child's primer.

'No.' She was silent for a while, like a criminal weighing up the options of confessing. 'Actually.'

'Actually?'

'I had to leave as well. Personal stuff.'

He tried hard to remember her son's name. He made a stab at 'Archie?'

'No. My cat.'

He didn't respond to that in case he said the wrong thing (he'd learned something from being with Julia for two years). 'So *four* people left the scene of the crime?' he puzzled. 'That must be a record.'

'It's not funny.'

'I didn't say it was.'

'An astonishing thing happened that I thought you'd like to know about.'

'Astonishing things happen all the time,' Jackson said. 'We just don't notice.'

'Oh, please. You'll be telling me you believe in angels next and everything that happens is meant. They got Terence Smith for Richard Moat's murder.'

'Everything that happens is meant.'

'You don't sound as surprised as I would have liked.'

'I'm surprised, trust me.' He wasn't, he had received a phone call, no more than a murmur in his ear, a murmur with a Russian accent. He had no idea how, but Tatiana seemed to know everything. He wondered – if you had sex with her, would she kill you

511

afterwards? He thought there was a possibility that it might just be worth it.

'Jackson?'

'Yeah.'

'Your Terence Smith was a one-man crime wave.'

'He wasn't mine.'

'He was also your basic moron, left trace evidence everywhere. The tech boys got bits of Richard Moat's blood and brain matter from the baseball bat. He had Moat's phone in his pocket and when they searched his flat they found Martin Canning's laptop, which is where he got his address from, I suppose. So it looks like he killed Moat by mistake, that he might really have been looking for Canning after all. Revenge for throwing his briefcase at him, but he got Richard Moat instead. Who knows?'

'This is all very neat,' Jackson said.

'Well, not that neat. We still haven't found anything to connect him to your non-existent dead girl, nothing in his flat or in the Honda.'

'She exists, believe me. Terence Smith killed her on Graham Hatter's orders. He used Hatter's car to dispose of her – find that and you'll find the evidence. Hatter's probably sipping cocktails with Lord Lucan now in South Africa or wherever murderers on the lam hide out these days.'

'And this is all on the word of a Russian call-girl who no one except you has ever met. Oh, and Gloria Hatter. Who is also *on the lam*, as you put it. There is nothing to link either Terence Smith or Graham Hatter to the girl. A girl who, I should emphasize, no one has missed.'

'I know people who miss her,' Jackson said. 'She was called Lena Mikhailichenko. She was twenty-five years old. She was born in Kiev. Her mother still lives there. She was an accountant back in Russia. She was a Virgo. She liked disco, rock and classical music. She read newspapers and crime novels. She had long blond hair and weighed one hundred and twenty-two pounds and was five foot five inches tall. She was a Christian. She was good-natured, kind, thoughtful and optimistic, they all say optimistic. She liked to read and go to the theatre. She also liked going to the gym and swimming and she had a completely misplaced "confidence in tomorrows" so perhaps her English wasn't as good as she claimed. I think that's another way of saying optimistic again. And parks. They all like parks, in fact they all say more or less the same thing. You can see a picture of her at www.bestrussianbrides.com where she's still up for sale, although she left Russia six months ago to see if Edinburgh's streets were paved with gold. That was when she fell in with Favours and met her nemesis in the shape of Graham Hatter. I think if you look you might find that our Mr Hatter was involved with Favours, as well as God knows what else.'

'You don't give up, do you? You have to come back.'

'No.'

'Jesus, Jackson.'

'No. I'm tired of being involved. I'm tired of being a witness.'

'Martin needs you to give evidence on his behalf, he killed someone. He saved your life. He's your *friend*.'

'He's not my friend.' There was a long pause. The

Supremes asked him to stop in the name of love. 'Anyway,' he said.

'Anyway.'

'Well, don't forget,' Jackson said, 'we'll always have Paris.'

'We never had Paris.'

'Well, not yet,' Jackson said. 'Not yet.'

55

SOPHIA'S SCOTTISH BOYFRIEND POUNCED ON HER AS SHE came through the door, tugging on the zip at the front of her pink uniform. He found the pink uniforms vaguely pornographic, as if Barbie had designed her ideal nurse's uniform. Sophia wore hers very short and he often wondered if there were men in the houses she went to who spent their time trying to get a glance up her skirt as she bent over or reached up. When he thought of her at work, feather dusters tended to be involved as well as leaning provocatively across beds or kneeling on floors to scrub them with her pert Czech arse in the air.

'Wait,' she said, pushing him away.

'Can't,' he said. 'I've been thinking about this moment all day.'

She wanted to take her jacket off, have a glass of red wine, eat beans on toast, wash her face, put her feet up, do a hundred things that were higher up her list of priorities. She'd had to work an extra hour today. 'New practices,' the housekeeper told them. The housekeeper was new too. The mean-faced Scottish housekeeper had disappeared overnight and now they had a tetchy Muscovite bitch in her place. Favours was 'under new management'. Sophia didn't think much of the new regime. She thought it might be time to stop working here, go home to Prague, take up her real life again. She imagined herself in the future, a top international scientist, living in the States, handsome husband, a couple of kids, imagined looking through the photographs that recorded her stay in Scotland – the Castle, the Tattoo, hills and lochs. She might remove the photographs of her Scottish boyfriend so that her American husband didn't feel jealous. On the other hand she might not.

'Come on,' her Scottish boyfriend moaned at her, tugging at her clothes. Sometimes when he was in the mood there was just no putting him off.

It was when he was pushing her pink uniform up around her hips that she felt something uncomfortable sticking into her back and said, 'Hang on,' to him so that he groaned and rolled over, his big pale Scottish penis sticking up in the air like a flagpole. She had nothing to compare it with, this being her first Celt, but she liked to imagine that this was what all Scotsmen were hiding under their kilts – even though the other maids shrieked with more knowledgeable laughter when she said this.

She found the source of her discomfort in one of the pockets of her jacket. The doll. One of the writer's matryoshka. She had a vague memory of picking it up amidst the horror of his house. It was a small one, although not the baby. She opened it, pulling it apart.

Like an egg, there was a secret inside. She frowned at it.

'Sony memory stick,' her Scottish boyfriend said. 'For a computer.'

'I know,' she said. Sometimes he forgot that she was a scientist from a sophisticated European capital city. Sometimes he behaved as if she farmed potatoes back in the Middle Ages. The memory stick had a label on it. 'Death on the Black Isle'.

'Greg upstairs has a Sony,' he said enthusiastically, his flagpole already limp and forgotten. He liked everything to do with computers. 'We can see what's on it. It must be important if it was hidden.'

'I don't think so,' Sophia said. 'It's just a novel,' but she was quite relieved when she heard him thundering up the stairs to Greg's flat. At least now she could kick her shoes off and get a glass of wine. She remembered the writer's house, how it was before the terrible thing happened in it. She could almost smell the roses in his hallway.

56

THE BODY WASHED UP A SECOND TIME AT CRAMOND, AS IF THE girl was determined to come back again and again to the same place until someone took notice of her. The pathologist at the scene thought she might have been strangled (*post-mortem lividity on the neck*) but they would have to wait for the post mortem to know anything more certain. Three days in the waters of the Forth surfing up and down the coastline hadn't done her any favours. Not quite Ophelia, washed down the stream, garlanded with flowers.

Cramond was under the flight path for Edinburgh airport and Louise wondered what they looked like from the air, little spiders scurrying around with no purpose, or a well-drilled army of ants working together? From the single policeman who had responded to the call, the number of people had expanded exponentially in the course of an hour. Her team, her case. *Her first murder*. They had found Hatter's car parked in the long-stay car park at Edinburgh airport. Jackson had been right, the boot was swarming with DNA – hopefully they would find matches to their corpse. Sooner or later they would find Graham Hatter.

They took the body away in a police launch but both the procurator fiscal and the pathologist elected to fly in the helicopter. Louise went on the boat with the body, like an honour guard. She touched the thick plastic of the body bag.

'Hello, Lena,' she whispered. She had been Jackson's girl all this time, now she belonged to her. She dialled his number. There were all kinds of things she would have liked to say to him but in the end, when he answered, all she said was, 'We found her. We found your girl.'

57

WHEN THEY LANDED AT THE AIRPORT IN GENEVA THEY TOOK a taxi straight to the bank.

Inside the cool interior, Tatiana spoke to a woman at a reception desk. 'This is Mrs Gloria Hatter, she is here to withdraw funds.' Gloria supposed that people who worked in Swiss banks probably spoke English better than the English did. She could have sworn that Tatiana didn't sound as Russian as she had done before.

The receptionist picked up a phone and murmured something discreet and French into it, and within seconds they were ushered into the plush interior of a private room.

'Nice bank,' Tatiana said appreciatively.

Half an hour later they were outside again in the sunshine. It was that easy. Tatiana had instructed Gloria to arrange for the money to be handed over in the form of high-value bearer bonds. The bearer bonds seemed rather flimsy to Gloria, she would have preferred the weighty reality of cash. *Loot*, Tatiana said and laughed.

They went to an old, expensive café and Gloria divided the bonds between them. 'One for you, one for me,' she said. Tatiana tucked hers into her bra and Gloria followed suit. Then Gloria turned her phone back on and listened to the messages on her voicemail. There was a message from the security company man wondering where she was and why her house was wrapped in crime scene tape. There was a message from Emily who seemed irritated by the imminence of the Second Coming. There was a message from the hospital. Gloria took a second phone out of her handbag and listened to the one message it contained. It was an announcement she had been expecting since Tuesday and it confirmed the message from the hospital.

It was a momentous and final thing.

'Graham's dead,' she said, but she was speaking to herself. Tatiana had gone.

Gloria took her time over her coffee. She had a very nice slice of something called an 'Eglantine torte' with it and when she paid she left a very good tip. She remembered that it was Friday, Beryl's day, and wondered if her ancient mother-in-law would notice that she wasn't there.

Out in the street she pushed the second phone deep into the first waste bin she came to. She was sure it would be emptied soon, the Swiss being so famous for their cleanliness. What she had seen of the country so far was very appealing. She imagined buying a little dark-wood chalet in the countryside, window boxes full of trailing geraniums in the summer, crisp white snow piled on the roof in winter. A basket of kittens sleeping by a log-burning stove.

There was so much work to be done. She would move through the world righting wrong. Legions of kittens, horses, budgies, mangled boys, murdered girls, they were all calling to her. *Blessed are they which do hunger and thirst after righteousness: for they shall be filled.*

She would be feared by the bad. She would be a legend in her own lifetime. She would be cosmic justice. That should definitely be said with capital letters. Cosmic Justice. Incontrovertibly and without argument, Cosmic Justice was a Good Thing.

58

JACKSON HAD GOT AS FAR AS SCOTCH CORNER BEFORE HE turned round and headed back north. He found that he couldn't, after all, just drive off into the sunset. Martin had asked for his help and he had said yes. The guy had saved his life and needed him to testify on his behalf and it wasn't possible to just walk away from that.

The Angel of the North came back into view, holding his rust-red airplane wings above the land like a great protector. Jackson had slipped from the righteous path but it was OK, he was back on it again now.

59

HE DIDN'T NEED THE GUN, AS IT TURNED OUT. THE ONLY explanation he could come up with for its disappearance was that Martin had taken it when they were in the hotel room together, before he slipped him the Mickey Finn. He should have checked it was there before he left the hotel. That was a mistake. There was no room for mistakes in his career. Maybe it was time for him to do something else, go in a different direction, do that OU degree, start an ostrich farm, run a B and B. Crazy talk, Ray.

When he had eventually opened up his bag, there was a Gideon Bible inside instead of the gun. The golfing trophy lay innocently on top, looking slightly skewed out of its original position so you knew the little chrome golfer was never going to be able to hit the ball straight. Ray had played golf a few times, had quite liked it, the force of the drive, the precision of the putting. It had appealed to both sides of his natural skills. He'd picked up the trophy in a charity shop. Some starving kid somewhere in the world benefiting by a penny from some old geezer's golf trophy. R. J. Benson. You had to wonder about him, who he was, what was his life? The trophy was dated 1938. Had R. J. Benson fought in the war, had he died in the war? Or had he outlived everyone he knew and died alone? Would that happen to him? No, he'd blow his own brains out first. Do as you would be done by.

You could imagine it happening to Martin though. Ray experienced an unexpected twinge of fondness for Martin. He had told him way too much about himself. Anything was too much, even nothing was too much. By the time Ray had returned to the Four Clans to look for him, to ask him about the gun, Martin had gone. He'd like to kill him for messing him about like that, but then the guy had saved his life, so he owed him. A life for a life.

A gun would be too obvious in this place and unnecessary considering that all he had to do was reach over and flick a switch. Basically, he could just turn the guy off. God knows what he was hooked up to, it looked like only the machines were standing between him and eternity. He could probably just let nature take its course, but better to be safe than sorry. As they say. And anyway, he'd been paid to do a job and so do the job he would.

It had been easy enough to get into the ICU. The fat nurse on night duty asked him if he was a close relative and he'd put on a sad face and said, 'I'm his son, Ewan. I've just flown back from South America,' and she'd put on a matching sad face and said, 'Of course, let me take you to your dad.' He'd sat with 'dad' a while, companionably, as if he really was his son. 'You're a hard man to find, Graham,' he said softly. He had been looking all over the place for him. There was no way for his client to get in touch with him once the job was put in motion. That was the way Ray liked it. Safe not sorry. A phone call at the beginning, a phone call at the end.

It was funny being back in the hospital. The A and E had been noisy and chaotic, not like here. It was peaceful at Graham's bedside, apart from the blinks and beeps of the machines. He had thought of him as 'Hatter' when he was hunting him down, but finding him like this, as helpless as a baby, the guy seemed to merit a little tenderness. He took out the syringe from the inside pocket of his jacket. Full of nothing. Air. You needed air to live, you didn't think of it as something that would kill you. The air would travel in his vein, find his heart, stop the pumping action, stop the blood flow, stop the heart. Stop Graham dead. It only took the littlest thing. He lifted the covers from Graham's feet and found the vein in his ankle. 'This won't hurt a bit, Graham,' he said. Ray of light, Ray of darkness. Ray of sunshine, Ray of night.

He replaced the covers. Graham's heart would go into cardiac arrest in a few seconds and all hell would be let loose, nurses running all over the place, even the fat nurse heaving her hips heroically along the corridor.

Time to go. He patted Graham's blanketed leg. 'Night night, Graham. Sleep tight.'

Outside it was beginning to spit with rain again. He made the phone call to his client. There was no answer so he left a message on her voicemail.

'Congratulations, Mrs Hatter,' he said. 'Our business is concluded.'

CASE HISTORIES
Kate Atkinson

'NOT JUST THE BEST NOVEL I READ THIS YEAR BUT
THE BEST MYSTERY OF THE DECADE'
Stephen King

Cambridge is sweltering, during an unusually hot summer.
To Jackson Brodie, former police inspector turned private
investigator, the world consists of one accounting sheet –
Lost on the left, Found on the right – and the two never
seem to balance.

Jackson has never felt at home in Cambridge, and has a
failed marriage to prove it. Surrounded by death, intrigue
and misfortune, his own life haunted by a family tragedy,
he attempts to unravel three disparate case histories and
begins to realise that in spite of apparent diversity,
everything is connected . . .

'AN ASTONISHINGLY COMPLEX AND MOVING
LITERARY DETECTIVE STORY . . . THE SORT OF NOVEL
YOU HAVE TO START RE-READING THE MINUTE
YOU'VE FINISHED IT'
Guardian

'TRIUMPHANT . . . HER BEST BOOK YET . . .
A TRAGI-COMEDY FOR OUR TIMES'
Sunday Telegraph

'PART COMPLEX FAMILY DRAMA, PART MYSTERY,
IT WINDS UP HAVING MORE DEPTH AND VIVIDNESS
THAN ORDINARY THRILLERS AND MORE THRILLS
THAN ORDINARY FICTION . . . A WONDERFULLY
TRICKY BOOK'
New York Times

9780552772433

BLACK SWAN